Also by Jeff Mann

Bliss (poems)
Mountain Fireflies (poems)
Flint Shards from Sussex (poems)
Edge (personal essays)
Bones Washed with Wine (poems)
Loving Mountains, Loving Men (memoir and poetry)
On the Tongue (poetry)
A History of Barbed Wire (short fiction)
Binding the God: Ursine Essays from the Mountain South (personal essays)
Ash: Poems from Norse Mythology (poems)
Fog: A Novel of Desire and Reprisal (novel)
Purgatory: A Novel of the Civil War (novel)
Desire and Devour: Stories of Blood and Sweat (short fiction)
A Romantic Mann (poems)
Cub (novel)
Salvation: A Novel of the Civil War (novel)
Rebels (poems)
Country (novel)
Consent (short fiction)

INSATIABLE

INSATIABLE

Jeff Mann

UNZIPPED

Insatiable

Published in 2017 by Unzipped, an imprint of Lethe Press, Inc.
6 University Drive, Suite 206 / PMB #223 ✦ Amherst, MA 01002 USA
www.lethepressbooks.com ✦ lethepress@aol.com
ISBN: 978-1-59021-637-8 / 1-59021-637-7

Set in Jenson and Kelt.
Interior design: Alex Jeffers.
Front cover art: Elizabeth Leggett.
Back cover author portrait: Ben Baldwin.
Cover design: Inkspiral Design.

LIBRARY OF CONGRESS CATALOGING-IN-PUBLICATION DATA
Names: Mann, Jeff, author.
Title: Insatiable / Jeff Mann.
Description: Maple Shade, N.J. : Unzipped, an imprint of Lethe Press, [2017]
Identifiers: LCCN 2017042617 | ISBN 9781590216378 (pbk. : alk. paper)
Subjects: LCSH: Vampires--Fiction. | GSAFD: Erotic fiction. | Fantasy fiction.
Classification: LCC PS3563.A53614 I57 2017 | DDC 813/.54--dc23
LC record available at https://lccn.loc.gov/2017042617

The earlier adventures of Derek Maclaine were published in *Devoured*, a novella included in the anthology *Masters of Midnight: Erotic Tales of the Vampire* (Kensington Books, 2003); a collection of short fiction, *Desire and Devour: Stories of Blood and Sweat* (Bear Bones Books/Lethe Press, 2012); "Snow on Scrabble Creek," a short story included in *The Bears of Winter: Hot and Hairy Fiction*, edited by Jerry L. Wheeler (Bear Bones Books/Lethe Press, 2014), and "Spring on Scrabble Creek," a short story included in *Threesome: Him, Him and Me*, edited by Matthew Bright (Lethe Press, 2016).

A version of the first two chapters of this novel, "Summer Solstice Sacrifice," was published in the Halloween 2014 issue of *Glitterwolf Magazine* and in *Blood in the Rain: Seventeen Stories of Vampire Erotica*, edited by Cecilia Duvalle and Mary Trepanier (Cwtch Press, 2015).

For Cynthia Burack,
in return for thirty-five years of wonderfully simpatico friendship.

For John Ross,
in return for home.

For Anne Rice,
whose books I've savored for decades.

In memory of Larry Gibson, environmental activist.

CHAPTER ONE

The long sun of the summer solstice has finally set. Now twilight fills the high mountain forest, and darkness thickens beneath the boughs of red spruce. Between temple-column tree trunks, I move toward flickering light and the musky scent of a man.

At forest's edge, I stop, snuffling the air. He smells beautiful, as beautiful as anything I've ever seen. My fang-teeth lengthen. Bare-chested and barefoot, clad for the hunt in nothing but kilt, sporran, and dirk, I lope through the orchard, past the gnarled shapes of apple trees. I pause on the border of the lawn. Here, incongruous for a ridge-top in West Virginia's Potomac Highlands, is a circle of standing stones very much like those in my native Scotland. Beyond that looms a rambling farmhouse with a turret.

He sprawls on a couch on the house's back patio, sipping aromatic mead in the light of many candles. He's wearing nothing but baggy gym shorts. The scents of his armpits, his sweaty skin, and his crotch flood me, stiffening my cock and speeding my pulse. Through shadows I move closer, drawing my dirk. I study his shaggy brown hair, stubbly cheeks, thick sideburns, and bushy goatee. I savor the big muscles of his arms, the beefy mounds of his fur-coated chest. What a treasure he is.

He takes another swig of mead, wipes sweat off his brow, and stretches. Fondling his prominent nylon-covered crotch, he takes a deep breath. Folding his brawny arms behind his head, he closes his eyes.

The dirk is older than I am, an heirloom given to me by my father on my sixteenth birthday. Now I rest its long thistle-etched blade against my prey's throat. "Keep very still," I whisper.

His hazel eyes flash open. He stares up at me and swallows hard.

"Who the hell are you?"

"I'm Derek Maclaine," I say, running honed metal over his windpipe. "You smell very, very good. What's your name, boy?"

"Matt. M-Matt Taylor. W-whaddaya want?"

"I want you to do what I tell you. Will you do that for me?"

Matt licks his lips. His thick eyebrows bunch up. "Y-yeah. Long as you don't stick me with that big damn knife."

"Good boy." I run the tip of the dirk over Matt's chunky chest, making swirls in the mat of chestnut-brown hair. Then I open my sporran and pull out the rag. It's a rolled-up camo bandana with a fat knot tied in the center of its length.

"Gag yourself. I want you nice and quiet for what's to come."

"Aw, no. Please, man, no." Matt shakes his head.

I lower the dirk, ever so gently probing his plump, furry belly, then resting the knife's tip in his navel. I hold out the rag. "Do it. Or else."

Matt takes the bandana. He looks up at me, looks at the dirk's long length. His mouth trembles.

"Go on now," I say, shifting the dirk-tip from his navel to his left nipple. "A man so big-built and butch was born to be obedient."

Matt swallows hard. He pushes the camo knot between his teeth.

"Pull it tight, good and tight. A little tighter. Good boy. Now knot it behind your head. Yes, there you go. Perfect."

Matt looks up at me, eyes glassy with humiliation. He bites down on the cloth and bows his head. His shame at being mastered is delicious.

I lift the dirk and step back. "Now lie down on the floor and put your hands behind your back. If you give me any fight, I'll gut you."

Matt sits up very slowly. He slips off the couch, falls to his knees, and lies down on his belly. He crosses his wrists together in the small of his back.

Gently I tap the tanned, muscled skin between his shoulder blades with the dirk. "You're going to behave?"

"Um. Ummm huh," my captive mumbles, nodding.

I pull handcuffs from my sporran. Bending, I lock them around his wrists. "Roll over," I say.

He does so. I stand astraddle his chest. "Now you're helpless, aren't you?" I say, slipping my dirk into the sheath buckled around my waist.

"Ummf." Matt stares up at me and flexes his muscled arms.

"Can't get loose, eh?"

Matt strains, inhales, exhales, and shakes his head.

I press a bare foot into the cleft between his pecs. Curling my toes, I tug his chest hair. "You're wondering what I'm going to do with you now that I have you helpless, aren't you?"

"Mmm hm." Matt's chest heaves. Moving my foot from his torso to his loins, I press my sole against his crotch. Beneath the fabric, his prick's already hard, but now, beneath my weight, it grows harder still.

"We're going to celebrate the summer solstice, my boy. Today was the height of the light. Tomorrow, the sun begins to wane. The God of the Waning Year conquers the God of the Waxing Year, just as I now intend to conquer you."

I work his prick. He moans.

I remove my foot. Bending, I grip him by the arm and haul him to his feet. "You'll be my Sacred King tonight. You'll be my sacrifice," I say, leading him off the patio and into the grassy darkness.

We enter the standing stones. Matt stumbles and sways, drunk on mead. In the center of the circle, a post of oak wood stands. I push him back against it. With thin cords I pull from my sporran, I bind him to the column, one tight length just above his meaty pecs, one tight length just below them.

I step back, taking in the splendid sight of manly strength made powerless. "Ahhhh, yes. You're not going anywhere, are you?"

Long eyelashes blinking, he glares at me. Taking a deep breath, he strains and twists against his bonds, mumbling what are no doubt muffled obscenities. Then his struggles end, and he falls still.

"My little Hercules," I whisper, gazing into Matt's wide eyes. Cupping his bushy chin in my hand, I kiss his gagged mouth. I brush unkempt hair from his sweat-filmed face and nuzzle his neck. He tenses against me, trembling. I slip a hand inside his gym shorts, clasp his stiff cock, and stroke it. I fondle the ooze-wet tip; I grip his ball-sac and tug till he's wincing.

Moving my focus to his pecs, I knead the dense meat there, running my fingers through thick auburn chest hair, flicking and pinching his nipples between my fingernails. "Just a little hurt," I sigh, nudging his bearded chin with mine. "Don't you want a little hurt?"

He nods, tightening his chest mounds and whimpering as I twist and tug the tender tit-flesh. His hard cock bumps my thigh. About us, fireflies gather, winking like a restless galaxy among the stones.

Stepping back, I unsheathe my dirk. "I own you, do I not?" I say, running the blade-tip over his ribs.

Transfixed, Matt's eyes gaze into mine. Slowly he nods.

"And what you have is mine to take, is it not?"

He bites down on cloth. For a few seconds he struggles again, his muscles bulging against their restraints, then, with a bass groan, he slumps against the post in surrender.

"Are you ready to be taken?"

Matt bows his head and nods.

"Tonight the darkness masters the light," I say, drawing the tip of the dirk across his left pec, leaving a thin line of blood. Matt grunts and trembles. I cut his right pec next. Matt chokes back a deep sob. Blood scrolls down his chest.

Teeth aching, I sheathe my weapon. Wrapping an arm around my captive, I bend to his breast. I lap up the blood, running my tongue over his wounds, over the thick fur there. I clamp my mouth down on the welling furrows and slurp. Gripping Matt's cock, I begin a slow stroking. His hips buck. He heaves a series of gagged whimpers and then a sharp yelp as I sink my fangs into his left nipple and commence a hard sucking.

Matt struggles and shakes. He tosses his head and moans, hair falling over his face. I move to his right nipple, piercing it, drawing up rich mouthfuls from the deep well of his strength. Inside my grip, his cock pulses and slides. Dropping to my knees, I jerk down his shorts, run my tongue over his prick-head and down his shaft. I deep-throat him till he's groaning low and pounding my face, and then I sink my right fang into his cock and suck up the sweet liqueur it yields.

After a lengthy supping, I rise. Weakened, eyes closed, Matt sags in his bonds. I kiss him on the brow, leaving a ruddy mark. He looks up at me, clearly dazed, and pants against his gag.

"I need more of you. Will you give me more?" I cup his rough cheek in my hand.

Matt nods jerkily, drunkenly. I unknot the cords binding him to the column. He slumps against me, knees buckling. I lift him naked into my arms. Walking the perimeter of the circle, I cradle and rock him as I whisper the invocations: Great Eagle of the East, Fiery Lion of the South, Sea Serpent of the West, Black Bull of the North. In the circle's center, I call upon the Dark Lady, the Falcon-Feathered One, the Stirrer of Fate's Cauldron, and the Lord of Storm, the Horned God of the Wild.

In the west, lightning flashes, and there's the rumble of thunder. A cool breeze pours over us. Matt lies limp in my arms, his eyes dreamy, mumbling words I can't make out, his sweaty head pressed against my shoulder. Blood still oozes from his punctured cock.

I lower him onto the grass in the circle's center. He rolls onto his belly and cocks his butt, a mesmerizing invitation. I peel off my kilt before kneeling beside him. I run my hand over the soft skin and softer fur of his plump ass, then sink my teeth into his right buttock and drink deep. With spit and blood, I moisten his asshole, then, lying on top of him, I position my cock between his buttocks, find his fur-bordered aperture, and slowly enter him.

Matt moans and nods, bucks and sighs, as my prick's length slides inside. He clenches his ass-muscles around me and claws at my belly hair, urging me on. I ride him, slow and shallow thrusts at first.

"You need to be used, do you not?" I snarl against his ear. "You love a big man's hard prick-dirk sheathed in your ass?"

"Uhhhhh huuuhmmm!"

"Harder? May I use you harder?" I rake his shoulder with a fang.

Matt nods frantically, gripping my cock from within.

"Sweet, sweaty savior," I breathe against his hair. I clamp a hand over his mouth, twist his gore-wet nipples, and give it to him harder and deeper. He shouts and growls, writhes and rears like the wild mount he is. When he spreads his thighs wider still, I begin a brutal pounding.

"My chalice," I sigh, nuzzling his neck, breathing in his scent, fisting his cock, and driving into him. "My bloody grail."

Matt rocks beneath me, sobbing and moaning, bucking his beefy butt back against my groin. When I sink my teeth into his neck, he stiffens, heaves a hoarse moan, and comes in my hand. I've taken only a couple of draughts from his carotid before he sighs, shudders, and passes out. I retract my fangs, grip his shoulders, shove into him savagely—in and out, in and out, in and out—soon shooting deep inside him. Drowsily, I lick his welling neck wound, call the storm closer, and fall asleep upon his broad back.

Chapter Two

The thunderstorm's given way to soft rain by the time Matt wakes. Unbound, he's curled naked in my arms upon the patio couch.

"Uhhh. Whoa." Matt shakes his head and tries to rise. "Weak."

"I drank quite a bit. It is a Sabbat holiday, after all." I pull him closer. "Rest here and enjoy the night. In a little while, I'll bandage you up and help you in to bed."

"Mmmmm. Okay." Matt snuggles back against me. "Rain feels good. So cool after all the heat lately. Did you—?"

"Call the storm? Yes. But that's not all I called. Look."

Matt lifts his head and gazes out over the lawn, dimly illuminated by receding lightning flash. "Jesus. A whole herd a' deer?"

"Not Jesus. Cernunnos."

Matt grins. "Right. Wow. They're beautiful."

For a few minutes we lie there in the rain, watching the stags, does, and fauns graze the lawn and nip at bushes. Every now and then they pause, regarding us with calm-eyed curiosity before returning to their meal. Eventually they drift off, past the standing stones and into the apple orchard, where they're lost to sight.

Matt rolls over with some effort. "Wuuuufff. I can barely move." He kisses my breastbone and buries his face in my chest hair. Somewhere a tree frog chirps. "I think you're gonna have to carry me to bed this time around."

"Be glad to. You know how much I love to throw you over my shoulder."

6

"Yep. Makes you feel all butch and strong and protective." Matt fondles my bushy black goatee. "My big ole ferocious caveman."

"Exactly. A caveman with fangs. So how did you like the 'mysterious intruder' scenario?" I ask, stroking his wet head. Upon his temples, streaks of gray frost his hair's auburn hue.

Matt chuckles. "You know the answer to that."

"Yes, I do. You were hard throughout."

"Yep! It was hot, hot, *hot*. Having me gag myself. Tying me to the post. The knife-play. Getting butt-plowed in the grass. I'm damn lucky I met you, Laird Maclaine." Matt takes my hand and kisses the back of it. "Little did I know, that spring night in Eppson Books so many years ago, that I'd meet a leather-daddy vampire I was going to spend the rest of my life with."

"A monster who binds and gags you with regularity and drinks your blood till you're too weak to stand. Sure you don't have any regrets? Wouldn't you rather have a human lover?"

"Don't get started. You know the answer to that too. I give to people I love. I love you. I don't mind giving you my blood. It turns me on when you bite me, man. And I don't mind being so weak. It's like when you have me tied up. I get to stop being strong for a while." Matt rubs a cuff-chafed wrist. "You know what I mean? I get to forget responsibility and just…be powerless, knowing that when I'm helpless, it turns you on."

"I feel the same way when you top me. I felt the same way with the few vampires I've submitted to—Sigurd and Marcus, that Roman aristocrat I told you about."

"It's a relief sometimes, ain't it? And I know you'll take care of me. I love it when I'm weak or tied and you hold me in your arms. I know you'd take on the world for me. You know I'd do the same for you, right?" Matt gives my ponytail a gentle tug. "Anybody wants to fuck with you'll have to get past me first. I know I ain't no powerful vampire, or a werewolf, like our lil' buddy Donnie, but still…I'd die for you, Derek. You know that, right?"

"I do. But that's not a parting that appeals to me. I've already lost too many men I loved…Angus, then Mark, then Gerard. I have no interest in losing you."

Matt sighs, tugging at the Thor's hammer pendant about my neck. "Sometimes I wish I was as strong as you. Then I could defend you just as good as you can defend me."

"You're warrior stock, that's for sure," I say, squeezing Matt's gym-hard biceps. "I still remember you tearing into those Leviticus Locusts."

Matt sniggers. "Well, gay-bashers piss me off. Speaking of warriors, did I tell you about that Civil War reenactment I went to down in McDowell?"

"You didn't tell me much. Something about a new crush you have. 'The Rebel Otter,' you called him."

Matt grins. "Ohhhh, yeah. His name's Hunter Hedrick. He was so damn cute. Lean lil' thang. Gray Confederate pants, suspenders, high black boots, kepi cap. Green eyes, pretty red lips, full chestnut-brown beard. High proud butt! I couldn't keep my eyes off his ass. One minute he was playing his guitar and singing 'Lorena' so sweet and sad, and the next he was brandishing his rifle and charging the Yanks. Donnie says he's gay, 'cause he's seen him at some Roanoke Mountain Bear runs. I chatted with him a little bit—"

"Flirted with him, you mean?"

"Well, yeah. You know I cain't help but flirt when a guy catches my eye. And this one.... Woooooofff!"

"I can tell you've fallen hard," I tease. "Find out where he lives, and maybe...."

"You'll mesmerize him? That'd be hot. We could spit-roast him the way we do lil' Donnie." Matt wipes raindrops from both his beard and mine. "Speaking of which, Donnie and Timmy are coming up next weekend to help in the garden. How about we have a hot-tub party? I could mix up some sangria or margaritas, grill some burgers, cook up some peas and new potatoes, make some wilted lettuce, maybe a meringue pie."

"And afterwards we could have a four-way?"

"You read my mind." Matt's grin is sheepish.

"No need to. I just know you too well. Hot-tub four-way it is."

"You gotta admit they're both pretty yummy young guys."

"Which is why they're our fuck-buddies and my thralls."

"Yep." With a fingertip, Matt traces on my left shoulder the tattooed face of the Horned God. "Derek?"

"Um. Don't like your tone of voice. What?"

"Mark Carden and Gerard McGraw, those men you loved after you turned vampire. I know you don't like talking about 'em, but...did you ever think about turning them?"

"I did."

"So why didn't you?"

"I wanted to be sure of my feelings for them. I wanted to be sure of their feelings for me. After all, immortality…centuries together.… They were both young men in their twenties. I guess I was waiting for them to mature a bit more before I…."

I roll over onto my back and pause. The rain is so gentle, as if Thor's beard were brushing my face.

"And then, dammit, with their stubborn warrior hearts…hearts very much like yours…they were dead. Why do I always fall in love with fighters and risk-takers? Angus was much the same."

"Why? 'Cause you're a warrior yourself, you damn fool." Matt gives my side a gentle punch.

"I guess so. At any rate, you know what happened. Both of them enlisted in the wars of their time, though I begged them not to. Mark fell at Chickamauga, and Gerard in the Battle of the Bulge. I followed them into those conflicts, but I couldn't save them. They both died in daylight. I was asleep, holed up like some sort of sinister grub, when Mark was shot in the head and Gerard bled to death in one of those damned Belgian trenches."

Matt rests his head on my shoulder and drapes an arm across my belly. "Derek, honey?"

"Matt, honey?"

"We've been together for over a decade. You're sure of my feelings for you, ain't you?"

"Oh, yes." I tousle Matt's wet locks.

"And you're sure of your feelings for me?"

"Idiot. Of course. I adore you, Matthew. You're everything to me. My undead life would be echoingly empty without you."

"So, you ever think about changing me? Earlier, you talked about parting. You talked about losing those guys you loved. You're gonna lose me sooner or later. Got all this gray in my beard, in my hair, even here." He plucks ruefully at the patch of silver between his pecs. "You, if you don't feed for a while, you get all gray too, but all it takes is a few minutes with your teeth in my neck or in my butt…." Matt rubs his ass and smiles. "And you're all black-haired and age thirty again. Me…different matter."

"I don't want to talk about this, Matt."

"Why? You're a big, strong guy. You're strong enough to face the truth, ain't you?"

I take his hand. "Yes. Do you want me to change you?"

"Yes. No. I don't know. Isn't…what you are kinda unnatural?"

"I don't think so. Otherwise, how could I command aspects of nature, like animals and storms? I'm a different kind of nature, perhaps. A distilled, intense form of nature."

"That makes sense. Well, I don't wanna get any older, that's for sure. My joints hurt me when I lift weights, so I gotta take that glucosamine. Got high cholesterol. Piss stream's slower and slower. All the shitty little details of getting older that you sidestepped. A coupla drinks, and I have problems getting it up. Ugh. I'm amazed you still want me. One of these days, maybe you'll take up with some tasty young guy like Donnie, or Timmy, or that Rebel reenactor, and I'll be put out to pasture."

"Bullshit."

"It could happen. Time flies, man. Before we know it, I'll be an ole geezer. Won't be able to keep up the house or the garden. Won't be able to chop wood or guard you while you sleep, or kick an intruder's ass. Useless. Useless. You'll send me off to some ole folks' home and start up courting some hairy cub to replace me."

"You think so little of my loyalty?"

"Naw. I'm just shitting you, I guess. But still…."

"You do know what you'd be giving up if I turned you?"

"Shit, sure. Sunlight. Doughnuts! Mac and cheese! Beer!"

I laugh. "Blood's infinitely more delicious than any of that, I promise you. I just fear…do you remember what I told you at Kanawha Falls, that snowy night you decided to take a chance and be with me? Be an undead monster's lover?"

"Yeah. Kinda. Been a long time. Tell me again."

"Well, tonight, when we celebrated the solstice, me as embodiment of darkness and you as embodiment of light…. I'm afraid if you became a vampire too, that chemistry, that tension between opposites might be canceled out. The erotic magnetism that flickers between our polarities might fade."

"Now *I* say 'Bullshit.' You sound like those hetero…those backward heteronormative…?"

I chuckle. "That's right. Big word for a Summers County redneck."

"Sure is. I got a smart boyfriend I've learned a helluva lot from. Anyway! You sound like one of those heteronormative old-fashioned Wiccans who says you gotta have man/woman polarity or nothing'll work. There's all kinds a' tensions and polarities, Derek. Didn't you feel major 'erotic magnetism' between you and Sigurd, that big ole Viking who turned you? Or that sexy Eye-talian, Marcus?"

Matt gives my right nipple a nibble, then strokes my limp penis. "You *really* think if I sprouted me some big ole fangs that I wouldn't be cocking my hungry butt up in the air every time you got nekkid?"

"That *is* hard to imagine. Well, it would make fighting for Top significantly more interesting."

"I'm not sure I want to change, but…. Let's just think about it, okay? I wanna stay your boy, Daddy, not become your gray ole Daddybear."

I say nothing. The thought of turning Matt has always disturbed me, and I can't say why. He's right. If I don't turn him, inevitably I'll lose him, just as I lost Angus, Mark, and Gerard. I didn't have a choice where they were concerned. This time I do.

Matt rubs his brow and sighs. "Wow, I'm so tired." He rolls over, his back to me. I take the hint, wrapping an arm around his chest and spooning him from behind. A screech owl calls in the orchard, an eerie quavering. The rain slows and stops. When Matt starts to snore, I lift him into my arms and carry him into the house.

CHAPTER THREE

I wake, comfortably curled in my "Daddy nest," as Matt calls it. The sun, I sense, is just about to set.

When I went missing after the attack that left my lover Angus dead and me mortally wounded, my father, Lachlan Maclaine, assuming the worst, had a fine coffin made for me. It served me well as a sleeping place from 1730 until nearly a year ago, when Matt decided I needed a more spacious bed in the cellar crypt, so that he might cuddle with me during the day, if he so chose.

Thus the nest, which handy Matthew built for my last birthday. It's the equivalent of a huge dog's bed, with plump pillows, a wide mattress set inside a low wood frame, and blankets in my clan's tartan. I sleep in it in nothing but my kilt, or, more often—Matt's strongly expressed preference—in nothing at all. The tartans are delightful to nestle against, and sometimes I wake at sunset to find Matt in the nest with me, naked as well and eager for a romp.

Tonight, however, my burly husbear's not by my side. I buckle on my kilt, push aside the crypt's secret panel, stride past our dungeon play-space full of leather-sex paraphernalia, and on up the basement stairs, sensing him neither in our house, Mount Storm, nor on the lawn, nor in the woods beyond.

Perplexing. It's a Sunday. He only works his Forest Service job during the week. If he isn't curled up beside me or sucking my cock as I come to consciousness, he's usually in the den, pouring drinks, or in the kitchen, whipping himself up an Appalachian feast. Tonight he's simply not to be found.

When I open the liquor cabinet, I find a note wedged beneath the bottle of Tobermory, a single malt I'm partial to, distilled on my native Isle of Mull. I unfold it and read:

> *Hey, Hot Daddy!*
> *I figured you'd want a drink. Man, I'm sore today. Thanks for the rough workout last night!*
> *I'm down in Monterey. My cousin Dillon from Boone County—The miner? You met him once in Charleston, remember?—is passing through, and he wanted to meet me for dinner at the Allegheny Café. He sounded stressed out. Who knows what's up? I'll be home around 9.*
> *Hairy-Chested Hugs,*
> *Your Bad Boy*
> *PS. Maybe we can spend some time in the hot tub tonight before I head off to bed? I'm thinking I need to gulp your big load. It'll help me get through another week of work.*

"Horny little bastard. Praise Eros, Cernunnos, and Pan," I mutter, remembering the aroma of Matthew's pubes, the vivid honey of his blood, the tightness of his ass. With any luck, he'll get himself a good meal tonight. Knowing him, it'll be brown beans and cornbread, or country-fried steak with mashed potatoes, or his all-time favorite, barbecue. My boy surely does like to eat. What would I do without his furry beer belly to rub? Feeling fortunate, I pour myself a Scotch, then sit out on the front porch to feel the high mountain breezes and study the stars.

I hear the crunch of gravel and the thrum of Matt's pickup engine, then there's the flash of headlights ascending the mountainside. It's nearly ten.

He's driving fast. Bad sign. I slip into the kitchen and pour out a glass of Woodford Reserve, his favorite bourbon. I suspect he's going to need it.

I'm standing in the driveway when Matt pulls up. He climbs out, slams the truck door, wipes his brow, and glares at me. "Goddamn it, Derek. I really need—"

"Here you go," I say, presenting the tumbler of whiskey. "Get naked and join me in the hot tub. Then you can tell me what's happened."

"That farm's been in our family for five generations," Matthew says. Naked, still bruised and marked from our solstice sex, he sinks down into the bubbling water of the hot tub and takes a swig from his second glass of bourbon.

"Buddy, you know you get stumble-drunk when you drink in the hot tub. You have to go to work tomorrow. Maybe you ought to slow down?"

"Too damn angry." Grimacing, Matthew pushes hair off his brow. "But you're probably right. You're always right, damn it."

"Yes, I am. You don't want a hangover tomorrow. So tell me."

Matt takes another taste, this time a sip, not a swig. "Evening went great for a while. Our favorite wolfie-beast, Donnie, waited on us. Good food, as usual. Dillon made small talk, waited till we'd eaten before he told me what he came to tell me. I guess he figured the news might spoil my meal or make me lob things against the wall, and he was right."

"You do have a temper, Mr. Aries."

"So do you, Mr. Leo."

"Yep. Fire and fire. I'm surprised this whole damn mountain hasn't burst into flames in the years we've shared here. So then what?"

"Dillon told me that a few months ago, a goddamn mining company, Alpha Coal, bought up a huge buncha acres just over the mountain from him."

"Alpha Coal? Timmy used to work for them. He hates their guts. After he became my thrall, I burnt down their headquarters in Kanawha City."

"That's what I thought. Scared some guards while you were in wolfie form too. Nice work! Anyway, Dillon says the noise is terrible. Dynamite. Chain saws. Big frigging machines. Those motherfucking draglines with scoops that could pick up a bus. They're tearing all the mountaintops off to the south of him. And they've been pressuring him something awful to sell to them. Can you fucking imagine that? Greedy assholes."

I sigh. Slipping under the water, I douse my head, then rise to the surface and wring my beard and hair out. "Yes, I can imagine that. MTR. Mountain-top removal mining. I've bat-flown over those sites a few times. They look like a cat's litter box, or the surface of the moon. That kind of crap has been going on in this state for years now, Matt."

"Yeah, you're right. I've thought about it, and I've heard folks complain about it and protest it and try to raise money to fight it. But now it's personal. Cousin Dillon, he's got a great little place, kinda like Mount Storm here—on a ridge top, surrounded by trees. So pretty in the autumn, all the maples go-

ing fiery, the sourwood leaves like red stained glass. There's even a little grave-
yard there, where some of my aunts and uncles are buried. He don't want to
leave his land. And he don't want to listen to all that goddamn racket. Hell,
he's so tore up about it all, he even said he'd considered suicide. Suicide! That
sweet guy I used to go fishing with on Bluestone Reservoir! Can you imagine some assholes coming in here and tearing up the landscape and trying to
force us off Mount Storm? I'd shoot their goddamn heads off."

"That's not going to happen. There's no coal around here."

"That's not the point. This is my *cousin*, Derek. A guy I grew up with. I think
I should go down there tomorrow and see what's up."

"Tomorrow? I have to sleep, and you have to work."

"I'll take me a personal day. This is important."

"If you drive the van tomorrow, I could go along."

"Naw, you stay here. I wanna see all this shit in the daytime."

"Are you sure? I know you, Matt. I know what kind of temper you have.
You're only going to make things worse if you get into a fistfight with someone."

Matt grins. He scratches his chin. He knocks back the rest of his drink and
places the empty glass on the rim of the tub. "Yeah, as tempting as that sounds,
that ain't the way to do it. Thanks for letting me talk. It's made me feel better
and think clearer. After I check out the site, maybe I'll drive in to Charleston
and see if I can chat with some environmental action groups Dillon's gotten
involved with. Maybe they can tell me how I can help. But for tonight…."

Matt moves closer. "You told me once that vampire come helps a human
keep his youth and strength, and I'm thinking I'll need all the vigor I can get
for tomorrow's adventure. How's about you get up outta that water, Laird
Maclaine, and I blow you?"

"Anything to contribute to the cause," I say, hoisting myself onto the edge of
the tub. Matt grips my biker-bushy black goatee and pulls my face down to
his. Our kiss is long and deep. Then he hunkers down between my thighs and,
humming with hunger, takes my cock into his skilled and eager mouth.

CHAPTER FOUR

Timmy Kincaid wipes beer foam from his mustache. "I used to work for the assholes. I can tell you all about 'em."

Timmy and Donnie, snuggled together on the candlelit patio couch, are snacking happily on junk food. Both are burly, bewhiskered country boys. Newly lovers, they could be brothers. Timmy sports a brown goatee, and Donnie's proud of his ink-black beard. Neither hides his redneck nature. Timmy's wearing tight jeans, cowboy boots, and a wife-beater; Donnie's camo shorts are threadbare in the crotch and his baggy black tank top veils his ample belly.

Both men are aromatic enough to make me salivate, and both are exactly my type, which is why I made them my thralls. They'd service me with the slightest mental suggestion, but I didn't ask them up here tonight for sex. No, while we're waiting for Matt to get home from his exploratory trip to his cousin's property, I'm quizzing Timmy for information about Alpha, since he'd worked for them briefly before I enthralled him.

"Bastards fired my ass as soon as they caught wind I was gay." Timmy pulls a potato chip out of the bag in his lap and offers it to Donnie before kissing the salt left on his lover's lips. "Not that who I fuck means I can't mine like a madman. I kinda miss it…the drift kind—that's got some skill, some pride, some legacy to it. But blowing off mountaintops, that's brutal. Nothing good's left behind."

Donnie nudges Timmy's shoulder with his. "I don't want you mining, man. Too dangerous. He's, uh, he's a real good cook at the café," Donnie offers. "You should taste his rolls and scalloped taters and coconut pie."

"Matt's raved about this boy's culinary prowess many times. But stop distracting me with talk of treats. Tell me more about Alpha."

"Way I heard it, a few years back men from Alpha appeared all over West Virginia. One lil' girl told me they had the slickest business cards they'd thrust into everyone's hands, whether you drove a beat-up Ford pickup or a Mercedes-Benz. 'Cards felt so thick, so creamy, so gilded, you'd think they were inviting you to the governor's third wedding,' she told me. And sometimes clipped to the back of the card was a folded-up hundred-dollar bill."

Timmy pauses to sip his beer. "Pretty soon they'd bought up half the mining companies in the state. And I suspect they have men running the trucking companies and the coal plants."

I sit back, thumbing a fang. "They must have friends in high places. But who might hate them, who might their enemies be? That would be useful to know."

"Bunch of folks have brought legal action against 'em for ruining the water and ignoring environmental regulations, but they have slick lawyers—"

Donnie interrupts. "Lots of people who've filed in court or protested, well, some of 'em have had a run of bad luck. A few of 'em, their houses have been robbed. A few have gotten anonymous death threats; a few got their truck tires slashed. One guy's son got framed: locked up after being caught with a vial of crystal meth, even though the kid was a high school athlete who got tested regular and was no way a user. Most people who raise a ruckus against Alpha find it easier to move away."

"Our very own coal cartel. Where are they headquartered? Who's the man in charge?"

Timmy laughs, sliding out of his lover's arms. "Don't you and Matt read anything in the *Gazette* besides restaurant reviews?" He strides over to a stack of papers Matthew's got piled on the patio ready for recycling, riffles through them, and brings one over.

"Here's the weasel." Timmy stabs an index finger at a photo on the front page of the Business section. "CEO Stanley Sodeski. Their new headquarters—after you burnt the old one down, and, man, was that a pretty sight on TV!—it's right in Charleston, in one of those prissy ole mansions in the East End. Near the Capitol. Hell, if they had their way, their office would be *in* the Capitol. Might as well be. The governor's always giving 'em all kinds of breaks."

"Are there any other names you could give me? In case I'm in the mood to lean on someone the next time I get to town? In case I'm in the mood to interrogate someone and then dismember him?"

Timmy grins. "I wouldn't want to cross you, sir. Indeed I wouldn't. Or him neither." He angles a thumb at his boyfriend. "At least during the full moon."

Donnie flushes. "H-hey, now. I cain't help it. Don't tease me."

I chuckle. "You two are very cute together. Downright adorable. Which one's the Top?"

It's Timmy's turn to blush. "I, uh, manage."

Donnie pats his thigh. "You manage right well."

"I think you're both going to get plowed hard this weekend when you come back up to help around the grounds. Matt has a big cookout and a hot-tub party planned. Back to Alpha. Names?"

"Yeah. Sorry. My boss was Shorty Bennett, but he dropped dead about the time I left. He was the asshole who told 'em I was gay and had me fired. The head security officer's Dick Blankenship. We called him 'Dildo' behind his back. He's a real prick. Great big bald guy with muscles popping out all over."

I smirk. "Lot of good those muscles will do him if I—ah, hold on. Here comes Matt up the mountain. He's not driving fast, as he was the other night. That's a good sign, I hope."

"Yep." Donnie nods, cocking his head. "I can hear his truck, all right."

"Wow. I don't hear nothin'. You…uh, special-skilled folks sure have sharp ears." Timmy shakes his head, bites into a pepperoni roll, and pops open another beer.

The three of us fall silent, waiting for Matt's arrival. Fireflies flicker about us. A high breeze grieves through the eastern line of pines.

In a few minutes, Matt's truck pulls into the driveway. The door slams. Dressed in a tight gray T-shirt, jeans, and hiking boots, he appears around the corner of the house. He shuffles up onto the patio. He sits heavily in a chair, his face blank. He rubs his temples, pushes hair off his face, and leans back. He props his feet on the coffee table, swallows hard, and closes his eyes. "Damn glad to be home," he croaks.

Timmy and Donnie stare at him. "Jesus, Matt," Timmy blurts. "What the hell's going on?"

"Hey, guys. Glad y'all are here," Matt mumbles. "Derek…."

"I got you," I say, rising.

"Not bourbon. Moonshine this time. Please."

Oh, Goddess. What's happened now? I hurry into the kitchen, pull the jar from the cabinet—corn whiskey a biker buddy of Matt's fetched him from Franklin County, Virginia—and pour a healthy slug before moving back outside.

"Thanks, honey," Matt sighs, taking the glass. He takes two big swallows. Then he sits up and gazes over at us. I've never seen him in such a dazed state of shock.

"Well, boys, I saw it. I saw it all," Matt mutters hoarsely. "Jesus, did I see it. And I talked to some people."

"So tell us." Timmy wraps a protective arm around Donnie as if in the face of approaching threat. "What did you see?"

"Will in a minute. Derek, I gotta ask you something first."

"Sure, Matt. Ask away."

"If I quit my job, would that be all right? Would we be all right?"

"Absolutely. Between the money I've amassed over the centuries and my publishing company and investments, we're more than all right. I've told you for years now that you don't have to keep a job if you don't want to."

"Eager to have a kept boy, huh?" Through the pale mask of shock, a little of Matt's customary humor shows through.

"Exactly. Just keep this in mind," I say, smiling. "As long as you're paid, by God, boy, you'll keep spreading your butt-cheeks for me."

"You've been waiting years to say that, ain't you now? I'm serious, man. You're sure it's okay?"

"Abso-fucking-lutely, as you would say. But why do you want to quit your job?"

"'Cause…well, the reason I kept my jobs, first that park job I had when we met, and then the National Forest job, is because, well, a man's gotta have a purpose. Do some good, y'know? But now…I think I got another purpose. And it's more important than any I've had before."

Matt pauses, taking another sip of corn whiskey. "So, I went to Dillon's first. Long drive up Cabin Creek. The approach to his property looked normal. Right pretty. Thick woods. Tulip trees, oaks. Road wound up and up, and there we were atop that ridge. I hadn't been there since I was a kid for family picnics. Dillon's mother, my Aunt Doris, used to make the best goddamn fried chicken I ever…."

Matt clears his throat. "She's buried up there. But if Alpha has their way, she won't be no longer." He swigs some moonshine, slams the glass on the table, and stands. He begins to pace.

"Dillon has a coupla sweet lil' log cabins up there in the woods. So high up. Away from people, from traffic. What a great getaway from the goddamn noisy mess of the world. Or it was."

Matt grimaces. He spits over the side of the patio. "I get out of the truck, and we shake, and then he says, 'Right pretty up here, ain't it? But now I'm gonna show you what you came to see. Now I'm gonna show you the mouth of Hell.'"

Matt stops pacing. He looks out over the standing stones, the orchard, and the forest back of the house. Other than tree frogs and wind in tree boughs, it's utterly silent. "His mountain, Keystone Mountain, it was like this once. Now...."

"Go on, Matt. Tell us. The sooner I know what we're dealing with, the sooner I can help you fix it."

"Fix it? I don't know, Derek. Even you...."

Matt takes his seat again, lying back with a huff. "Okay. This is hard to say. I'm gonna tell it slow. So, we walked through the woods, all green and glossy with high summer, wildflowers blooming, birds flying around. I thought of the Green Man, Derek, y'know? It's like he was everywhere."

"Green Man?" Timmy says.

"That face made of foliage they got hung up there." Donnie points to the plaster mask on the patio wall. "The guy who has tree leaves for his hair and beard."

"Yep." I nod. "He's the pagan embodiment of vegetation. He's the god of plant life in the same way that Cernunnos is the god of animal life." I pat my left shoulder, the stylized face with stag horns and beard, then touch the hammer hanging about my neck. "The way Thor's the god of storm." I gesture toward the steeps of the Potomac Highlands surrounding us. "It's the power and the spirit of the Green Man that leafs out the millions of trees and shrubs that coat these mountains. Sorry for the heathen sermon, Matthew. Please go on."

"Yeah. Okay. So, the Green Man. He was there. And then he wasn't. Dillon led me along the trail, and the woods just ran out. Where the rest of the mountain used to be...there was nothing. All of a sudden, we stood at the top of a long drop, a cliff face of several hundred feet. Right behind me, little plants were flowering—lady's thumb and wild strawberry. Before me…was a huge, huge hole, like a volcano's crater, miles wide. Miles and miles of torn-up earth. And way, way below were a few trucks parked and some big black pools of who knows what kinda sludge? I looked out over all that, what used to be forest, what used to be mountaintop, and I almost puked."

Matt takes a sip of 'shine and clears his throat. "So I stand there on the edge of that big fucking mess, that huge pit of destruction…. Pit, yeah, like the pit of Hell. Dillon was right about the mouth of Hell. Smoke rising here and there from trees they'd cut down before they dynamited…they don't even sell the trees for lumber, they just burn 'em up…and some cedar waxwings come flying out of the woods behind me and get only a few feet into the empty air over that crater and then veer around like they're saying, 'Holy *shit*! What *is* this?' like they know evil when they see it, and fly back into the woods, and Dillon says, 'Usually it's so noisy with machines and dynamite you cain't bear it. Today we got some reporters coming up the mountain, though. Those Alpha sons a' bitches must have heard the press was coming, so they ain't working today.'"

Matt digs at his brow as if he's trying to exhume the memory. "Boys, part of me wanted to fall down on my knees and cry. And part of me…."

"Part of you wished you had a shotgun," I say.

"Yep. Yep. It was fucking obscene." Matt takes another swig and grits his teeth. "I wanted to track down the SOBs responsible and blow their brains out. Then Dillon says, 'You see what happens to the land. Now I wanna show you what happens to the people. You picked a good day to come, 'cause there's a convocation down in town.' So he leads me back the way we came, and, God, was I glad to turn my back on that monumental frigging mess, and then we climb in his truck and he drives us down to Charleston. We go to this environmental activist office, a group called the Mountain Partisans, down on Quarrier Street. Turns out they were having a meeting, and some folks who live in the coalfields, folks whose lives have been screwed up something awful by that kinda mining, they'd come in to tell what it was like. Some of 'em had already given up and sold their property to Alpha, but most of 'em don't want to leave, no matter what. Like with Dillon, their land's been in the family for generations."

Matt leans back and stares up at the stars for a long moment before resuming. "Those coalfield folks, they talked about the coal dust everywhere, and the water tables messed up, so folks' wells dry up, and the valleys and streams all filled up with 'overburden,' as those Alpha bastards call the earth they tear up to get to the pissant bits of coal that's left. Cancer rates rising…some researchers are saying the rates of cancer are twice as high in communities near those mining sites. And kids getting sick 'cause their school is near coal storage silos. And another school…Alpha's built a huge slurry pond with an earthen dam just behind a grade school. Can you imagine if that dam ever breaks? It'd be like that awful Buffalo Creek flood back in '72."

Timmy nods. "My daddy used to talk about that. Over a hundred people killed."

"Yep. Can you imagine living around the dust and smoke and racket? Jesus, I'd go stark raving mad. And the water's fouled up too. One lady had brung in a jar of water from her house. Said it was undrinkable. That it stank of chemicals. It was brown. Full of all kinda crap, particles of shit."

"Like that big spill a few years back in Charleston," Donnie says. "That was Alpha's fault too. My cousin Denise in the West End couldn't drink her water or take a shower or brush her teeth for weeks and weeks."

"Exactly." Matt nods. "I was going to get all macho and open the jar and take a sniff, but the lady said, 'Don't, mister. Don't even smell it. It'll make you sick to your stomach.' So, after the coalfields people spoke, Dillon and I hung around. I talked to some a' those environmental organizers, the Mountain Partisan people, and they said they sure could use some help fighting those coal-industry fuckers, and I thought, 'Well, shit, the Forest Service don't need me half as bad,' so I told 'em if they had a position—and they did, a part-time one—I might take it."

Matt leans forward, rests his elbows on his knees, and gazes at me. "Whaddaya think, Derek? Those people living in the middle of that manmade hell have complained and complained and hired lawyers and brought legal suits, but nothing seems to do any good. I really want to help 'em. I mean, those Alpha bastards are fucking with my family now."

I rub my chin. "I don't know, Matt. It all sounds a little quixotic. How would you help? What would you do?"

"Hell, I don't know. Try to raise money? Speak to civic groups? 'Raise awareness' was the phrase the activist folks used."

"You've certainly got the energy and charisma to be an activist. But what about our life here? Would you have to move back to Charleston?"

"We could rent a lil' house, maybe. I'd just spend a few nights a week down there and be up here otherwise." Matt grins at me. "Don't want you to get all starvacious. You might eat these two boys up entirely." He cocks a thumb at Donnie and Timmy, who respond with nervous smiles. "Don't worry, honey. Just 'cause I got a new crusade doesn't mean anything's gonna change between us."

"I say you tear 'em up," says Timmy. "I fucking hate 'em. Thanks to them, I was unemployed and heading for the poorhouse before Derek saved my ass."

"I think you better be careful," Donnie says. "Whoever those guys are who run that company, they have a lot of money and power on their side. If you piss 'em off...."

"Donnie has a point, Matthew. Earlier this evening, he told us that some people who've given Alpha trouble have had suspicious runs of bad luck."

Donnie makes a face. "I didn't get to the worst part. A few have come to mysterious ends."

Matt scowls. "Mysterious ends? Like what?"

"One guy burned up in his trailer, and another had a heart attack. Another'n had a real bad car accident on Gauley Mountain and is all crippled up now. And a real outspoken lady from Sylvester just up and disappeared." Donnie swigs his beer and sighs. "None of it could be connected to Alpha, though folks tried to prove—"

"Maybe it's all coincidence," Matt says. "Not like Alpha could cause a guy to have a heart attack."

"Stress could," Timmy points out. "Or maybe some kinda drug."

"Matt, I don't like the sound of all this," I say, stroking my goatee. "I don't want you to get hurt."

"I can take care of myself, honey." Matt makes a show of flexing his biceps. "Besides, I got a special kinda bodyguard, don't I?"

"Yes, you do. At night. Not during the day. And if you're in Charleston while I'm here...."

"Okay. There might be danger. Whenever a guy goes up against money and power, there's gonna be some risk. But that's no reason not to stand up for what's right, is it? You're always calling me your butch little warrior. Sure, I've punched out a few gay-bashers, but otherwise I've spent my life making a paltry living in state parks or national forests. That wasn't war. This, *this* is war. This is something worth fighting for, ain't it?"

Matt stands, crossing his arms across his chest. God, I love the masculine heft of him.

"Ain't we talking about fighting for the Green Man? And for your Horned God? Your Lord of the Animals? Think of all the critters that used to live where those mother-fucking mining sites are now. Where the hell are they? One pretty little gal at the meeting today talked about all the species being run out and endangered. Tiny little bird called a cerulean warbler…population's dwindling fast. Ain't this a crusade you can get behind?"

The thought of my partner putting himself in harm's way makes me vaguely ill, but what can I say? He's right. His conviction and courage are two of myriad things I love about him.

I rise too. "Yes, Matt. All right."

"So I got your support?"

I step forward and grip his hand in mine. "Yes. Always."

"And you two?"

"*Hell*, yes," says Timmy. "I hope you help to bury 'em deep as the streams they've covered over with crap."

"Yep, yep," says Donnie, snuggling against his boyfriend. "Just be careful, for fuck's sake."

"Hell, I ain't got nothing to worry about." Matthew grins. "I got a vampire and a werewolf to back me up. And a mean ole ex-miner with a vicious right hook. Christ, now that's decided, I'm starved. Gimme one of them there pepperoni rolls."

CHAPTER FIVE

The night of Samhain, I wake in my nest, parched with thirst. The scent of man-sex floods my nostrils.

Naked, I rise, leaving the crypt and climbing the basement stairs. The kitchen's full of cooking odors, and the lamps are low in the den. Outside the picture window, a few scattered snow flurries slant. A wood fire's warmed the house, but the fireplace has been closed up.

"Matt?" Following my senses, I ascend to the second floor. Sex-aroma grows richer and thicker with each step I take. In the master bedroom, there's the slap of flesh against flesh.

There on the bed are my three boys, deliciously intertwined. Burly little Donnie's on his hands and knees, getting fucked in the ass by his boyfriend Timmy, getting fucked in the mouth by my sexy husbear.

Matt grins over at me as he rides Donnie's face. "Damned pretty, ain't it? Nothing like a were-cub who loves getting screwed at both ends at once. Happy Halloween! Why don't you join us, Daddy?"

"That's a fine idea," I growl, stroking my stiffening cock. I kneel on the bed behind Timmy, lube up his hole, and open him up with my fingers. "Please, my lord," Timmy grunts, pushing back against me.

"So eager," I chuckle, edging my prick-head into him. "I love it when you call me 'lord.'"

"Ohhhh, yeah. Feels so good. Thank you, lord," Timmy gasps, adjusting his hips' rhythm so as to accommodate my thrusts while continuing to pound

Donnie's ass. I sink my teeth into Timmy's neck and drink deep. He climaxes inside his lover, falls to the side, and faints.

I push my cock into the were-cub next, cupping his fur-plastered pecs in my palms, working his nipples hard and then fisting his dick. Donnie moans around Matt's erection as I bite his throat and start a powerful sucking. In minutes, Donnie's come in my hand and passed out.

"Now you," I snarl, throwing Matthew onto his back. I hoist his legs over my shoulders and drive into him. He cups the back of my head, kissing me passionately while jerking himself.

"Damn, yes. Fuck me, Daddy," Matt pants. "Use my hole. Pump your seed up inside…. Uh! Uhhhh!"

Matt stiffens, grunts, and spurts onto his belly. Another few seconds, and his pulsing ass finishes me off.

I pull out, bend to slurp up his semen, then embrace him, trapping his arms against his sides, and push my fangs into his neck.

"Yeahhh. Yeahhh. Drink me," he moans, sagging against me. "D-drink me, Daddy."

I retract my fangs when his muttering trails off and his head begins to loll. We cuddle for a while, Matt drowsing in and out. Timmy comes to long enough to wrap an arm around Donnie, then passes out again and starts to snore.

After a short nap, Matt yawns and stretches. Smiling, he runs his fingers through my goatee. "Your hair's all midnight-black." He rolls onto his side and tries to rise.

"Ooooffff! Mighty weak yet again. Help me downstairs? I'm real thirsty and I ain't had dinner yet. It's still early evening. How about we leave these boys to snooze and go enjoy the fire?"

I help Matt to pull on a pair of sweatpants and a V-neck undershirt, a garment I savor since it highlights the brown hair foaming over the pit of his fang-marked neck. When he staggers and sways, I lift him into my arms, ignoring his feeble protests, and carry him down the stairs.

"Lemme just set up a plate," he mutters when we reach the kitchen. I lower him to his feet, and he doles out his usual Samhain feast: French beef stew with bacon and mushrooms, scalloped potatoes, salad, and homemade French bread slathered with butter. It's all accompanied by a big glass of Pinot Noir.

"You've gotten to be quite the international cook and wine connoisseur," I say, steadying him as we head into the den.

"Yep. Just don't know why I cain't lose weight," he says, rubbing the swell of his belly and grinning sheepishly at the large portions of his meal.

"It is indeed a mystery." I open up the fireplace, add a log, and poke up the flames. "You eat like a bird. Was that *clafoutis* I saw cooling on the counter?"

"Yep. Hey, it's a holiday! I gotta celebrate with dessert. Must admit I've gained ten pounds since I quit my job last summer," Matt grouses, taking a seat on the leather couch. "Desk work at the Mountain Partisan office and speaking engagements across the region don't exactly burn calories."

He flashes me a bold, hungry look as he adds pepper to his stew. "Look at you, all muscled-up and nekkid. You're just perfect. Always the same. Just the right proportion of definition and heft. All that black body hair, umm umm umm! Me, I'm just a grizzled, fat ole bear. If you do decide to turn me into a vampire, I wanna go on a six-month diet first."

"Bullshit. I love you just the way you are. What would I do without your fuzzy belly to rub after I give you a good fucking? I thought you looked mighty handsome at that Elkins environmental conference last week. You and your cousin Dillon both gave fine speeches. Moving and persuasive."

"Don't know about my speech, but, yeah, Dillon was great." Matt pauses to chew some stew. "Dillon, in less than a year, he's gone from wanting to shoot himself to being one of the biggest opponents Alpha has. He's a real good orator. Has all those coal bigwigs pissed off. He's cussing 'em out on the news seems like every week. Hey! Did I tell you? In January, right after New Year's, he's going up to Washington to speak to some hearing committee. Maybe he'll turn things around. If he can just convince some politicians in the Capitol… though that's gonna be difficult. Big city people have never much cared about hillbillies and our quality of life."

"It sounds to me like we should follow your cousin Dillon to DC. I'll put you up in the Tabard Inn. That's where I—"

"I remember. That senator, Tobias Crockett. Wish there'd been some other way to stop that guy. I hated him, but—"

"But the anti-gay laws he helped push through made your cousin Chet drown himself. There was no other way, Matt. The man 'needed killin',' as you'd put it."

"Yeah, maybe. Anyway, what about DC?"

"We should go together. I have a thrall up there who could arrange a nest for me during the day. You should talk to your co-workers at Mountain Partisans and come up with a list of politicians, men I can mesmerize, men whose decisions might put an end to Alpha Coal and all the destruction it's causing. Or, even easier, isn't it high time I track down all of Alpha's main players and do away with them?" I extrude my fangs and lap them. "It'd be a delightful lark."

"Now, no, Derek. You know I don't like you doing stuff like that. I don't want you killing nobody. Let's do this the right way. Some a' that glamouring, mesmerizing stuff you do, that'd be all right. Besides, my suspicion is that Alpha's a frigging hydra. Cut off one head, and a bunch more sprout up."

"Mmmm, maybe. Still…."

"Now you listen to me, Laird Maclaine," Matt says, waving his spoon. "You behave. Or one evening you'll wake up in silver handcuffs."

"Promise?" Grinning, I thumb a fang. "I could do with a long, hard butt-pounding. You haven't taken a turn on top since last spring."

"I'll pound ya, all right. In the head, if you don't listen to me. I'm serious, Derek. Don't you run off and slaughter somebody. Those poor bastards working those MTR sites are just trying to make a living, albeit at one of the most destructive jobs this earth has ever seen."

"I would never touch a miner, Matt. I'm talking about the executives. If a few of them died at the right times, perhaps the company would collapse."

"It's a hydra, I told you! Some other company would just take Alpha's place."

"I'm not convinced. Why not take advantage of your secret weapon here? Or what about, during the next full moon, we send Donnie after them just to shake them up? I think I can control him now. He and I in wolf forms, causing unholy havoc…. God, what fun."

"Derek! Sometimes you're a little too bloodthirsty for my taste."

I roll my eyes. "My nature is bloodthirst, and I adore your taste."

"Stop joking around, dammit," Matt says, forking up salad. "You can be so casual about hurting—"

"Y'all talking about me? I heard my name." Donnie stumbles into the kitchen, dragging Timmy behind him by the hand. Both are dressed in nothing but flannel boxer shorts.

"Damn, what's all this you got cooked?" says Timmy. He's a mite too pale after my overeager blood-drinking earlier.

"It's a Halloween feast, boys," Matt says. "Derek's enjoyed his dinner. Now let's enjoy ours."

"Set them up, Matthew." I pour myself a glass of wine, grateful for both the interruption and an opportunity to change the subject. "After my heavy supping, I suspect all three of you need to get your strength up." Stepping into the den, I bend down to stir up the fire.

CHAPTER SIX

The moon's rising over the eastern wall of German Valley, and I'm sitting on the front porch in the chill December night, sipping Tobermory and sharpening my dirk, when I hear Matthew's truck making its way up the mountain. Since last June and the start of his job with the Mountain Partisans, he's been staying over in his little rented house in Charleston on Tuesday, Wednesday, and Thursday nights, but today, Friday, he's due home for the weekend. Next month, his cousin Dillon is speaking to that hearing committee in Washington, so Matt and I have planned a follow-up glamouring jaunt to DC. It will be deeply delightful to bend a few politicians to my will.

First, though, I have good news for him, something that should please him enormously and improve the foul mood he's been in over new mining permits that Alpha Coal has managed to wrangle. After Internet stalking and some bat-winging, I've tracked down Hunter, the little Rebel reenactor he has a crush on. The boy lives in nearby Petersburg, West Virginia. I'm thinking a carefully arranged "accidental" meeting one winter evening soon, an invitation up to dinner and the hot tub, some casual mental manipulation on my part, and I can sit back and watch Matthew ride the boy till he's raw.

When Matthew pulls up, I meet him in the driveway. "Welcome home. I have some good news. I found—"

I stop in mid-sentence, my stomach clenching at the sight of his tear-streaked cheeks. "Derek," he rasps, his handsome face contorting.

"Matt?" I wrap him in my arms. He embraces me, leans his chin against my chest, breaks down, and sobs.

"Honey, what is it? What's happened?"

"Dillon's dead!"

A chill suffuses my spine. Alpha? "How did he die? If anyone's to blame, I'll gut them."

Matt takes a few moments to compose himself, sucking in ragged breaths, wiping his eyes, and choking back sobs. "Heart attack, they th-think, just like that other guy who pissed off that goddamn company. He was s-supposed to attend a Partisan meeting this afternoon, but when he never showed up, we went looking. Found his truck halfway up Keystone Mountain, slammed into a big ole oak, with him slumped over the wheel. He must've had the attack and run off the road. Oh, hell, I cain't believe he's gone!"

I wrap an arm around Matt and lead him into the house. "Do you think that coal company had anything to do with it?"

"Not if it was a heart attack. They ain't sorcerers, far as I know, though they might as well be in league with the devil, considering all the damage they've caused. But the stress they put him under, that was the indirect cause, for sure. Goddamn them."

In the den, Matthew pours a drink, knocks it back, then takes me by the hand. "I ain't done crying, honey. I haven't felt a grief this deep since my mommy died. How about we go upstairs, start up the bedroom fireplace, get naked, and you just hold me?"

I kiss his cheek. "You've got it, boy." What I want to say but don't is that the timing of this death is too convenient, mere weeks before Dillon was scheduled to speak at that Washington hearing committee. Whether Matthew likes it or not, it's time I took a hand in this. I won't have a bunch of slick, fat, rich coal company men making my husband frustrated and miserable if I can do anything about it. What good is power if you can't use it to punish your enemies and protect your loved ones?

CHAPTER SEVEN

The lawyer's office on Kanawha Boulevard is full of Matt's few living relatives and Mountain Partisan activists, all seated in uncomfortable metal chairs. Luckily, January's early nightfall has allowed me to attend the reading of Dillon Taylor's will. We're all curious as to who will inherit his controversial property. If it's his younger sister, Darlene, a woman Matt assures me is both pious and gutless, she's sure to sell to Alpha as soon as possible, which will upset Matthew to no end after all the struggles Dillon suffered to keep the property from them.

"You look very sophisticated in a suit and tie," I whisper, as the lawyer pulls a folder of papers from his desk.

"Shit," Matt murmurs. "I hate this stiff monkey suit. Too tight around the belly. Any sophistication this hillbilly's got rubbed off on him thanks to a Scottish laird from the Inner Hebrides." Matthew smoothes the gray fabric of his dress pants. "I wish they'd just phoned folks after the will was probated and told us who gets what. Why this big public scene like on TV?"

"All right, folks," the pudgy lawyer says. "Let's get this started."

The chatter around us dies down. "I need a drink," Matt groans.

"I've been sober for twenty-two years, Mr. Taylor, and so your only options are tap water and Pepsi. This won't take very long, I assure you, so you won't be at risk for any delirium tremens. First, let me read a note the late Mr. Taylor left as preface for his will."

The man clears his throat. "'Howdy, folks, I'm sure you're sitting there in your finery missing me up a storm. Sorry for the big public reveal. After a lifetime of being a nobody, I must admit I kind of relished all that media attention over the last few months. If you're hearing this, though, I guess the attention's over for me, except for this last hurrah. I asked my lawyer to gather you all together to hear the big news, and I even invited some Alpha Coal folks. I suspect they're lurking in the back of the room right now like the slick weasels they are.'"

"Holy shit," Matthew mutters. Everyone in the room turns, and there, yes indeed, are two men in black suits standing against the back wall, watching the proceedings with grim eyes. One's thick and middle-aged, ill-favored in the face and wearing a buzz-cut. The other's in his thirties, lean, handsome, and stylish, with angry blue eyes and wavy yellow hair. A very close-cut blond beard shades his angular face and frames his stern-set mouth.

"Ummm," I growl beneath my breath. "That one at least…a snack for later? After some vigorous punishment?"

"Behave," Matt begs. "Hush."

"Now for the will. It's very short, simple, and to the point," continues the lawyer. "'To my nephew Travis, my dirt bike. To my niece Annie, my banjo. To my sister Theresa, my oak dining-room table. To my sister Darlene…my cut-glass collection, and those pieces of Blenko glass she's always coveted with salivacious intensity.'"

"'Salivacious.' Very nice," Matt whispers. "Dillon always liked to fiddle with words."

"'To my favorite cousin, Matt, my house and property on Keystone Mountain. Don't ever sell it to the coal folks, Matt, or I'll haunt you.'"

"My God," Matt whispers. "I cain't believe it." Loudly, so everyone can hear, he says, "Hell, no, Cousin Dillon! I won't sell."

"Oh, Law! That cain't be right," Darlene squeals. She's an emaciated middle-aged woman wearing a calico dress and sporting a prominent chin. "All that house-cleaning I did for him? All those church-supper leftovers I brought up? Ingrate!"

The lawyer clears his throat again. "There's one last item. It's a little…impolite. 'To all you greedy SOBs at Alpha Coal…you're not fit to tote guts to a bear, and if there's any way I can fuck with you from beyond the grave, well, you best believe I aim to do so as soon as I can scale those gates.'"

"Lawdamercy, how vulgar," a lady to my left mutters.

The lawyer rises and slips the papers back into his folder. "That's it, folks. Mr. Taylor, if you'd stay a few minutes, we have a few fine points to discuss."

The shocked silence is shattered. Everyone rises and mills about. Darlene rushes over and smacks Matthew on the arm with her purse.

"Did you know he was going to do this?"

"Hell, no, ma'am. I had no idea."

"The two of you, hanging out the last half a year, traveling together all over the state, trying to make trouble...you *convinced* him to leave it all to you."

Matt grins. "Darlene, honey, you know as well as I do why he did what he did. He knew you woulda sold to those bastards back there." Matt jabs a thumb at the two coal company men still standing in the back of the room. They're glowering at us, their arms crossed across their chests, their legs spread, as if they intend to create a wall of force that will forbid our exit. "You woulda sold that family property in an instant."

"And why not? Half the mountain's already in ruins. Only a fool holds on to half a lottery ticket. Those gentlemen would have given me a slew of money to—"

Again Matthew raises his voice to make sure everyone in the room can hear. "Well, they can offer me as much money as they want. No way in holy hell I'll sell to the likes of them. I'm gonna enjoy being the bone that sticks in their craw just as much as Dillon did. You just watch me."

"Bone in their craw?" Darlene rolls her eyes. "You better watch out, cousin. They just might swallow you instead. Pride goeth before a fall. And the wages of sin is death."

"You're welcome to spare us your Bible verses, ma'am," I purr, resting a hand on Matthew's shoulder. "We've both had more than enough of that."

"And who is *this* gentleman?" Darlene regards my ponytail, bushy goatee, and the steel hoop in my left ear. "Some sort of hippie or biker trash?"

"Ma'am, really. You hurt me deeply."

"This here is Derek. He's my partner," Matt says without missing a beat. He wraps an arm around my shoulder and kisses me on the cheek. "My lover. My husband. I figured family gossip would have told you all about him. We've been living together for over a decade. You should see him nekkid. Built like a brick shit-house. Sexy tattoos all over. Hairy as a bear."

"Dear Lord," Darlene mutters. "Disgusting. Just disgusting. Y'all are sinners bound for the fire. The Lord will make sure you reap your just deserts." Head shaking, she turns and hurries from the room.

"You love to shock people, don't you?" I say, patting Matt's rump. "Go on and talk to the lawyer. I'll wait for you outside."

Matt nods. When I turn to enjoy a little mesmerizing or intimidating of the Alpha men, they're nowhere to be seen. They no doubt headed out in a frustrated huff. Smart move on their part, the bastards. If Matthew hadn't forbidden violence, I might have enjoyed drowning them both in the Kanawha River. Instead, I step outside to look out over black water and feel winter wind on my face.

CHAPTER EIGHT

The front steps of West Virginia's grandiose Capitol building are crowded with people, all of them carrying candles in memory of Matt's deceased cousin. It's a cloudy mid-March night, with a cool breeze off the river. The Klines, a husband-and-wife duo of folk musicians from Elkins, are performing a set of mining songs, accompanying themselves on guitars. Standing on the sidelines, beneath the neoclassical columned portico, Matt and I hum along to "Coal Tattoo," then "Coal Miner's Grave."

"I've nervous as hell," Matt murmurs, gazing out over the sea of flickering flames. "I hate being in front of a bunch of strangers. Hell, I'm just a Summers County redneck from the sticks. What the hell am I doing here, about to speak on the steps of the Capitol?"

"They're not strangers. They're people who believe what you believe. You'll be fine, Matt. You'll be more than fine. With your good looks and charm? Just think of Dillon. He'd be so proud of you."

Matt gives my hand a quick squeeze. "Thanks, honey. I sure hope you're right."

The set ends. The crowd applauds. Matt takes a deep breath and straightens his tie. "Okay," he says, stepping forward. "Here I go."

My handsome husbear takes the podium. He looks out over the audience, looks down at his note cards, then looks back at me. I can feel his anxiety.

Do it, I say, making my voice sound not in his ears but inside his head. *I believe in you. This is important. A man like you can cause great change. Do it.*

Be my warrior. Be a crusader for the Green Man and the Lord of the Beasts. Do it. Save your homeland.

Matt smiles at me, then turns back to the audience below. "Howdy, folks," he says into the microphone. He clears his throat. "I'm real glad to be here. Well, actually, I'm sorta scared. My talent ain't in giving speeches. I'm better at telling you which tree's a beech and which tree's a sugar maple. I'm pretty good at making a tasty pot of pinto beans and a hot skillet of cornbread. And I sure prefer to wear camo shorts or denim overalls than this outfit." He tugs his tie and rolls his eyes. "Can any of y'all relate?"

There's a ripple of laughter and a nodding of heads. Oh, you sweet, furry charmer. You were born to do this.

"So, I'm Matt Taylor. You probably never heard of me. But I'll bet you heard of my cousin, Dillon Taylor. The guy who owned Keystone Mountain? He's why we're all here tonight. I wanna talk about him a little bit, if y'all don't mind. Him and me spent lots of summer vacations together when we were kids. He'd come on down to Summers County, and we'd catch us some bass in the Bluestone Reservoir or the New River, and about get eaten up by gnats in the process." Matt swats at the air around his head in mock irritation. "Or I'd go on up to Keystone, and we'd spend long days outside in the woods, playing guitar and banjo, sipping on lemonade…or the occasional swiped beer, I gotta admit. It was kind of an Eden up there, with the quiet, the breezes in the leaves, the wildflowers, my aunt's fried chicken…fireflies and June bugs…."

Matthew pauses. "Well, folks, as just about all of you know, it ain't like that no more. About a year ago, Alpha Coal bought the other half of the mountain from an elderly neighbor of Dillon's, an ole guy who was chewed up with lung disease and needed to go into a nursing home…and his family convinced him to sell to Alpha, 'cause you know they musta offered him a heap of money. It's all about heaps of money with Alpha. So now that half of the mountain's gone."

Matt brushes shaggy hair out of his eyes and bows his head for a long moment. "Now, there is…and I hope you ladies will forgive my language…. I'm just an ole country boy with a bad temper and occasionally coarse…well, very frequently coarse language."

He gives them a big grin. "Y'can take the boy outta the country, right?" He gestures to the grand building behind him, then toward the lights of tall buildings downtown. "But…well, y'all know the rest: cain't take the country outta the boy."

His face grows serious again. "*Now*, folks, half of Keystone Mountain is a shit-show. It's a damned mess. A big horrible nasty pit with smoke and din and dust. Something Satan must have thought up. A nightmare. A hell on earth. Those folks, those outsiders, those rich guys who make the money off that business—and it ain't the miners making the big money, folks, it's the owners—they don't care about human life, animal life, or plant life. If they had their druthers, the whole state—Hell, the whole region! Hell, maybe most a' the world!—would be nothing but ruination except for the sweet spots they buy with all their millions. They wanna live up north somewhere, some big mansion with a gate, far from the mess they're making down here. They wanna sip cocktails on their yachts. One thing's for sure, they sure as hell don't care about us."

Matt waves an arm over the crowd. "Us. You and me. All of y'all. All of us who live here. Whose families have been here for generations, loving and tending these hills. Folks, I'm not really a religious man. I don't go to church, and I'm sure that disturbs some of y'all. But I believe in God. All folks' gods are the same one, I think. In fact, I have no doubt. Christian, Muslim, Jewish, whatever. All those ways to the center, as someone said, all those ways are right."

Matt points up at the sky, then at the Kanawha River right behind the crowd, then at the black face of the mountain on the river's far side. "I believe in God, and I believe He made this earth, these mountains, that river, and He's given life to all of us. And not just us. To the critters in the woodlands and the sea and the sky—the white-tailed deer, and the cerulean warbler, and the blue whale. All the...."

His voice grows hoarse now, as it does when he's brimful of emotion. "All the beautiful things the Lord has given us. He's given us the grace of being here, on this planet, in this beautiful state. He's given us all the kindness and loyalty we find in friends and family and clan."

He looks back at me long enough to grin and wink. *I love you. I love you so much*, I sigh inside his mind.

"And, oh God, I am so, so, *so* thankful for all of it. I truly am. And I'll bet all y'all are thankful too. Ain't you? Ain't you?"

Affirmative murmurs arise. More nodding of heads. A bevy of "Amen's." A baritone "Hell, yes!"

He brushes hair off his face and clears his throat. His smile fades. "I also believe in evil. Evil to my mind is pure selfishness, stoked to new depths by greed. Evil doesn't care if it inflicts suffering on mankind or destroys God's creation. What vast, inexcusable *ingratitude*. Ripping open a mountain like it was a living thing and spreading its guts all over the place! *That's* evil!

"'It creates jobs,' Alpha Coal would say. Lord God!" Matt sneers. "It seems like anybody can get away with anything, even murder, in West Virginia as long as they can claim they're creating jobs. Yeah, MTR creates jobs. For a handful of specialists. Compare that number to the number of folks living in those mining regions, folks whose lives are turned upside down. You know what they have to endure. You've heard all about it, thanks to Cousin Dillon. The noise, the pollution, the dust, dynamite and burning trees and flying rocks raining from the sky! Compare those few jobs to the environmental consequences. Air full of crap, water full of poisons. How many of y'all remember the big chemical spill? The weeks and weeks you couldn't use your water supply?"

Again the crowd responds. "Right!" "Bastards!" "Send 'em to prison!"

"Prison? Now there's a thought. Except the coal industry has had the legal system in this state in its back pocket since about 1880. And that, by God, needs to change."

"*Hell*, yes!" sounds the baritone voice again. "Testify, brother!" It's our buddy, Timmy Kincaid. He and Donnie are standing in the front row, smiling up at Matt.

Matt strokes his beard. "Brother, thank you. I *will* testify. Those MTR types can talk reclamation all they want, but nothing can put that land back the way it was. 'We leave the land nice and flat,' they say, 'nice space for more strip malls and car dealerships.' Jesus *Christ*, who the *hell* needs more a' that?"

"Not a soul!" a tall woman near Timmy shouts. "We want pastureland and bottomland and gardens! We want clean water! We don't need any more asphalt!"

"Thank you, ma'am! You're absolutely right. So now, listen here. I don't want to hold you here any longer. Me, to be honest, it's been a long day, and I'm tired and I'm sad and I'm ready for a beer. Or three. I just wanted to thank y'all for coming here, to convocate and honor my cousin Dillon. And I wanted to confirm some things that are important. It's true that I inherited Dillon's property up on Keystone Mountain. We just found out a few weeks ago. The Alpha Coal folks haven't contacted me yet, whining for me to sell to them, so right now I'm just going to save them the trouble."

Matt takes the microphone out of its stand and steps from behind the podium. From the top step, he scans the audience. He peers into the dimness on either side of the crowd. "Y'all here, Alpha? Y'all here? You always seem to have guys lurking around. Y'hear me, Alpha? I got news for you. You killed Dillon Taylor. That heart attack he had was your fault after all the misery you put him through. And I wouldn't sell to you for anything in the world. Tell you what I am going to do, though."

Matt squares his shoulders and pushes his broad chest out. "I'm gonna continue doing what Cousin Dillon did. I'm gonna be speaking and traveling and pushing a long stick in that nasty hornet's nest. I'm gonna speak to those folks in Washington, the ones he never got to meet. I'm gonna make as much damn trouble for you as I can, you bastards. Hell, I think I might even run for office. Too many legislators in this town, in this very building...." Matt beckons to the great dome above and behind us. "Too many delegates and senators kowtowing to you, Alpha. I may just be a good ole boy from a hick town in southern West Virginia, but, by God, I know I can do a better job than's been done by most of those politicians."

The crowd erupts in excited shouts. "Senator Taylor," someone shouts. "Governor Taylor," someone else responds.

Matt blushes, returning to his place behind the podium. "God bless y'all," he says. "I much appreciate your enthusiasm. So, look, I'm gonna end with this. Alpha Coal's pushing for more mining permits, despite lots of folks' complaints and a bunch of pending legal actions and clear violations of a slew of environmental regulations. I say a bunch of us picket their offices tomorrow and show 'em they can't push us around. How 'bout it, folks? Are you with me? Let's show 'em they can't take a piss on us mountaineers no more!"

There's a chorus of shouts. Candles are raised. The applause is wild and hearty. Matt, face red, waves, nods, and hurries back into the shadow of the portico. Someone at the podium, after announcing the end of the program, begins the state song, "The West Virginia Hills," leading the audience through the tune. "Oh, the West Virginia hills! How majestic and how grand...."

"Oh, man, I'm so glad that's over," Matt gasps, throwing his arms around me.

I kiss him on the nose. "Seems to me like a star is born."

"Star? Ha! Well, they seemed to like me. And I got to say my piece and not flub up. Let's get back to my lil' house, honey. Like I said, I'm dying for a beer."

"I think you should step out there once the song ends and talk to your future constituents. Especially if you're going to lead a protest tomorrow. Especially if you want to be a politician."

"Hell, I guess I ought. Got carried away, I guess, with all that talk about running for office."

"Sounds like a good idea. Except that you'll be needing to hire a bodyguard during the day. At night…."

"At night you got my back. Okay, lemme go talk to some folks. I won't take too long." Grinning, Matt slaps me on the butt and heads back through the great columns.

I step to the side of the portico and watch with pleasure as Matthew shakes hands with a long line of folks eager to speak to him. Senator Taylor? Possibly, despite his past as a very, very out gay musician singing queer-positive songs all around the state. I'm contemplating men's clothing stores in Charleston where I might buy him a few new suits and ties when my sharp senses warn me of a threat.

Fangs tingling, I step back into the deepest shadow of the portico and scan the Capitol lawn. Yes, as I suspected. There, to my left, a man over beyond the great trees and the statue of Stonewall Jackson, on the far side of the street. A man talking into a cell phone. He looks familiar. One of Alpha's employees?

I simply can't resist. I've slipped off the portico, sped through the shadows, and come up behind him in a matter of seconds. He is indeed one of the Alpha men from the lawyer's office, the older, ill-favored one.

"May I help you, sir?" I say with drawling congeniality.

He whirls around. "H-huh? No. Just watching the proceedings."

"Mr. Taylor's quite the speaker, isn't he?"

The man shrugs.

"Are you with Alpha Coal?"

The man stiffens. "And if I am? So what?"

"So you'd better stay away from Matt Taylor. All of you."

He clenches his fists. He's bigger-built than me by a little bit, not that that matters. "Or what?"

"What do you think?" I smile. "Or else."

"Are you threatening me?"

"Yes, indeed. I am indeed."

"Who are you? Taylor's bodyguard?"

"In a manner of speaking." I'm not in the mood for a glamour. He's not worth the effort. Perhaps his younger, better-looking colleague might be, but not him. I think I'll quietly throttle him and dump his corpse into the river. Thanks to Matt's scruples, I haven't killed someone obnoxious in a long, long time, but this Alpha business has put me in a foul mood, and my anger's long overdue for an outlet.

I move closer. He steps back.

"You better not fool with me," he says, patting his suit coat. A gun, most likely. That just means I need to move fast. The sound of a gunshot would ruin the festive atmosphere of the evening.

"I'm not fooling, I promise. I'm dead serious," I say, tensing to spring.

"Derek!"

Dammit. Matt. He's crossing the street.

"Howdy, Matthew," I say, turning toward him.

"What's going on?" he says, moving between the stranger and me.

"This gentleman represents Alpha Coal."

"Yeah?" Matt rests his hands on his hips. "What d'ya want?"

"Nothing." The man's smile is cold. "Just listening to your pretty speech."

"Glad you liked it. I hope you recorded it and sent it to your bosses."

"Actually, I did," the man says, holding up his phone. "It impressed them very much."

"Good," replies Matt. "Might prevent misunderstandings in the future."

The stranger chuckles. "Based on what I've witnessed tonight, I don't think so. You're a fool to go up against us, Taylor. I think your fate might already be decided. The only surprise will be *how* it's gonna come down."

"Is that a threat?" I snarl. The urge to tear his throat out is overwhelming.

"To quote you, 'Yes, indeed.' Who is this guy, Taylor? If he's your bodyguard, let me give you a little advice. If you're going to keep pissing Alpha Coal off, I'd recommend more intimidating protection."

Matt chuckles. "He's a lot stronger than he looks. And he's not my bodyguard. He's my boyfriend. My partner."

"Really? You two are…?" The man shakes his head, looks us up and down, and laughs. "Never would have guessed that."

"What's so goddamn funny?" I spit.

"Not a damn thing. Good evening, guys." With a tip of his hat, he moves away down the street.

"You were going to hurt him, weren't you?" Matt turns to me, frowning.

"That was undecided until you showed up and he threatened you. Now I want to tear him limb from limb and feed his parts to the fishes."

"Derek, dammit." Matt heaves a long sigh. "C'mon, Monster Maclaine. I'm more than ready for that beer."

CHAPTER NINE

"That guy lurking on the edge of the crowd tonight and taping Matt's speech, that's Baxter Moore," says Timmy. "And the blond guy he runs with is Jon Fain."

Donnie, Timmy, Matthew, and I are relaxing with Scotch ales in Matt's tiny rented house in Charleston's East End, ironically only blocks from the offices of Alpha Coal. Before us, a gas fireplace exudes yellow heat, no doubt most welcome to their human frames on such a chilly night.

"Yes, Moore was with a tasty blond in the lawyer's office during the reading of the will," I say.

"Fain's a good-looking guy for sure, but a real bastard," Timmy says. "Back when I worked for Alpha, I'd see him around the mining sites sometimes, all sleek in three-piece suits, bossing men around. He lives up in South Hills, one of those new mega-mansions. Guess his employers pay him real well."

"No doubt," says Matt. "Derek, I know that look in your eyes. What are you planning to do? You're not gonna hurt anybody, are you?"

"Me? Never."

"Don't shit me, honey. I told you—"

"I know, I know." Wrapping an arm around Matthew, I give him a hard hug. "I was just thinking about some supping and mesmerizing. I think it's time we got a little more information on our opponents."

"Sounds good to me," says Timmy, grinning vindictively. "Fain treated me like a dog four or five times. Want me to show you where he lives?"

I finish my ale and stand. "I do believe I do."

"Derek!" Matt stands as well. "*Don't* hurt anyone."

"I promise that Mr. Fain will live to see the morning, albeit in an enfeebled state," I say, patting Matt's cheek. "I've got to feed, don't I? Might as well get some information too. Right?"

"Okay," Matt mutters, still clearly dubious. "Just be careful, okay?"

"Both of you be careful," Donnie adds. "Those Alpha guys play rough."

"Careful? What can harm me?"

"Derek!"

"*Yes*, I'll be careful. Let me fetch some, uh, accouterments, Timmy boy, and we can head out. I haven't had a ride in your pretty new Ford Ranger yet."

"Go on back to Matt's now," I say. We're sitting in Timmy's idling truck, sheltered behind a huge blue spruce, watching March drizzle spot the windshield. Lights glow on every floor of Fain's huge three-story house: lots of wasted electricity powered by coal, no doubt. The place has one of those port-cochère-style front driveways you could fit an elephant under. The man's clearly into conspicuous consumption.

"Sure I cain't help you? Maybe you can hypnotize Fain into kissing my hairy Rebel ass?"

"I'd be glad to kiss your hairy Rebel ass myself…before I fuck it," I say, climbing from the cab. "You're sure he lives alone? No fragile wife or adorable spawn to terrify?"

"Sure as I can be. I even asked some good ole boys I used to work the mines with. The prick ain't married yet, though my guess is, as good-looking and rich as he is, he gets himself plenty of pussy."

"No doubt. Get on now. I'll see you boys this weekend at Mount Storm."

Timmy reaches over and squeezes my hand. I close the truck door quietly. He drives off. I watch him disappear around a corner, then turn, stroking my rain-wet graying goatee. It's been several nights since I've fed, but I intend to make up for that abstemiousness tonight.

I circle the house, peering in windows. The house is isolated on a jutting ridge overlooking the Kanawha, so I don't have to worry about neighbors catching sight of a mysterious stranger wearing a long black Western duster ranging around the lawn. Fain's nowhere to be seen in any of the first-floor rooms. But somewhere…somewhere underground…I can hear faint music with an annoying, erratic rhythm. When I bend to the house's foundation, I can detect the scent of cologne mixed with sweat. He's in the basement. And here, flanked by boxwood bushes, is the basement door.

Locked. There's an alarm, no doubt, poised to begin its banshee keening if I were to tear the door open. As I shift, my frame glows green and my edges smudge and fade. In mist-form I slip under the door, streaming past piled storage boxes and toward a brightly lit room where music throbs and sweat-musk emanates.

It's a basement gym, nice and roomy, with a punching bag, stationary bike, and racked free weights alongside several lifting benches. Fain has his back to me. He's dressed in blue nylon gym shorts and a white muscle-shirt that sweat has stuck to the skin of his back. He's jogging on a tilted treadmill. His even breathing tells me that he's in fine shape, that he's regular and disciplined in his use of this well-equipped gym.

I move closer, breathing in the scent of him, savoring the steady beat of his heart, the coursing of his blood. The man's a little taller than me and nicely built. Too thin for me, really, but his long legs are coated with golden hair and the muscles in his arms are prettily defined. I wait till he's stopped the machine to take a long swig of water before seizing him from behind.

Fain yelps, curses, and squirms. "Good boy. Give me a little fight," I say, tightening my grip about his chest. Clamping a hand over his mouth, I sink my teeth into his neck.

Fain groans and shudders. He lifts his head and blinks up at me. His sapphire eyes go wide. When he tries to sit up, he fails. Mumbling what are no doubt frightened and frustrated vulgarities, he begins a feeble thrashing around on the segmented pads flooring his gym.

I've got the coal thug naked, trussed, and silenced, just the way I like a handsome man. His hands are cuffed behind his back. His ankles are roped together. Several layers of duct tape are wrapped around his head. The tape covers his pretty Cupid-bow lips and most of his neat blond beard, unfortunately, but it's worth the visual sacrifice to see him so powerless, to savor how completely I've stolen his speech.

"Later, we're going to have a long talk," I say, slipping out of my clothes item by item. "Right now, though, I want to hear you sob and shout for help against that gag. I want to admire how frigging hot you are with all that tape plastered over your mouth. Go ahead now, Mr. Fain. I know you're very weak, but still. Scream for me. Struggle. Get even sweatier. I like to taste a man's sweat almost as much as I like to taste his semen." I find a bit of almost-dry gore in the nook between my first and second fingers and lap it clean. "And his blood, of course."

The mention of blood encourages my captive to obey me. He howls for help. He rolls around in that deliciously fettered and thoroughly helpless and hopeless way that gets me unendurably hard. His heart is racing. Blood wells from the marks on his neck.

I lick my lips. "I'm tempted to drain you dry, but then you'd be of no use to me whatsoever," I say, pressing a foot down upon his heaving fur-dusted chest. "Instead I'm going to rape you. Have you ever had a big hairy man's cock up your shapely rump?"

Fain's eyes go wide. He swallows hard. He shakes his head and wails.

"We all have fetishes, do we not?" I say, gripping him by the arm and pulling him to his feet. "Mine are fairly simple. I love to bind and gag a man, hurt him a little, get him to break down and weep, and then take him up the ass. I've been enjoying such delectable scenes since 1730."

I brush his wavy golden hair, lick a trickle of sweat off his temple, and drag him across the room. "You, Jon Fain, are next. Next in a long, long, long line of lucky lads, musky lads, furry lads in need of mastery."

When I shove him down onto his knees and bend him over the bench press, he starts struggling again. When I clutch an ass-cheek and finger-probe his hole, he goes wild, screaming and writhing beneath me.

"You're my thrall now, though you don't know it. I could calm you. I could make you want this. But I think you deserve a little punishment before I give you the gift of acquiescence."

To my delight, Fain stops shouting and begins to sob. Sweet muted pleas. Copious tears. Just what I wanted. I spit-moisten first my cock and then his exceedingly tight and no doubt virgin hole, lap tears off his tape-swathed cheeks, and drive mercilessly into him.

The bed's luxurious, in a capacious bedroom decorated in shades of gray and blue. I've just finished supping on the soupçon of asshole gore my savage ravaging inspired and am licking his wounded neck, mightily tempted to drink from him again, when my cuffed captive moans and shifts in my arms. His pretty blue eyes flicker open. He regards me with an expression of terror.

"There you are, Jon. May I call you Jon?"

Fain nods, the look of fear fading into dazed confusion. I stroke his mussed hair. "Good, good. No reason to be frightened. I ravished you, Jon. Thank you for such pleasure. Your ass was superlatively tight. Are you sore?"

Jon nods.

"Badly?"

Jon nods, his brow creasing.

"Good. That's as it should be. Did you enjoy having me inside you?"

Jon shakes his head.

"Ah, I don't think you're recollecting rightly. You loved it, did you not?"

This time Jon nods. A single tear forms at the corner of one eye.

I chuckle. "Before I leave, you want me to lift your long, shaggy-haired runner's legs in the air and plow you again, don't you?"

Jon nods.

"Excellent. But first let's get all that tape off your pretty lips. You have information I need."

I pick and peel the gag off, amused by his pained wincing. "Thanks, sir," Jon mutters, licking his lips.

"Do you know what the word 'thrall' means, Jon?"

Jon cocks a golden eyebrow. "Thrall? Like 'enthrall?'"

"Exactly. You'll do whatever I tell you to, won't you?"

Jon hesitates, looking perplexed, then surprised. "Yeah. Yeah, I guess so. How did that happen? What do you want to know?"

I kiss him firmly on the mouth. "I want to know everything you know about Alpha Coal."

Chapter Ten

His name's Stan Sodeski, the president and CEO of Alpha Coal. He's a gray-haired, jovial-looking gentleman with glasses and a white mustache. He doesn't like gay people or believe in same-sex marriage, facts he's made clear through frequent irate letters to the *Charleston Gazette*. A few years before he became CEO, he sent hateful anonymous email to several gay activists and authors across the Appalachian region, messages that Matt's friend Bobby, a techno-savvy bear-chaser at Virginia Tech, was able to trace to him. Complaints about that harassment never came to much, thanks to his friends in judicial positions, and certainly didn't slow his rise to power.

He apparently isn't any fonder of snakes than he is of queers, at least judging by the squeals of fright he's emitting in the living room of his Kanawha Boulevard condo this warm April night. I'd promised Matthew not to hurt anyone, but what my husband and his version of absolute morality don't know won't hurt them…meaning that there are at least two timber rattlers mixed in with the passel of black rat snakes Mr. Sodeski gets to enjoy. It's herpetological Russian roulette: which species will get to him first? After several minutes of frantic side-stepping, Sodeski finally makes it onto a couch, only to feel the largest rat snake of all wrapping around his calf. Under my direction, it gives his ankle only the tiniest of nibbles, but the portly Sodeski faints anyway. He'll live to suffer at my hand another day.

On to the board of directors.

his name's Robert Massey. He's a gray-haired, stern-looking gentleman who cherishes his expensive vacations and believes "those old bitches" down in Sylvester complaining about the immoderate amounts of coal dust in their community should get the hell off his back.

At this point, he'd also like to get the spiders off his back. He's never seen— or felt—so many of them. He lies on his considerable belly in bed, paralyzed with terror, puling like a choleric infant, as they explore his mole-speckled expanse. What an admirable plethora of species: Carolina wolves, goldenrod crabs, dark fishing spiders, bold jumpers, barn funnel weavers, the striking black and yellow garden spiders, and a couple of black widows, just to spice up the possibilities.

When a hairy black wolf spider jumps onto his forearm, Mr. Massey promptly pisses himself. I can barely suppress my laughter. When one of the glossy widows bites him on the thigh, he screams, rolls out of bed, and crawls to the bedroom door. Soon, clad only in underwear, he's staggered into the street of his suburban neighborhood, begging passersby to call 911.

his name's Dan Philips. He's a devout churchgoer, a proponent of family values and the death penalty. A sporty-looking man in his forties, red hair going a little gray at the temples, he's fond of seersucker suits.

He's less fond of his patio guests. As night descends, buzzards one by one take up residence there, perching on the couch, chairs, and railings. They hunch, dark-winged and bare-necked, birds of ill omen. When he tries to shoo them off with a broom, they create a waddling, hissing circle around him, then spatter him with noisome, carrion-scented vomit.

er name's Linda Flint. She's a hard-nosed lawyer during the day, an ador- ing mother at night. She prides herself on her collection of sleek pants suits and professionally severe blouses, her full head of auburn hair.

Right now, however, she's wishing that lovely hair were cut as short as a butch lesbian's, for it's snagged with shrilling bats. She screams and claws at the wee beasties. Others of their kind flit and swoop about her dining room. Her two daughters, keening with fear, huddle beneath the dining table. Her husband, pale and ineffectual city dweller, swings at the erratic animals with a fly swatter while dialing 911 with a shaking thumb.

his name's Jimmy Holden. He's a cadaverous insurance executive with a summer home in Newport, Rhode Island, and a passion for golf and the latest high-tech gadgets. He thinks that any environmentalist nut who believes in climate change and who dares to criticize Alpha ought to be sent to jail and put in solitary for a couple of months.

A solitary cell, however, would be more welcome than what he finds in his kitchen tonight. All he wanted was a midnight snack and some quiet. Instead, he finds rats. Hundreds of them. They stare at him from counter and breakfast nook, cabinet top and stovetop. When he backs up, skin prickling with disgust, they all leap to the floor and follow him. It's like having a multitudinous official escort. He tries to keep calm and move slowly, but when they start pouring furrily over his bare feet, he shrieks, turns, and runs. By the time he makes it out the front door, his bare feet are bloody from a score of savage bites. If the medical help he finds isn't wise enough to give him rabies shots, he'll be frothing at the mouth in a matter of weeks.

CHAPTER ELEVEN

"**B**een busy, ain't you?"

My husbear's sitting on the patio couch, finger-picking his guitar in the twilight when I emerge from the house. He's barefoot, wearing old jeans and a gray Mountaineers tank top. The latest issue of the *Charleston Gazette* is spread across the coffee table before him. Down the slope sound the argent chimings of spring peepers. The orchard and woodlands behind the house are covered with April's chartreuse leaves.

"'Her hardest hue to hold,'" I mutter, quoting Robert Frost, studying the silver hair on Matthew's bearded chin. I take a seat beside him and squeeze his knee. What's about to happen I well know. In Freudian terms, the Superego is about to scold the Id.

"Busy?" I play innocent. "Did you work in the garden today? Looks like the white oak leaves are as big as red squirrel ears. And the dogwood's blooming. Doesn't all that mean it's time to plant corn?"

"Yep," Matt sighs. "I got in four rows." He picks out the first few bars of "Dixie."

I try to make distracting small talk. Chatting about food is always a good delaying tactic. "Beltane's coming up in a couple of weeks. Do you want to have the boys up? You always make German food for that holiday. Donnie loves your potato salad with bacon."

"Gonna make all that, yep. Sure, let's have 'em up."

Matt shifts the tune. Now he's plucking the dour notes of "The House Carpenter," the Appalachian version of what's called "The Demon Lover" in the British Isles. He played it the night we met, during a performance with his country/folk band, the Ridgerunners.

"*Well met, well met, my own true love…*" he sings, his baritone voice deep, rich, and husky.

"Well met. Do you still believe that? I know you're about to chastise me something awful."

Matt lifts the instrument off his knee, places it gently in its lined case, and closes the clasps.

"'Well met?' Hell, yes. 'My own true love?' Hell, yes. But that doesn't mean you don't drive me crazy sometimes. You like to piddle with people so much—and maybe I would too if I had the powers you do—that sometimes you do stupid, or unwise, or cruel things. Even when I ask you not to. You need more self-control, honey. I mean, hell, you've had since 1730 to learn how to rein yourself in."

"You're right about all of that, Matt. And we've had this conversation many times before. It's just that I love you so much that…when someone crosses you, I want to hurt them. I want to send them far, far away, or—"

"Or make them cease to exist. Which would be so easy for you. But sometimes the consequences, the long-range effects.…"

Matt shakes his head. I steel myself for the berating tirade that's sure to come. Instead he guffaws.

"Shit. I try and try to be stern with you about these things, but there's just enough of you in me that.… Okay, I would love to have been there when you sent those rat snakes after that motherfucking Sodeski."

"It was pretty priceless," I admit, relieved by his amusement and by the fact that the press somehow didn't report the presence of rattlesnakes.

"There were articles in the *Gazette* today about all those, uh, zoological visitations. Those board a' director assholes are shaken up bad. One was treated for shock, one nearly had a stroke, another had to have rabies shots, and another's in the hospital after a black widow bite. Some crazy preachers are even saying a powerful demon's after Alpha."

"A powerful demon *is* after Alpha," I say, flexing an arm and preening.

"You cain't resist a little supernatural showboating, can you? A little terrorism?"

I take his hand in mind and pat it. "No, I can't. So what's next in your crusade to stop Alpha?"

"Those bastards managed to get yet another permit, this time to tear up a mountain near Blair, so we're having a protest march down in Logan County next week."

"In the afternoon, I assume? Be careful. No night-walkers to back you up."

"I will. Been real cautious since I started getting hate mail. Plus a bunch of us Mountain Partisans are planning to go to DC in June. We're gonna try to convince the politicians up there that MTR and the chemical industries are fucking up Appalachian water supplies real bad. A whole slew of coalfield folks plan to testify. After that shit-storm of river pollution that happened in Charleston a while back, maybe this time those Capitol Hill bigwigs will listen. Maybe you can go with me, the way we'd planned last winter, and you can pull some of that fancy fanged hypnotism. How about it?"

"Absolutely. I'll help in any way I can."

"That's kinda what I'm afraid of." Matt grins. "So what about *your* plans?"

"What plans?"

"Please. What's the next step in your crusade to protect me and stop Alpha? And don't tell me you don't have plans. You can be one of the slickest liars I know, but rare is the time that you can fool me."

I chuck his silvery chin. "I got some handy security codes off Fain. How about I sabotage some of their facilities? Hit them where it hurts the most: in the pocketbook? Do you know how much some of those mountain-gutting machines are worth? I could cost them millions of dollars."

Matt gives me conflicting signals, smiling and shaking his head at the same time. "You remind me of a teenaged boy: addicted to explosions. Kinda like me at sixteen. Nearly lost a finger to some faulty fireworks."

"I promise not to lose any fingers."

"I don't think I wanna know about it. You might give the Partisans and all the other folks against MTR a bad reputation."

"Maybe. You certainly will need to have alibis during the times I have my fun. Since Dillon died, you've become one of Alpha's most vocal opponents. I don't want law enforcement bothering you or regarding you with suspicion."

"You gotta remember that the important thing is to stop any future mountain-maiming. This ain't about giving you the opportunity to enjoy lots of violent fun."

"What? It's not? Hateful!" I cross my arms in a mock-pout, then nod. "You're right. So how about we divide up the duties? You stick to the straight and narrow with your speeches and public protests and awareness-raising, and I indulge in a little destruction? Wear down Alpha's morale a bit? They can't eviscerate mountains if their machines are in shambles, can they?"

"You got a point there," Matt admits. "Like I said, I don't wanna know what you're up to. If your shenanigans get too showy or widely publicized, I'll encourage the Partisans to issue a statement denouncing such 'outrageous illegal behavior' so we can distance ourselves from the crazy vigilante sabotaging pore innocent Alpha's operations."

"Expect showy. Denounce away. The information I've gotten from Fain is just too good not to use."

"Part of me's scared of what you'll do to Alpha." Matt gives me a weary smile. "You're *determined* to be wicked, ain't you? I feel like a parent who's just too tired to punish you or force you to behave."

"You're welcome to punish me any time you want," I say, leering at him. "There's all that silver chain in the basement, you know. It's been a long time since you got mean and dominant with me. I could do with a change of pace. Get as rough as you please. Make me hurt."

Matt chuckles. "Don't tempt me, bad boy. I just might do that. And I know how fast you heal…."

"Top me some other night." I pull Matthew to his feet. "You're making me hungrysome. Tonight, I'm going to ride your rump till you're good and sore." Heaving him over my shoulder, I stride through the French doors into the house.

chapter twelve

After weeks of reconnoitering, I'm finally ready to test the latest codes Jon Fain gave me. Tonight, *Walpurgisnacht*, May Eve, I'm relieved to discover that each of them works like a charm.

First, the security cameras about the Keystone Mountain mining site flicker off. Now, so do nine-tenths of the glaring spotlights, leaving the loathsome crater conveniently dim for my purposes. Now the locked door to the hut of hoarded dynamite snicks opens beneath my touch. I'm about to enter when I hear a man's gruff voice behind me and the click of a gun's safety catch.

"Who the hell are you? Put your hands up."

I dissolve into mist, giving him no chance to see my face. If anyone recognizes me as the man who accompanied Matt to the reading of Dillon's will and to the candlelit memorial service at the Capitol, my human, all-too-human husbear might be in serious trouble.

"What the fuck? Where'd he go?" shouts another man. Holding a flashlight, he's moving in from the left. Animate vapor, I drift across the barren landscape, over inky pools of pollutants and oil, counting my foes as I go: five men in security uniforms and carrying firearms.

Don't hurt anyone, said Matt. Shit. All right. Tonight may not involve slaughtering fun, but it will certainly include scare-the-shit-out-of-them fun, the same sort of amusement I enjoyed with those guards at the Alpha Coal building I burnt down in Kanawha City right after I enthralled Timmy.

I mist around the object of tonight's quest, the looming machine nick-named Don-Don. It's a dragline, the several-hundred-foot-tall monstrosity they use to move tons of earth above the coal. I focus, shifting yet again. The bestial form I take is nearly twice the size of normal *Canis lupus*. Fangs bared and slavering, I lope out from behind the machine, glowering at the startled guards.

"What the hell is that?" one man shouts, training his flashlight on me.

"Shit, look at the size of that dog," shouts another guard. "It looks mean." He flaps his hand at me. "Git! Git on outta here!"

Hackles rising, I lope closer.

"Well, hell. Just shoot it," directs a third.

The man who'd pulled a gun on me earlier sighs. Raising his pistol, he levels it at me and fires.

Right in the shoulder. I recoil, snarling. Shit. Hurts. Shit. If those bullets were silver or rowan wood, I'd be fucked. As it is....

Snarling, I race toward the man who shot me and leap upon him. Tearing his throat out would be proper punishment, but Matt's words stand between me and murderous satisfaction, so I settle for sinking my fangs into the man's forearm. He screams, trying to shake me off.

Gunfire kicks up gravel near my front paw. I drop my first prize and race after my second. This one I seize by the calf, worrying the plump mouthful of muscle for a few pleasant seconds before heading off after prize number three.

"Shit!" This one drops his gun and runs. I'm about to leap upon his back when another bullet stings into me, this time in my hip. I wince. I turn. I scowl.

My assailant is several hundred yards away, carrying a rifle. He's young, probably no more than twenty-five. He's tall, good-looking, thin-hipped and broad-shouldered. His sharp features and neat reddish beard look familiar. He seems to know how to aim a rifle, even in very dim light and at a good distance, for now another bullet catches me in the neck, making me yelp.

"Good job, Nate!" one of the other men yells. "Put that rabid bastard down!"

Nate? Dammit. I met this boy several years ago, down at Charleston's bear bar, the Tap Room. Matt and I engaged in some heavy flirtation with him that never went anywhere. He's gay, albeit fairly closeted, from what I can recall. What the hell is he doing working for Alpha?

Shaking off my surprise and the pain of the bullet wound, I sprint toward him.

"Goddamn you," Nate shouts, aiming again. He sounds like Matt, speaking with the same mountain drawl. Another bullet pierces me, this time in the chest.

"Bull's eye. That'll do you, you big bastard," he says, waiting for me to collapse.

But of course I don't collapse. I dash toward him, glaring. I bare my teeth again, growling low in my throat.

"Shit. Shit. Die, dammit," he says, backing up.

He's aiming once more when I smash into his torso, knocking him onto his back. The urge to sink my fangs into his neck is immense. Instead I look into his terrified green eyes, growling huskily. I nuzzle his beard. When I lick his neck, I can feel his pulse racing against my tongue.

"Jesus! Get off!" He's only able to roll out from under me because I've decided I'll let him. Staggering to his feet, he darts off into the darkness. Soon I hear car engines revving amid a confusion of shouts.

A few minutes of spinning wheels, and they've fled down the mountain. No doubt they're on their cell phones, calling for backup, so I need to work fast.

Alighting on the steeply pitched rooftop of Dillon's larger cabin, I fold my black-leather wings against the wind and watch from a distance. The explosions begin, orange and white, furling open in the tattered, concentric patterns of chrysanthemums. Their force rocks the structure beneath me.

The first shatters the dragline bucket. The follow-up, erupting only seconds later, uproots the huge crane. It sways, teeters, and falls. Before it can hit the ground, the third blast rips the dragline's cab into pieces. Small postscript, the final explosion takes out a high voltage grid that powered the great machine when it was in operation. The few lights left on the site wink out.

Now, on that desecrated land there is darkness, save for the glow of small fires inside the twisted metal. Now there is silence, except for the crackle of those fires. I launch off the roof, spiral through the air, lick my fangs, and laugh low in my throat. For a few gratifying moments, I circle the smoking mess of my triumph before jetting off beneath spring constellations toward Mount Storm.

CHAPTER THIRTEEN

When I emerge from the basement of Mount Storm the following night, I find my boys lounging on the patio, enjoying the balmy evening and preparing to scarf up a Beltane feast.

Matt's tong-lifting fat bratwursts off the grill. The patio table's heaped with Germanic cuisine: home-baked pumpernickel bread and butter; cucumber, onion, and sour cream salad; pickled herring; spiced sauerkraut; marinated green bean salad; warm potato salad with bacon; pickled beets; and big steins of beer. The sound system's playing Chris Young's country baritone down low. Candles burn along the patio railings.

"Here comes the conquering hero," Matt says with a crooked smile. I can tell he's seriously conflicted: part of him's probably dismayed at the havoc I wreaked, and part of him's delighted. After all, he hates Alpha even more than I do.

"Hooray!" Timmy jumps to his feet and seizes me in a big bear hug. "You tore their asses up, now didn't you?"

"Let's just say I inconvenienced them," I reply, tousling his brown hair.

"Looks like you made the papers, man. Congrats." Donnie hands me a copy of the latest *Charleston Gazette*. The headline blares, "Mysterious Sabotage on Keystone Mountain. Eighty Million Dollar Dragline Blown to Bits."

"Your own little May Eve mountaintop bonfire, huh?" Matt hands me a stein of beer. "Come and get it, guys."

I settle down at the table with them and sip my beer while they gobble enthusiastically. "I do love to see burly, bearded boys eating good food," I say.

"I ain't gonna be so burly if I end up on a prison diet," Matt says, frowning at me. "Cops came to the Mountain Partisan office this morning and grilled a whole bunch of us."

"I was afraid of that. So, what happened?"

"Well, most of us were real honest about being glad the sabotage happened, but we all had alibis, except for Judy, and she's a grandmother, so they don't really suspect her. I was down at the Tap Room with these boys here, just as you suggested, helping to plan the Mountain State Bear Contest coming up soon. All sorts of people saw me there." Matthew doles out more helpings before slicing up his second sausage and adding mustard.

"Good. You might have to arrange another alibi soon."

"So you ain't done?" Timmy's clearly joyous at the prospect.

"No, I'm not done. Not at all. Fain gave me a detailed list of Alpha's properties. I plan to work through them, one by one. I'm going after the MTR sites at Elk Run and Marfork next. The fewer draglines they have, the less damage they can do. Isn't that right, Matt?"

Matt rubs his forehead and gulps a big slug of beer. "Yeah, that's right. I cain't believe this is happening."

"I cain't either," says Donnie. "Eighty million dollars…."

"Do you want me to stop?"

"Hell, no, don't stop," Timmy says.

"Those assholes fired Timmy and they're ruining the mountains all three of us grew up in. I say don't stop," Donnie adds. "They gotta be the ones sending Matt all that hate mail. He got another nasty letter today, telling him they were gonna exterminate him like a cockroach."

"Matt? Is that true?"

Matt kneads his jaw and takes another swig of beer. He nods but says nothing. Instead, he sits back and looks out over the lawn.

"Your group is doing a lot of good, Matt. The protests, the newspaper articles, the lobbying, the upcoming trip to DC. But while you work to change things through legal channels, more mountains are being torn to pieces. And, since Alpha has so many politicians and judges in their pockets, they're simply ignoring the environmental restrictions that have been passed. Didn't they get yet another new permit, this time to mine Justice Ridge?"

Matt swallows more beer and stares at me, his bushy eyebrows knitted up. "You know what? Fuck it. You're right. Don't stop." He stabs a piece of sausage with his fork and pops it into his mouth. "I hate those sons a' bitches more than anybody I've ever hated in my life. You do what you want to do, honey. Just don't hurt any miners. Poor bastards are just trying to make a living at a time when jobs are few and far between…no thanks to that lying retard in the White House. Don't everyone know that coal ain't coming back?"

"Speaking of miners struggling to survive, do you remember that hot otter—Nate was his name—down at the Tap Room? The one we tried to seduce one evening? Tall guy with a red beard?"

Matt nods. "Nate Palmer. I wanted to top him bad. He'd look mighty fine on his elbows and knees—"

"Getting plowed, yes. We constructed quite a few fantasies about him that night."

"Yep. I wanted you to glamour him, but he left early, and we never saw him again. Later, I found out why from a few gossips around the bar."

"Oh? Why?"

"He's religious, and I think he listened to his preacher more than his libido. He stopped coming out to the bar and crawled back into the closet. Moved to Chelyan. What a waste. Why you bringing him up?"

"He's one of the mine guards at Keystone. He's a good shot. He put three bullets into me."

"Damn. Really? Aw, shit. He's working for Alpha Coal? I repeat: what a waste."

"If I ever run into him again, I promise to reform him."

"You damn well better. There's always room for one more in the hot tub."

"And room for a few more in my harem of hot thralls. Speaking of which, are you still planning to go down to McDowell for that Civil War reenactment? To see your Rebel boyfriend, Hunter?"

"Count on it," Matt says. "I'm gonna lay on the charm. That lil' guy's gonna be putty in my hands. Okay, boys, y'all had enough, or do you want thirds?"

"Stupid question," Timmy says, lifting his empty plate. "Thirds, please."

"Me too," says Donnie. "Especially the tater salad."

"Glad you like it. Boys, your appetites are downright gratifying, in and out of the bedroom. Just save room for German chocolate cake. I made it this afternoon."

CHAPTER FOURTEEN

"They've changed the security codes, just as you expected," Jon Fain mutters. "But I brought you the new ones."

A week after my Keystone Mountain spree, my new thrall and I are enjoying glasses of port in his cavernous living room. He's dressed in an expensive business suit. Anxiety, I can sense, keeps welling up in him, flickers of potential disobedience I have to mentally tamp down.

"Good boy," I say, taking the note card from him. "What are your bosses saying about the Keystone Mountain sabotage? Whom do they suspect?"

Fain hesitates. "I'm not sure. They have folks following Matt Taylor and Jack Gunnoe and Buddy Gibson…."

"Really?" I scowl, tonguing a fang. "So they suspect them?"

"Not really. They're all too much on the up and up. No, the Alpha higher-ups think there's some crazy vigilante on the loose. Someone like you. I really want to tell them about you, but I can't. I don't know why."

"Because you don't want to tell them. Right?"

Fain finger-taps his knee nervously. "Right. I don't. Right."

"Stop tapping. It's irritating. Loosen your tie. Take off your shirt."

Blank-eyed, Fain does so. I run my fingers through his golden chest hair and pinch his small nipples. He closes his eyes and sighs.

"What do you say?"

"Thank you, sir."

"Good boy. What else have you learned at work?"

"Not much. I'm not as close to the inner circle as you seem to think."

"Sad to hear. Perhaps I should have enthralled someone else…but none of them I've glimpsed is as pretty as you."

"They seem to think that…if the saboteur comes after them again…somehow they're confident that…uhhhh, that feels good, sir. No one's ever played with my nipples before."

"Then you've been bedding the wrong people." Bending, I run the tip of my tongue over Jon's left nipple and suck it softly.

"Don't mind me. Go on."

I sink in a fang. Jon flinches and trembles.

"T-They seem to th-think that they can w-ward off other attacks."

"How?" I mumble, mouth filling with blood.

"Don't…ahhh! Don't know."

"They're sadly mistaken." I drink for a few more minutes, gulping down his youthful strength. Removing my fang, I sit erect and spread my thighs. "Suck me."

"Yes, sir." Dizzily, Jon drops to his knees and begins sloppy, unskilled fellatio. I tolerate that only briefly before changing our course.

"Get naked now. Then go fetch a pair of your dirtiest underwear and stuff them in your mouth. Then bend over the back of the couch and put your pretty little butt in the air. You haven't been half as useful as I'd hoped. My fault, I guess, for choosing you instead of one of your homelier but more knowledgeable colleagues, but still…I think you need to be punished. Tonight, I'm going to slap your butt red, and then I'm going to fuck you using nothing but your own spit while I drink from your neck. Is that all right with you, Jon?"

"Sure it is." Jon stands, giving me a mindless smile. "Everything's all right when you're around, sir." He peels off his clothes before staggering off in search of the laundry hamper.

CHAPTER FIFTEEN

Soaring as high as I can, so as to get the widest view possible, I flap over southern Kanawha County and on into Boone County, amazed at the amount of devastation. One hundred and eighty degrees of wooded West Virginia mountains roll before and below me, but there's the sprawling blight of a mountaintop removal site every ten degrees or so, broad brown patches of torn-up earth, like holes ripped in a great green quilt. There and there and there and there and there and there and there and there. Alpha Coal and its predecessors have been successful at taking exactly what they want, human and ecological consequences be damned.

More of the same, I know, awaits me further south, in Logan and Mingo County, southeast in McDowell County, southwest in Lincoln, and on into southwest Virginia and eastern Kentucky. No point in ranging further. I'm so angry I'll richly savor what I'm about to do.

Turning, I arc through the clear May night toward the MTR site at Elk Run. According to Fain's information, it should be located only a few ridges over from Keystone Mountain. Below me, set between and beyond the amoeboid blots of MTR sites, the lights of homes glint in hollers. God knows what sicknesses have been spawned in those folks' flesh by their proximity to such a vile industry.

Ah, there it is. That must be Elk Run, garish with spotlights, just as Keystone was. It's another extensive lunar landscape of shattered shale, and, yes, there in its midst, like a long-necked, predacious bird, is tonight's prize, the Elk Run dragline.

Tonight, I remain in bat form, my fastest, most agile option. Feeling those bullets during the Keystone visit irritated me considerably. As big as I am—gray-backed, with a black three-foot wingspan—my powers of intimidation are considerable, even without the bulk and slavering teeth of a giant wolf. I circle the area, counting, to my surprise, only three foes. After what happened at Keystone, I expected that Alpha would beef up security at all its sites.

No matter. I veer down, fangs bared, and dive-bomb the few guards I see.

One man shoots at me and misses. When I hover over his head, clawing at his face, he dives beneath a truck. One runs away screaming, only to trip and fall face first into a puddle. One flees the compound, hops into his car, and tries to start it. As is appropriate for something resembling a scene from a horror film, the engine won't turn over. I fly against his windshield, bumping the glass and hissing, before the car finally starts. He slams the vehicle into gear and tears down the mountain. His wailing friends depart as well, scurrying off into the woods.

Regaining human form, I punch in the codes killing the security cameras. I'm about to do the same to the lights when a fourth guard steps from behind a huge truck, aiming a pistol at me.

"Hey! What the hell do you think you're doing? Put your hands up, or I'll shoot."

To my immense pleasure, it's Nate Palmer, Matthew's red-headed otter crush. He must have been reassigned to this site when I took out the Keystone dragline.

"Howdy, Nate." I step forward. "Sorry to scare you." I lift my hands into the air and smile.

"How do you know my name?" Keeping his weapon trained on me, he edges closer.

"We've met."

"You're shitting me. Where?"

"The Tap Room. You were quite the flirt."

He frowns. "I don't go there anymore." He moves closer still.

"That's too bad." I gaze into his green eyes and reach for his will. Someone torn between his homosexuality and his conservative faith is bound to be confused, conflicted, and easy to dominate.

Yes. He's a mental mess, poor boy. He's been waiting for someone like me to make things simpler—much simpler—and relieve him of his terrible doubts, his self-loathing, his painful resistance to natural desire. I sink mental fingers into his brain's convolutions, tickle, probe, and squeeze. He steps back and shakes his head, fights me just a little, then sighs, rubs his eyes, and lowers his gun.

"That was easy. There we go. That's better, isn't it?"

He gives me an addled smile. "Yes. Yes, it sure is."

"Come here, Nate."

"Yeah, sure," he mumbles. Sheathing the gun, he stumbles forward.

"Things are going to get very interesting up here in a manner of minutes," I say, taking his hand. "You need to drive far, far away as fast as you can. Do you understand?"

"Shit, I can't. I rode to work today with Jerry, and he just drove off without me, the moron."

"Then you'll walk. Stick to the road. I'll follow you after I'm done here and make sure you get down the mountain safely. You're a comely boy, Nate. I'd like to see you again. Would you like to see me again?"

Nate's grin is that of a very buzzed drunk. "Hell, sure. I remember you now. You're one hot daddy."

"And you're one hot otter. But you won't tell your bosses you saw me up here?"

"No. No way."

"Good boy. Let's seal the deal." I open my arms.

"Yeah. Sure." Nate shambles forward and takes my hand.

"Aren't you proper?" Wrapping an arm around his waist, I nuzzle his neck and extend my fangs.

I wait till enfeebled young Nate has lurched down the road and out of sight before turning the great lights off. I set the dynamite, then retreat to the edge of the immense earth-wound to watch. Again the concatenation of metal-splintering, fiery chrysanthemums, the bucket breaking into shards, the tall crane creaking and toppling like a fallen redwood, the huge cab of the dragline exploding into pieces. One more machine that will never destroy a mountain again.

Rubbing my hands with satisfaction, I'm gathering my energy to take bat-form and rise into the air when an unwelcome tingling and a noxious, industrial stink make me pause. Something else is here. Someone is watching me.

I spin about. There, atop a tall pile of shale, on the far side of the dragline cabin's smoldering ruins, lurks something gray and amorphous. It's like nothing I've ever encountered before. It looks like a fog bank, but I can feel its malevolence. Part of it seems rooted in the maimed earth it rests upon, but I can sense its mind moving out to explore me, much like the way I slip inside my thralls' brains. It's a glaucous-gray nexus of threat, a throbbing ash-heap of energy. It contracts and then expands, snaking a tendril down the shale pile in my direction. The movement seems somehow less exploratory than aggressive. The chemical reek hits me again, making my nostrils flare and sting.

For a split-second, I think about charging it, but it's something beyond my ken, and I can't say that about much of anything after nearly three hundred years of existence. That fact suggests caution. Besides, the fetching Nate Palmer needs safe escort. He's staggering down the mountain in the dark, weak and disoriented with blood loss and newly bestowed thralldom. Antoine Saint-Exupéry was right: "You become responsible forever for what you have tamed."

I regard the entity—it looks like nothing so much as a corpulent paramecium—then spit on the ground. "Not tonight, you loathly blob," I mutter before focusing, shimmering, and taking wing.

CHAPTER SIXTEEN

I wake with a jolt, naked and powerless, unable to move my limbs. Silver. I'm bound with poisonous silver. I can feel its burn, cutting into my flesh, sapping me of strength.

I roll onto my side, frightened and stunned, and begin a weak thrashing. Somehow, while I slept, someone who knew of my weaknesses has breached my crypt. My hands are locked behind me in silver cuffs. Scorching silver chains wrap my torso, trapping my tattooed arms against my sides, and tightly fetter my ankles together. A rubber ball coated with silver has been strapped into my mouth. When I sink my fangs into it, my mouth burns.

For the first time since Marcus cuffed and ravished me atop the Palatine Hill, I find myself helpless. That time, helplessness graded into surprisingly delicious submission. This time, it makes my torso heave with terror. What threat has invaded Mount Storm, and what's happened to Matt?

I struggle madly, blood-sweat filming my brow, chest, and back, all the while knowing that my restraints are inescapable. The hated silver weakness floods through me. I lift my head and call for Matt, but the shout I try to emit comes out only as a muffled moan. I try to extend my senses, try to gauge if my husbear is nearby, if he's hurt, or—gods forbid—dead, but the touch of the poisonous moon-metal stings too badly for me to gain sufficient focus.

Matt. If those bastards at Alpha have hurt him…. The thought simultaneously makes my eyes grow wet and my chest tighten with rage. I will gut them.

Somehow I will escape these chains. I will pluck out their eyeballs and feed them to the birds of the air. I will—

Footsteps thud outside the crypt. The lock clicks. The door opens. I tense, wishing I could spring but knowing I can only lie here and face my fate.

Matt steps into the room holding a lit candelabrum. He's shirtless, wearing a black leather vest, black jeans, and black boots. Around his beefy biceps, studded black leather armbands glint.

"You little bastard," I curse. The gag makes my words unintelligible but I repeat them nonetheless. "You little bastard."

"Surprise! Did I scare you?"

It takes much of the energy I have left to lift my head, growl at him, and nod.

"*Fuck.* You look *hot.*" Matt places the candelabrum on a shelf and kneads his crotch. "I need to top you more often." He sits on the edge of my nest and runs a finger through my chest hair, down my belly, along my chain-restrained biceps. "I've really got you now, huh? You cain't hardly move, can you?" he says, pinching a nipple.

I toss black hair out of my eyes and shake my head. I flex my muscles against the chains and try to rise. Wincing, I fall back onto the bed.

"You remember a few weeks back, when you said I could punish you any time I wanted? You said you deserved it? You wanted it rough, you wanted it to hurt?" Reaching down, he strokes my cock.

"Umm hmm." I grin around the ball gag. I've gone from enraged and frightened to thrilled and aroused in less than a minute. Inside his fond hand, my prick grows stiff.

"Well, tonight's the night." Bending, Matt gives my cockhead a soft lick. "I spent half the afternoon in the police station in Charleston, answering a bunch of fucking questions…*despite* the fact that I had the neat alibi of being at the Tap Room last night, this time helping with plans for the Pride Parade, while you were having your fun up Elk Run. I'm riled up, and I feel like working off some hostility. I feel like working you over good."

"Do it," I mumble, prick-pumping his hand. "Do it."

"What's that, bad boy? Can't understand a thing you're saying with that big fat ball in your mouth." Matt grins triumphantly.

One of the pleasures of being a kinky telepath is that you can enjoy the feeling of powerlessness a gag creates but still communicate if necessary. *I* said, "Do it." *Beat me. Torture me. Pound me raw!* I do my best to shout inside his head, despite the way the silver diffuses my power.

Matt taps his temple. "Tricky prick! Nice. Loud and clear. Let's get you up now."

My burly and beloved captor helps me sit up. I shake my head against the dizziness as he unlocks the chain around my ankles. He padlocks another chain around my neck, a silver slave collar, and pulls me to my feet.

"Let's go," he orders, dragging me toward the door. I take a couple of steps, then sink to my knees.

"Man, you really are weak. C'mon, I'll help you."

Matt helps me stand. Thighs shaking, I lean into him. He wraps an arm around me and leads me into the room just beyond, a dungeon playroom lit with more candelabra. The sound system's playing some movie soundtrack: dark, eerie, orchestral, throbbing.

"I like this, you weak and me strong. You said you wanted a change of pace." There's a chain thrown over a rafter, one end dangling, the other end attached to a hook in the wall. Matt leads me to it. He locks my slave collar to the chain, then tightens it, hauling me up onto the tips of my toes. I stand, limp and swaying, suspended from my neck.

"You look like the Tarot's Hanged Man," Matt says, sniffing my armpits.

Odin on the tree. "*I know that I hung on the windy tree...wounded by a spear...and offered to Odin...myself to myself...*" I repeat fragments of the Eddic poem.

"Odin on the tree, Christ on the cross. After all the boys you've crucified—those dark-haired little Jesuses you dote on—and all the nights you've tied me up and roughed me up and fed on me, it's past time you were the one strung up. Tonight, you're gonna be *my* suffering savior, my hot and hairy bottom," he says, fondness, cruelty and satisfaction mingling in his face. He fingers my ribs and fondles my navel. "You can take this?"

Foolish boy. My mockery fills his head, prodding him, I can only hope, to new heights of sadism. *I can take anything you inflict.*

"Yeah. I know. That's what's going to make this fun."

Do your worst. I gnash the ball and glare. Saliva gathers in my burning mouth, spills over my lips, and moistens my goateed chin.

"Okay. Here we go."

"How's that feel? Good?"

I grunt and nod. The work boot sways between my thighs, hung from a ball-stretcher buckled around the base of my scrotum. Matt nudges the boot, causing it to swing, increasing the gravity-drag on my testicles.

"You're so much fun to top," Matt says, untying my ponytail, letting shaggy black hair fall around my face. "No way hanging a guy up by his neck would be a safe scene with a human, but you…. You really are looking like Christ right now, big guy. A very inked-up Christ. How you like this nifty gag?" He taps the ball between my lips, then buckles it in a couple of notches tighter till it digs into the corners of my mouth. "I made that thing a few months ago, just for a scene like this. It was kinda hard to find paint made with real silver that would affix to that ball, but I finally found it. Man, you're drooling and slobbering up a storm." Matt runs a forefinger over my spit-spattered torso and sighs. "How about we punish those tasty tits first? How about we get 'em good and raw?"

Matt spends a good long time pinching my sensitive nipples. Then he applies a series of discomforts even more delicious: he bites my tits till they swell and bleed, then affixes alligator-teeth clamps, tightening them slowly, and then finally adds leaden weights to those clamps. I bite down on the corrosive ball and groan as the tender flesh of my nipples burns, stretches, and distends.

"Now for that curvy butt of yours," Matt says, brandishing a short leather flogger. Disappearing behind me, he warms my ass with a few gentle strokes before moving into a sharp series of blows. I growl and sway, too weak to do more than cock my butt, inviting an even harder beating. My prick's achingly hard, reveling in the perverse and inexplicable ways that pain meshes with pleasure.

Matt pauses. "Ummmmmmm mmm! You should see your butt-cheeks now. Flushed all nice and pink." When he runs a hand over my rump, the sudden tenderness makes me jolt.

"Yum. So warm." Reaching around me, he tugs hard on my weight-stretched, painfully clamped nipples. I flinch and grunt, rubbing my bare ass against his desire-thickened dick.

"You need it bad, don't you?" Matt chuckles low in his throat. "Table's turned tonight. A little silver, and suddenly the ferocious, all-powerful vampire's a helpless prisoner. I can hurt you as hard as I want, cain't I? I can use you any way I please."

I groan and nod, slobber dripping off my chin. *You got me, boy. Make me suffer. Tear me up. Mark me. Use me till I howl.*

"Ohhh, man, you bet I will. We're just getting started, Daddy. Let's move on to the heavier floggers. This next one's gonna make you feel like someone's balled up his fist and punched you in the rump."

By the time Matthew's done beating me—a good half-hour's worth—I'm slumped and whimpering, hanging limply from the chain around my neck.

Matthew tosses the flogger onto the floor and fondles my burning butt. He wraps his arms around me, runs his fingers through my chest hair, tugs my agonized tits, and sighs.

"Damn, that was glorious. What a release. I needed that bad. Thanks, Daddy."

You bet, boy, I reply, pressing back against him. *Any time. Thank **you**.*

Matt kisses my shoulder. "You got some major welts back here. They'll be all healed up here in a few minutes, won't they?"

I nod, tickling his belly hair with my cuffed hands. *Just think of me as your own bloodsucking Wolverine.*

Matt snickers. "Yep. With fangs instead of claws." He grips my cock and works it till I'm just this side of shooting. Then he slaps me across the butt and pulls a padlock key from his jeans.

"Time for the paddle bench, Dad," he says, freeing my slave collar from the rafter-chain. "I got a wooden frat paddle and a wooden cane with your name on 'em. I'm gonna bruise you up real, real bad before I take you up the ass."

I'm lying on my belly on the foam-padded central bench, straddling it, my knees resting on its side supports. The pressure of the bench against my still-clamped nipples makes them burn even worse. To my pain and pleasure, I'm still gagged, cuffed, and chained. Now Matt uses rough hempen rope to tie me down to the steel structure and slips a blindfold over my eyes.

"All healed up," Matt says, patting my butt with the frat paddle. "Guess I've got to start all over again."

Matt begins slowly, just as he did with the flogger, but soon he's steadily slamming the solid oak paddle against my ass. He works up a rhythm: left cheek, right cheek, left cheek, right cheek, left cheek, right cheek, both cheeks together. Swamped with pain, I yelp like a startled dog, struggling weakly, salivating copiously, gritting my teeth around the ball gag.

"Yeah, oh yeah. Nice." Matthew pauses, panting. "Your butt's downright cherry-red. Starting to bruise up." He plays with the hair in the crack of my ass and rubs my hole. "In a little bit, I'm gonna ride you like the big pig you are. But first…ready for the cane? I'll bet my big strong Daddy can take a *lot* more torment."

You're damn right I can. Bring it on! I lift my ass and bow my head.

There's a swishing sound. Matt's teasing me, slicing the air with the long, thin cane. I tense and tremble, straining against the silver locked around my chest and arms. I grunt with pain as the first blow cuts across my ass.

It's been a while since I've been treated to the luxury of dungeon torture, courtesy of my handsome husbear. It's been even longer since he's caned me. It's just as I remember it: exceedingly painful, exceedingly arousing. I shout against the ball and thrash against my bonds of silver and hemp as Matt slashes steadily at my buttocks.

"You got you some pretty parallel welts," Matthew murmurs. "Let's see if I can make that supernatural skin of yours bleed."

He lays it on even harder. The thin cane cuts into me again and again. Stinging anguish builds. I thrash, drool, gnash the gag, and roar.

"Want me to stop?" Matt says, pausing.

I shake my head and cock my ass.

"My Hebridean warrior," Matt sighs. "God, I love you. I love your endurance, and I love your strength, and I love your pride."

Again, there's that swishing sound. This time the cane breaks the skin. I lift my blinded head and groan, snuffling the scent of my own blood.

"There you go," Matt enthuses. He canes me a few minutes more, till I can feel thin rivulets running down my butt-cheeks.

"Beautiful. Beautiful."

The blows cease. Matt's tongue flickers over my wounds, lapping at the blood.

"Who's the vampire now?" he says, emitting a soft laugh. "Tastes pretty good. Makes us blood brothers all over again, huh? God *damn*, you have a pretty butt. Bright red and all tore up. I have got to chow down on your hole."

The agony's long faded, replaced with a flood of delight so vast I lose all track of time. Matt might have been rimming me for half an hour or five hours. I can't tell. But now he stops.

"Umm, your asshole tastes terrific." Matt licks his lips noisily. "I think my tongue's got you opened up just right. Now you're gonna get the ass-fucking of your undead life."

I can hear him removing his boots and jeans. He kneads my buttocks, and then there's the sound of lube squirting into his palm. He applies the cool liquid to my butthole. I spread my thighs, moan, and nod.

"You're always saying you want warrior sex, barbarian sex," Matt says, pushing two fingers into me. "This evening been barbaric enough for you?"

Oh, yes, I sigh inside his mind. *Gloriously barbaric. Just what I wanted. Just what I needed.*

"Good to hear. You want to be my come-dump, poor trussed and gagged Daddy? You want me to shoot my big load up your hole?"

God, I love his dirty talk. *Hell, yes. Hell, yes. Plow me raw.*

Matthew obliges. This time he doesn't start slowly, as he did with the flogging and paddling. This time he simply shoves his cock into me and starts pounding. For half a minute, it feels like he's ripping me in half: his cock isn't as long as mine but it's much thicker. But then the familiar pleasure of being filled full washes over me, then Matthew adjusts his thrusts to nudge me in just the right place deep inside, and now I'm writhing ecstatically beneath him.

"Yeah? Yeah, monster man? You're loving my big fat dick up your ass, ain't you now? Hitting your sweet spot, huh?" Matt tugs on my boot-stretched balls and drives even deeper. I grunt against my gag, wriggling my ass against his groin, urging him on.

Wrapping his arms around me, he rests his sweaty-furred chest upon my back, and the brawny weight of him makes me feel possessed, protected, and loved. He pulls out, then slams into me again. This feeling of utter carnal completion I only achieve when my cock's pushed deep inside his ass or his cock's pushed deep inside mine. What incredible luck, to have found yet again what I had with my lost love Angus. *Thank you, Horned Lord,* I pray. *Thank you for this hairy, musky man, for this virile, cruel, kind, and loving grace.*

"Yeah, here's that rough ride you been wanting," Matt growls, slapping an ass-cheek and twisting a clamped nipple. "Damn, Derek. Yeah, squeeze me with your hole. Ohhh, yeah, that's right. God, Daddy, you're so tight."

His thrusts speed up. He shifts his hand from my nipple to my cock and jacks me so fast that my climax begins to crest in seconds.

"You close?" Matt mutters, biting my shoulder and squeezing my pulsing penis.

I grunt and nod, bucking back onto his transfixing prick.

"Good. Good. Oh. Oh, yeah. Oh, yeah. Here...we...go. God, Derek, God," he gasps, kissing my hair, my chain-trussed arms and heaving shoulders. "I love you so much."

Roaring, I climax in his hand. Seconds later, with a shout and a shudder, thrusting savagely, Matt pumps me full of come.

Panting and shaking, he collapses along my back. "Jesus. Amazing. Just amazing," he groans. He snuggles atop me for a long time before pushing himself to his feet.

"Okay, time to let you loose. You need to feed, and I need to cuddle."

CHAPTER SEVENTEEN

We lie together and listen to the night. Today must have been warm, for the house is stuffy, but now—it's nearly midnight—high mountain breezes waft through the bedroom's window-screens and cool our nakedness. Outside, moonlight illumines the lawn, nocturnal insects sing, and pines sadly sough.

Matt snuggles back into my arms, sighing as I drink from his neck. When I'm done, he drowses against me. I stroke his hair, feeling vastly fortunate.

After a short nap, he wakes. "So how'd you like all that?" he asks, taking my hand. Every time Matt tops me, he insists on a point-by-point review of his prowess, and tonight's no exception.

"A-plus, all of it. Tit-torture, flogging, paddling, caning, fucking. A-plus. It reminded me of our first six months together, when you were so afraid I'd lose control and drain you that you bound me in chains every time we made love. You're a superlative dominant. Every time you top me, I tell you that, but you never seem to believe me."

"Just making sure you had as much fun as I did. I sure was in the mood to hurt on you a little. I sure as hell needed to give your pretty butt a lengthy pounding."

"You certainly did. Your come is trickling out of my ass as we speak."

"Yeah?" Matt rolls over, slips a finger between my buttocks, and probes. "Oh. Yep. Hot." He works his finger up my hole while chewing gently on a raw nipple.

"Oh, yeah, Matt, that's great," I sigh, rocking my butt back onto his finger, arching my chest forward against his face. "So…uhhhhh, yeah…do the police really suspect you? Or any of your Mountain Partisan cohorts?"

"Naw. Don't think so," Matt breathes against my pec. "It's just that the mysterious vigilante has been pretty clever at leaving no clues. No security camera footage. No fingerprints. Do you even have fingerprints?"

"I don't know. I don't think so. I shape-shift so much that… Uuuuff! Oh, man, that's good. Yeah…."

I bend a leg, allowing his finger to probe my hole deeper. "Who knows? I do know that if I have prints, they aren't on file in any law enforcement agency. It's not as if anyone's been able to arrest me after one of my adventures and take my fingerprints."

"True. Well, I think the cops are just grasping at straws." Matt sinks his teeth into the flesh of my left pec and sucks my nipple hard before continuing our conversation. "They know that Alpha has a really clever enemy, and they know that 'dangerous wildlife,' as they call it—a huge wolf and a big bat—have apparently been trained by the vigilante to attack the security guys…so they're just harassing us Partisan folks 'cause we're Alpha's most public critics." He shifts to the other nipple and sucks it for a few sweet seconds. "Damn, your tits are tasty," he mumbles.

"Damn, your mouth is skilled. And have you seen Alpha spies following you, as Fain said they were?"

Matt rests his cheek against my chest and sniggers. "Yeah. They're not very good. They follow me around Charleston, but when I head out into the country on the way back here, I elude 'em pretty well on the back roads. But what if one day they follow me up here?"

"Good question. Perhaps we need our own security guard, especially since you keep getting anonymous hate mail. I think I have one in mind."

"Really? Who?"

"Someone who already has experience in the business. After last night, he'll be more than willing."

"Who the hell are you talking about?"

I kiss Matt's forehead and grip his stiff cock. "I'll tell you if you fuck me again."

"Derek, you're insatiable. At this age, I don't know how I keep up with you." Grinning, Matthew rolls me onto my back, hoists my legs in the air, and pushes his prick up my wet hole.

Five minutes of steady pounding, and he's filling me with yet another load while I jack off on my belly. Finished, he rolls off onto his back, panting happily. Reaching over, he wipes up my come and licks it off his fingers.

"I'm loving this submissive mood you're in. You can keep being the bottom as long as you like."

"Fine by me," I say, resting my head on his shoulder and rubbing his solid belly. "Your blood in my mouth, your semen in my mouth, your semen up my butt: it's all earthly paradise to me. I can smell my ass-musk in your beard."

Matt chuckles. "I do like to bury my face between your butt cheeks and go to town. So, the security guard? Who do you have in mind."

"Nate Palmer. Last night I mesmerized and fed on him. Now he's my thrall."

"Really?" Matt rises on one elbow and grins. His enthusiasm's adorable.

"Yep. All mine. All ours. Moving into his brain was an odd experience. It was as if his backward and self-hating religious beliefs were a drab, fragile fabric someone had draped around a stately statue. It took very little effort to rip it off. Beneath that false dogma, he's a very passionate, lonely, and confused boy. I think he'd benefit greatly from our companionship, both in and out of bed. How about you two have dinner when you get back to Charleston and offer him a job up here? I suspect he'd be more than glad to quit the Alpha position."

Matt bumps a fist against my breastbone. "Are you telling me, your husbear of many years, to ask a hot young otter out on a date?"

"I am. Get to know him. See if you like him well enough. If you do, invite him out for dinner. Seduce him. Tie him down to the bed, slap a piece of tape over his mouth, and play with him until I can join you."

"Yum. You got it. He seemed to be into both of us that evening at the Tap Room. Too bad he got God and pulled a disappearing act."

"True. He once was lost, but now he's found."

"Now maybe we can share his amazing grace, huh? You think he's a Top or a bottom?"

"From what I could sense, a bottom. A voracious one, I think."

"Ummmmm, great. So he's your thrall? How many does that make? I've lost count."

"Well, not many. Donnie and Timmy."

"And that guy Nick in Edinburgh, and that guy Steven in New York City, and that guy Ross in DC, and that guy Robbie in Glasgow...and that guy Francesco in Rome. And that guy Fain in Charleston."

"And that IT otter down at Virginia Tech."

"My buddy Bobby? The computer expert? When'd you do that?"

"Last spring when I went to Hemlock Lake to feed on that mandolin player again. I've been meaning to tell you. After I had the musician, I was still hungry, and Blacksburg wasn't far from there, so...I paid Bobby a visit. He was the one, remember, who figured out that Sodeski was e-mailing anonymous threats to local gay activists. I thought Bobby's IT skills might be useful."

"Did you fuck him?"

"What do you think? Let's just say he looks mighty endearing bound and gagged with several yards of duct tape. His hairless chest makes the tape's removal far less painful than with furry boys like you. After I took him, he broke down and wept in my arms, which was exquisite. The boy's hung like a stallion."

"Bobby? Yeah, the lean ones usually are. I'll bet our Mr. Nate's got a horse-cock too. Now that he's your thrall, I guess we'll find out. Any other mesmerized sex-slaves you'd care to list?"

"Ah. Well...just a few."

"Damn. You're a real pig, ain't you? You got a butch butthole in every port?"

"It's purely altruistic." I give a sheepish shrug. "I have such a rampant thirst that, well, if I limited my feeding to any one man, he might.... It's just better for everyone if I spread my blood-drinking around."

"And your butt-fucking too? 'Altruistic.' Right! You're sooooo fulla shit," Matt says, tugging on my goatee. "I guess I oughta be jealous of your harem of thralls, but actually I think it's hot."

"You benefit from it, remember? Weren't you the one urging me to glamour were-cub Donnie after we met him at the Allegheny Café? Weren't you the one asking me to enthrall that Rebel reenactor you have the hots for?"

Matt licks his lips and growls. "Sweet lil' Hunter? Guilty as charged. I went to that reenactment of the Battle of McDowell last week and saw him charging across the field like some kinda adorable avenging angel. We even talked for a while around his tent. He's real, real shy, but he did agree to have coffee sometime." Matt fist-taps his beefy breast and heaves an exaggerated sigh. "I must confess that I have fallen deeply and hopelessly in love."

"That happens just about every time you leave the house, doesn't it?"

"Just about. I guess I'm just as horned-up as you, but without the supernatural seduction skills. You're my vampire Casanova, my undead Don Juan."

"I might be all that…but you still scared the shit out of me when I woke up to find myself cuffed and chained."

"I think that scaring the shit out of you is physically impossible, ain't it? What with your, uh, preternatural, uh, physiology?"

"True." I can't help but grin. "But, seriously, I was terrified that someone had broken into the house and done away with you."

"Hell, I'm sorry. I thought you'd enjoy the whole kidnapping scene."

"I did, once I realized you were the one who'd bound me. I enjoyed it enormously. But until you entered the room, I was…I don't remember the last time I was so frightened. Not for me. For you."

"But no one's ever threatened us up here, honey. Not in all these years together. Why you so skittish all of a sudden?"

"Part of it's your crusade against powerful men like those bastards at Alpha and the hate mail you're getting. That's all making me more cautious and anxious than usual. Part of it…."

"Yeah?"

"Part of it's something I saw at the Elk Run site." I slip out of bed. "I'd like to sit out on the porch, since it's such a beautiful night. Would you like some Scotch?"

"Talk about changing the subject. What's got you so worried? You're never worried. You're always striding through the world like some kinda cocky demigod."

"Let's get those drinks, and then I'll tell you."

"It's so beautiful here," Matt sighs, resting an arm across my shoulders. "So isolated and quiet. I'm so happy to be living here with you, Laird Maclaine."

He's certainly right about the beauty of this place. We sit on the front porch swing, looking out over the lawn and down over the deep forested expanse of German Valley. The sky's bejeweled with stars. A moon slips in and out of intermittent clouds.

"So you gonna tell me? What you saw?"

I take a sip of Tobermory and nod. "After I'd fed on Nate and sent him away, I blew up the dragline machine."

"I'd sure like to have seen that. Those machines are fucking satanic. Then what?"

"Then…something very strange. In my many years on this earth, I've encountered other vampires, several werewolves, a handful of witches and sorcerers, but nothing like this before. Have you ever read H.P. Lovecraft?"

"Sure. Creepy stuff."

"What I saw was what I see in my head when I read some of his work. It was a…a Lovecraftian blob. Like some kind of plump protozoan—an amoeba or paramecium—but twice the size of your pickup truck."

"That big? What the hell?"

"I have no idea what it was. But I could sense several things about it. It was somehow…attached to that site. It was studying me, gauging my identity, my power. And it was malevolent. Had I approached it, I feel sure it would have attacked."

"You didn't attack it, I hope?"

"No. When the terrain's unknown, the warrior indulges in a little reconnaissance first, right? I'm going to hit Alpha's Marfork site next. If it shows up there, I'll fly over it in bat form and scrutinize it from a safe distance."

"Shit. Just be super-careful." Matt gulps his drink and rises. In the moonlight, his face distorts with disgust. "All that exercise I got treating you to sweet punishment and rough plowing had me all hungry for a midnight snack, but I think I just lost my appetite. So, atomic bombs create Godzilla, and now MTR creates a microbe bigger'n a pickup truck? Ack. Ugh. C'mon, let's go to bed. I got a long day of meetings tomorrow. I just hope I don't have nightmares all damn night."

CHAPTER EIGHTEEN

Matt's looking very handsome in his dress clothes. I'm far more used to seeing him in sexy redneck-wear: camo pants or cargo shorts, muscle-shirts or wife-beaters, cowboy boots or work boots. Today, though, he sits at his desk in the Mountain Partisan office, wearing tan dress pants, a blue dress shirt, and a red tie. He's catching up on e-mail. Bright sunlight brings out the reddish hue in his chestnut hair.

Why am I seeing sunlight? This can't be real.

As I admire him, something about him begins to change. His chest's growing transparent. I shouldn't be seeing that either.

There's his heart, pumping steadily. But now the sunlight fades. He lifts his head and shakes it, as if dizzy.

There…something like a claw in his chest, a spidery something made of smoke that seems gradually to solidify.

It wraps fingers around his heart. His pulse speeds up beneath the pressure.

An expression of panic fills Matt's face. He rises and staggers toward his office door. Then he flinches. His hazel eyes fly wide. He drops to his knees, clutching his chest.

He falls to the floor. His face contorts. His eyes close.

Inside his transparent torso, the spidery fingers tighten until his heart pops like a pink balloon and deflates into a limp bag.

I scream his name and leap from shadow into sunlight. Before I can gather him into my arms, my skin ignites.

I jolt up from my nest. Horrible, horrible dream. I want to rush upstairs to make sure that Matt's all right, but I sense that the sun's yet to set. I lie back, ball up the tartan blanket, and wrap my arms around it, as if it were my hus-bear, as if I were in a position to protect him both day and night.

Matt's naked, curled up on the floor of the den, deep in sleep and smil-ing.

He's surrounded with menace. A chemical-scented serpentine smoke cir-cles him, lunging at him again and again but bumping up against some sort of invisible wall. The entity hisses with frustration as each onslaught's repelled.

Now, whatever that shield is, it's no longer invisible. There's a white circle drawn around Matt with sugar, salt, or flour. It's flickering with a low flame. A sphere of violet light encloses Matt.

I move closer. The entity swirls around my right ankle, gnawing it like a peevish weasel. I shake it off, cursing.

"Off, you rank imp. Off, you pox!" I snarl, reaching for my lover.

When I touch the purplish sphere, it gives me a vicious shock. The smoke-demon is not the only one who can't enter the circle. Neither can I.

"Matt. Matt!" I shout.

Matt rubs his eyes and rolls onto his back. Even in these unsettling circum-stances, I can't help but admire how brawny his pecs are, how prominent his nipples.

He looks up at me and grins. He lifts a clenched hand and opens it, display-ing an item in his palm. It's a flat blue stone lying in a tiny puddle of blood.

He presses it against his heart, rolls onto his side, curls up again, and falls asleep. Around me, the foul-smelling smoke sputters and disperses.

This time when I wake, the sun's set. I pull on my great kilt and, barefoot and bare-chested, hurry up the cellar stairs. The last time I had dreams like that, dreams of that lucid, urgent texture, they were images sent by some-one more powerful than I. They turned out to have been precognitive, warn-ing me of coming danger. These dreams, I'm fairly certain, are of the same caliber and from the same source.

Matt isn't home, making me fear the worse. But the phone machine...the message light is flashing. I push the button and start the message.

"Hey, Derek." It's Nate Palmer's voice, sounding strained. "Matt told me to call. He knew you'd be worried. We're running a little late, but we'll be home in a bit. See you soon."

Flummoxed and relieved, I hang up. Matt must be all right, but what's he doing with Nate Palmer? Well, a few nights ago I did ask Matt to meet Nate and get to know him. Maybe they had a nice meal in Charleston. They must have really hit it off if Matt's bringing him up here. Fine by me. A slender otter snack would be a distraction more than welcome this evening. I've already tasted Nate Palmer's blood. Now I want to taste the rest of him.

I'm on the front porch smoking a cigar and sipping a mint julep when Matt's truck pulls up. I lope over to the driveway only to find, to my surprise, Nate in the driver's seat. He cuts the engine, hops out, then helps Matthew from the cab.

"Cut it out, I'm fine." Matt swats at Nate's hand.

"You're not fine, Mr. Taylor. Let me help you," says Nate, wrapping an arm about Matt.

"You're one bossy boy," Matt grouses. "Just looking for an excuse to hug me, ain't you? Hey, honey. Got a couple of them drinks for me and our guest?"

"Absolutely," I say, frowning. Something's clearly happened, and it isn't good. "As long as you tell me what's up."

"I'll tell you, Mr. Maclaine," Nate says. "We were up at that Keystone cabin that Mr. Taylor inherited—"

"Call me Matt, for Christ's sake. Derek, let's get settled on the porch, and I'll tell you all about it."

Matt's slumped on the swing and Nate's standing by the porch rail looking out over German Valley when I return bearing their drinks.

"Thank you," Nate says, taking his glass. "You sure have a pretty place up here. Bet you have a great view come daylight."

"You'll be finding that out," Matt says, smiling wearily and taking a long sip of julep. "You don't have much choice but to spend the night. As kind to me as you've been today, tomorrow I'm gonna get up early and make you biscuits and sausage gravy."

"That sounds great, Mr. Taylor, but—"

"*Matt.* And that's Derek."

"You can call me 'sir' if you feel like it," I say, smirking.

"Matt. Uh, Derek. Ah, sir. Okay. But shouldn't you sleep in? You seemed pretty shaky today, and the doctors said—"

"Doctors?"

"Yes, Derek. Calm down and stop worrying. You gotta have something to worry about, don't ya? You cling to any worry that comes along, the way a drowning man grabs a piece of driftwood. Here's what happened. Me and Nate here, we had a nice lunch at Blossom Dairy and shared a good talk. He's been wanting to quit Alpha for a while but really couldn't afford to. So I offered him the security job up here and he took it. Gave Alpha his two-week notice."

"Good. Welcome to Mount Storm," I say, shaking Nate's hand. "We have several guest rooms. Take your pick. Tomorrow night, we can discuss your duties. Right now…get to the doctor part, Matt."

"Okay. Okay. Can't rush a West Virginia storyteller, right? So then I take the afternoon off and drive Nate up to the Keystone Mountain place, 'cause he'd heard a lot about Cousin Dillon and his property. So we're walking around, looking down into that awful pit and admiring the blasted-to-smithereens remains of that dragline machine…when I, uh, didn't feel too good."

"He nearly fainted, sir. It's like he took a fit."

Those arachnoid fingers in the dream, clutching Matthew's heart. Damn it.

"I don't know what it was, honey. Sometimes I get the weak trembles, as Granddaddy used to say, if I don't eat, but I'd just had a tasty Reuben sandwich at the Blossom. My vision got blurry. My chest felt tight. So Nate here pretty much carried me back to the truck—he's stronger than he looks—and drove me down to the emergency room in Charleston."

"He cussed me all the way into town," Nate adds.

"No surprise there. He hates hospitals. So what did the doctors tell you?"

"They said that my symptoms suggested a heart attack or stroke. But when they ran tests, they couldn't find indications of either. Last physical I had, my doctor said I was in pretty good shape, thanks to the time I spend in our lil' basement gym, working out and riding the stationary bike."

Matt can't resist treating Nate to a little show, flexing his thick biceps and grinning. "Not bad, huh? Plus you know I hike a lot. Every chance I get. I've never had heart problems, despite my perpetual plumpness." Matt gives his beer belly a couple of rueful pats.

"Did Dillon?"

"Heart problems? Naw. Heart ailments don't run in our family."

"But he died of a heart attack, remember? As he was driving down Keystone Mountain."

Matt shakes his head. "I never understood that at all."

"I think I might."

"What? Tell me."

"I will. But first…Nate, come here."

"Yes, sir." Giving me the acquiescent smile I savor in handsome thralls, the rangy boy strides over.

I take him by the shoulders. "You're not afraid of me, are you?"

"I was. But I'm not now."

"Do you know what I am, Nate?"

Nate pauses. "You're someone I serve. Someone I need to protect."

"Right. I'm a little bit more than a normal man."

"A lot more," Matt corrects. "In all sorts a' ways."

"Thanks, honey. You know I have talents that other folks don't have, don't you, Nate?"

"Yeah."

"Well, I have a friend who has even more talents than I do. Her name is Cynthia. Sometimes she can see the future. She can make folks see the future in their dreams."

Nate nods. "My great-aunt Beulah, she was psychic like that. She predicted a few deaths in her day."

"Good. Now, one other thing. Do you know how to make a mint julep?"

"No. Sorry."

I take Nate by the arm and give him a firm pat on the ass. "I'll show you. It's a skill you'll need if you live here. Come with me. We're going to require another round of drinks for this next part."

Nate's sitting on the porch swing now, between Matt and me. We're sipping our mint-fragrant bourbon as I describe my dreams of the day before. A soft rain's begun, falling melodically on the roof.

"So, those dreams about Matt's heart, they were like the precognitive visions I had the year he and I met. I'd dreamed of that window full of odd office furniture, that alley of yellow brick, before I ever saw them. I'd seen that miserable gang of gay-bashers, the Leviticus Locusts, beating Matt up and murdering him. The dream showed me what Matt's fate would be, were I not to intervene. But I did intervene."

"And Derek saved my ass. I did some damage to 'em," Matt admits, "but Derek slaughtered 'em."

"Slaughtered them?" Nate says. "Like…literally?"

Matt's face is grim. "Yes. Literally. Then Derek sent a sea of rats to eat them."

"Jesus. Rats? You can control rats? How is that possible?"

I gaze into Nate's wide green eyes. "You'll be calm, won't you? If you're going to be our security guard, I'm going to have to share some of my secrets, but none of them will frighten you, will they?"

"Yes, I'll be calm. No, none of your secrets will frighten me," Nate repeats.

"And you want to be here?" Hoping for an honest answer, for a few seconds I give him back his will.

Nate nods, looking pleasantly surprised. "Yes, I do. You're both pretty cool dudes, and you're both mighty handsome. I'm glad to be here. I feel at home somehow."

I resume the glamour just to make sure he won't bolt in the face of the next piece of information. "Here's one of my secrets. I was the wolf you shot at Keystone Mountain. I was the harrying bat who ran off your fellow guards at Elk Run."

"Yeah? Wow. Okay. That's cool." Only the power of my glamour, I sense, is causing him to casually take in such an unbelievable claim rather than calling me insane.

"You're connected to a very, very powerful man now, Nate buddy. Derek'll take care of you," Matt assures him.

"Now you're part of my clan," I say, patting Nate's lean thigh. "Now your enemies are my enemies."

"I've been mighty lonesome lately. I could sure do with a clan," Nate sighs. "All those years the preachers had me convinced I was damned. What a waste…."

For a few minutes, the conversation dies. I wrap an arm around Nate. Nate closes his eyes and leans against me. Matt cups Nate's knee.

"So something's after me," Matt says, breaking the silence. "And if we don't do something, I'll have a mysterious heart attack like Dillon did. So whadda we do?"

"We find someone who knows something about sorcery. About protective spells. And we need to do it soon, before whatever the hell is out there gets to you."

"Sorcery? Tall order. Except…." Matt's face lights up.

"What? Tell me."

"Okey. I'll bet Okey could help us."

"Who's Okey?"

"Okey…."

Matt stands, takes a long sip of his drink, then steps to the railing and extends a hand into the rain. "Love the storms up here. 'Mount Storm.' You named this place well, honey. Okay, so. Okey and me met at some gay pride event in Charleston in our twenties and got to be buddies. He's a big guy… stocky, six foot two. He's…man, such a warm, sweet, funny guy. He's a drag queen, and like many a drag queen, tough as nails. He used to carry a damn brick in his purse in case some asshole messed with him. He gave a lotta shows at the Grand Palace before it closed."

"He sounds very interesting, but what good could he—"

"He's a witch, Derek. He knows all kinds a' things about all that stuff. If anyone around here can find me a blue stone like that one in your dream, something that wards off that smoky spider thang, it's him. We're Facebook friends now. He lives in Huntington. He teaches sociology at Marshall University. I'll drop him a note before we head to bed."

"Great. Tomorrow night, let's head up to Huntington, and—"

Matt interrupts me. "Uhhh, Derek, you're a vampire. What if—"

Nate interrupts Matt. "A vampire? Is that what you are? Yeah, I thought that you…." Nate takes my hand wonderingly. "Yeah, you…at Elk Run, you kissed my neck. I could feel your goatee, so soft against my throat, but then… you bit me?"

"Exactly. You gave me your blood with whimpering pleasure, and, as you did, you came in your pants. Remember?"

Nate blushes. "Yeah, I do. Creamed my jeans pretty bad."

"If I were to feed on you later, would you come for me again?"

"Yeah. Oh, sure."

"Derek, we'll bed this boy here in a bit. Back to Okey, please. God, you're easily distracted."

"Hungry, I guess. So you don't want me going with you to—"

"As I was trying to say—before *you* distracted *me* with that tasty tale about Nate here coming in his pants—was that maybe Okey will be able to sense what you are, and maybe he don't trust your kind. Don't that make sense?"

"Yes," I admit. "The few witches I've encountered have, well, made me feel most unwelcome."

"So tomorrow, Nate and me will drive up to Huntington and confer with Okey. Hopefully, he'll be able to help. But if he cain't...."

"If he can't, we'll find someone else. I need to get hold of Cynthia and see if she knows more. Last I heard, she was located in Columbus, Ohio."

"Okay. Good to have another option to fall back on. So, look, guys." Matt finishes his drink. "I still feel pretty weak from that fainting spell, and, honestly, I'm scared. I hate to admit it, but I'm really scared. I ain't in the mood for sex, but I sure could use some serious cuddling. Okay? I'd love to nestle between you two and just have y'all hug on me all night long."

"Absolutely," I say. Undoing the brooch holding my great kilt together, I strip. At a mental suggestion from me, Nate does the same. Jointly, Matt and I admire the boy's broad shoulders, tight chest and flat stomach dusted with fur, narrow hips, chestnut pubes, and long, furry legs. His cock's impressive, rearingly hard.

"Let me echo Derek's words: welcome to Mount Storm, Mr. Nate. Some night when I ain't so wiped out, I'd like to help you out with that big ole thang. As it is, tonight I'm gonna be glad to settle for a sweet snuggle-sandwich."

Smiling tiredly, Matt strips as well. I wrap one arm around the burly bear, another around the slim otter, and lead them both in to bed.

Chapter Nineteen

It's a flat shard of lapis lazuli in the shape of a rhombus. I hold it in the palm of my hand, just as Matthew did in my dream, and stroke it with a finger. I can feel power radiating from it. It makes my arm tingle.

Matt and Nate have just returned from Huntington. Tonight, we sit out on the patio enjoying microbrews while potatoes bake in the oven and Matt marinates rib eyes for a late dinner.

"So, we got to Huntington about lunchtime and met Okey at Hillbilly Hot Dogs for lunch. Goddamn, I love that place. Had two hot dogs and some scrumptious fries with blue cheese."

"You're sure your doctor assured you your heart was healthy?" I ask, arching an eyebrow.

"Yes!" Matt snorts. "I may have a gut, but I'm in good shape. While you're snoozing the day away in your crypt, I'm working in the garden or hiking, or I'm in the basement gym lifting weights or biking miles and miles on the stationary bike."

"While watching gay porn," I add.

"Yeah? So what?"

Nate grins. "You watch porn while you ride the exercise bike?"

"Hell, yes. Logan McCree and François Sagat and Trent Locke? Those boys make the time go a *lot* faster."

"You're so frigging cute sometimes I can't stand it. Back to Okey," I urge.

"I told him everything. Except, uh, for your special condition. He said he was eager to meet you, so we'll have to cross that bridge when we come to it. I also didn't tell him you'd blown up a dragline, though, knowing what a liberal and environmentalist Okey is, he'd probably give you a gold medal. Anyway, once he'd heard about the dream and the blob-thing on that MTR site...and the fact that I'd suffered that fainting spell, and the fact that you had a clair-voyant friend who'd sent you dream-warnings before, he was convinced that some nasty kind of supernatural shit was after me, so he grabbed his cell phone and made some calls. By the time we got back to his house down near Ritter Park, there were four folks there, waiting on his porch. A coupla thin lil' twinky gay guys and a coupla big ole butch lesbians who'd probably whip my ass in a wrasslin' contest."

"His coven?"

"Yep. So we all went inside, and we all had some sweet tea while he caught 'em up on everything. Then we went into his ritual room and he got out that piece of lapis. They put down a circle of white river stones—reminded me of our ritual circle of standing stones out there in the yard—and they called the Quarters the way we do."

Matt pauses to gulp down beer. "Then Okey got out his Book of Shadows and had me sit in the center of the circle. He stood at the lil' altar and did some stuff with candles, and then some stuff with a red cord he knotted again and again while his folks chanted things, some of it about the Moon Goddess and some of it about that Horned God of yours." Matt indicates my Cernun-nos tattoo.

"Then they all got out their knives, their athames, and they put the points on the blue stone and chanted some more. Then they pricked their fingers and daubed blood on it. They had Nate and me do the same. They said the blood was a symbol of kinship, that the more folks added their blood to the charm, the stronger the protection would be...the blood forces would meld together, make a kind of...barbed wire fence? And that fence'd defend me, the way the power of a clan protects each member. You're always talking about your clan, Derek. This charm's built to focus the power of a clan to ward off evil."

"Okey used that word? Clan?"

"Sure did."

"Sounds like a true hillbilly to me. I expect that he and I are going to get along fine. For now, let's just add a little more power to that amulet."

I fang-gash the ball of my thumb and allow my blood to drip over the stone till the blue lapis sits in a palmed pool of red, just as in my dream. For a few seconds, nothing happens, but then the stone grows warm and starts to steam, and the blood begins to bubble. Both Matthew and Nate gasp.

Gradually, the blood recedes and then disappears, as if the amulet had absorbed it. Now the stone pulses in my palm. The power of it seems to have increased fifty-fold.

"Wow. Did you see that?" Nate says.

"Damn," mutters Matt. "Amazing."

"Vampire blood can be pretty potent in magical workings, I've been told. You keep this in your pocket, hot stuff," I say, handing the lapis to Matt. "I can tell it's going to be effective. It'll keep the Lovecraftian blob away from you, and whatever sort of malignant forces Alpha's sent against folks like your cousin Dillon."

"So you think Alpha's behind this? A coal company with black magic on its side?"

"Who else? People have been calling the coal companies demonic for years. Perhaps Alpha's made the metaphor a reality. Donnie told us about all those people that gave Alpha trouble who moved away abruptly or came to mysterious ends."

"True. So Alpha hates me so much they're going after me with sorcery? Now I'm really scared. Especially since Okey told me that the amulet has an important limitation."

"Well, shit. What's that?"

"It deflects nasty magical attack real well—so no sudden heart attack for me, with any luck. But it doesn't do much against a determined physical attack."

"I repeat: Shit. Shit, shit, shit. I want you to stop going down to Charleston so much. Can't you get your work done off-site? Telecommute?"

"Naw. The face-to-face meetings with other activists are too important."

"Matt, don't be stubborn. I can protect you here. At least during the night. During the day, Nate here can watch over you. Right, Nate?"

"Yep," Nate replies. "I'm a damned good shot, and I have a passel of guns. I know I'm not as muscled-up and bulky as you bears, but I'm pretty good at street fighting and a few martial arts too. I worked in security at Alpha for years, and I hated every minute of it, 'cause I saw the mess they were making of the mountains. Protecting you would be a welcome way to make up for that time working for them."

"Thanks, guys, but…. Derek, honey, you can't keep me at home like a parent afraid his kid'll get hurt if he goes out into the world. The reason Alpha hates me is 'cause I'm getting work done. I'm succeeding in interfering with 'em, slowing 'em down. I'm doing good stuff, honey! This ain't no time to retreat and go hide. It's a time to work even harder and make 'em squirm."

"That's heroic and idealistic, but you're risking your life. Let someone else do that."

"Someone else? Why someone else? It's as much my responsibility to stop Alpha as anybody's. Why should I hide up here and let other folks take all the risks? That'd be cowardly."

"What if you get yourself killed?" I swig the rest of my beer and stand.

"That ain't gonna happen. Nate, how about you be my bodyguard? Instead of hanging up here, patrolling property miles and miles from anything or anyone, how about you come to work with me? We'll tell the Partisan folks that you're my personal assistant, or some such BS. You can stay over with me in that lil' house I rent."

"Sure," says Nate. "That sounds great. I'll take care of him, Mr. Maclaine. Count on it."

"You'd damn well better. Matt, I have half a mind to chain you up in the basement and keep you there till all peril is past."

"The only way peril will pass is if Alpha's stopped, and I'm gonna help stop them. How about tonight we chain Mr. Nate up instead and have our way with him?"

"Don't change the subject," I growl. "This is serious."

"Derek, don't look so sour. You're always expecting the worst."

"True. So that, if the worst occurs, I might be prepared for it."

"You got a bad case of siege mentality. Relax, honey. It's a beautiful night. I got my protective charm from Okey. We have this handsome otter on our side. Besides, Nate and I have an announcement to make."

"Yeah? He blew you in a rest stop on the drive back from Huntington, and now you two are running away together?"

"Naw, I got him to agree to compete in the Mountain State Bear Contest this weekend. He's gonna go for Mountain State Bear Cub, and I'm gonna compete for Mountain State Bear. Whaddaya think? Think we stand a chance of winning those coveted black-leather sashes?"

Normally, such news would make me smile. Instead, foul as my mood is— the thought of Matt putting himself in further danger is intolerable—I roll my eyes. "Really? You can think of something so silly and trivial at a time like this?"

"I figure grim times call for a few fun distractions. We're gonna get Nate a pair of leather pants to show off that tight lil' butt of his, and we're both gonna wear harnesses. You gotta come. Hell, you oughta stop feeding for a while and get a pretty silver beard going, and maybe you could win Mountain State Daddy."

"No, thank you. I need to keep my strength up for more serious matters. In fact, after you boys have your meal, you need to provide me with mine. Tomorrow night, I plan on hitting another MTR site."

CHAPTER TWENTY

The Marfork site is much the same as Keystone and Elk Run: glaring lights, parked trucks, an immense moonscape of upended earth surrounded by security fences, and a dragline easily twenty stories tall. I soar over the dusty chaos, reconnoitering. There are no security guards in sight, a fact that makes me nervous. Perhaps there's a different kind of guard I can't see yet: the protozoan from hell.

Was that slovenly thing the source of the malevolent magic Matthew's new amulet is keeping at bay? I champ my teeth at the thought. If so, then it, like a mad dog, is liable to be put down, and I'm just the undead warrior to do it.

Gliding down to the security hut, I regain human form long enough to punch in the long series of numbers that will cut the surveillance cameras. Earlier this evening, Jon Fain, after a tedious and petulant show of reluctance, gave me the newest codes. The man was so irritating that I taped his mouth, beat his ass with his own belt, and fed on him nearly to the point of no return. Pretty he certainly is, but perhaps it's time I replaced him in my eldritch employ. Perhaps it's time I made a different Alpha employee my slave. Surely there's at least one more fuckable man who works for that evil company.

Damn it. The cameras stay on. The code doesn't work. It's definitely time to replace Fain. Well, then, tonight I'll do my destructive work the hard way, and I'll give those bastards a grand show while I'm at it.

Shifting into wolf form, I race across the compound toward the dynamite hut. Snarling, I slam my shoulder into its door.

The door thunders. The structure shakes. The entire hut's built of corrugated metal. Steel? Tin? Who knows? Who cares? As long as it isn't silver.

I back up and leap again, smashing my several hundred pounds of wolf weight against the door. It bends. I back up and leap again. It dents.

These are the fuckers who're threatening Matt, I remind myself. My Matt, my sweet husbear, clutching his chest and slumping to the floor, that loathsome smoke-spider clawing at his heart. I back up and leap again. Again. Again.

The door flies backward off its hinges and hits the ground with a resounding clang. There, in the corner of the ceiling, hangs a camera. Launching myself into the air, I seize the thing in my jaws, rip it from its anchor, drop to the floor, and worry it as if it were the face of my worst enemy. It is, I guess. At least one of my foe's many eyes. The camera spits sparks and smokes. I flip it out the door before taking human form again.

Here's a nice cache of dynamite. I've lit the first stick—once again my Bic lighter is useful for more than the sudden urge for a cigar—when my nose fills with the chemical stink I smelled at Elk Run. It's not the odor of must, musk, or rot, for those are natural, organic. No, this is the stink of laboratories, unnatural compounds, industrial pollutants, the foul acids only a misguided science could make. That foul fog-thing is here.

I spin around, glaring. A glaucous gray form looms, only yards beyond the hut's entrance. Dropping the lit stick, I shade into bat form and dart from the hut before the thing can trap me there. Rising a good ten feet above the unseemly mess, I circle it, fangs bared. Thin cilia several feet long rise from it, resembling the stamens extruding from a flower. Again I have the distinct feeling that it's assessing me, trying to determine my weaknesses.

Dare I try to bite it? It doesn't look sufficiently solid to pierce with my teeth, plus, Gods, the stink of it is repugnant enough. I have absolutely no desire to discover how it tastes.

Hell, the dynamite. It's still burning, no doubt, and likely to explode any minute. Can't let that go to waste. I dive-bomb the pulsing putrescence, causing it to contract the way an amoeba will if you poke it with a pin. Hideous mess, it probably has no more sense than a microbe. Suddenly the entire thing flattens, and then a long tentacle of its animate fog lengthens, tightens into a series of overlapping circles, like a flexible metal spring, and snaps out at me with amazing speed.

I veer at the last second and the tentacle misses me by inches. Damn it, I don't have time for this. I dive-bomb it again, then wing into the hut, snatch the stick of dynamite, and shoot back out.

Do I drop it on that odious mess or on the dragline? The fuse is short, as is the time for decision. I race for the great craned machine, dropping the stick onto the top of the dragline cabin before flapping away as fast as I can.

The roar of the blast is deliciously immense. Again there's the satisfying sight of metal shards flying apart, the crane crashing to earth, flaring petals of flame, and another destroyer destroyed. Having achieved a safe height, I circle, laughing deep in my throat. Poet William Blake called industrial England's early factories "satanic mills." What would he say if he could see this?

Far below, the great lumpy thing shifts from gray to green to crimson to green to gray. It's like an angry man's face going livid with rage. Glimmering spots of light arc and wink inside it, like overheated meteorites. Is the poor thing throwing a hissy fit? I glide over the smoking ruins of the dragline, savoring the show, then head back toward Charleston. The codes Jon Fain gave me were incorrect. Tonight he'll be made to pay.

CHAPTER TWENTY-ONE

For the second time tonight, I find myself drifting over smoking ruins, but this one isn't a pleasurable sight, it's a perplexing one. Jon Fain's house is a heap of wet ash and blackened walls.

I swoop down into the limbs of a tree at the edge of the yard and observe the chaos: fire trucks, police cars, the squirt of high-powered hoses. I wait for nearly an hour, listening to assorted conversations long enough to determine that if Fain were in there, he couldn't have survived.

Someone has done my work for me. Why? Perhaps the codes Fain gave me tonight were wrong not because he was resisting my will but because he'd been given codes that were deliberately incorrect. If so, that would mean that his employers figured out that he was not to be trusted and decided to dismiss him in the most extreme way possible.

Too bad. He had a very pretty mouth. Launching myself off the branch, I rise into the sky.

Mount Storm's dark. Only a lamp in the den is on, turned low. Upstairs, Matt's characteristic snores sound.

I pad up the steps and enter the master bedroom. By Eros, what a sight. Matt and Nate, both naked, are curled up upon the four-poster, Nate nestling inside Matt's thick arms. Rope, a dog collar, a butt plug, two used condoms, a roll of duct tape, and a tube of lube are scattered across the floor, evidence of the romp they must have shared.

"Sweet boys," I whisper. "I hope you fucked for half the night. You're worth any battle, any risk."

I sit on the bed and watch them sleep, fingering Matt's graying beard and Nate's lightly furred pecs. Normally, I'd be tempted to feed on one or both of them, but seeing that gruesome amoeboid horror earlier has dulled my appetite.

I'm about to rise when Nate's long-lashed eyes flicker open. "Hey, Derek," he murmurs. "How'd it go?"

"Good." I stroke his cheek. "Did Matt screw you silly?"

"Yes, sir. He pounded me pretty hard. I'll be walking crooked tomorrow. But he said he'd make it up to me with a fancy breakfast. Some kind of Cajun dish called grillades and grits."

"You'll enjoy that, boy. Get back to sleep now," I say, sliding off the bed.

"Hey, Derek? Thanks. Thanks for choosing me. For making me see what's important. For giving me a job and a home. I'm real happy here."

How much of what he says would he say were he not my thrall? I don't know. It doesn't matter. He is my thrall, and only death or my decision to release him will change that. Still, his happiness feels genuine. Destroying my enemies is a true delight, but making a handsome man happy is even more of a pleasure.

It's nearly dawn. I'm sipping Drambuie and reading Ovid in the tower room, the isolated part of the farmhouse where I go to savor complete solitude, when my iPhone buzzes. I recognize the ring tone, and it's most welcome.

"Hell vixen," I say.

"Rabid bear," Cynthia replies. "Did you get my dream-message?"

"Ohhhhh, yes. Were I still capable of wetting my pants, I might have done so. Thank you for the warning. I owe you a lot. Matt's upstairs, safe in bed, snuggling with a new slave of mine."

"So you managed to find the right witch and the right amulet? Lapis?"

"Yes. As usual, a simple phone call would have sufficed."

"Where's your sense of melodrama? You bears are just humorless."

"You lesbians are just humorless. Strident and humorless."

We laugh simultaneously. "I've missed you," I say. "A lot's been going on around here, and I could use your advice."

"I have much advice to give. In person would be best. I have a fine home in German Village, a neighborhood of Columbus. Wing up here some evening and spend a night or two. There are all sorts of scruffy, tattooed cubs I'm sure you'd savor at Club Diversity, my favorite gay bar. We could sit out on the back deck beneath the great maples and sip huge martinis while we commiserate and confabulate."

"A visit to Columbus would be a great change of pace. Are you still with Lara?"

"Yes, indeed. Since she got her promotion, she's been living in DC, so we get together on the occasional weekend. Last spring I had a short affair with Nancy, a hot butch bottom...."

"Butch bottoms, God, yes. Aren't they the best? Just like my lovable husbear."

"Just like you when you're in the mood."

"True, true."

"At any rate, that passion had an unfortunate ending. Nancy began to resist my will and then spurned me, so I fear I had to do away with her...and her wife. Their poor children saw it all. Now the brats vacillate between the madhouse and the orphanage. These days, I'm following in your footsteps, so to speak, and spreading around my sharp kisses and sweet favors. At this point, I have somewhat of a Sapphic harem. Rebekah's my present favorite."

"Excellent! Never too many thralls. I'm always telling Matthew that no one man should have to bear the burden of my thirsts."

"A fine excuse. Gluttony and erotic abandon all around! Sluts and studs forever! You must meet Rebekah. She's all curvy black elegance, with stylish glasses and gowns and kissably full crimson lips. Her blood's so sweet and feral. 'Black wildflower honey' would be the metaphor you'd use. I believe you have someone similarly feral in your pack of bear-boys, do you not?"

"Do you mean Donnie? Rebekah's a werewolf like him?"

"Yes. She looks lovely, naked and locked in a cage in my basement during the full moon."

"Can you control her while she's in wolf form? I've managed to do that with Donnie, after a good year's practice."

"Yes. I sent her after the preacher of a local mega-church. He was harping a little too much on the 'queers are bound for hell and should be executed' sermons. Poor man was found frightfully dismembered in his back yard."

"How tragic. Outspoken Christian fundamentalists do seem to come to bad ends when you and I are around."

"True." Cynthia laughs softly. "Miss Rebekah, she's more than a handful, even in human form. A lusty bisexual. Every now and then I catch her holed up with some hipster boy and have to punish her. That leads to all sorts of delectable scenes."

"I can imagine. Why don't you collect a couple of those naughty boys in that basement cage for me to snack upon during my next visit?"

"I'll do my best. When can you get here? Soon, I hope. I've had visions of that monstrous fog-microbe you've encountered, and I'm doing my best to determine what it is by indulging in research with local occultists."

"So what have you discovered?"

"It's a demon, most definitely. I think it's somehow feeding on those mining sites. If so, the more that vile industry expands, the more likely it is that the demon will grow bigger and stronger. If we wait too long, it might become so powerful that it can't be stopped."

"Makes sense. It seemed to be protecting those sites, and it was, uh, colorfully irked when I destroyed the last dragline."

"Get up here as soon as possible, Derek. We need to discuss the situation in person. At this point, I have no idea how to stop it. Matt's not out of danger yet, you know. He won't be safe until Alpha and that thing—"

"The Lovecraftian blob, I call it."

"Nice. Until Alpha and the Lovecraftian blob are destroyed."

"Yep. That's what I'm afraid of. I'm pretty convinced the amulet will protect Matt from supernatural threats, but the coal company he's riled up no doubt has dozens of minions armed to the teeth. They've been following him around Charleston and sending him death threats. Have you had any more specific visions of Matt in danger?"

"No. I've tried to see more, but my clairvoyance is spotty and uncontrollable. Nothing specific. Just a feeling of impending threat. Ah, here's Rebekah now. Excuse me a second. I can't resist her red lips."

I can make out the wet sounds of vigorous kissing before Cynthia gets back onto the line.

"I'm famished, Derek, so I'm going to go now. Rebekah says that you should bring your wolf cub up here with you. She'd love to meet you both."

"I'll do that. We have a travel van Donnie could drive. I'll put my coffin in the back. This weekend, Matthew and Nate, my new otter-thrall, are competing in the Mountain State Bear Contest. After that, I plan to demolish another dragline. Then how about Matthew, Donnie, and I all come up for a few days? Do you have sufficient room?"

"Oh, yes. It's a huge brick house overlooking Schiller Park. We can send our humans out to explore the city while we contemplate ways to put that vexatious amoeba out of its misery."

"Sounds good. See you soon."

"Yes, indeed. Come here, my dear," I hear Cynthia say to Rebekah as she ends the call.

I pocket the phone, open the book, read a few lines of Ovid, turn to a lengthy end note, then, too restless to read, flip the book closed.

Standing, I gaze out at the night. So peaceful here, while, in the coalfields to the southwest, Alpha desecrates more land and that shambling demon ranges over the ruins, growing plumper on the ecological carnage. Having Cynthia on my side will prove enormously helpful. Not only is she clairvoyant, she's twice as strong as I, having been turned in the 1400s in Krakow.

The fog-slob, who knows how powerful it is? By the time this is over, I might have to ask for help from my maker, Sigurd, or my Roman friend, Marcus, who's older and more powerful still. Perhaps Matt can get his witchy friend Okey to help us as well, if Matt can convince him that working with a crew of vampires is in his best interests.

"A gathering of the shadow clans," I mutter. Outside, the east grows pink, so I head down the tower's corkscrew stairs toward the master bedroom. I want to enjoy a few minutes of being surrounded by my boys' naked, furry warmth before I retreat to the chilly cellar crypt for the day.

CHAPTER TWENTY-TWO

Tonight, Charleston's Tap Room is packed with queers of all stripes: a few handsome lesbians, a few gaudily dressed drag queens, bears and cubs of all ages and sizes, even a handful of nattily dressed businessmen and curious twinks. This year's Mountain State Bear Contest is a raving success.

I stand in the darkest corner—my preferred perspective point—sipping a beer and watching the show. I'm dressed in my usual summer leather-bar garb: olive drab pants, biker boots, and a tight black muscle-shirt. Upon my right wrist I wear the studded black leather band that Matt gave me in this very bar, the night we were attacked by the Leviticus Locusts and I took rich pleasure in dispatching all five of them before making their remains a feast for sewer rats.

The contestants for Mountain State Bear are several. I especially like barrel-chested Ken—with graying beard, blue eyes, mischievous grin, and impressive shoulders—and black-goateed Jeff, with extensive tattoos, shaved head, and gym-hardened pecs.

But of course Matt's the most fetching of all. Downright toothsome. He struts up onto the stage last, exuding the same cocky charm that made me fall in love with him years ago. He's shirtless, wearing tight black jeans, cowboy boots, and a black leather vest that shows off the hair-matted cleft between his pecs and his equally hairy beer belly. He swaggers and grins, flexes his arms and wiggles his butt. The crowd responds with deafening hoots of enthusiasm.

The judges must share that enthusiasm, for now Matt's proclaimed the winner. A drag queen drapes him with the sash and kisses him on the cheek. Matt indulges in an awkward little celebratory jig before climbing off the stage. He joins me in my shadowy corner, seizing me in his arms for a crushing hug as the Bear Cub part of the competition commences.

"Ain't lost it yet, have I?" he says, swigging a beer and squeezing my ass.

"Stupid question. You're hotter than you ever were." I squeeze his butt right back. "I figured you might cut back on your very-out-and-queer public persona now that folks are wanting you to run for political office, but here you are, strutting around in a leather vest like a porn star extra from *Where the Bears Are*."

"Hell, it's not like the *Gazette* covers this. But it will cover the Pride Parade, and I'm gonna be a prominent part of that. Shit, Derek, I couldn't go back in the closet even if I tried. When you met me, me and the Ridgerunners were performing all over the state, singing openly gay love songs. That caused all kinds of ruckus. People don't forget stuff like that. Everybody knows I'm queer. I don't think that'll make one bit a' difference if I run for office. It's my stand on mountaintop removal that folks care about, not who I sleep with. Speaking of which, lookee there. There goes Nate. Ain't he hot? Damn, I hope he wins."

Nate's a pretty arousing vision, that's for sure, all pale skin and ruddy fur. He's wearing the tight black leather pants that Matt bought him, plus a studded dog collar. His bare pectorals, red-brown chest hair, and small nipples are accentuated by a tight leather harness. Leather bands adorn his sinewy upper arms. The erstwhile Alpha employee doesn't strut the stage with confidence the way Matt did. He's much more tentative and shy. But that shyness is hopelessly endearing. When—after one more contestant, a boy with far more avoirdupois than I find appealing—Nate is announced the winner, Matt emits a long, high "Yeeeee haw!" before bounding toward Nate and grabbing him in his arms.

"Congrats, man!" Matt yells over the thump of resuming disco music.

"Thanks. Wow. I can't believe it," Nate says, plucking at his sash. "Just a few weeks ago, I was sitting in a pew being told what a sinner I was, and now, thanks to y'all...."

"You stick with us, man. We'll take care of you." Matt steps between Nate and me, wrapping an arm around each of our waists. For a few minutes, the three of us simply stand there, watching the motley crowd and swaying to the music.

Matt squeezes Nate's shoulder and swills the rest of his beer. "Look, guys, I gotta meet with some folks over there." He indicates a crew of young men dressed in Oxford shirts and chinos. "We gotta plan a few fine points of the Pride Parade coming up. Why don't y'all git on back to my place and get to know one another better?" Matt winks, plucking at the fine tendrils of red hair in the pit of Nate's throat.

"Gladly," I say. "Except I don't want you walking home alone."

"Come on. It's only a few blocks. I'm a big boy. I'm a ferocious redneck, and Mr. Mountain State Bear too. I've whupped some ass in my time, yes, sir, I have."

"Yes, but…. Ummm, I don't know."

"I'll be fine, I promise. Get this pretty bottom-boy ready for me, Derek. The way we discussed. Okay?" Grinning, Matt pats Nate's ass. "I want him all nice and lubed up and open when I get home."

Nate fidgets and blushes. "Damn, you'll say just about anything."

"Yep, I will. My mommy used to tell me I was vulgar, and ain't nothing much changed since then. Don't worry, guys. Git on now."

"All right, all right. So bossy." I slip a finger into the D-ring of Nate's dog collar. "Come along, Mr. Mountain State Bear Cub. The night's just begun."

"Uh oh," Nate says cheerfully. "Guess I'm in for it now." Obediently he follows me out.

Matt's rented house on Lee Street is small and cozy, four rooms built around a central set of fireplaces that have been converted to gas, plus a kitchen addition. The bed's king-sized, deliberately chosen to accommodate three grown men when the lucky occasion dictates.

I pull off my muscle-shirt, light a few candles, and take a seat in a chair by the bed. "Get naked," I order. "But leave the harness and dog collar on."

"Yes, sir," Nate mutters, head bowed in that show of surrender I so relish in a hot man. Slowly, he undresses. He stands before me now, hands clasped behind his back, his prodigious cock bobbing in the dim light.

"You tall, lean boys are nearly always hugely hung, aren't you? Come straddle Daddy's lap."

Nate does so. I wrap my left arm around his back, and with my right hand I grip his prick. He embraces me. We kiss, messily and deeply, till his neat beard and my wild goatee are both moist with spit and his dick's oozing pre-come.

Reaching over, I take up a roll of duct tape off the dresser. I gaze into his eyes, questioning. Nate swallows hard and nods.

I peel off a short strip of tape and apply it to his mouth. I peel off more, wrapping it around his head till three layers and several feet of it silence him.

"Oh, yes," I say, tossing the roll on the floor. "I've been wanting to see you like this. Do you like being gagged?"

Nate nods.

"There are few things I enjoy more than kissing a gagged man. May I kiss you now?

Nate nods again. Cupping the back of his head, I pull him to me, pressing my mouth against his tape-sealed lips. I work his nipples between my fingernails till he's groaning, then sink my teeth into his neck.

By the time Nate comes to, I'm stretched out atop him, driving my cock deep into his ass. He's belly-down on the bed, his wrists bound together and tethered to the headboard.

"It would have been politer, I know, to wait till you wakened, but your butt was just so small and round and tight and white, with all that musky fur in the crack, that I had to get inside you." I kiss his pale back, stroke his face, and prick-probe his hole. "I hope that's all right? I figured a good plowing would be a hot way to wake you up."

Nate grunts and nods, rocking inside the force of my thrusts.

"I'm not hurting you, am I? I used lots of lube and took my time working my way inside."

Nate shakes his head. The telepathic connection between master and slave allows us mental conversation, much like that I had with Matt the night I woke to find myself in chains. *It doesn't hurt, sir. It feels wonderful. Please don't stop.* Lifting his hips, he pushes backward, giving me greater access to his snug, slick depths.

"Good boy. I could sense that you'd be an eager bottom."

I give him a few more vigorous prods before pulling out my prick. I slap his ass-cheeks till they're warm and pink, then spread them, nuzzle my face between his buttocks, and push my tongue up his hole. He cries out, squirms, and humps the pillows piled beneath his groin.

After a lengthy session of having his ass eaten, Nate's ready for more dick.

Please put it in me again. Please put it in me again!

"Most assuredly," I sigh. Hauling him up onto his elbows and knees, I position my prick and slam inside him again. A good ten minutes of that deliciously submissive posture, then I roll Nate onto his back, hoist his long legs in the air, and bend him double, kissing his brow, nose, and taped mouth while riding him hard.

You're so, so tight, boy. Milk my dick. That's right. That's right.

You're so big, sir. Man, you fill me up. Fuck me harder. Please fuck me harder.

I'm nearing release when I hear the front door open. In another minute, Matthew's standing by the bed, grinning widely.

"Goddamn," he says. "Whatta sight. I gotta get me some a' that." Hopping about, he pulls off his cowboy boots, then his pants and jock. "C'mon, Derek, gimme a little time in that saddle."

"Yep. Real soon. I'm…about…to…."

I grit my teeth, pressing my face against Nate's and madly hammering his hole. Another rapt moment, and with a roar I'm pumping come deep inside the trussed and tape-gagged boy.

Oh, God. That was good. That was amazing. Nate rubs his sweaty cheek against mine. Between our bellies, his cock is dripping with excitement. *Thank you, sir. Thank you, sir.*

"Thank *you*, boy." I kiss his taped lips before pulling out and lowering his legs. "'Amazing' is right. Next?"

"You're damn right I'm next," says Matt, working Nate's cock briefly before patting his slender hip. "On your belly, kid. Act Two's about to begin."

CHAPTER TWENTY-THREE

The cellar of Matt's house is moist and musty. I rise from the make-shift bed of old blankets, eager to get back to my dry, neat nest at Mount Storm.

When I lope up the cellar stairs, no one's about. Not Matt. Not Nate. No note telling me something reassuring: "Hey, Derek, we're having a late dinner at Sitar of India," or "Hey, Derek, we're taking in a band down at Eppson Books." I reach out with my mind, rummaging through what I suppose the occultists would call astral energies and auric traces, trying to detect their presence in the city.

Nothing. Could they have gone back to Mount Storm? No. They'd never do that without me. After all that's happened lately, they both know that I'd be worried sick.

As I am now. I slip into the bedroom, dig my iPhone out of my discarded pants, and punch in Matt's number.

Nothing. Nothing. Nothing. Has something horrible happened to him or to Nate while I lay senseless? By Thor's hammer, if Alpha's hurt either one of them...Alpha or that viscous monstrosity....

I dial Timmy's number. "Hey, man," he answers. "What's up?"

"Timmy, listen. I can't find Matt. Did you hear from him today?

"Naw. 'Fraid not. Donnie and I have both been here at the Allegheny Café. Say, that lil' Rebel reenactor came in today for lunch. He's mighty cute. No wonder Matt—"

"Timmy, I can't talk about that now. Matt and Nate are nowhere to be found. They were supposed to spend the day in meetings at the Mountain Partisan office and be at Matt's house when I rose, but they aren't here. And they didn't leave a note."

"Oh, shit. That ain't like Matthew. Whaddaya want us to do?"

"You two get to Mount Storm and check the place. Have Donnie stay up there to let me know if Matt shows up or calls the house. You get the van and head down toward the Kanawha Valley just I case I need you. I'm going to fly around Charleston and see if I can pick up some trace of him."

"Derek, calm down now. Things are probably fine. You can count on Donnie and me. We're just about to end our shifts. We'll get up to Mount Storm as fast as we can."

I hang up, trying to tamp back the rage and panic rising in my throat. Timmy's right. I need to stay calm. Now is the time for a cool head. I've always been best in times of crisis, and this, I fear, might be one of those times. Leaving the house by the back door, I step into the dark backyard and take to flight.

For hours I wend my way over the Kanawha Valley. Charleston, then down the river to South Charleston, Dunbar, Institute, Nitro, St. Albans, then back over the Charleston suburbs to the south, then up the river to Belle, on as far as Montgomery and the Kanawha Falls, where Matt once sat by me in the wintry garden of the Glen Ferris Inn and agreed to give our relationship a chance. I can feel them nowhere. My boys have simply disappeared.

Cursing, I range farther, to Keystone Mountain, to Elk Run, and to Marfork. I can sense nothing unusual. Not even that poisonous, bloated germ.

I return to Charleston. In an alley near the Tap Room, I shift to human form long enough to check my phone—the only message is one from Timmy telling me that he and Donnie are at Mount Storm but there's no sign of Matt—and to seize a stubble-faced college-aged boy off the street for a strength-replenishing snack. Then I take once more to the air.

I'm drifting over Kanawha City, sick with despair and ready to give up, to return to Matt's house on Lee Street and try again tomorrow night, when I hear it. A small, small voice, barely a flicker in my head. Before I can gauge its direction, it stops. Then it starts up again. It's Nate Palmer, and he's in deep distress.

I move south. It's like trying to pin down the weakest of radio signals. Then I dip over a ridge and the voice is clearer: *Derek. Please help me. I can hardly breathe. Please, Derek. Help.*

I'm close, boy. Speak to me. Help me find you.

They buried me, sir. Please....

He's down there. By the darkest of gods, it's a landfill.

I shoot down to the ground, leaving off bat form. Nate's near. Very near. Here, right here, beneath this upside-down couch, buried in the earth. I seize the malodorous piece of furniture and hurl it behind me, and then I smell Nate's blood. Lots of it. Frantic, I begin to dig.

Nate, I'm here. I've found you. Hold on, boy. Hold on.

No response. He must have lost consciousness. Or, God forbid, expired.

Only a foot beneath the surface of the soil, I find it. It's a freezer, the sort of capacious home freezer in which country families store sides of beef or pork or venison. Several strips of duct tape—the very silver-gray substance with which I took such concupiscent delight in gagging Nate last night—are wrapped around it, sealing the lid shut. I claw at the tape, ripping it away. I hurl open the lid.

Nate's curled up into a ball, his hands cuffed behind his back. He's covered in blood, and he's unconscious, but he's still breathing. Barely breathing.

I lift him out of the makeshift coffin and carry him out of the landfill. I lower him with great care onto a patch of dewy grass, snap the cuff-steel between my fingers, and examine him for injuries. He's been shot in the right shoulder. Thank the Goddess he's still alive.

Nate opens his eyes, licks his lips, and gives me a faint smile.

"Derek. Hey. You found me."

"I'm here." I take his hand. "What happened, boy?"

"They...grabbed us, Matt and me. We were down...at Daniel Boone Park, just shooting the shit, watching the sun set. We were just...just about to head...home to w-wait for you to wake...when they pulled up in a van. Six of them. They shot me before I could pull my gun...and they b-beat Matt down. They cuffed us and...th-threw us in the van. I passed out. Next I knew, we were out here, it was night, and they...were f-forcing me into that damn f-freezer. I passed out. Came to and started...started calling for you. I was afraid I'd suffocate. I can't b-believe...b-believe you found me."

"I almost *didn't* find you. What have they done with Matt?"

"Don't know."

"Did you recognize any of them as Alpha employees?"

"Naw. All strangers. Derek…."

Nate passes out. I've got to get him to the nearest hospital. The one down-town has a heliport. Perfect. Shifting, I grip Nate in my claws, then rise into the night.

CHAPTER TWENTY-FOUR

alf an hour after depositing Nate on the roof of the hospital and making anonymous calls to both the emergency room and 911 to alert them to his presence, I'm circling Dick Blankenship's pretentious mega-mansion in South Hills. Months ago, soon after Timmy told me that Blankenship was Alpha's head of security, I located the man's house for future reference. Tonight, that knowledge has proven exceedingly valuable. I'm afraid time's running out for Matt, and I've got to find him before dawn.

I descend onto the Italianate back terrace. My rage is in no mood to fiddle with home security systems, but it is in the mood for a dramatic entrance. I simply slam my shoulder against one of the French doors, shatter the glass, and throw it open.

A buddy of Matt's, a former Marine who used to meet us down in Franklin for a beer, used to talk about "situational awareness," how soldiers are trained to rapidly assess their surroundings and gauge the strategic benefits and advantages thereof. Heighten that awareness by twenty-fold—fifty-fold, for the really ancient ones like Sigurd or Marcus—and you have the keenness of my senses. In a split second I know that the domestic tableau I've interrupted within couldn't be more convenient for my purposes.

The family sits before the television, staring at me, all frozen in attitudes of shock. A husband, a wife, and two children, a boy and a girl, both younger than ten.

Blankenship is just as Timmy described: bald, stern-faced, clearly an aficionado of weight-lifting. He's a massive man, no doubt accustomed to intimidating everyone around him. The details of his wife's and children's appearance are irrelevant. The only thing that's important here is that this man probably knows where Matt is—indeed, he might have ordered the attack—and that this same man probably loves his wife and children and would mourn horribly if they were to be harmed.

"What the hell?" Blankenship jumps to his feet. "Who the hell are you?" His wife grabs the children and moves around the couch to hide behind her husband's considerable breadth.

"No shrilling security system? It isn't armed? You thought you were safe in such a fine neighborhood. Wrong." I point to a grandfather clock against the wall. "It's late. Isn't it time those precious bundles were put to bed? I'd hate for them to have to see what's coming next."

Blankenship darts to a closet, throws it open, and rummages on a high shelf. A weapon, no doubt. Fine. No reason to interfere with his efforts. The more dramatic the struggle, the more entertaining the evening.

He spins. Gripping a pistol with both hands, he points it at me.

"Ah, yes," I say, crossing my arms and smiling. "The requisite weapon. The patriarch defending his family."

"Susan, call 911," he says, voice low and steady. "Tell them a stranger's broken into our house and I'm holding him at gunpoint. Tell them to hurry."

"I wouldn't do that, Mrs. Blankenship. I need to speak to your husband about a very important matter, and I don't want any interruptions."

"Go, Susan. Now." Blankenship takes a step toward me. "If you move an inch, I'll put a bullet in your heart. Kids, stay behind me. Susan, go."

He ushers her toward a phone in the corner. She makes a tentative move in that direction.

"I said not to do that." Frowning, I stride closer. Blankenship steps back and fires.

The bullet slams into the center of my chest. I double over, growling, and then, shaking off the jagged pain, I straighten. The predictable effect, one I never fail to savor: my attacker looks stunned by the apparent impossibility.

He grits his teeth and fires again. This projectile tears into my belly.

I clutch my gut. I wince and shudder, shrug off searing discomfort, and smile.

"You're as good a shot as the boy your thugs tried to bury alive," I say, before leaping through the air.

I catch Blankenship by the throat and shake him hard. The gun goes flying. I lift him with one hand, then toss him across the room. He smashes against the mantelpiece and thuds onto the floor. Before he can begin any attempt to rise, I've torn the phone out of the wall, tossed the gun through the open door through which I came, then seized him again, punched him in the face five times, and thrown him against the couch. It tips backward with his weight and deposits him onto the carpet, where he lies groaning for a few seconds before going limp.

Mrs. Blankenship begins to scream, as do her spawn, who huddle behind her. I can't resist. Turning to them, I bare my fangs. The decibels increase exponentially.

Chuckling, I sheathe my teeth. "Your terror's delightful, but your cries are not. Please be quiet. I can't abide noise."

This request is not honored. Shrill hysteria continues.

"Be silent," I snarl. Beneath my basilisk gaze, the mother stops screaming. Seconds thereafter, the children follow suit.

"Much better. Mrs. Blankenship, some of your husband's colleagues took from me someone I love very much. Did you know that?"

"I did not," she says, face blank as a turnip. "That's awful."

"You wouldn't want to suffer the same, would you?"

"Certainly not."

"Do you have a basement?"

"Yes. Yes, we do."

"I suggest you take shelter there from this unnatural disaster. And take your little darlings with you. You won't use the phone to call anyone, will you?"

"N-no," she says.

"Good. Go now."

Mrs. Blankenship takes her children by the hands and shambles away. "Daddy!" the girl squeals as she and her sibling are herded from the room.

I return to Blankenship, who's coming to consciousness. Again, I clutch him by the throat. Hauling him to his feet, I shove him down into an armchair.

"Who the hell are you?" he rasps. His eyes are swollen and his right cheek's lacerated and bleeding. He clutches his side. Hopefully, he has a broken rib or two. "Where are your wounds? I shot you twice."

"Yes, you did. I guess I'm too mean to die."

He studies me. "You're half my size. How'd you…."

"Throw you around the room the way a terrier does a rat? It's a long story, one I don't have time to tell. I want you to tell me where Matt Taylor is."

Blankenship probes his side and grimaces. "Who?"

"You fucking swine." I step closer.

Blankenship cringes. "I don't know anyone by—"

"You're a bald-faced liar. Matt Taylor, you daft troll. The man who's been harassing your company very publicly for months."

"I have no idea where he—"

"I have ways of convincing you that are subtler, but instead…I'll do this." Seizing his right forearm and hand, I snap his wrist.

Blankenship thrashes and howls. In the bowels of the house, I can hear his wife responding in kind. I take him by the neck once more and run a forefinger down his cheek.

"You're a stupid fucker. Matt Taylor was the one person standing between me and my desire for an epic bloodbath. But now your people have him somewhere. Let me be crystal clear about this. If you don't tell me where Matt is, I will gouge out your eyes and lap blood from your empty sockets. Then I will break your neck and watch you spasm, soil yourself, and expire. Before the blood's cooled on my lips, I will go downstairs, where your family awaits. I will twist your wife's head clean off before your children's wide eyes, and then I will lift your bairns like poppets and brain them against the walls until Jackson-fucking-Pollack would offer me a Scotch."

I shake him violently and extend my fangs. "Then I'll torch this vulgarity you call a home as a warning. Because I intend to visit every member of Alpha's board of directors one by one, and I will end them in the most horrible ways I can imagine. The corporate office will reek like an abattoir. I will dynamite every one of their earth-destroying machines until no one would ever think of taking up so much as a spade in the name of Alpha. Unless…unless you tell me where Matt Taylor is. Now."

"Oh, my God," Blankenship gasps. The smell of urine wafts from his groin. "You have animal teeth. You're not human. What kind of fucking monster are you?"

My fingernail's a ragged talon as I tap his cheekbone, puncturing the soft skin. "One you've made furious. Now tell me or your right eyeball's gone."

Blankenship groans and squints. "He's in an abandoned Alpha warehouse at our Mammoth site. Near Cedar Grove."

I tap his cheek again. "Is he still alive?"

"Yes. Beaten up pretty badly, but alive, last I heard from the guys holding him."

"When was that?"

"About an hour ago."

"Why did you have him taken?"

"To interrogate him. We thought he might know who's been blowing up our draglines." His eyes widen. "Was that you?"

"Heaven forfend. I'm a great champion of pollutants, environmental holocausts, and fossil fuels. What do they plan to do with Matt after they get the information they want?"

"I don't know. I—"

I tighten my grip around Blankenship's throat, cutting off his breath. He squirms and gasps in my grasp. "Tell me," I say, licking a fang and loosening my hold.

Blankenship coughs and shakes, sucking in air. "They're going to shoot him in the head and bury him in the woods."

I heave a hoarse growl. I want to snap this man's neck so badly. "Who told you to abduct him?"

"If I tell you that, they'll kill me."

"If you don't tell me that, you'll be dead before they get a chance to kill you, and so will your wife and children."

"S-Sodeski told me to have it done. Alpha's CEO. At first, he thought he could have Taylor taken out the way they did his cousin, Dillon...."

"How was that?"

"I don't know. Really! I swear! The guy had a heart attack, but I think my superiors had something to do with it, because I overheard them boasting about putting an end to 'the Dillon Taylor trouble.' There's this funny little man with a white beard I've seen with Sodeski at company parties. I think he's a scientist. Maybe he developed some kind of new poison."

"Go on."

"So then, when that way didn't seem to work and Matt Taylor stayed healthy, the higher-ups decided to kidnap him, question him, and then get rid of him the old-fashioned way."

"Right. The way their predecessors got rid of Sid Hatfield and Ed Chambers in the 1920s: a few well-aimed bullets. Where I can find Sodeski? His Kanawha Boulevard apartment?"

"No, he moved out of there after a weird snake infestation. Usually he lives outside DC. Lately he must be at his local place, since he's been calling lots of meetings at our Charleston office due to the dragline sabotage. It's down in Boone County. I don't know exactly where. The last few years, Sodeski's been secretive about all kinds of things."

"I'll find him, never fear. Do you have a computer here?"

Blankenship looks puzzled. "A computer? Yeah. A laptop back in the study."

"Get up," I order, dragging the battered man to his feet and propelling him before me. "We're going to take a look at that Mammoth site on Google Maps. Then I'm going to lock you up with your family in the basement, after I tear out every phone line in the house and smash every cell phone to bits. I very badly want to put an end to you, but I won't tonight. But if I get to Mammoth and find out you're lying, I'll be back, be sure of it. Next time, I'll massacre you all. And I'll start with your children."

Chapter Twenty-Five

I f ever my vapor form were handy, it's right now, as I slip under a side door of the rundown warehouse at Mammoth and begin hasty reconnaissance. I can't detect Matt's mind calling out to me, as he surely would be doing in these circumstances, so he must be unconscious. The alternative cause for his silence I refuse to contemplate. He is in this building, though. I have no doubt, because I can smell him. The scents of his sweat and blood usually have me salivating with lust and thirst. Tonight's different. Tonight, those odors portend fear, struggle, and injury.

The front rooms are pitch-black and empty, except for a few piles of trash and some scattered coal. All the loss and pain and sickness and terror, just so greedy men can harvest this black rock and the prehistoric sunlight locked inside it. I think it's time to invest in some solar panels for the roof of Mount Storm.

There's light in a back room, showing under a door, and the raucous sound of television. I glide closer, straining for the sound of Matt's heartbeat. There it is! My beloved's still alive, thank the Horned One. All the human men I've loved in my long life—Angus, Mark, Gerard—came to violent, untimely ends, and I was unable to save them from their fates. This time, this time will be different.

I ooze under the door. There's Matt, in the far corner of the room. Goddess, I feared I might never see him again. I sift up the wall and along the ceiling, then hover over him.

Matt's stripped to the waist. His head's slumped on his chest, his face framed with shaggy hair. He's unconscious, breath shallow and uneven. His hands are cuffed behind him. He's lashed to the back of the chair with rope. There's a rag tied in his mouth. Normally, as an enthusiast of erotic sadism, I would find these details arousing, especially if we were back home in our basement dungeon. As it is, I'm only further enraged. This isn't a scene of consensual dominance and submission. This is a scene of brutal torture. Matt's handsome face has been battered. His eyes are swollen and blackened, as are his lips. His gag's sodden with fresh blood. What appear to be cigarette burns scatter his bare chest. There's another burn on his puffy left cheek, just above his beard line.

With some effort, I turn my attention from the physical evidence of his suffering to those responsible for it. There are six of them, as Nate had reported. They're all solidly built and nicely dressed, the latter detail quite ironic, considering their activities of the last few hours: burying one man alive, beating another into insensibility. Two sit at either side of a desk, playing games on their phones, one sipping a beer, one sipping a bottle of water. Three sprawl on a couch, watching a basketball game on a little television. The sixth stands by an open window and smokes.

I'm poised to swoop down into carnage—the retribution I've been aching for ever since Matt came home in tears with the news that Dillon was dead—when a cell phone buzzes. The man at the window digs around in his pocket, pulls out his phone, and answers it.

"Yes. Yes, sir, this is Randy. Yes, the Palmer kid's done. That's what he gets for betraying Alpha, right? Yes, sir. No, we tried. Yes, we did our best with Taylor, but…hold on."

Randy pauses, addressing his cohorts on the couch. "Would one of you assholes please turn that damn TV down? Thanks."

One man obliges. Randy continues.

"We hurt Taylor pretty bad. Beat him. Burnt him. It didn't do much good. The guy's fierce. And tough. And mean. Even threatened us. Told us someone worse than any man we've ever met would be coming for us if we didn't let him go. Yeah. Yeah, real dramatic. Spat on us, cussed us. Wouldn't stop cussing us, so we gagged him and beat on him some more. He— No, nothing. Wouldn't tell us anything. You want us to use the acid next? Right now, he's passed out, but once he— Huh? Okay. Yeah. That sinkhole out back, all right. Lots of gravel to cover him. Yep. All right. Hold on a minute."

"Hey, Lee," he says. "Shoot him."

"Now?" says the man who'd adjusted the television. "Can't we wait till the game's over?"

"Now. Mr. S wants to hear the guy die. He agrees that any more interrogation is a waste of time. Shoot him. Let's get this over with. It's nearly three a.m. I gotta get some sleep. My kid has peewee football practice tomorrow."

"Well, hell," Lee whines, pulling a handgun from his suit jacket pocket. "We didn't even get to use the acid I got from—"

I've heard enough. Shifting into human form, I drop from the ceiling into their midst.

"Holy shit!" Randy says. "Where'd you—"

I truncate both his sentence and his life, snapping his neck between my hands.

I turn toward Lee, knock the gun from his grasp, and backhand him across the room. His head hits the wall with a crunch. He drops to the floor, twitches, and lies still.

I leap upon another, tearing open his neck with my fangs. Another shoots me in the back. I turn, take him by the throat, and throttle him into unconsciousness.

Two are left, cowering against the wall. One's unprepossessing. The other's vaguely handsome, his round face shadowed with stubble.

"Easy choice," I say, seizing the latter and sinking my teeth into his neck. His frantic heart pounds, speeding his salty, ferrous essence across my tongue and down my throat. I drain him till he collapses.

The last man's fled. I race through the door and into the night. His panicked panting sounds just ahead of me. Seizing him by the back of the neck, I throw him sideways into a tree, knocking him out.

I haul him up and throw him over my shoulder before returning to the warehouse. Inside, I make a heap of unconscious men and corpses in the center of the room. Randy's cell phone lies open on the floor. On it, a voice squawks. I pick up the device and press it to my ear.

"Hello," I say. "May I help you?"

"Randy? Is that you? Jesus. What in God's name is happening there?"

"Which god? Mars, the god of war? This is not Randy. Randy can't come to the phone right now. Randy's dead."

"Who the hell is this?"

"Randy's dead. Lee's dead. In a few minutes, all your men here will be dead. I'm going to build a bonfire. A sacrificial bonfire to the gods of justice."

"Bonfire? Who the hell are you? Are you the crazy bastard who's been ruining our properties?" The voice sounds white, middle-aged.

"Are you the CEO of Alpha Coal? Mr. S, Randy said. Mr. Sodeski, I presume?"

No answer.

"Let me tell you something, whoever you are. You've never dealt with anything even close to resembling me. I don't care what kind of slimy, obese imp from the pit you have on a leash. When I get hold of you, I will tear you into pieces. I will rip your heart from your chest and squeeze blood from it like a sponge. I will fillet your flesh from your bones. I will—"

My interlocutor hangs up. How rude. No number to call back: the phone's screen says BLOCKED. Well, I'll deal with him later. Time to rouse Matt and get the hell out of this place. It's too close to dawn for me to risk flying us back to Mount Storm—the many miles between Pendleton County and the Kanawha Valley have proven inconvenient more than once—but I phoned Timmy with an update after leaving Blankenship's, so he should be here soon.

After all that's happened, I won't leave Matt in his Charleston house. Anything might occur tomorrow while I sleep. And after what happened to Nate, I don't want my other thralls in harm's way. In fact, Nate might still be in danger. We'll need to fetch him in tomorrow, if his physical state permits. Who knows what Alpha snakes might have infiltrated that hospital? Plus Nate, unlike Matthew, has no amulet.

"Sweet man," I say, shaking Matt's shoulder and patting his injured face. "I've come for you. Please wake up." When he doesn't respond, I take the plastic bottle of water off the desk and pour it over his head.

"Mmmm!" He comes awake with a jolt and a gasp. He looks around in confused panic, starts writhing in his bonds, and then his glance rests on me. His eyes well up, and he begins to cry.

"Oh, Matt. Sweet Matt," I soothe. "It's all right now."

Tenderly I remove the bloody rag from his mouth, then the ropes about his chest. Last of all, I snap the cuffs between my fingers.

"Derek! Oh, God, Derek," Matt sobs, grasping my hand. He tries to stand, only to fall back into the chair with a grunt.

"Easy now. I got you." I lift him into my arms and carry him out the door and into the clean, cool night. "How badly are you hurt?"

"B-burnt. They knocked loosh a tooth, I think," he says, gulping back tears. His mouth's so swollen he's slurring words. "Bruised a few ribs, or broke 'em. Cain't tell. Man, Okey was right when he tol' me that charm'd keep off black magic but not vicioush morons."

"The amulet, do you still have it?"

Matt fumbles in his pocket and nods. "Shtill there, yeah. Please, honey, get me outta here. I was so scared I was g-gonna die before you could get to me. They wanted to know…the draglines…."

"I know. They wanted to know who destroyed their precious earth-eaters. And you told them nothing."

"Hell, no," Matt whimpers. "I tol' you I'm one tough hillbilly. The mother-fuckers couldn't break me. Gemme home, Derek. Gemme me home."

"The emergency room first, I think."

"No! They'll come for me there. Pleash take me home. Oh, Jesus! Nate! They buried him alive. They—"

"I found him in the nick of time. Relax. Timmy's on his way with the van. He'll fetch us home. Sleep now." I kiss his puffy cheek and tweak his mind.

"Yeah, shleep," he mutters, head lolling.

I lower Matt into the grass and stroke his wet hair. Then I head off to find what I need to turn the warehouse and the men inside into first a conflagration and then a pile of ashes.

CHAPTER TWENTY-SIX

The next evening, I'm pacing in the master bedroom of Mount Storm, listening to Matthew's soft snores, counting the extensive number of his bandages, and waiting for him to wake, when I catch the unmistakable sound of Donnie's ramshackle car ascending the mountain. I head downstairs, meeting Timmy in the den. Together we step out onto the front porch. It's a drizzly night. Were Matthew not assailed with more pressing concerns, he'd be pleased that his summer-parched garden is receiving some rain.

Donnie pulls up and cuts the engine. The car emits pops and sighs, as if glad to find its efforts at an end. Donnie climbs out, and I stride over to help Nate from the passenger side. He's moving slowly, and his right arm's in a sling, but otherwise he appears to be in decent shape.

"Thanks, sir," Nate says, leaning on my arm. "I'm so relieved to get out of there. I think I saw some Alpha thugs in the hospital hall."

"Don't want you buried alive again or having a mysterious heart attack," I say, helping him up onto the porch. "Did the police question you?"

"They did. But Timmy had called this morning and given me your instructions. I told them I had no idea how I got on that heliport and that I didn't recognize my assailants—which was true—and I didn't mention Alpha or Matt."

"Good boy. Things are complicated enough without law enforcement sniffing around us. I don't want them connecting your abduction with the men who died in that fire at Mammoth or suspecting any other members of my Mount Storm clan."

"Come on, otter boy, you look hungry," says Timmy, poking Nate's flat belly. "Let's get you fed. Since Matt's down for the count, I'm the cook in charge. You like Tex-Mex? How about some quesadillas and chile con queso? Margaritas too. Won't take long at all."

"Sounds wonderful," says Nate, following Timmy into the kitchen. "The hospital food was pretty foul."

"Thanks for fetching Nate," I say, bending to give Donnie's broad shoulders a hug. "I know that's a long drive."

"Four hours down and four hours back. No problem. Nate's a cool, a real cool dude. Hey, Derek? Can we…can we talk?"

"Just for a minute. I want to get back upstairs to Matt."

"Yeah, okay. Well, look. I been thinking…you and Matt have done a lot for me. I owe you, man. I was all alone in my little trailer, scared to death every time the full moon approached, scared of what I'd find the next time I woke up nekkid in a field with blood on my hands and in my mouth, scared I'd torn up some poor kid or old lady…and now you keep me in your dungeon when I change so I cain't hurt anybody…and I'm happy with Timmy, and we both have nice jobs, and we're part of your…bear den, I guess you'd call it."

"Mountaintop man cave. Harem of hirsute, bearded, brawny beauties. Yep. Go on."

"So you're gonna go after the folks who hurt Matt, ain't you?"

"I sure am. As soon as Matt's back on his feet."

"Look, I've heard about that blob-monster." Donnie's black-bearded face twists with disgust. "You don't know how strong it is. What it can do. It might have been the thing responsible for…what happened to those enemies of Alpha, including Matt's cousin, right?"

"All that's true. But I'm going to put it down like a rabid dog."

Donnie scowls and paces.

"Why should you be the soldier all the time? We…we're all members of this crew. We should help each other."

"You've already helped. You drove all day to get Nate out of harm's way. I think the Lovecraftian blob gets its power from the devastation in the coalfields, and Mount Storm is far from all that. As long as you boys stay away from the Kanawha Valley and the coalfields, you should be safe."

"What if I don't wanna be safe? If you can wait till the next full moon…now that you can control me in my wolfie form…why don't you and I go on a raid together? A little nocturnal bushwhacking? We could both tear 'em up."

I kiss Donnie on the forehead and tweak a beefy pec. "Matt and Nate almost died. I don't want any of you taking further risks until I put Alpha to the sword."

"Just think about it, okay? You wanna do damage, right? I can do damage, long's it's a full moon."

"Yes, you can. Right now, though, I want you to go on in and enjoy a meal with Timmy and Nate. I need to go check on Matt. Oh, one thing. Would you like to accompany me to Columbus soon? My friend Cynthia has someone she wants you to meet. A black lady named Rebekah. She shares your unusual experiences come the full moon."

"She's a wolf too? Damn! I've never met another, other than, uh, uh, my daddy."

"She *is* a wolf, apparently. And that's the first time you've mentioned your family since we met you."

"Yeah, well, too much to tell, and most of it bad. Sure, Derek, I'd love to go on a road trip and meet Rebekah. Biggest cities I've ever seen have been Charleston and Roanoke."

"Hey, were-cub," Timmy shouts from the kitchen. "This dip is mighty good. Git in here before this ravenous otter eats it all up."

When I return to the bedroom, Matt's awake. He's lying back on doubled-up pillows in dim lamplight and staring blankly at the wall. He's bare-chested, and the covers are pulled down to his waist, giving me a view of his many bandages. A big one's wrapped around his ribs; smaller ones plaster his burns. The sight's more than sufficient fuel for my fiery hate. Soon, soon, I must find Sodeski's no-doubt-palatial residence and tear him to bloody bits. First, though, time to comfort Matt.

"Hey, stud," I say. "Welcome home. Did you sleep all day?"

Matt's blackened eyes brighten. He smiles at me. His swollen mouth looks better than it did last night. "Hey, honey. Yeah, I slept away most of it."

"Nate just got back from the hospital. His arm's in a sling, but he's safe now." I sit on the edge of the bed and take Matt's hand. "How do you feel?"

"Physically? Really shaky. Emotionally? Really grateful. Really, really, really grateful. You got to both Nate and me in time. We both coulda died. You're our knight in shining armor."

"'Your knight in ebony armor,' Cynthia once put it. My timing was Norn-sent, that's for sure. A few more minutes in the freezer, and Nate would have suffocated. I think that's why those bastards only shot him once. They were saving him for a significantly more horrible end since he'd 'betrayed Alpha,' as one of your captors put it. They were just about to shoot you when I arrived. They'd grown weary of your redneck stubbornness."

"Hell, I figured you'd've done the same after all these years."

"Not possible. On the other hand, that stubbornness does keep landing you in trouble. This isn't the first evening you've been lying in this very bed all bandaged up after getting beaten up by sons of bitches."

"True. The Leviticus Locusts. But that evening ended great, didn't it? That was the first time you and I made love."

"Yes." I brush hair from his brow. "And as soon as you heal, we'll make love again."

"Who bandaged me up? You?"

I nod. "I learned a few things about tending wounds when I was a young man in Scotland, ranging around the country with Angus and getting into brawls with hostile clans. I learned even more following Mark around from battle to battle during the Civil War. Former houseboy Bob taught me a few Cherokee tricks too, before he and Kurt moved to DC. I'm not entirely a demon of destruction, you know."

Matt grips my hand. "I know that better'n anybody in the world. You're my savior, Derek. My healer. My warrior. My protector. So what happens now?"

"Now you all stay here. As I was telling Donnie earlier, I think you're safe as long as you stay far from the MTR sites that are feeding that blob from hell. You all stay here and circle the wagons, so to speak. While you and Nate recover, Timmy and Donnie can keep an eye out and guard the property. Meanwhile...."

"Meanwhile, you're going to kill as many people as you can. I saw the newspaper this morning. Those guys who kidnapped me, you burnt 'em all up, didn't you?"

"You're damn right I did, and I'm not going to apologize for it. I restrained myself for months while you and the Partisans conducted your lobbying and meetings and protests. And what happened? Alpha tried to kill you with black magic probably siphoned from that repulsive demon, and when that didn't work, thanks to the amulet Okey and his coven created, they abducted you and nearly shot you through the head."

Matt shifts and winces. "I ain't asking you to apologize. But what if Alpha comes up here with an army? Or the cops find some sort of evidence and come up here during the day with a search warrant? If they find you, you might end up with a stake through your heart or get dragged out into the sun to die. I don't want you taking crazy chances. I know how irrational with rage you can get. Why don't you wait and gather reinforcements?"

"I can't wait that long. Last night, when I found out that you were missing, I tossed Alpha's head of security around, and he admitted that that fucking CEO, Stan Sodeski, was the one who had you abducted. And one of your captors was on the phone with a 'Mr. S,' who's got to be the same man. To-night, I'm going to call IT Bobby. He's sure to be able to track down where Sodeski lives. Tomorrow night, I'm going to break into Sodeski's home, run him through with my claymore, then dismember him and feed him to the fishes, just as I did Angus's slayer. For far too long, my sword's been growing dull on its mount above the mantelpiece. It's thirsty for justice, and so am I."

"But what about the demon? What if you encounter it again?"

"The thing looks like a beanbag and moves like a sloth. I'll evade it. Or I'll drop a stick of dynamite on it. After I destroy a few more draglines, I'm going to confer with Cynthia and her occultist friends in Columbus. Maybe they'll know how to do away with it for good."

Matt sighs. "Dammit. Stubborn."

"Pot. Kettle. Black. Few things can hurt me, Matt. I'm the last person you should worry about."

chapter twenty-seven

I study the Sodeski compound from the air. It's huge, a gated community in the middle of nowhere.

In its center, like the nucleus of a malignant cell, stands the mansion, an ostentatious confection built in a bastardized combination of styles. Just what I expected from a fabulously wealthy coal magnate: the vulgar taste of the nouveau riche. It's surrounded by high white brick walls. Several expensive cars line the driveway before a huge garage. Beyond the back patio and pool are a horse barn, a terraced series of rose gardens, a few outbuildings, and a tennis court. In the woods, a good distance outside the encircling security wall, stands a little huddle of cheaply built homes where ramshackle vehicles are parked. Perhaps the employees who keep up the place live there, Sodeski's version of slave cabins.

What's unexpected about Sodeski's compound is its location. As my activist husbear has explained many times, throughout the history of the coal industry the absentee landlords who've extracted coal with little to no concern for the ecological consequences or the lives of local inhabitants have always lived outside the region—Pittsburgh, Philadelphia, St. Louis, Richmond—far from the messes they've made. True, Sodeski's principal dwelling is in the sprawling tangle of the Northern Virginia suburbs, near Washington, DC—probably so he can have useful congressmen over for dinner and conspiratorial chats—but for some reason this second home's located on a mountaintop near Madison, reasonably far from the unpleasant noise and dust of any one MTR site but surrounded at a far distance by many of them.

I think I know why: Alpha's hell-slug. If it feeds on devastation—burning trees, acrid smoke, broken shale, and coal dust—and if Sodeski's controlling it, no wonder he's built another home here, in the region where his pet gains its power. That won't do him any good. Tonight, I run the man through.

I conduct another few rounds of flitting-bat reconnoiter. Many, many men with guard dogs patrol the property. Alpha seems to be on the defensive now that Matt's kidnappers are burnt corpses, now that Blankenship's no doubt told everyone about the super-strong stranger who broke into his house and tossed his formidable frame about with the greatest of ease. I could've erased the Blankenship family's memory, but I'd rather they live in fear and infect Blankenship's Alpha cohorts with that fear. Plus there's one other small detail that must be increasing their paranoia: the honeyed promises I hissed over the phone two nights ago when I had the redoubtable Mr. S on the line, something about pulling his heart from his chest and squeezing it like a sponge.

Circling the house, I peer in windowpanes. No one's inside except for a cook slaving away in the kitchen and, upstairs, in a salmon-colored bedroom, an immensely fat woman in a hot-pink muumuu watching television. Mrs. Sodeski, perhaps. But is her husband at home?

I veer off toward what appear to be the employees' cabins. Perhaps I can gain information and a good meal at the same time.

From lit window to lit window I move, hunting for an appealing victim. Woman. Homely man. Woman. Old man. Skinny man.

Aha! I stop abruptly. Hovering in the darkness, I lick my lips. I can almost hear how Matt would chide me were he here: *Anyone'll do in this circumstance. But no, you're always obeying the dictates of your dick.*

True enough. I'm not a beggar; ergo I can be a chooser. I choose this one. He's so much my type that for a second I fear that Sodeski's somehow studied my patterns and set a trap for me. I've seen the medieval tapestries: the fabled unicorn is lured in by the bait of a naked virgin, then brought low by the hunters' arrows. In this case, it would be not a unicorn but a perpetually horny vampire, not a virgin but a plump, hairy hillbilly groundskeeper. For a split-second, my innate warrior-caution imagines the worst: I'm drinking deep when suddenly I fall dead from silver-laced blood.

Can you lace a human's blood with silver? I don't think so. Grinning—as much as a dark-snouted, needle-toothed bat can grin—I sill-perch outside the man's window. He's sprawled in a recliner, smoking a cigarette and watching television. To my pleasure, he appears to be alone in the house.

He's about thirty-five, I'd guess, a short, stocky slab of a man with a brown buzz cut balding at the front and one of those voluminous country-boy beards that always get my salacious saliva going. Wide shoulders descend to a huge chest and a thick waist. He's barefoot, wearing oil-stained denims and a wife-beater that shows off his dense arms, chest pelt, and fat pecs. He reminds me of a younger, plumper version of Matt.

I'd like to tie the man up and feast on him all damn night. I'll bet his ass is as coated with fur as his torso. Lust has, after all, always been one of my primary motivators. Tonight, however, is not about lust but revenge. After I'm done with Sodeski, perhaps I'll come back and take my time with his employee.

I make the process as efficacious as possible, misting under the door, taking man-form behind him, and tipping his recliner backward. He yelps as I seize him and sink my teeth into his sweaty throat. I drink till I'm pulsing with his considerable strength and he's limp with unconsciousness.

Picking him up—quite an armful—I carry him to his bed and lower him onto it. I play with the cloth-covered nubs of his nipples for a few moments and press my nose into the bush of one mouthwateringly smelly armpit before patting his whiskered cheek and shaking him.

"Wake," I say.

The man's eyes flutter open. "Howdy," he says, as if we've been buddies for years. "How yew?"

"I'm fine. What's your name, handsome?"

"Zac. Zac Black."

"Black? The Blacks were a sept of my clan back in Scotland."

"Scotland? That why you're wearing a kilt?"

"Yes. I'm from the Isle of Mull…a long time ago."

"Kilts are great." Zac nods drowsily. "I had a super time at last year's Celtic Festival in Parkersburg. Almost bought me a Utilikilt."

"You'd look good in a kilt. You're alone here?"

"Yep. Wife dumped my ass about a year ago."

"That was stupid of her. Was she blind? Where you from, Zac?"

"Logan County. Near Blair."

"West-by-God-Virginia, huh?" I take his moist hand. He looks down, surprised. Then he interlocks fingers with me, looks back up, and smiles.

"That a sword?" he says, beckoning toward the sheathed claymore buckled around my waist.

"That it is."

"Man, that's a helluva pig-sticker. Bet you could do some damage with that thang. Who're you?"

"I'm Derek. What are you doing up here on this remote mountaintop, Zac?"

"Used to work construction, but then a buddy got me into his landscaping business, and then I got this job with Sodeski, keeping up his grounds."

"How do you feel about Sodeski? What kind of man is he?"

"He and his wife treat me like trash. They treat all us workers like trash. But the pay's good."

"Would you be sad if he went away forever?"

"Naw. I'd miss the money. Wouldn't miss the man. He's a highfalutin, greedy prick, and his company sure makes a mess of the mountains. Hey, is it true what they say about guys in kilts? No underwear?"

"No underwear." I lift up my kilt long enough to show him.

Zac grins. "You got a chubby going. Why is that?"

"Because you're so burly, hairy, and handsome. You smell really good, too, and I'd like to get to know you better. Right now, though, I need some information. Is Mr. Sodeski at home?"

"Yep. Far as I know. Is there a big white Cadillac in the driveway?"

"I believe there is."

Zac nods. "That's his. He's here then."

"Does he usually have so many guards about?"

"Naw. Don't know what's up. I was mulching the rose gardens this afternoon when a whole bunch of security guys drove up."

I stroke his thinning hair. "Have you ever kissed another man, Zac?"

"Huh-uh." Zac looks up at me and grins. "But for some crazy reason, I'd sure like to kiss you."

Talk about easy glamour. I think I stumbled onto a repressed bisexual. Perhaps my gaydar's growing keener? "Just one kiss for luck," I say. "You can make it as soft and sweet as you crave."

"Yeah," Zac sighs. Reaching up, he pulls me down to him.

The widow's walk is one of a dozen mismatched architectural features to this house, and it provides a fine podium from which to control the guard dogs. One by one, they turn on the men guiding them. Soon, the broad lawns all around the house are full of screaming security guards and snarling canines.

I sift through an open window screen on the third floor and drift in mist form down the stairs, looking for tonight's prize. A few security guards, guns pulled, are on the second floor, all of them pressed to the windows, watching the amusing spectacle outside.

"The safe room, Mr. Sodeski," yells someone downstairs. "Let's put you in there till we can figure out what's going on."

I want man-form for the rest of this. Solidifying, I bound down steps to the ground floor. Across the room, the portly man I recall from the night I sent my delegation of peevish serpents is stumping toward the rear of the house, followed by the huge woman in the muumuu and a small-framed elderly man with a stringy white goatee. Surrounding them is a protective pack of six men with pistols in their hands, hustling the two into a wood-paneled study.

I speed forward into the room. Seizing two of the men by their heads, I smash their faces together, then fling them to the side. Another guard shoots at me at point blank range, catching me in the shoulder. Snarling, I shake off the sharp pang, then angle my knuckles and drive his nose back into his brain. The next man I take by the throat, throttle till his eyes are bugging, and toss over my shoulder.

Panting and wailing, Sodeski throws open a door. Beyond that is the head of what appear to be stairs descending into a cellar. His precious safe room must be down there. A vain hope. After another few yards and two more bodyguards, he'll be mine. I might just have to decant his heart's blood into a wine glass and enjoy it on his back patio, then celebrate his messy demise by ass-fucking his gloriously chunky groundskeeper in every possible position. As for Sodeski's wife and what is most probably Sodeski's sorcerer-for-hire, they should make fine feasts for the guard dogs.

I seize the next to last man, sink my teeth into his throat, twist my head, and rip. Arterial blood spatters everywhere. Mrs. Sodeski looks back, screaming, and thuds down the stairs after her husband. I take a quick drink, then lift the guard over my head and lob him across the study into a gold-framed mirror, shattering it.

One more guard. I clutch him by the shoulder, the last obstacle between me and the exquisite reprisal I've come for, when another pistol sounds behind me.

Uhh! Pain between my shoulder blades. Not the dull, quickly fading pang of a normal bullet. It's sickeningly sharp, making my limbs quake. Rowan-wood bullets, may the Sky-Thunderer damn them! I haven't felt this burning enervation since I tore a ridiculous vampire hunter to pieces on Inishmore half a century ago.

I whirl, snarl, and leap, tearing my attacker's weapon from his hand and snapping his neck. I'm about to return to my pursuit of the Sodeskis—if their panic room is air-tight, they might be able to escape me—when another rowan-wood bullet embeds itself in my calf, sending spasms of agony up my leg. Just beyond the study door stand two men, pistols drawn. How do they know what I am? How do they know of my weaknesses? Now four more men join them, and another wooden bullet stabs into my ribs.

Gods damn them. By now those porcine Sodeskis must be huddled in their safe room. A few more of those bullets, and I won't be able to get out of here.

"I'll be back," I hiss at the staring clutch of men, baring my fangs. "Count on it. And when I return, I will offer up your entrails and eyeballs to Lord Odin's ravens and crows."

Another bullet sings past me as I shift. Riddled with rowan-anguish, I'm barely able to achieve sufficient focus to regain bat form. I rise and wing painfully over their heads, able to manage only half my normal speed. Another poisonous rowan-wood bullet grazes my wing as I hurl myself toward a picture window, smash through it, and zigzag skyward.

I perch on a chimney, catching my breath, torn between options. Below, the dogs I'd controlled, released from my will by this weakness that swamps me, have collapsed atop the men they were savaging. Guards pour out of the house, looking for me and shooting at shadows.

I can't give up now. Perhaps I can find fuel sufficient to burn the house down around Sodeski and his safe room. If I have the energy, which is doubtful. I don't recall the last time I've been so severely wounded and so weak. One of those wooden bullets in my heart might end me.

Dammit! So close. Cursing, I'm about to retreat into the surrounding woods when a familiar reek envelopes me.

It's here. The hell-slug. It's billowing over the back patio far below, that familiar flabby cumulus cloud in which erratic lights arc like comets. Enraged,

I launch off the chimney and veer toward it. That's when it puffs up at both ends. The center goes concave, then purses like a pair of bulbous lips and spouts a stream of gray, roiling gray like smoke but fast as water shot from a fire hose. By Herne, the fucking thing is spitting at me!

Wounded, limbs stiff from rowan-toxins, I'm too slow to dodge it. The substance slams into my chest, foul-smelling as its globular origin and burning me like acid. It's the astral equivalent of toxic industrial waste, mine drainage, befouled water tables, carcinogenic pollutants, all distilled into a searing venom that makes my undead skin blister as human skin might if spattered with napalm.

I lose altitude, circling downward. Six feet from the ground, I lose winged form, then hit the patio, shattering flagstones. The thing spits again, catching me in the ribs with another fiery gout of poison just as another sharp rowan-bullet hits me in the right shoulder. Snarling with agony, I stagger to my feet, my tartans smoldering around me, then limp off the patio inside a hail of bullets. Three more dig into me: my left thigh, my right triceps, and the back of my neck.

My strength's nearly gone. I must get out of here. I will not be captured by these vermin. With the last of my power, I shift back into a bat and flee into the forest as more weapons resound behind me.

Panting with pain and effort, I've zigzagged through a quarter mile of trees when the mountaintop abruptly ends and I'm soaring over a deep valley. I make it over the next swayback ridge before the rowan-poison stiffens my limbs into uselessness. Slipping back into man-form, I drop like a rock toward the treetops below.

CHAPTER TWENTY-EIGHT

I come to consciousness and massive misery, riddled with wounds. I'm lying on my back. Surrounded by wood, lying on wood. It's cut into stove lengths. I'm in a woodshed? When I look up, the roof-aperture through which I crashed yawns above, a black gap full of stars.

My kilt and sporran are in ruins, nothing but scorched shards of leather and wool that fall from my frame when I roll onto my side. Now I'm naked, with my claymore still buckled around my waist.

A sudden light blinds me, and I squint, shielding my face with my hands. A woman is standing in the shed's open door. She's training her flashlight on me, mouth agape.

"Lord, Lord. Mister, are you all right?" The woman's fearless, moving toward me, a burnt, naked stranger who's dropped out of the sky. She's thin, in her fifties, with long graying hair, a gingham blouse, blue jeans, and cowboy boots. A cross hangs about her neck. It's made of silver, which only increases my bodily woe.

I open my mouth, try to speak, and fail. The only sound's a dry croak.

"Oh, you're hurt bad. Can you get up? Let's get you inside."

I rise to my knees, swaying. When I try to stand, I can't. I drop back down onto hands and knees. The rowan-wood embedded inside me has me almost immobilized.

"Can you crawl?"

I try to do so and find that I can. I can crawl. Very, very slowly. All my Hebridean warrior glory reduced to this? I've got to recover fast. I need to get to Cynthia and her crew of occultists. They'll help me find a way to flatten that demonic spitting sowbug into oblivion. I'll make it pay for this humiliation. I'll make all of Alpha pay.

"This way, honey," the woman says. "Across the lawn. It's not far. Let's get you to a bed, and then I'll go fetch help."

Like a crippled child, I make my way. Grass. Grass. Set of steps, an agony to ascend. Back porch. Kitchen linoleum. Stuffy hall. Tiny bedroom. The woman has to pull and shove to get me into the low bed. It's very warm in here, but still she tugs up a corner of the sheet to cover my exposed genitals.

I lie back, amused by her modesty. What's unsightly isn't my limp cock and balls but my plethora of rowan-bullet wounds, already festering, and the demon-blistered skin on my chest and ribs.

"Let me just fetch you some good sweet well water."

I nod. Closing my eyes, I take deep breaths to steady myself against the pain. Each inhalation racks me. The rowan-poison's spreading through me. I need someone to cut these fucking bullets out. I need blood to help me recover. I need a dark place to sleep away the day. I need my clan. Were-cub Donnie was right. As much as I hate to admit it, I need help to end Alpha and its Satan-slug.

The woman returns with a glass of water. I take it from her, fingers shaking, and gulp it. Only her kindness and the damnable silver around her neck keep me from gulping her blood as well.

"Thank you, ma'am," I rasp. "That's good. Thanks so much for helping me. I'm Derek Maclaine."

"I'm Eddy Johnson. Where you from?"

"Pendleton County."

"A mountain person like me." She smiles. "It's mighty pretty up in those Potomac Highlands. Here, let me get you another glass, and then I'll fetch you an ambulance. The phone lines have been down the last few days, after a big storm we had around here, so I'll have to drive down the creek to Uneeda to call them."

"Please don't go to that trouble. I have friends who would do me more good." I take her hand and look into her eyes. Can I manipulate her mind while I'm in such a feeble state?

"You're awful bad off. We really need to get some paramedics up here."

My mesmerism's as shaky as my limbs. The toxic rowan-bullets are resisting my natural healing powers, but the acid burns across my torso are itching, meaning they're already on the mend.

"Please, ma'am." I smile, putting on a show of haleness I'm far from feeling. "I'm just a little stiff."

"You're burned bad on your chest, and you've got wounds all over you!" She bends closer, examining first my injured thigh and then my ribs. "Are those bullet wounds? Did someone shoot you?"

"Yes, ma'am, I'm afraid so."

"Then we'll need to call the police too." She checks her wristwatch. "Nearly three in the morning."

"When does the sun rise?"

"Around six, honey. Why?"

No way for Timmy or Donnie to get to me by dawn, even if I were to convince her to call them instead of an ambulance. I'm going to have to take shelter from the sun here.

"Do you have a basement, Mrs. Johnson?"

"Call me Mizz Eddy. I have a root cellar."

Bringing up the topic of vampirism in this dire situation does not seem advisable. "I, uh, I'm a sufferer from a rare disease. Porphyria. Have you heard of it?"

"Yes, I have. I was a nurse in Boone Memorial Hospital for thirty years till I retired. It's a blood disease, isn't it?"

A nurse? Thank Thor, I seem to have fallen into the right woodshed. "It is. It makes me very, very sensitive to sunlight. I may have to take refuge in your root cellar before daybreak."

"The root cellar? For heaven's sake, you need to get to a hospital, and we need to call the police. You just lie back and stop arguing. I'll be back in about an hour. I hate to leave you alone, but—"

I seize her hand. Now that weakness has robbed me of the skill, imposing my will upon humans and controlling their minds suddenly seem far more valuable than immense strength or shapeshifting. I'll have to use simple persuasion instead.

"Ma'am, *don't*. Listen to me. Men are after me. If I go to a hospital, they may find me. My best chance of survival is to hide here till my friends can fetch me. Please believe me. Don't call an ambulance."

"But what about the police? Surely they—"

"For all I know, they're on the payroll of the men who shot me. In fact, I feel sure they are."

She shakes her head. "Who shot you then? Who has so much power around here? Why are you naked, by the way? And why are you wearing a sword? And how'd you fall through the roof of my woodshed?"

I'm tempted to say that I'm a clumsy exhibitionist angel with a knife fetish but think better of it. Instead, I change the subject and take a chance.

"Mizz Eddy, how do you feel about mountaintop removal mining?"

The expression that crosses her face instantly convinces me that telling the truth—at least some of it—is in my best interests. She looks like she's ready to spit on the floor.

"I think it's detestable. The good Lord made these mountains, and the forests covering them, and the animals that dwell in them. Those men are blasphemers, destroying God's creation. All they care about is money. I've seen those awful mining sites. Dynamite exploding, rocks flying around. A child down in Virginia was crushed by a boulder. Then there was that slurry spill down in Perry County…that chemical spill in the Elk River. All sorts of wells in this county have been poisoned or dried up, and mine might be next. The coal industry's become a pestilence. Used to be, men in my family made an honest living in the drift mines, in West Virginia and Kentucky, but these big machines now…. I voted for that Giardina lady back in 2000, when she ran for governor against the coal interests, and I give money to that ILoveMountains organization whenever I can afford it."

Thank Cernunnos. There's my answer: a Christian I can agree with.

"Have you heard of Stanley Sodeski? He's the CEO of Alpha Coal."

"I have. He doesn't live far from here. Just a few hollers over. I hate to say it, but he ought to be flogged for all he's done. I know that's not merciful or charitable, but…."

"He's the one whose guards shot me. I tried to go after him and teach him a lesson."

"Are you *crazy*, boy? You went into that place with nothing but a sword? No wonder you're all torn up. You mountain men are always going off half-cocked and getting yourselves maimed or killed."

"I guess I was a little rash. Should have taken a bazooka instead. So you won't call the police? Or the paramedics?"

She rubs her chin. "No. But if you won't get medical help, then at least let me examine you. I don't understand why you aren't in worse shape with all those wounds. Keep still now."

I lie there, acquiescent, while Mizz Eddy inspects my injuries. The urge to seize her and drink from her is great. Only my weakness, the silver around her neck, and a deep sense of being beholden keep me from acting on my violent thirst. Somewhere, and soon, I must have blood, or I might pass out. As it is, my head's swimming with rowan-illness.

"Seven. You have seven bullets in you," she says, shaking her head. "The wounds are foaming. I've never seen anything like it."

"Ma'am, before the sun rises, you have to cut them out. They're poisoning me. Please cut them out. Will you do that? You said you'd been a nurse. I trust you to—"

She's not listening to me. She's staring at my torso. She lifts a veined hand and touches my ribs, eyes full of wonder. "Your burns aren't there anymore. They're healed. How could that have happened? That isn't possible."

Supernatural miracles tend to make humans very nervous. I need to win her over before she figures out I'm not quite human and she bolts. Taking her hand, I give mesmerism another try, slipping psychic tendrils into her thought.

"I'm gifted in strange ways. Gifts I've inherited from my bloodline. Does that make sense?"

She smiles. "I suppose so. God's gifts are many."

"True," I say, digging deeper. Ah, there we go. I can feel her mind go malleable. For a moment, I think about asking her to take off her cross, but that might end in messy, murderous ingratitude I would gravely regret. I've got to take blood from someone else.

"Do you have neighbors nearby?" I ask.

"Just the Houchins, down at the mouth of the holler. They're sweet old folks."

Old won't do. I need someone young, strong, someone I can enthrall....

By Herne, I'm a fool. I know just the youth I need.

"Ma'am, are you willing to remove the bullets? They're treated with some kind of poison that's burning me from inside. I'm feeling weaker and weaker, and nauseated too."

Mizz Eddy looks dubious, so I nudge her mind again.

"Well, I suppose so. I don't have a scalpel, but I have a hunting knife. We'll have to get you good and drunk on moonshine. I have some in the cupboard that I keep for medicinal reasons…and for when my honey Harry visits. It's still going to hurt real bad. If you start to jerk and struggle, I don't think I'll be able to hold you down."

"I know a friend who can help. Why don't you go get ready and I'll call him?"

"But there's no phone, honey. How can you call anybody?"

"You'll see. Please go on and get ready, ma'am."

Eddy shrugs and leaves the room. I lie back on the bed, close my eyes, and focus what strength I have. "Zac," I whisper. "Handsome Zac. I need you badly, Zac."

Chapter Twenty-Nine

I'm very, very drunk, lying atop the dining room table under the bright ceiling light, when a heavy knocking fills the house. Eddy rushes off to answer it. In another few seconds, my latest thrall is standing over me, face drawn with concern. He's dressed as he was earlier, in dirty denims and wife-beater, smelling just as fine as he did before.

"Damn, boss, you look awful." Zac studies my oozing wounds and grips my hand. I can sense his dedication to me. It's already vast. What luck to have found him. The lonely men, those are the ones who take to my glamour and thralldom the best. Eros knows there are many such isolated, frustrated gay men in these fundamentalist-blighted mountains. It's as if there were a great emptiness in him waiting for my coming, waiting for my call. Thank the Horned One. Without Zac so close nearby, and the kindnesses of Mizz Eddy, I might have perished tonight.

"I heard all the guards shooting at someone. That was you?"

"Yes. Thanks for coming." I want to lift the burly bear's wrist to my mouth and feed, but at this point, the weaker I am, the better the makeshift surgery will go for my human caretakers. "We don't have much time. You need to tie me down so I don't thrash around and I don't hurt either of you."

Mizz Eddy fetches rope, and Zac ties me spread-eagle to the table. Normally, I'd snap rope with little effort, but tonight's a different matter. If the rowan-poison's permitted to flood my system much longer, I might be completely paralyzed.

"Do it," I say. "Cut the bullets out now. Cut out as many of them as you can before the sun rises. If I pass out, carry me down to the root cellar before daybreak. That's crucial. And Zac? Guard me while I sleep. Understand?"

Both Zac and Eddy nod. Zac stands at the head of the table and grips my arms. Then Eddy lifts the knife, newly sharpened on her whetstone, and begins probing the wound in my right shoulder. I grit my teeth, gasp, and try to keep still as the blade digs into me, jostling the noxious rowan-shard.

Endure, Derek. After all you've been through, this is nothing. Think of Angus, and Mark, and Gerard, and all they suffered. Think of Matt and all your boys: little were-cub Donnie, and faithful Timmy, and rangy otter Nate…and now this broad-shouldered man, big-bearded Zac, holding you down. You've got to survive. Someone's got to protect your clan and stop Alpha. Who else but you?

The knife digs deeper. "Ah!" Mizz Eddy says. "There we go." With tweezers, she draws the bullet out.

"It's wood?" she says, regarding it.

"Yes, ma'am. Rowan wood. Nasty stuff," I say, giving her a weak smile. "Six more to go. I can take it. Go on, ma'am. Get it over with."

"God give me strength," Eddy sighs. "After this is over, I might just finish the rest of that moonshine myself." Retrieving the knife, she starts work on my ribs.

I wake to the scents of mold, potatoes, and earth. I'm lying on the floor of what must be the root cellar, wrapped in a blanket, my sheathed claymore at my side. The pain that interfused my body like a constricting silver net has faded into simple exhaustion. Mizz Eddy must have had the time to remove every one of the bullets. I may just buy her a new home or a new car. Maybe I'll do both. Hell, I'll even make a donation to her church.

Beyond the door, the last light's failing. Zac's hunched in a cane chair just inside the cellar, a shotgun in his hand. I can feel his tension and determination. The sight of him makes my parched throat ache.

"Zac?"

"Hey!" Turning, Zac carefully lays the gun on the ground. "How you feeling, boss?"

"I'm very hungry. Is there danger about?"

"There was. Not now."

"Is Mizz Eddy safe?"

"She is. She got all the bullets out, and then I carried you down here like you asked. There's some clothes there for you. She said she thought they'd fit you."

"Is the door locked?"

"Yep."

"Get naked."

"Uh, sure." Zac checks the lock on the door, then peels off his wife-beater, unlaces and removes his boots, and shucks off his jeans and briefs. Nude, he resembles Matthew even more: the same beefy barrel chest and plump belly, thick arms and thick thighs, the entire curvaceous expanse plastered with dark brown hair.

"There ya go," Zac says. It's almost as if his voice were blushing.

"Come here," I say. "Lie down here beside me. I'm sick and weak. You're healthy, strong, and young. Hold me, Zac. I'm cold. Lend me your warmth."

"Sure, boss. Be glad to." Kneeling, Zac climbs under the blanket with me. He's barely slid an arm around me before I've embedded my fangs in his throat.

I took more than I meant to but not half as much as I wanted. Still, the important things are that my latest slave is still alive, albeit insensible, and that I'm stronger, albeit a long ways from my full strength. I hold sleeping Zac in my arms, nuzzling his nipples, kissing his wounded throat, kneading his hairy ass, and thanking the Lord of the Animals for such warm mammalian comforts.

Zac sighs and groans. He rests his head on my chest and flings his arm across my hip. "Wow, I'm weak. Feel like I got hit by a truck. What happened, boss?"

"I fed from you. A little too much, I'm afraid. I'm sorry. It was necessary."

Thralls are always marvelously understanding. "Ah, that's all right. Whatever you need, I got."

"That's very generous of you," I say. "Have you ever cuddled naked with another man before?"

"Naked?" Dazed, Zac looks down at our intertwined bodies. "Oh, yeah. Guess we are. Cuddle? Uh, naw. Uh, yeah. A buddy of mine in high school used to suck me off in the barn. We'd head out there when it looked like a storm was coming up so we'd be stuck there and no one would be likely to come out and bother us. We'd lie there together in the straw and listen to the rain on the tin roof. That was mighty sweet."

So that explains his easy acquiescence. He's probably been eaten up for years with repressed yearnings for the touch of another man. "You mentioned there was danger earlier. What happened?"

The contentment drains from Zac's face. "Some of Sodeski's men came by here around noon, looking for you. Luckily, Mizz Eddy had cleaned up all the blood, and they didn't notice the hole in the woodshed roof or the little door to this cellar, which she'd hid behind some brush. She was pretty nasty to 'em, and they were downright ugly with her. She cussed 'em so bad that they left pretty damn quick. They didn't see me, 'cause I was already down here holed up with you, but they might've recognized my Jeep. I think you and me need to get outta here as soon as possible, just in case those pigs come back."

"You want to come with me?"

Zac grins. "Don't want to bail on this adventure halfway through, do I?"

It's painfully tempting to take this stocky beauty with me rather than sending him back to serve as my spy. If the men looking for me did indeed recognize Zac's Jeep, he might be in trouble or at least under suspicion if he returns to the Sodeski compound. On the other hand, if he comes with me, he'll be in as much danger from Alpha as Matt and the others.

"You don't want to go back to the Sodeskis? To your job there?" I loosen my hold on his will just long enough to allow him free choice in the matter.

"Hell, no. I've had enough of them damn Sodeskis. Let some other poor bastard spread horseshit on their rose gardens. I'm thinking we need to get somewhere safe and far away."

Gently I tug his beard, delighted to discover that his fondness for me is at least somewhat genuine. "I have just the place in mind. It's about four hours' drive from here."

"Sounds good, though I don't think I'm strong enough to drive just yet. I'm real dizzy. You wanna...."

"I'll drive. Absolutely. I—"

There's a tapping on the root cellar door. "Boys?"

It's Mizz Eddy. "Get up here and have some dinner. I got some brown beans and chowchow, and cornbread right out of the oven."

"Come on, Zac," I say, patting a fuzzy shoulder. "You need to get your strength back. Then we're going to take that drive. A pretty place way up in the Potomac Highlands might be standing in need of a groundskeeper. There are some great men there I want you to meet. We'll treat you better than the Sodeskis ever did."

"Those fit you tolerably well," says Mizz Eddy, as I help her clean the kitchen after dinner. In the living room, Zac's snoring on the couch, full from a good meal and still weak from my fang-feast.

I'm bare-chested and barefoot, squeezed into denim overalls that used to belong to Mizz Eddy's father. Her boyfriend Harry must be a very small man; none of his shirts or shoes would fit me. Oh, well, Matt's always savored the shirtless-and-tattooed-country-boy-in-overalls look. Maybe that'll help when I get home, when I tell him what happened and he proceeds to berate me for hours on end.

"That big boy can really put down a meal. You, though, you didn't touch your food," says Mizz Eddy, drying a bowl. "Don't you like soup beans?"

"My apologies. I don't mean to seem ungrateful. I'm just still nauseated after my ordeal. Zac and I should leave soon. He's afraid those men might come back, and I want to be gone if they do. The longer I stay here, the longer you'll be in danger, and, after how kind you've been to me, I don't want to put you at any further risk."

"Well, let me get that boy up and see if he wants some blackberry cobbler before y'all go. He's acting as if he's sleeping off a hard drunk." Wiping her hands on a towel, Mizz Eddy steps into the living room, flicks on a lamp, and bends to Zac, shaking him gently.

"Zac, honey, wake up. You want some cobbler and ice cream? Derek says that y'all need to—"

She falls abruptly silent. Dammit. She's staring at the wound on his neck. "Lordamercy, it looks like some kind of animal bit this boy. But when?"

Turning, she fixes her gaze on me. Dammit. A shirt, a shirt, my kingdom for a shirt.

"Your wound. The one in your shoulder. That was the first bullet I took out. But there is no wound. No bandage." She shakes her head, as if driving off a horsefly or a cloud of gnats. "I forgot. Your burns. They're gone too. You made me forget. How did you do that? And you never answered…. How did you fall through the roof of the woodshed?"

No hypnotic compulsion this time. After all she's done for me, I owe her the truth.

"Have I given you reason to fear me?"

"No. But...."

I smile. "Would you like to fetch Zac's shotgun first?"

Mizz Eddy purses her lips. "Don't think that would make much difference, would it? You had seven bullets in you, but now you're fit as a fiddle."

"Let's go out on the porch and let Zac sleep for a little longer."

Mizz Eddy nods. We slip outside. Eddy takes the swing; I take the rocking chair. The year's first fireflies flicker around the yard.

"Did you bite that boy?"

"I did. I had to in order to begin the process of regaining my strength. I bit him, and I drank his blood. Carefully, so as not to cause lasting harm."

"So you drink blood." She's strangely calm. Mountain woman are often made of sterner stuff than mountain men. "And you heal with amazing speed. And you avoid the sunlight. And you.... The woodshed roof. You fell from the air? You...flew?"

"Yes, ma'am."

"You aren't fiction. You aren't a legend. I know how solid you are. I cut into your flesh. Your blood was on my hands."

"I am more than legend, yes."

"Demonic? Damned?"

I sigh. "I would say none of those. Others might feel differently. I'm definitely part of nature. I'm human and animal, like you, like Zac, but I'm something more too. I'm dedicated to nature, and to some small extent I control aspects of it."

Sitting back, I focus my thoughts on the glimmering fireflies in the yard. They gather into a cloud, stream onto the porch, and circle Mizz Eddy's head seven times before drifting back into the dark.

"My sweet Lord," she whispers.

"I was human once. I was born in Scotland in 1700. I died in Scotland in 1730. I had a lover, Angus. Men murdered him. I chose to become what I am to avenge his death."

"You're gay?" That fact seems to surprise her more than the claim that I died nearly three hundred years ago.

"I am, ma'am," I say, stroking my goatee. "Does that disturb you?"

"Honey, no. Not all Christians are backward and hateful. My little niece Joyce is as gay as they come. We're all God's children. Though in your case, I'm not sure that's true."

"Oh, I'm a child of God, but not the Christian god. The god of the animals, the god of the storms, and the dark goddess."

"Honey, God's God."

"Yes, I think you're right. I'm trying to do God's work. I'm trying to punish the men who are savaging Appalachia's mountains. Sodeski and his company are trying to kill Matt, my partner—"

"Good Lord. Matt Taylor? I remember you now. You were with Mr. Taylor at that vigil at the Capitol, weren't you?"

"Small world. Yes, that was me."

"Are you…are you the one who's blowing up those draglines?"

"I am."

"You've killed men. Those Alpha guards who came down here today looking for you said that a bunch of men died the other night at the Sodeski mansion when an intruder broke in. You're a murderer."

"I am. I've murdered many men over the centuries. Most of them have been evil. Some have been innocent, men so handsome and desirable that my thirst got the better of me. Sometimes I regret that. But the men I've slain lately have been Alpha thugs, men who're helping that company commit what I believe you earlier called blasphemy: the rending, gutting, and flattening of mountains."

"They're sinners, there's no doubt of that. But murder is a sin too. 'Thou shalt not kill' is one of the Commandments."

"I don't believe in sin. And how much killing did the Israelites indulge in?"

"Christ brought the new word. That supersedes the Old Testament."

"I admire your Christ's gentleness and compassion, but I fear I have much more of a Hebrew Bible mindset. My ethos is that of *The Iliad* and *Beowulf*, the Icelandic Eddas and sagas, the Scottish Highlands that birthed me. I believe that heroism, honor, and a brave name live on. I believe that those who threaten my clan and kin must be punished."

I rise. "You asked if I were demonic. I am not. I know nothing of Satan or Hell or the afterlife. There *is* a demon in this particular saga, however. It's protecting Sodeski."

"Sweet Jesus. You've seen such a thing?"

"More than seen it. I felt it, more's the pity. It was the thing that burned me, that caused those blisters that covered my chest and ribs. I don't know how Sodeski raised it, how he found it, or how he controls it, but I intend to destroy the thing, and I intend to destroy Alpha as well. Will you help me stop their depredations? Will you agree to keep my secret?"

"What if I won't? Will you murder me?"

"Absolutely not. You've helped me far too much for me to harm you. If you hadn't cut out those rowan-bullets, I might have perished. I'm as much of a mountain person as you, Mizz Eddy. I know when I'm beholden."

"You're not going to hurt Zac, are you? He helped you too."

"Zac? Oh, no. When I bit him, he became connected to me, devoted to me. He's like kin now. He'll protect me, and I'll protect him. I'm going to take him to my home high atop a mountain near Franklin. He'll be safe there."

Mizz Eddy falls silent. She rocks in the swing. I rock in the chair.

"I'll keep your secret. It'll be a burden, but I'll carry it." Her thin hand grips the cross hung around her neck. "God sent you here for a reason. He guided you to me, and He led me to help you. I trust His plan."

"Would you rather forget me entirely? I could arrange that."

"No, honey. I want to remember you. You're a marvel and a monster. But God has His reasons for creating monsters. He has a purpose for you just as much as He has a purpose for me. I'll pray for you. I'll pray that the Lord works His will through you."

CHAPTER THIRTY

Zac sleeps all the way back to Mount Storm. At first, he's slumped against my shoulder as I drive his Jeep along dark country roads. Eventually, he nudges his head onto my lap and curls up on the seat on his side, snoring loudly. What a lovable package he makes. I caress his beard as I steer. What with my new security guard Nate, and now my new groundskeeper Zac, my harem has nearly doubled over the last few months. Only seven more, and I could print a Derek Maclaine Seraglio Calendar, with one bear, cub, or otter for every month of the year. Then again, perhaps five is enough, even for a man of my considerable appetites.

What with the long drive, it's nearly three in the morning by the time I park in Mount Storm's driveway, but lights are burning in most of the windows. I've thrown Zac over my shoulder and am lugging my dozing bundle up onto the porch when the front door flies open. They all stand there, fully dressed, staring at me: Matt, Donnie, Timmy, and Nate.

"Oh, thank God!" Matt says. "We thought we'd lost you!" Limping forward, he gives me a hard hug before shifting his attentions to Zac. "Trading me in for a newer model?"

"Not at all. This is Zac. You know I'm a big fan of 'and,' not 'or.'"

Matt's grin is weary. His face is still bandaged, still bruised and swollen from the beating he received only days ago. "As in, 'I'll take Matt *and* Zac *and* Donnie *and* et cetera'?"

"Exactly."

"Christ." Matt shakes his head and runs a hand over Zac's buzz-cut. "Well, you know how to pick 'em." Matt gives me another hug before leading the way inside. "I'm just so glad you're all right."

"I'm very glad to be home," I say, surveying the den's wooden walls and leather furniture.

"We're damn glad you're back," Timmy says. "We were afraid you'd come to a bad end. Why didn't you call? We were worried sick."

"My phone burnt up with my kilt. Then I was—by necessity—incommunicado for a while."

"Your kilt burnt up?" Matt says. "Good God, Derek, what did you get yourself into?"

"That explains the overalls," says Nate, arm still in a sling. "What every well-dressed rustic blood-drinker wears."

"It isn't funny, Nate," Matt snaps.

"Don't you think I look studly in these? I thought you were a sucker for shirtless men in overalls."

"Cut it out, Derek. You're not gonna flirt your way outta this. What went on at Sodeski's?"

"Tell us what happened," Donnie urges.

"All right, all right. Calm down, boys. Earlier tonight, I had to feed on Zac, and he needs to sleep it off. Let me tuck him into one of the spare beds. Then I'll tell you everything."

When I return to the den, each one of them gives me a huge hug before allowing me to sit back on the couch and tell my tale.

Matt's face is red by the time I'm done. "You idiot. You *idiot*. You could have been killed."

Donnie frowns. "You shoulda waited till the full moon so I could go with you. Rowan-wood bullets wouldn't hurt me, would they?"

"I don't know. I don't think so. Silver bullets might end either one of us. I guess they decided to go for the cheaper option. What I want to know is how did Sodeski realize that a vampire was after him? How did they know the effects of rowan-wood on my kind?"

"And that demon thing," says Nate. "Where'd it come from?"

"Damn you!" Matt blurts. "You cocky prick. You flew right into a trap."

"Matt, don't nag me. I'm sorry."

"I'm nagging you 'cause I love you. What would any of us here do without you? If that thing had covered you with acid, or that lady hadn't been able to get those fucking bullets out.... You cain't wage this fight alone, don't you see that now?"

"Yes, I do. Tomorrow, I want Donnie here to drive me to Columbus. While Cynthia and I confer about demonology, Donnie can chat with a werewolf Cynthia knows, Rebekah."

"Cool, bud," Timmy says, giving Donnie a hug. "You'll get to meet a were-wolfstress. Is that a word?"

"I'll go too," Matt says. "At this point, I'm afraid to let you out of my sight, you big brat. I'm afraid you'll do something stupid and rash again."

"No, you won't go. You're still recuperating, and so is Nate. Stay here and rest. Help Zac acclimate."

"Why'd you bring him home anyway?" Matt rolls his eyes at me. "Don't you have enough houseboys?"

"He wanted to come with me. If he'd gone back to the Sodeski compound, I was afraid he might have come to harm. He's a landscaper. How about he stays here and helps you around the grounds? You've been so busy with the Mountain Partisans that this place is going to hell in a handbasket."

"It is not! I've been meaning to—"

"I'm teasing! The place looks great, but wouldn't you like a little help with it?"

Matt shrugs.

"I'll send Zac away if you want."

"Naw. Don't do that. I like the way you take in orphans, the way you rescue sad, lonely guys."

"Like me," says Donnie.

"Like me," says Timmy.

"Like me," says Nate.

"Yep. You've created a real bear-family here, honey. I'm sorry I got so angry. I just want you to stop taking such big risks and stop trying to do everything yourself. Talk to Cynthia. Get hold of that Roman guy, Marcus. Or your maker, Sigurd. Put yourself together a little army before you face Alpha again. Gather your strength before you go after 'em. Be smart, not hot-headed."

"I'll do all of that, I promise. But right now, I'm tired and I'm hungry. I haven't regained my full strength. Would all of you boys come with me?"

"What d'you have in mind, sir?" Timmy asks.

"I want you all to come upstairs, get naked, and climb into bed with me. No sex. Just snuggling. Matt, I'm not going to feed on you. You neither, Nate. You're both still recovering. But you two plump morsels...." I wink at Timmy, then at Donnie. "You'd spare your ole Daddy a little nourishment, would you not?"

"Yes, sir," they say in unison. "Gladly," Donnie adds.

"Hey, boss. Where'd you go?"

It's Zac, wandering down the unfamiliar hallway in the dark.

In here, I think rather than say, unwilling to wake my bedmates.

Zac staggers in. He stops and gapes at us, five hairy, bearded men, our nakedness lit by the gleam of one votive candle. Matt drowses on his back to the right of me, his head on my shoulder. To my left, Nate lies on his side, his head on my chest. Donnie spoons him from behind. Timmy spoons Donnie from behind.

"Ohhhhh, man." Zac rubs his eyes. "Wow. Is this an orgy?"

No, it's therapy. Welcome to Mount Storm, Zac Black. Would you like to join us?

CHAPTER THIRTY-ONE

C lub Diversity's on the edge of German Village, the charming neighborhood where Cynthia's latest lair's located. Occupying a brick
brewmaster's house built in the nineteenth century—high ceilings,
big rooms, and woodwork—it's far nicer than the gay bars Matt and I have
patronized in West Virginia. While Donnie fills up a big bowl with popcorn,
I order two martinis from a good-looking bartender with a gray-streaked
beard who gives me a flirtatious wink. Donnie and I saunter out the back
door toward the gazebo where Cynthia and Rebekah await. Night breeze
rustles maple leaves high above.

The two women are a study in contrasts. Cynthia Skala's very pale, with high
Slavic cheekbones. She's wearing her usual short, chic lesbian haircut, asym-
metrical earrings, a man's black dress shirt, and slate-gray slacks. She's been
my occasional compatriot for years, helping me cut down annoying wooden
crosses that a pious millionaire erected along Appalachian interstates. We're
also fond of helping each other dispatch gay-bashers and rapists. I haven't
been so fond of a woman since my beloved sister Morna, back in the 1700s.

Rebekah, on the other hand, has dressed to emphasize her feminine vo-
luptuousness. She's buxom, wearing a red dress with an Empire waist that
matches her red-framed glasses. Her lips are full, painted red as well. Her
skin and shoulder-length hair are glossy and dark. How she can walk on sti-
letto pumps that high should be listed as one of the great mysteries of the
American Midwest. And she's looking at Donnie as if he were a bar snack she

were about to snap up. Right. Cynthia said she was bisexual. Well, she has good taste in men. Donnie's looking especially huggable tonight in his tight black T-shirt and gray camo shorts. Chest, belly, butt: the boy's plump and curvy in all the right places.

"Predacious horror," Cynthia says, gathering me into a hug.

"Ruthless virago," I reply. "And this fetching lass must be Rebekah."

"Laird Maclaine, I'm so pleased to meet you," Rebekah says, taking my hand. "Who's this precious little thing?"

"I'm, uh, Donnie, ma'am. I, uh, hear, uh, you and I have some things in common."

Rebekah plucks a piece of popcorn from Donnie's bowl and nibbles at it. "Let's leave these warlords to make their plans of mass destruction, sugar. It's about time for karaoke. Will you sing with me?"

"Ma'am? Uh, I'm kind of shy. I don't know if—"

"Shy? With that deep, sexy, rumbly voice of yours? Why, you could be the next Josh Turner or Chris Young. I'd fuck either of them, wouldn't you? Come along now, let's do that duet, 'Endless Love.' Finish that martini, and I'll buy you another."

Donnie gives me a look of desperation. He takes a big swig of his drink as Rebekah leads him away. Cynthia watches them go, chuckling.

"She's incorrigible. She likes the same sort of boys you do: butch, bearded, and built. Speaking of which, the timing for your visit is excellent. I have a meal for you caged in my basement. I caught him last night. He's gift-wrapped in the perverse way you savor."

"Really? I was just kidding when I said—"

"What kind of hostess would I be to invite a country boy into my big city and not have some kind of menu planned? From the looks of you, you need to feed."

"I'm not at my best, I must admit. Still recovering from rowan-wood bullets and demon vomit."

"Hm. Yes. I saw some of it."

"Another vision? Oh, excellent. Another witness to my humiliation."

She rubs my arm. "Don't worry. We'll rectify all. By the way, if you don't want to wait till we get back to my place for a meal—really, Derek, your skin's looking quite pasty—one of the bartenders tonight—his name's Craig, the guy with the beard—he's been very eager to meet you."

"Ah, the fellow who winked at me? He made our martinis. He's handsome."

"I told him that I had a bear-daddy friend coming to town. He's a randy fellow. You might be able to lure him off duty for a few crucial moments."

Inside, a small crowd's gathered before the karaoke machine. Donnie and Rebekah are doing a fine job with "Endless Love." My were-cub seems to have cast off his inveterate shyness, intoning into the mike as if he were born for it.

Craig's grinning at me from behind the bar. I'd use some glamour, but my energy's low. Besides, supernatural persuasion might not be necessary, if the way he's looking at me is any indication. The tight gray jeans and torso-hugging black tank top I'm wearing seem to help.

"Howdy," I say. "I'm Cynthia's friend, Derek."

"You sure are. I love all your ink. Not to mention those pecs. How can I help you?" He's wearing a black baseball cap, a black muscle-shirt, and baggy cargo shorts. The smell of him—man-musk mixed with Old Spice—reminds me of how famished I am.

"I do believe I need another drink."

Craig looks at my nearly full martini and cocks an eyebrow. I finish it in two gulps.

"Keep that up, and you're going to be staggering out of here," he says, taking the empty glass from me.

"I have a driver." I indicate Donnie, who's grinning at Rebekah while they launch into another duet, this one "If You See Him," the song Brooks and Dunn recorded with Reba McEntire.

"He's a hot little number. You two an item?" Craig pours out gin and adds ice.

"I pound his ass every now and then. My husbear Matt and I have an open relationship."

"Really?" Craig grins. "How long you going to be in town?"

"Only a night or two."

"I get off at midnight. Want to join me for a nightcap at my place? It's just around the corner."

"I'm afraid I can't. Cynthia and I have some pretty pressing business."

"You sure?" Craig hands me my drink and flexes an arm.

"Are you hairy? I love hairy men."

Craig gives me a big grin and pulls his muscle-shirt up to his neck, exposing his chest and belly, both of which are dusted with salt-and-pepper hair.

"Nice," I say. "What else you got?"

Craig looks around. No other customers are at the bar. Everyone's staring at Donnie and Rebekah, who're arm in arm, belting out the chorus. Grinning wickedly, Craig slips his shorts down, giving me a glimpse of his half-hard cock.

"Vulgar. Outrageous," I say with deep approval. "How about the ass?"

Craig obliges, turning his back on me and dropping his shorts even further, giving me a long look at his smooth, tanned butt.

"How's that drink?" he says, zipping up.

This man's more than willing, but leaving a bloody bite-mark on his neck might not be a good idea. Luckily, necks are not the only body part fun to suck.

"The drink's great, but it's not sating all the thirsts I'm feeling. Take a break. I really want to blow you. I really need for you to come in my mouth."

Craig's eyes widen, clearly delighted that he's found a man who's as bold a sex-pig as he is. "Hugh! Can you cover the bar for a minute? I need to make a call."

"Sure," shouts a younger man serving beers to a table of middle-aged men.

Craig slips out from behind the bar. "C'mon, big boy. I got a load more than ready for you." He grabs me by the hand and leads me up a wide staircase to the second floor.

"In here," he says, nudging open a door. I follow him into a dim storeroom. He closes the door and locks it. Then he shoves me up against the wall, pulls up my tank top, pinches my nipples hard, and pushes his tongue into my mouth.

"That's right," I say, rubbing his beard with mine. "Get rough. I love my tits torn up."

As requested, he twists and tugs my nipples, then cups the back of my head and nudges me down onto my knees. "Suck me," he says, pulling out his cock.

It's one of the biggest dicks I've ever seen. I take it into my mouth and apply nearly three centuries' worth of fellating skills, licking, sucking, deep-throating, and nibbling him. He grips my head, grunting low and fucking my face so hard my temples throb.

"Christ, you're good," he gasps, after only a few minutes of steadily riding my mouth. "I'm gonna shoot."

As soon as he begins spurting onto my tongue, I sink a fang into his erection. He winces but keeps pumping my face. I suck hard, fortified by both blood and semen.

When he's done, I take his hands and draw him down onto the floor beside me. Wrapping an arm around his waist, I nuzzle his scrotum. He grips me by the hair and shoves his cock back into my mouth. I keep sucking as, thrusting gently, he softens inside me, his glans seeping post-orgasmic juice. He strokes my ponytail, humming and sighing.

"You bit my cock?"

"Ummm hmmmm," I mutter around dick-flesh before releasing him. "I tend to get a little wild."

"Wild's more than welcome."

"Good to hear."

"Can you come back tomorrow night?" Craig slips a finger down the back of my jeans. "I'd love for us to take turns bent over that bench there, pounding each other's assholes raw."

"Next time I'm in town, it's a date." I pat Craig's butt before getting to my feet. Gripping his hand, I haul him up. "I'd better get downstairs. Bad manners to keep a lady waiting. Will you mix me another martini, please?"

Cynthia's lounging in the gazebo when I step outside. When I take a seat, she lifts her beer bottle in salute.

"Dipsomaniacal dyke," I say, lifting my martini in return.

"Rampant man-whore. Insatiate satyr. I can smell Craig's crotch in your goatee. Well done."

"Can I help it if all these tattoos are man-magnets? 'Twas a memorable snack to hold me over till later tonight. I can't believe you have a man waiting for me in a cage in your basement."

"Not a willing one—he's no doubt wailing and thrashing around as we speak—but one you're welcome to drain completely. Abstemious little sips from this man and that aren't going to get you over the lingering rowan sickness. You need to gulp down an entire life force."

"Drain completely? Really? It's been a while since I've allowed myself that murderous luxury."

"Really. The bastard deserves it. I'll tell you all about him when we get home. Right now, to work."

"Yes. So, your occultists. I thought they'd be here."

"Vampires make them nervous. It's all I can do to convince them to treat with me. With two of us around—plus a pair of werewolves—the poor things might soil themselves."

"So squeamish. They do sound delicate. City folk have over-refined sensibilities."

"I like my cities. I know, I know: you Highland barbarians prefer trees to people."

"We do indeed. Barbarian? I love it. Marcus called me that."

Cynthia smiles before taking a swig of beer. "Before he pummeled your rump on the Palatine Hill?"

"Why do I tell you everything?"

"Tonight, I'm here to tell you that, according to those squeamish occultists, the demon's name is likely Aldinach. It was first summoned by the ancient Egyptians. It's the embodiment of technology run amuck, when it becomes an end in itself, when it grows so powerful and solipsistic that it becomes anathema to organic life. It feeds on destruction, then causes more destruction in order to feed on that."

I sip my drink, then look up at the maple leaves whispering above us, and, beyond them, the stars. "That sounds about right. Poisoned water tables, burnt trees, mountains gutted like swine...."

"Mountaintop removal is just Aldinach's latest manifestation and its latest feasting table."

"Fucking draglines. I need to take them all down."

"You won't be able to do that until you're rid of Aldinach."

"And Alpha. I got my immortal arse kicked the last time I wrangled with them. How did they know to use rowan-wood bullets? And where did Aldinach come from?"

"It's probably been around ever since human beings began to damage the natural world around them. As for this particular incarnation, the same source responsible for the rowan-wood bullets is no doubt responsible for raising Aldinach. A ceremonial magician must be working for that company."

"I've suspected that myself."

"Indeed. Not all occult practitioners love Father Sky and Mother Earth. For more and more of them, it's all about money. Making money and the world be damned. Someone at Alpha went looking for a desperate mage adept at manipulating astral energies but with terrible money-management skills. Dime a dozen nowadays."

"So what do we do?"

"My contacts won't be of much direct help. They're afraid of enraging demons or powerful companies, no matter how wicked the men who run them or how richly they deserve to be put down."

"Like a bad breed of dog."

Cynthia smiles. "I love that expression. But they say that the witch who gave Matt the lapis amulet can help, especially if he has a coven. They spoke of a charm that might diffuse the force of Aldinach. A blood-charm, I think. You need to speak to that witch and—"

"That witch, according to Matt, doesn't like our kind any more than your occultist friends do."

"Take Matt along. They're friends, right? Matt should be able to persuade him. Meanwhile, we need some brothers and sisters in arms."

"Indeed. 'A little army,' Matt said. Alpha has one, so we need one too. So, you're willing to fight beside me?"

Cynthia rolls her brown eyes. "What do you think? We ferocious bulldaggers are always up for a brawl."

"We'll need a lot more help. I fear I've become a bit of a recluse, living up on my mountain. Whom do you suggest?"

"There's my Dykes-on-Bikes buddy, Felon. She's always up for kicking wealthy corporations in the balls. How about your Roman gentleman? He's very old and very powerful, is he not?"

"Marcus might help, though he strikes me as the type who'll only join us if I can convince him that it's in his best interests. Donnie has agreed to help if we attack during the full moon."

"Rebekah will help as well. She may look like a fashionista, but she's absolutely savage. What about Sigurd?"

Shrugging, I tug the Thor's hammer around my neck. "I haven't heard from him in years. He's even more reclusive than I. Last I saw him, he was living near Stromness on Mainland Orkney, the island he came from. We celebrated the summer solstice amid the Stones of Brodgar, the prehistoric circle in which he was turned. But that was nearly twenty years ago. Since then I gather he's dwelt in Iceland."

"What would you say if I told you he's no longer in Iceland, that I know where he is, that he wants to see you?"

"What? Where?"

"He still adores volcanic islands. This past April, Lara and I vacationed on the Big Island of Hawai'i. I sensed him one rainy night near Hilo Bay, then encountered him when we were both hunting in the Puna district. He was quite hospitable. He has a grand abode in Puna, overlooking a black-sand beach, with two huge Hawai'ian thralls and a beautiful altar to Pele, the goddess of volcanic fire."

"It would be wonderful to see Sigurd. Matt's never met him."

"You should call for him when you need him, he said. Call him now. Call Marcus too. You've shared blood with both of them, have you not? They should be able to hear you, no matter how far away they might be."

"All right, I'll try."

Closing my eyes, I concentrate, calling out to Sigurd Magnusson over America's central plains, over the jagged Rockies, the western deserts and the coastal ranges, over the chill Pacific. *Maker, great Viking, you who gave me life anew, help me now. I have foes aplenty. Come to me. Or lead me to you.*

I shift the focus of my plea, aiming east, over the Appalachians, the Tidewater of Virginia, and the rough Atlantic, calling on Marcus Colonna. *Aquila Aurea, Splendidus, Roman lord to whom I owe my fealty, I have foes aplenty. Lend me your favor and your strength. Come to me. Or lead me to you.*

Opening my eyes, I gulp the rest of my drink. "I hope that worked. I'm not yet at full strength, and I'm still hungry. Speaking of which, shall we fetch Donnie and Rebekah and head back to your home? I'm curious to see your house, and even more curious to see what delicacy's waiting for me in your basement."

"In a minute." Cynthia lays a hand on my arm. "First, there's something else I need to share with you. I had another vision."

"Something threatening Matt?"

"Something threatening all of us. I saw what would happen if Aldinach isn't stopped."

A cold nausea grips my gut. "Yes? What was that?"

"I think you can imagine. Picture those MTR sites. Picture them expanding exponentially like budding yeast, snaking out over the hills that remain. Picture rivers frothing and steaming with poison. Picture the green diminishing and shattered shale mounting, animals fleeing and plants expiring. Picture forests burning, filling the sky with smoke. Picture all that you've seen of those mining sites and then increase it a hundredfold, a thousandfold. Picture the humans, both those we care for and those strangers who nourish us with their blood. Picture them sick, wasting away, dying of exposure to toxins in the air, water, and food."

"Appalachian Ragnarök," I whisper.

"It won't be confined to Appalachia. Soon—"

"Hey, Derek!" Donnie bursts out the bar's back door. "Rebekah wants to take me to a deli up the street for dinner and then to a late viewing of the latest Godzilla movie. Turns out we're both dorks about sci-fi stuff. You mind?"

"That would be best," Cynthia says beneath her breath. "Considering the noisy and reluctant guest I have waiting for you."

"Go on, cubster," I say, giving him a weak wave before turning to Cynthia. "It's time for that invigorating repast now. After what you've told me, I'm going to need all the strength I can get."

CHAPTER THIRTY-TWO

Cynthia's house is a huge brick edifice with a front porch overlooking the manicured lawns and flowery plantings of Schiller Park. Stained glass adorns many of the windows. Inside, the rooms are airy, furnished with comfortable antiques in dark wood.

Cynthia leads me to a door beneath the carved-wood staircase. "You can sleep downstairs with me in the crypt when dawn comes. After your thirsty frolic, I'm sure the cellar will be dead silent by then." She unlocks the door to reveal steps sloping down into darkness, then ushers me to go first.

I descend to a flagstone floor. Both the sound and the scents are titillating: a man's muffled shouts, a man's spilled blood, piss, and fear-sweat. I move down a low hall toward those stimuli. The hall ends in a big windowless room with a furnace at one end and a steel cage at the other. The cage is probably eight foot square. Inside it writhes tonight's sweaty, wide-eyed banquet.

The boy's lean, lightly muscled, and in his late twenties, by the looks of him. Coincidentally, he's dressed much like me—black tank top, gray jeans, and biker boots—with one important difference: his crotch is sodden-dark with piss. His arms are sinewy, the left one sleeved in tattoos. His hair's cropped short, his brown beard's cut close and neat, and big black hoops adorn his earlobes.

"An early summer solstice present," Cynthia says, unlocking the cage door before handing me the key. "He reminds me of the way you're looking these days: biker chic."

I growl low in the back of my throat, my usual expression of violent lust, knowing with sweet certainty that that lust is soon to be sated. I step into the cage and take a deep breath, snuffling his scents. His mouth's sealed shut with both ball gag and duct tape, but the noises of outrage he makes are piercing nonetheless. His hands are bound behind his back with a combination of rope and tape, as are his elbows. His wrists are chafed and bleeding, making my fang-teeth ache, and his booted feet are taped together. When he tries to kick me, I press my own booted foot into his chest and bend down to him, gazing into his wet brown eyes. He has the thick eyebrows and long lashes I dote on.

"Behave, boy. Keep still and keep quiet, or I'll make your ending pure agony."

He stares up at me, face twisted with fear, and obeys.

"Fragrant. Glorious. And what a nice job of gift wrapping." I bend to the boy, touching his inked shoulder. He jolts, shakes his head, and wails.

"I knew you'd approve. His name's Brantley, and he's committed many sins. I'd list them for you, but why don't you ask him yourself?"

Cynthia pats me on the back and heads for the stairs. "I want you at full capacity for the war to come. Finish him. I'll dispose of what's left tomorrow."

As soon as Cynthia disappears, I strip. As soon as the bound boy sees my erection, he begins to cry. Naked, I stretch out beside him and take him into my arms. I stroke his short hair, nuzzle his beard, and lick tears off his cheeks. He fights me, shaking and sobbing.

"That's right. Let it all out. Fear. Grief. Regret." I rub my face over his until my beard, forehead, nose, and cheeks are wet with his saline sorrow.

As soon as his fit of weeping recedes, I rip off his tank top. Again he jolts and wails against his gag.

"What a beautiful body you have," I sigh. His torso's well-defined, firm little pec mounds I gently knead. A light coating of hair covers his chest, thicker around his tiny nipples. His belly's lean and smooth, sporting a vague six-pack. A dark line of fur begins at his navel and disappears into the top of his jeans, which are slung low around his narrow hips, in the way of this decade's young. He stiffens, sniffles, snorts, and trembles as my fingers explore every detail, this terror-racked landscape of pale skin and soft brown fur.

"Don't want you to suffocate and end this fine evening too soon." I peel off four layers of tape and then unbuckle his ball gag. He gasps, draws in air, and flexes his jaw.

When I try to kiss him, he grimaces and shakes his head.

"No. G-God, no. Get off me, you f-freak."

"Lie still and let me kiss you, or I'll break your neck."

Whimpering, he does as he's told. I kiss him, sucking hard on his lips and tongue, till both our beards are sodden with my saliva. I badly want to sink my teeth into his pulsing carotid, but Cynthia indicated that the boy had a few confessions to make, stories that will probably make it easier for me to end him. Ever since I settled down with Matt, he's been insisting that I resist my occasional urge to kill except when self-defense or defense of clan requires it. Tonight will be a welcome exception, something Matt has no need to know about.

"Why don't you tell me why you're here?" I say, fingering the miniature nubs of his nipples, gone hard in the cellar chill.

"N-no way," he stutters. "That crazy c-cunt said that once you heard all I've done that you'd...you'd drain me like a spider does a butterfly, whatever the f-fuck that means. I'm not g-gonna tell you jack-shit."

Hmmm. After that crying jag, he seems to have gotten his courage and defiance back. Thick Southern accent. Georgia? Pure redneck, just the way I like my men. Probably a restless country boy led astray by the hedonistic delights and wicked ways of the big city.

"I think you will tell me," I say, flicking my tongue over his right nipple. "You taste good. You're getting me hard."

"S-stop that shit, you queer. Don't touch me. I hate your kind. You f-fucking c-cock-sucking son of a—"

I give him points for valor, none for discretion. "If you want to make me angry, you've succeeded."

Clamping a hand over his mouth, I sink my canine teeth into his right pectoral. Young blood oozes into my mouth, and I nudge that slow yield into a steady trickle by grinding his nipple between my incisors. He squeals and squirms, his heartbeat pounding against my cheek, only making my cock harder. I pause long enough to kiss him on the brow, then give his left pectoral and nipple the same brutal treatment, savoring the way he shouts against my palm and kicks with frantic fury.

Enough delicate sipping. Ravenous, I wrap an arm around his chest and embed my fangs in his throat. He shrieks and thrashes, his fear and powerlessness as heady as his blood.

I drink and drink, feeling strength's welcome warmth coursing through my limbs, till he's limp, his screams have faded into whimpers, and his eyes are glazed.

I retract my fangs, lie back, wipe a trickle of blood from my mouth, and pillow his head on my chest. "I'll ask you again," I say, caressing his fang-torn torso. "Tell me why you're here."

His brain's dazed, easy to compel. "I l-like to beat up queers. I even...I've killed a few and g-got away with it."

I can't help but snicker. Cynthia knew I needed a full meal to recover, and she knew that Matt's scruples have been trammeling my rage and bloodlust for years, and she knew the one crime that would enflame me to the point of murder. She knew I would see what I see right now, in the depths of my memory: Brodie MacDonald and his thugs attacking Angus and me in Lochbuie's standing stones, yelling that hateful line from Leviticus as they stabbed us again and again.

"Go on, boy, go on. Tell me all about your conquests."

"There was a scrawny f-fag in high school...we kicked his face in. He had to have surgery to build his j-jaw back. There was the b-black drag queen some friends helped me throw...into the Olentangy River a c-couple of years ago. This month, we caught a few...after gay pride events...and b-beat the hell out of them."

"'We?' There's a band of you, of course."

"Well, sure. My buds got my back. So, l-last night, I was out on my own...I was real drunk and ran across this hot b-black chick at a beer garden...and we started flirting...but there was this swishy guy across the room, so I told her about how much I hated queers...and the b-bitch called me names and told me she was bi and had a g-girlfriend...and she threw her beer in my face and walked out...so I followed her home...slipped onto the b-back porch...and then somebody threw me against the wall...woke up to f-find myself here."

"And what were you going to do to the black lady you followed home?" I ask, fondling his abs.

"Hell, man, s-show her what a real man feels like. Rape her."

"Funny you should mention rape," I say, abruptly rolling Brantley onto his belly, jerking down his jeans, and digging my fingers into a plump butt-cheek.

"Oh, Jesus! Oh, n-no!" he blurts, just before I stuff the ball gag between his teeth and buckle it tight. He writhes as I slap his ass, probe his crack, and shove two fingers up inside him. He yelps and pleads as again and again I sink my fangs into his smooth white buttocks.

I drink from him and finger-fuck him till he's sobbing brokenly, with no fight left. Then I climb on top of him, moisten us both with spit, and force my cock deep inside him. He slumps there, rocking beneath me, grunting, flinching, and whimpering, breathing hard through his nose. As I approach my climax, I pierce his throat again and again drink deep. By the time I've come inside him, my victim's spasmed, shuddered, and stopped breathing.

ChAPTER ThiRTY-ThREE

omething's wrong. Lifting my head from the near-paralysis of day-sleep, I extend my awareness as best I can.

It's far too soon for Donnie and me to be home: we left Cynthia's just before dawn, less than an hour ago. Yet someone's removing my travel crate from the van.

Humans. Several of them. No voices I recognize. Someone's hijacking me, and there's nothing I can do until the sun sets.

Donnie? Is he all right? I've fed from him many times, so we have a psychic connection, but I sense no fear, I hear no struggle or objections on his part. He's nearby, and he's uneasy…but not afraid. He seems to be willingly handing me over.

Now my crate's deposited. I must be in another vehicle, for the engine sounds distinctly different. Now we're moving. Now I sense Donnie no longer. Anxious, angry, I try to open my eyes and fail. Instead I clench my fists, snag my left fang on my lower lip, mumble curses, and lose consciousness.

hen I rise, poised to teeth-tear the windpipes out of my abductors, I find myself on a plane. I step through a hanging curtain into a spacious fuselage, where a human, a middle-aged gentleman in an elegant suit, reclines in one of the roomy seats. Behind him, a curly-haired, olive-skinned girl's rattling ice in the service section. Everything's exquisitely appointed.

This is clearly a millionaire's plane. In such surroundings, I feel somewhat shabby in last night's bar garb.

"*Buona sera,* Signor Maclaine," he says. "Would you like a drink? Gin and tonic? Campari and soda? Black sambuca?"

I sense no danger, so I smooth my beard and swallow my rage. "The latter, please. I'd also like some explanations. Who are you? Why did you take me from my friend? Where are we going? And whose is this plane?"

"Maria, would you pour Signor Maclaine his drink?" the man says before turning back to me. "Please take a seat. Those are queries most easy to answer. I am Eduardo Assisi. We took you because our employer told us to. We are soon to land in Hilo, Hawai'i. And the man who owns this plane is—"

"Marcus Colonna," I say, taking a seat.

He nods. "Mr. Colonna is eager to see you again. But first he thought you might enjoy a few days catching up with your Norse friend, Sigurd Magnusson. This should explain everything."

Assisi hands me an envelope with my name written on it. When I open it, I find what appears to be a handwritten note sent through a fax machine.

> *My redneck Enkidu, hairy forest lord,*
>   *This trip will come to you as a surprise. Forgive me. After I heard your call, I conferred with Sigurd. We decided to treat you to this brief holiday so that you and he might meet and deliberate. Afterward, you should come to Michigan's Mackinac Island in mid-June. I will be staying at the luxurious Grand Hotel, and I will be presiding over a convocation of our kind. I gather you have need of help against a particularly pernicious set of foes. Perhaps the convocation can be convinced to give us our aid. Bring any friends you want. It will be my pleasure to treat you all to several nights on that beautiful island. In mid-June, the lilacs are at their height.*
>   *Mithras bless you,*
>   *Marcus*

I pocket the letter. "This answers everything, thank you."

"Good, good. Mr. Magnusson's men will meet you at the airport. Once you two have had your talk, we will fly you to Charleston, West Virginia. Now I will leave you to your thoughts. Unless you have need of anything else?"

"I'd like to assure my mate of my well-being. Have you a phone handy? One that can reach West Virginia?"

"Certainly. Maria will arrange that."

Assisi disappears behind a curtain. Within a minute, the attendant has brought me both a liqueur glass full of sambuca and a phone, then vanished herself. I sit back and gaze out on an immensity of dark waters glittering beneath the waxing moon, then dial the number for Mount Storm. It rings only once before I hear Matt's voice, hoarse with concern.

"Hello? Derek?"

"Yes, indeed. 'Tis I, your heroic husbear."

"Lord God, are you all right? Donnie said that that Italian vampire's men took you."

"They did, but I'm fine. When I was in Columbus, I sent psychic calls out to both Sigurd and Marcus, hoping they'd help us against Alpha. Marcus works fast. He must have had minions in Ohio. When they borrowed me from Donnie, they put me on a plane. I just woke. We're about to land in Hilo."

"Hilo?"

"On the Big Island of Hawai'i."

"You've got to be fucking kidding me. Me and all the boys have been pacing around, wondering what happened to you, and you're going to Hawai'i?" Matt's laugh is bitter. "Goddamn it. The things you pull. What the hell are you going to do there?"

"I'm meeting Sigurd for the first time in many years. I'm pretty sure he'll agree to help. Once I get home, I want us to visit Okey. Cynthia and I had a long chat, and she indicated that he and his coven will be invaluable."

"I sure hope so. Word is that Alpha just got two more permits to tear down mountains, so I'm feeling pretty useless these days."

"We'll stop Alpha, Matt. Count on it. After we meet with Okey, I need to go to Michigan. Marcus is having a big meeting of vampires on Mackinac Island, and I'm hoping to enlist their help."

"Really? You're gonna slam Alpha and its demon with a shit-load of vampires?"

"And werewolves. Cynthia's wolf friend Rebekah is willing to help, and so's Donnie. Maybe witches too, if Okey's coven turns out to be amenable. How's everyone at home?"

"Fine. We're all staying pretty close to Mount Storm, like you said. I told the Partisan folks that I've got a bug I can't shake, so I'm doing work for them at home. Nate's arm is still in a sling. My ribs are still bandaged up, but my burns are healing pretty well. Donnie and Timmy divide their time between helping keep this place up and working down in Monterey."

"And Zac? How's the new member of the household adjusting?"

"Pretty damn well. He sure likes to cuddle. He's actually in bed with me right now, fast asleep. Can't you hear him sawing logs?"

"I think I can," I say, picturing them, two brawny, bearded men with thick brown body hair curled up together.

Assisi steps through the curtain. "Signor Maclaine, I'm very sorry to interrupt, but we're about to land."

"Matt, I have to go." Out the oval window, I can make out lights twinkling in the distance, miniature stars dwarfed by the endless black of the Pacific Ocean. "I should be home in another couple of nights. Can you pick me up at the Charleston airport?

"You bet. Just call and tell me when."

"Bring the van, since I'll be in my travel crate. And get hold of Okey and schedule a visit, okay? Maybe the same day I land. We'll deal with his vampire phobia when we get there."

I finish my drink, untie my ponytail, and run my fingers through my hair. Sigurd always liked me shaggy. Once he saved me from death. This time, with luck, he will save me from defeat and my adopted mountains from destruction.

CHAPTER THIRTY-FOUR

A soft rain's descending as I exit the Hilo terminal. The air's humid, perfumed with flowers. Somewhere frogs are chorusing. A limousine waits at the curb.

The Hawai'ian who steps out is a splendid human specimen: around six foot four, with the broad shoulders, full chest, and thick arms of a bodybuilder. Dressed informally in a skin-tight T-shirt and board shorts, he sports a profuse dark brown beard and hair even longer than mine, hanging nearly to his waist. His skin's mahogany, his eyebrows sharp-angled, like dark wings.

"Aloha, Lord Maclaine. I'm Kanunu," he says, shaking my hand and opening the limousine door. "I'm one of Lord Sigurd's servants. Would you kindly come with me? He has chosen a very dramatic setting for your reunion. I would say the most dramatic in all our islands."

"Lead on, Kanunu," I say, repressing the urge to seize the man and make a luau of his body and blood. The looming bulk of him reminds me of Sigurd himself.

I climb into the limo and we're off. Soon the airport lights have faded behind us and the car is making a long, gradual ascent up a forested slope. I breathe in Kanunu's scent and close my eyes. It will be good to see my maker again after so many years.

Hawai'i Volcanoes National Park is closed, but Kanunu's pass gets us past the gate.

"We're on the summit of Kilauea. It's one of the most active volcanoes on earth. This road skirts the great caldera, which is several kilometers wide," Kanunu explains, gesturing to our left. Indeed, I can make out in the moonlight a huge depression in the earth. At the far end, a plume of smoke rises.

"There," says my driver, pointing. "That steam emerges from the pit crater of Halema'uma'u, where the fire goddess Pele has her home. Lord Sigurd waits for you there. The gases are too noxious for me to approach, but you, Lord Maclaine, should have no such handicap."

Another few minutes, and we pull into the parking lot of a visitors' center, closed for the night. When I step out, high mountain wind buffets my face. Above, the waxing moon gleams. Far below, a small pit in the much larger caldera, Halema'uma'u glows red and emits billows of smoke illuminated from beneath. Another vehicle is parked nearby, and another muscular, handsome Hawaiʻian—this one my height, clean-shaven, with short dark hair, full lips, deep laugh lines, and angular cheekbones—stands by the overlook. He's dressed much like Kanunu. Striding over, he gives me a faint bow and shakes my hand.

"Aloha. I'm Mano, Lord Maclaine. Down there, Lord Sigurd awaits you." He points toward the smoking crater. From this distance, I can see a tiny form standing on the crater's edge, silhouetted in the glow.

"Thanks, Mano. I'll join him now." I climb up onto the parapet and leap, taking bat form as I fall. Another few seconds, and I'm gliding over the immense caldera, relishing the stiff wind and the distant view of the sea. Another minute, and I'm gliding down to Sigurd's side. As soon as I've taken man-form, he seizes me in his arms.

"By Odin, you're looking good, boy. It's been too long." Sigurd slaps me on the back. Odd to see an Orkney Viking who used to wear a kilt dressed in a contemporary black silk shirt and beige linen trousers.

"Too long, indeed, sir." I gaze down over the edge of the crater. Far, far below, red-orange lava seethes and steams. The heat's immense, bringing out blood-sweat on my brow and chest. "By the gods, you've chosen a memorable meeting place."

"Halema'uma'u leads down into the heart of the planet," says Sigurd, awe in his voice. "The lair of the goddess. If ever I grow weary of living, I will come here and give myself to Her."

"A theatrical end that would be. I hope you're not...."

"Odin, no. I'm very happy here. After decades of Icelandic snow, I thought Pacific breezes would be a fine change of pace." He's as magnificent as ever, a Viking giant with long golden hair and a luxuriant beard braided at the chin. He must be feeding regularly, because he looks very young.

"Yes, I am." Sigurd smiles. "Feeding regularly. Don't you remember how well I read your mind? How do you like my thralls, Mano and Kanunu? They've made Hawai'i especially attractive."

"I'll bet they have. You always had fine taste in men."

"I do indeed. I turned you, did I not? Let's rejoin them. My home's not far. I've a full night planned: an ocean swim, tropical drinks, an entertaining spectacle, and a nourishing meal."

Sigurd gives me no time to reply. Shifting, he takes wing. Shifting, I follow him. We circle the glowing crater a few times before flapping back to the overlook.

Sigurd's gated compound sits on an isolated, idyllic spot, the edge of a sea cliff in the district called Puna. Ocean breezes rustle coconut palms about the property. The wide grounds are full of lush grass, fruit trees, bubbling fountains, and flowering plants. Frogs chirp steadily in the vegetation, much like the spring peepers back home. Waves break and boom on a black-sand beach far below.

"A swim first?" Sigurd asks, stripping.

"Absolutely," I say, following his lead. "I rarely get to the ocean these days."

"You're as fetching as ever, lad," Sigurd says, taking in my nakedness. "More tattoos, I see. And you still wear the Thor's hammer I gave you so long ago."

"I'd never part with it. And you yourself are more than glorious."

I speak not flattery but truth. My Norse maker, nearly a foot taller than I, is solid with muscle, his skin white and smooth, save for sparse dustings of golden fur around his nipples, along his trim belly, and upon his long legs.

Sigurd grips me by the shoulders, bends, and kisses my brow. "Come, son," he says, ushering me toward the precipitous edge of the patio. He leaps into the air, and I follow him. We take bat-form only long enough to skim over the beach. Once out over the water, we transform again, diving into the waves.

I surface, shaking out my hair and goatee. Soon thereafter Sigurd does the same. After the great heat of the volcanic crater, the water's cool and delicious, exhilarating, with rough wave-swell and strong currents that would drag anyone of mere human strength out to sea. Overhead, the sky is full of stars.

"Can you feel them?" Sigurd says, swimming closer, then floating beside me. "The gods of this place?"

"I do. I feel great natural presences much different from those I know at home—meaning both Scotland and Appalachia—but these are equally immense and equally divine. Tell me of them."

"Ah, there is my favorite, the volcano goddess, Madame Pele. She is beautiful, ancient, unpredictable, difficult. There is silvery Hina." He points toward the moon, vague behind a drifting cloud. "There is Namaka, the sea upon whom we float tonight. There is the shark god, and the god of the underworld, and so many more. I honor them all."

"As one should when one is in their land. Cynthia tells me you have an altar to Pele in your home."

"I do. Your friend and I had a fine time during her visit. The five of us—Cynthia, Lara, Kanunu, Mano, and I—went in to Pahoa for drinks. My thralls' exceptional looks served as bait for admiring island girls whom Cynthia then fed upon. Speaking of drinks, now that we've cooled off, let's enjoy some cocktails on the patio. We have much to discuss. After that, my slaves will entertain us."

Sigurd swims toward the shore, his broad white shoulders parting the water, and I follow suit. Together we stride out of the sea, up a steep slope, and onto the beach. I bend down, scooping up a handful of black sand.

"It looks like caviar," I say. "Amazing."

"The blazing innards of the earth, oozing up through volcanic rifts, poured out into spines of *ʻaʻā* and loops of *pāhoehoe* lava. Ground down over millennia into glossy black sand. A miracle wrought by fire and water. Black as your hair, my lad." Sigurd tousles my lank locks, then takes to the air.

Naked, we lounge on the patio, listening to wind in the palms. The servants, naked as well, serve up mai tais decorated with purple orchids.

"Nudity's the rule of the house," Sigurd explains, reading my mind again. "Men so splendid should wear clothes only when absolutely necessary."

"*Mahalo*, master," Kanunu says, smiling. He's heavily tattooed like me, with tribal markings scattered upon his torso, arms, shoulders, and back. His huge pecs are lightly hairy; his compatriot Mano's torso is almost as muscular but perfectly smooth. They make a winsome pair. As they pad off together, I admire their compact buttocks and lick my lips.

"You certainly know how to surround yourself with scenery."

"You appreciate them as well as I do," says Sigurd. "I expected as much. They were a couple when I met them, two beautiful boys street-hustling in Honolulu. I kidnapped and enthralled Kanunu first, but when I saw how badly Mano mourned his lover's absence, I decided he should join Kanunu in slavery. I am ever so slightly in love with them, and they seem very happy here. They dreamed of achieving fortune and luxury, and here they have found it. How do you like your drink?"

I take a sip, detecting amidst the mélange of rum and fruit flavors the faint taste of blood. "I heartily approve. Especially the secret ingredient."

"My slaves kindly enriched our cocktails with their own vein-liqueur, so to speak. Later, they will provide you with an amusement worthy of a Roman banquet and, after that, with more of their blood. So, tell me about your recent adventures. I gather from Marcus that you need considerable help."

"True," I sigh. "Thanks to the blood and semen you gave me when you turned me, I'm unusually strong for a vampire of my age. I've encountered few opponents that I've had trouble besting. But these foes.... To sum up, I ran into a trap. Someone working for my enemies was able to gauge that I was a vampire, so I was shot with rowan-wood bullets."

Sigurd grimaces. "Vile tree. I know how toxic it is from personal experience. It was a rowan-wood stake those accursed priests used to dispatch my maker, Medb."

"Yes, so I recall. Though you served them their quietus, did you not?"

"Most certainly. I still smile at the thought of that slaughter."

"As I smile at the memory of picking off Angus's killers one by one. At any rate, after I'd been hit by those bullets, then the demon they'd raised—"

"A demon? Those are exceedingly rare."

"Not rare enough. It took advantage of my weakness to spit its acidic essence at me, burning me badly. It's an Egyptian horror named Aldinach. I escaped with the last of my strength. Had I been caught...." I leave the rest unsaid.

"I must ask: why are you waging this war? Why do you care so much about the affairs of humans?"

"Two reasons. One is personal: sheer vengeance. My partner Matt's cousin was murdered by Alpha Coal, the company that's summoned the demon, and now Matt's on a very public crusade to stop them. Thugs hired by Alpha abducted Matt and were about to murder him. I found him just in time. They also abducted Nate, one of my thralls. Again, I rescued him without a moment to spare."

"Very altruistic of you. You remind me of a Mormon elder, with a clutch of wives. You mentioned two reasons you're fighting Alpha. Tell me the second."

"The second reason involves principle, and it's a principle that you and I, being pagans, share. This company is destroying the earth in the name of greed. Have you heard of MTR? Mountaintop removal mining?"

"I have. I'm deliberately isolated, but I'm not uninformed. It sounds detestable. Abominable."

"It is. You spoke of the nature deities of these islands. Imagine a practice similar to MTR here in Puna. Ground torn up, trees cut down...."

"There are far too many human beings on this planet. Our kind should have culled them more severely and more efficiently over the centuries." Sigurd exposes a fang and runs it along his thumb. "But I understand you. You have no need to convince me that Gaia and Hertha and Pan and Frey and Freya and other deities of woodland, farmland, and wilderness must be fought for."

"So now I'm seeking allies. I can't destroy this threat by myself, as much as I wish I could."

"You have my help, of course. But you will need more than me. Marcus—"

"Marcus hopes to convince his convocation of vampires to help me. Will you accompany me to that event?"

"I'd prefer not to. Crowds rack my hermit's nerves, especially when our fellow *draugar* are concerned...some of the most egotistical, vain, manipulative, and conniving creatures on the planet. You won't need me there. But keep in mind that Marcus might demand a price for his help. He's not the sort of man who does something for nothing. Are you willing to pay whatever he asks?"

"To protect my mate and my homeland? I will. If I have what he wants."

"There is an easier way to protect Matt, you know. Turn him. You've been together for how long? Over a decade, correct?"

"Why haven't you turned Kanunu or Mano?"

"Evading tactic, lad? That's different, and you know it. They've been my thralls for only five years. At some point, I may indeed turn them. They're both at the peak of their physical perfection. Isn't Matt approaching middle age for a mortal?"

"He's forty-seven."

Sigurd plucks the orchid from his drink and nibbles at it. "Do you want to lose him to age?"

"Matt makes it complicated. He's very ambivalent."

"I believe you're even more ambivalent."

"And why do you think that?"

"Because not once in the entirety of your *draugr* existence have you ever turned a human."

I slurp up the rest of my drink, rise, and stride over to the parapet. Far below, the dark waves, crashing and weltering, create a line of creamy white along the black beach. "I never got a chance with the men I loved."

"True. Your love life has been that of a tragic hero's. You gravitate to warriors, to men willing to risk their lives for a cause. Angus, then that boy you loved during the Civil War, then that boy you loved during the Second World War, and now Matt, fighting this dangerous coal company and its demonic associate. But this time you have a chance to save your beloved combatant from mortality and its human miseries, to armor him against most of this world's dangers, and to keep him with you forever."

"Yes. I know all that. All that has occurred to me. But…."

"But?"

I listen to the booming of the surf. "How does Matthew Arnold put it? 'The eternal note of sadness….'"

"'The turbid ebb and flow of human misery.' Yes. I've known you longer than anyone, Derek. I've seen your loves and losses, your triumphs and despairs, your more-than-human raptures and miseries. I have a theory about why you never turn your human lovers into *draugar*."

Our conversation pauses, as naked Kanunu appears with a second round of drinks. Staring at the swell of his enormous pecs, I make no bones about licking my lips and flashing him a fang.

Sigurd chuckles. "Soon, son, soon. You really didn't think that I'd dangle this muscular morsel in front of you but then deny you more tactile intimacies, did you?"

"That's a relief. I'm starving."

Blushing, Kanunu gives me a faint smile before lowering his eyes and lumbering away. Eyes locked on his bare ass, I heave a lengthy sigh of longing.

"If any man was ever born to be taken hard and ruthlessly from behind, it's he."

"Agreed," says Sigurd. "I told you I had a spectacle planned for later. Back to the topic at hand. I think you're still mourning Angus McCormick after all these decades. I think you blame yourself for his death, and I think you've convinced yourself on some unconscious level that you don't deserve love. And so again and again you have attached yourself to young men who take risks, who have come to their prime in times of war, when historical circumstances and their own courageous natures send them into the direst of dangers...men you could keep from death were you to turn them, men you choose to lose so that you may suffer again and be punished."

I shudder and shake my head. "Those years we spent in Vienna...while I was nuzzling *Schlagobers* off my pet anthropologist Friedrich's arse, you were smoking cigars and sampling cocaine with Herr Freud."

"I was, actually. He borrowed several ideas from me, including most of what became *Civilization and Its Discontents*. Don't dismiss me, Derek. I was there for you when Carden died, and I was there for you when McGraw died. I saw how you suffered. Talk to Matt again. This could be a graceful way of sidestepping his mortality forever. Why would he regret it? Do you regret your existence?"

"No, not at all, other than the sometimes very inconvenient limitation of avoiding sunlight. Twice now—once in 2002 and once a few days ago—my need for sleep during the day made Matt vulnerable to his foes."

"Every life pays its price. Every existence has its limitations."

"I accept that. But there's a savagery and selfishness in me that make this life as a nightwalker and blood-drinker easy. My soul is wilder than most. It's compatible with the life of a predator. Vampire existence would be harder for Matt. My compassion and loyalty are deep, but I reserve both—the milk of vampire kindness?—for those few I count as my clan. Matt's compassion is wider. As vast as an ocean."

"A brawny Christ, eh?"

"I suppose. He's a beauty when he's mock-crucified."

Sigurd stretches, fixing me with his blue eyes. Blond hair falls over his brow; he brushes it away. *I'm sorry for my elusiveness, silence, and absence. I've missed you, lad. Will you sleep with me? When day comes?* The request echoes inside my head.

Most certainly. It has been too long. Fold me in your arms. Let's drink from each other again.

"Cynthia said you'd become a recluse like me, living up on your West Virginia mountain. Is this true?"

"It is. I relish the solitude and the quiet. Cities have gotten intolerably loud. Stereos, cell-phone chatter, cars…. At Mount Storm, I have Matt, and my thralls, and the forests and great mountains of the Potomac Highlands…air and water that are still relatively clean, though acid rain is depopulating the red spruce…. More and more, I have all I need at Mount Storm, other than the occasional jaunt out for 'strange,' as Matt calls it."

"I certainly understand. I'm nearly six hundred years older than you. I need less and less. Less stimuli, less blood, less of the company of my own kind. You quoted an English poet earlier, Matthew Arnold. Let me quote another one. 'The world is too much with us,' said William Wordsworth. The human race is ruining this planet."

Sigurd strokes his braided beard and eats his orchid whole. "I know that you often choose to fight what you hate and abhor, and I admire that, but more and more, my choice is avoidance and withdrawal. I want to be here, far from humanity, save for the select few I've chosen, the beautiful men who serve me. I want great heights and wilderness, where silence allows me to feel and hear old gods in the *aina*, the land. To walk the snowy slopes of Mauna Kea, to circle above the caldera of Kilauea, to touch the blood-red blooms of the *'ōhi'a lehua* tree, to lie in the surf of the black-sand beach…."

"Yes. To perch on the highest pinnacle of Seneca Rocks, to fly over the evergreens of Spruce Knob…."

"Or walk alone amid Orkney's standing stones…."

"Or those of the Hebrides."

"Or stride the lava fields of Berserkjahraun or the glacier of Vatnajökull."

"High desolations where only gods dwell. I understand you, and I apologize if my visit's interrupted your solitude."

"Silly pup, I'm the one who should apologize. I relish your company, and I'm a fool to have lost touch with you. Perhaps your passionate fire will refresh my world-weariness. Would your mate enjoy a celebratory Hawai'ian vacation after we destroy Alpha?"

"He'd love it, especially if he's provided a voluminous buffet of native foods and time in bed with your slaves. He's nearly as much of a hedonist as I."

"So it shall be. Speaking of slaves, are you ready for your preprandial spectacle?"

"I am," I say, cupping my hands behind my head and grinning.

Sigurd claps. Immediately, the two thralls stride out onto the patio. When Sigurd points to me, they kneel at my feet, put their hands behind their backs, and bow their heads.

"Powerful men in a submissive posture? What a pretty picture. What now?" I say, sipping my drink.

"Now you tell them what to do, and they will do it. They are perfectly acquiescent. Afterwards, we will share their bed till dawn, doing as we please with them."

"This is indeed a paradise you have created, sir." Only briefly do I contemplate the delicious options before coming to a decision.

"Let's start slow. Then I'll be wanting something rough, painful, and perverse."

At first, Kanunu's admirably stoic. He sways on his hands and knees, long hair shrouding his face, grunting softly against the rag I've tied between his teeth. Mano beats Kanunu's ass with a belt till his skin's welted crimson, then lubes his own ridiculously large cock and Kanunu's hairy ass-crack. At my command, he enters his lover hard and fast. He fucks him fiercely, sweaty groin and sweaty rump slapping loudly together, pounding him till the massive man—much to my delight—whimpers with hurt between gritted teeth and breaks down, emitting low, hoarse sobs.

After Mano, roaring, comes inside Kanunu and Kanunu's ceased his weeping, Sigurd leads us all to the slaves' broad bed in the back of the house, where the four of us intertwine, kissing and grappling. Kanunu rolls onto his back, still gagged, and begins to masturbate, while I finger-fuck his sticky hole and drink, first from his great breast, then from his neck. Mano faces Sigurd, sitting on his cock and embracing him, while Sigurd drinks from his corded throat and jacks his prick.

Kanunu spurts into his hand and passes out. Mano spurts into Sigurd's hand and passes out. Sigurd and I lap up both thralls' pearly moon-sap before tucking them into bed.

"It's nearly dawn," Sigurd says, leading me down the hall to a reinforced oaken door and a windowless room beyond. A broad sarcophagus lies on the floor, lined with the tartan blankets we both favor. Sigurd climbs into it and lies down on his side. I slide in and stretch out beside him, nestling back into his arms.

"Ah, you make me feel safe, sir. At home, I feel such a constant need to stay strong. I feel responsible for my boys, so I'm always a little on guard. It's a luxury, a deep comfort, to have a *draugr* so much mightier than I hold me like this."

"Do you find the same comfort with Marcus?"

"I feel a true fondness for him. Not the centuries-long devotion I feel for you, but still something very strong."

"He feels something for you too, lad. I've been able to sense that during the few conversations he and I have had. I'm fairly sure he'll be able to convince his convocation to help you. Tomorrow night, before you go, let's put an offering of flowers on Pele's altar and ask for Her aid. For now, drink from me. You have need of my greater strength."

"Gladly, sir." I turn, lap his smooth chest, then push my fangs into the curved flesh of a pectoral. Sigurd trembles as I drink deep.

"Oh, yes," he sighs, rocking me in his arms. "Thor and Odin bless the night we met. Thank the gods I got to you in time."

CHAPTER THIRTY-FIVE

When I open the lid of my travel crate, I find myself in a familiar space: the back of the Mount Storm van. Matt, dressed in a Rebel-flag baseball cap, "Butch Built" T-shirt, jeans, and cowboy boots, sits in a foldout chair grinning at me.

"Back, huh? As nice as Hawai'i was, you had to get home to the hills of West-by-God-Virginny, now didn't you?"

"I had to get back to you," I say, seizing his hand. "You look good. How're you feeling?"

"Ah, a bunch of Alpha thugs ain't gonna keep Matt Taylor down. I'm close to back to normal, 'cept for some rib-ache and some scars." He fingers his face. "Guess they paid a high price for beating on me and burning me with cigarettes."

"Yes, they did." I smile cheerily. "Where are we?"

"We're parked right down the street from Okey's house. I picked you up at the airport like you said. Those Italian guys were mighty spiffy." Matt tugs on my goatee. "Time's a'wastin', Hell's handsomest angel. Alpha's poised to rip up another mountain. You ready to take your chances with a wary witchie?"

"Yes, indeed. Let's do it."

Matt pulls me to my feet and gives me a powerful hug before we climb from the back of the van. The night's humid and quiet. The street's lined with silver maple trees; lightning bugs wink here and there.

"This way. He's expecting us." Matt leads me down the block to a white frame house surrounded by high box hedges. Its porch light is on. The verandah's lined with potted hibiscus, mint, and basil.

Matt advances up the walkway. I follow him, only to feel an odd flushing heat. Then hundreds of stinging sensations prick my skin, as if I'd stepped on one of those yellow jacket nests that plague Matt when he mows the Mount Storm lawn. I yelp and jump back.

There's a line of salt glittering at my feet. I might have known. The witch has a protective spell encircling his house.

Before I can compose myself, the door opens and out steps a ponderous man about Matt's age, dressed in tan shorts and a sky-blue T-shirt. He's taller than me by several inches, meaning that he positively dwarfs Matt. Like Matt, he's bulky, thick, and powerful-looking all over, easily two hundred and fifty pounds. This is a drag queen?

The man spies Matt and smiles. "Why, honey, as I live and breathe! You've gotten so big and handsome. Look at those biceps."

The man's smile fades as he catches sight of me, standing on the edge of the lawn, scowling with the fading discomfort of astral stings. He scrutinizes me for only a couple of seconds before the welcome in his face turns to flushing anger.

"Well, I'll be damned. Matt Taylor, did you bring a frigging vampire with you?"

"Mr. Okey, now, listen," Matt begs.

Before Matt can continue, Okey steps back inside and slams the door.

"Okey! Please!" Matt raps on the door. "We really need your help. Derek would never hurt you. Okey, please!"

There's a long pause, and then the door flies open. Okey stands behind the screen, glowering, his arms crossed upon his chest. He must have just donned every piece of silver he owns: necklaces, rings, and bracelets. I wouldn't be surprised if he'd stuffed his pockets with silverware just in case.

"Talk fast. Why are y'all here, and why did you bring that thing along?"

"He's not a thing. This is Derek. He's my honey. He's the husbear I told you about."

"Oh, Lord." Okey presses a palm to his chest and peers at me. "What kind of damnation have you gotten yourself into, honey?"

"It's kind of a, uh, mixed marriage, yeah. But Derek's a good guy."

"A good guy? A vampire? Honey, you've lost your grip. Just 'cause he looks like the kind of dark, hairy, smelly biker trash you've always fallen for, that's no reason to trust him. He's a killer."

"No. Well, sort of. B-but not really. He only kills w-when—"

"Well, shit, Matt. Stop while you're ahead, why don't you?" I mutter. I poke a hesitant finger into the invisible force field and get stung again. "Damn it."

"See? Grade-A Killer. You get out of here, you undead creep!" Okey shouts, shaking a silver-bangled arm at me. "I know your kind."

"Okey, buddy, you *don't* know." Matt pulls open the screen door and grabs Okey's hand. "Please, man. We've known one another for decades, right? You've never known me to be dishonest?"

"I remember a hot little cub you stole from me at the Grand Palace one fateful night."

"That was 1995! And I've apologized for that again and again. I was real drunk and real horny, and, besides, the damn kid gave me the crabs. Wasn't that punishment enough?"

Okey sniggers. "I suppose. Especially with all that body hair you have. You looked like a big baby when you shaved it all off."

"Yes, I did. Which is why you couldn't resist buying me a pair of diapers."

"Not to mention inviting you over for a sumptuous feast of deviled crab." Merriment flashes across Okey's face before stern disapproval returns. "And speaking of clinging bloodsuckers, that *there* is a crab louse in human form. He'll drain you dry sure as shootin'."

"Oh, for fuck's sake," I sigh. "You're wasting our time, witch. I love Matt. He and I have been together for well over a decade. I'd do anything for him. Protecting him is why we're here."

"Honey, is that true?" Okey rubs a silver pentagram between his fingers, looking doubtful. "Y'all been together that long?"

"It is, friend. Derek's saved my life twice. Once when the Leviticus Locusts tried to beat me to a pulp, and—"

"Those retarded twats? Lord in heaven." Realization glints in Okey's eyes. "Those rats...."

"Yep," I say, grinning. "Nice way to clean up a mess, huh?"

Okey shudders. "I suppose. Nasty. Those Locusts were a hateful, hateful bunch...but there's just more proof that you're a killer."

"Okey, those men would have killed *me* if Derek hadn't intervened. And last week, Alpha abducted me."

"What?"

"Yep. The amulet you gave me kept off psychic attack just like you said, so the Alpha bastards decided to kidnap me, question me, torture me, and murder me. Derek saved my ass. I'd be dead without him."

Okey stares at me. "Really? Maybe he just hypnotized you. Made you think—"

"That's bullshit. Now look here." Matt pulls up the front of his T-shirt, exposing the red scars his tormentors' cigarettes made.

"Oh, honey, no," Okey gasps, his hand flying to his mouth. "Those pigs. I can't believe it."

"Believe it. Look, I know we ain't seen each other in a long while, but I think of you as a big brother, and—"

"And a big sister too?" Okey mimes the primping of an imaginary wig, but his eyes are solemn. Reaching over, he touches the scar on Matt's face.

"Yeah, that too. I didn't tell you everything about Derek 'cause I knew you might not approve. But now we need your help bad. Won't you please let Derek in?"

"Absolutely not."

"But you got all that silver on. He can't get near you."

Time to take another tack. "Okey, you're a priest of the Old Gods, right?" I ask.

"Yes, I am. I'm a witch. Witches worship the Goddess and God of the Old Religion."

"Would you come closer, please? I can't get past this protective circle you've got, and you're wearing all that moon-metal. I can't hurt you. Please come closer and let me show you a couple of my tattoos. And this necklace I'm wearing."

"This isn't time for an undead fashion show, Father Fangster." Okey waves me away.

"Please, Okey." Matt takes his hand. "For me."

"You charming little bastard. You think your swaggering redneck looks will get you whatever you want whenever you want. And I'm here to tell you...."

Okey pauses dramatically, then heaves an exaggerated sigh. "I'm here to tell you that tonight you are right. Lead me to your monster."

Matt pulls Okey along the path toward me. "Recognize this?" I say, pointing to my left shoulder, conveniently exposed by my tank top.

"I do. The Horned God. He's the deity of the witches."

"And this?" I point to the Thor's hammer design I have tattooed on the inside of my lower right arm, then tug at the Thor's hammer around my neck.

"The Thunder God. A little too boisterous and butch for my tastes, but certainly worth reverence."

"And this?" I point to my left forearm.

Okey squints. "A thistle? And thorny rose vines?"

"Rose vines or briers, it's all the same. The prickly vegetation of the Green Man, another face of the Old God."

"So you're a pagan too? That's not necessarily any reason to trust you."

"No. But what I'm trying to do for Matt and for this region is a big reason. I'm a priest of the Lord of the Beasts and the Lord of the Storm, and I venerate the Green Man, just as you do. What maims the earth I hate and execrate, and I know you feel the same. Alpha Coal is trying to kill Matt for his activism against them and trying to desecrate these mountains for its own ends. I want to stop them. And I want to stop the demon they have protecting them."

Okey blanches. "Matt said that you ran into what you thought was a demon. Are you sure?"

"I am. I've since encountered it again, when I invaded the home of Alpha's CEO. I'm nearly invulnerable, but it burnt me badly nonetheless."

"You're saying that a coal company has a demon mascot?"

"Seems apropos, don't you think?" I sigh and run my fingers through my beard. "I'm telling the truth, Okey. You sense that I'm dangerous. I am. Very dangerous. But not to you. And not to your coven. And not to anyone who is a friend of Matt's. Matt once said that you referred to the combined power of a clan when you empowered the amulet you gave him. I grew up in the Western Isles of Scotland a long, long, long time ago, before the clan system was eradicated. Mine's a clan mentality. If you're Matt's big brother *or* sister, then you're family to me. Please let me enter your home. Please let me explain all that's going on. I think that you and your coven can help us stop Alpha and its demon ally. If you don't, Matt might end up dead, and who knows how many more mountains might be blasted into rubble?"

Okey takes a deep breath and looks at Matt. "Ohhhhh, honey. What all have you gotten yourself into? You and your flair for the dramatic, for dark and mysterious studs with dreadful, dangerous secrets."

Matt snorts. "Buddy, do you really think I'd ask you to let Derek inside if I thought for a minute that he'd hurt you?"

"No. You aren't some kind of demon yourself, are you?" Okey says, regarding me. "A fiend with powerful glamour who's taking advantage of my little friend here?"

"Not at all. Just think of me as another large wilderness predator, like a puma or a wolf: not to be crossed, definitely to be handled with care, but one of the Forest Lord's creatures nonetheless."

"You're as full of shit as Matt. No wonder you ended up together." Okey peels five different silver rings off his right hand—even their gleam makes me queasy—and puts them in his pocket. Then he reaches through the charmed wall of protection, grips my hand, and pulls me forward. There's a split-second of cacophony in my head and a sizzling of my skin, and then I'm through.

Okey drops my hand only to poke my torso. "Hm. Matt, honey, you always were a sucker for big muscles and hairy chests. Then again, who isn't? He's probably got a humongous cock too. Well, if y'all are going to visit, we might as well do this right. I do believe we're standing in need of cocktails. Will blood orange cosmopolitans do? Seems apropos for the company."

"Y'got any light beer?" Matt says. "Or moonshine?"

"Peasant. I do not. However, I do have cheese straws and sausage balls. Baked 'em today. I also have ambrosia salad and a pineapple upside-down cake."

"Hot damn." Matt rubs his belly. "I'll take any and all of that. I'd forgotten what a fine cook you are."

"And I'd forgotten how much fun it is to feed you bears. Y'all are so appreciative, and y'all sure know how to eat. My drag-queen sisters are always watching their weight, trying to look like toothpicks, picking at goddamn melon and yogurt. Personally, I think a man wants a girl to have some meat on her bones. A girl not unlike myself. Come along, ursines."

Okey leads us inside, through a foyer and on into a den full of scented candles, crammed-full bookshelves, and comfortable-looking furniture. "Y'all have a seat, and I'll be right back. I have my reputation as a premier Huntington hostess to live up to," Okey says, disappearing into the kitchen.

We settle onto the couch. "Man, I was afraid he'd send us packing," Matt says, squeezing my knee.

"I think he's too much of a devotee of the Earth Goddess and a fan of a certain tasty bear I know to do that. I just hope he has some ideas about what to do about the Lovecraftian blob."

Soft music starts up in the sound system. In another minute, Okey's returned with a silver platter bearing china plates, silverware, a pitcher of drinks, and three martini glasses. He's placing it on the coffee table when he sees my stricken face.

"Oh, Lord. My grandmother's silver. Force of habit. I always bring it out for company. I'm sorry. How rude. I'm so embarrassed. I've never served one of y'all before."

Okey hurriedly places pitcher, glasses, and plates on the table, takes the platter back into the kitchen, then returns with a wooden cutting board upon which rest cut-glass bowls of snacks and tableware that's steel, not silver.

"That's better, isn't it?" he says, doling out tidbits and pouring out drinks. When he offers me a plate, I shake my head.

"The drink's more than enough."

"First bear I ever met who turned down my cooking. I guess you don't have to diet. Lucky monster. So, tell me about this demon and how I can help."

Matt takes a sip of his drink and pops a sausage ball into his mouth. "Okay, so, Derek has a friend in Ohio, Cynthia. She's the one I told you about, the clairvoyant who sends Derek prophetic dreams, the one who warned him about my potential heart attack and indicated that we needed magical help. She's the reason I came to you for the lapis amulet."

I pick up a cheese straw and feed it to Matthew before taking a sip of my drink. "I met with Cynthia just a few days ago. She has occult contacts that are too timorous to do more than advise us, but they indicated that the demon's name is Aldinach, that a ceremonial magician must have evoked him, and that a charm like the one you gave Matt could help, if you have the power of a coven behind you, and I know you do."

"Tell me what you know about Aldinach," Okey says, face full of trepidation and disgust.

"Aldinach's a living metaphor for mountaintop removal: its avatar, its embodiment. It's a shambling gray waste devouring the mountains' green and leaving poisonous dung behind. It's a chemical shit-heap, to be blunt. An ambulatory coal-slurry pool. Are you willing to help us? I should warn you: siding with us might be dangerous."

Okey tops off our glasses. "Let me cogitate." He strides off to the kitchen, returning with china bowls of ambrosia and a big plate of cut cake.

"Hallelujah," Matt mumbles. "Damn, Okey, you're going all out. Some of my favorite sweets."

"Honey, I always did love to see you eat. It does my heart good. Mr. Monster, as to your question, *hell*, yes, I'll help, and so will my coven. We're stewards of the Earth Mother, are we not, Wiccans and pagans alike? If we won't fight for Gaia, who will? Plus I won't tolerate any kind of sticky horror or malicious magic trying to hurt my little bear-brother here. I'll do some research on this demon in just a little bit, but already I'm thinking we should use something like the charm I gave Matt and charge it with...."

Okey pauses, frowning. "We Wiccans don't do much blood-magic. Though it's very powerful, it's unpredictable. We hold all life sacred, so to use enough blood to charge the amulet with sufficient force to rip that nasty hell-slime apart, we'd have to sacrifice critters, and I hate to do that, no matter how good the cause, 'cause they're children of the Goddess just as much as we are. Maybe you should talk to this Voodoo lady who's a friend of mine...."

"No, Cynthia's occultists seemed sure that your coven could do the job. What if.... When Matt brought me the lapis and told me about the ritual you'd used, I gave it my own blood, and in my blood theoretically resides the power of those I've fed upon. The stone heated up, steamed, and absorbed all the blood."

"What? Really?"

"Yes. What if I were to take the amulet with me to a great convocation of my kind—*draugar*, my Norse maker calls us—and convince them to add their blood to the charm?"

"Lord, I don't know. Vampire blood? I'd have to be present to be sure that—"

"That convention on Mackinac Island?" Matt says, spooning up ambrosia. "At that fancy hotel you told me about?"

Okey draws in a sharp breath. "Mackinac Island? Do you mean *Grand* Hotel?"

I nod. "One of the oldest vampires I know, a Roman aristocrat, is presiding over the convocation, and it's in that hotel. Do you know it?"

"Do I *know* it? Darling, I've been dying to go there all my life, 'cept it's so goddamn expensive, who could? Why, that's where Miss Jane Seymour and Mr. Christopher Reeve filmed *Somewhere in Time*! One of my favorite films. So romantic. A classic!"

Okey rises, rummages through a shelf of CD's, and pops one into the sound system. A poignant piano tune fills the house.

"I've read so much about that hotel, dreaming I'd go there one day. It's fabulously expensive. Everything's just as elegant as elegant can be. They have a very strict dress code. After six thirty p.m., men have to wear suits and ties—"

Matt groans. "Oh man, does that mean I'd have to take off my work boots and baseball caps?"

"Well, certainly. You can't go there looking like a rube. Especially with that redneck Rebel cap."

"I *am* a rube," Matt sighs wearily. "I *am* a redneck. You know that. Anyone who doesn't admire Lee and Jackson can just go *fuck* themselves."

"So belligerent. Are you drunk already? Are them pink sissy drinks a'gettin' to you? I can see you in Pickett's Charge, slumping onto the field of Southern valor with a bullet in your head. What useless bullshit. You butch boys just seem determined to die."

"You're the guy who carries a brick in his purse, bud."

"True. And that one time you and I were jumped by nasty rednecks, that brick was mighty useful. Though you, lil' thang that you are, did help me kick their—"

"Yes, I did, though you did a lot more damage than I could. But watch it! *I'm* a redneck. Don't use the word that way."

"Sorry, honey. By the Goddess, you've gotten touchy. 'Jumped by nasty, uh, bigots,' is that better? The War Between the States is long over, and, speaking of Lee and Jackson, I don't see why you butch Southern boys can't get over it."

"'Cause we got our *asses* kicked," Matt growls. "*That's* why we can't git over it. Don't *fucking* tell me to git *over* it!"

"Oh, shit, here we go. The Rebel rant."

"You're goddamn right. Look here now. The Rebel flag—"

"Honey, my last husband—of two weeks—raved much the same. Back to the present. Back to pineapple upside-down cake. Back to Grand Hotel. Their fancy website says that 'ladies must wear their finery,' and, mercy, I have soooo much finery I've never gotten to wear. Mr. Mahnnnnnnnnnn-ster, are you going to that place?"

"I am. Very soon, at that. Marcus, my Roman friend, told me to bring any companions I wanted, that he'd treat us all to several days on the island."

"Treat you? He'd pay?"

"Yes. He's fabulously wealthy, to use your adverb. Matt, would you like to come?"

"Uhhhmmm, naw. Sounds too hoity-toity for an ole country boy like me."

"Honey, are you mad? You'd look so handsome all cleaned up in a suit and tie."

"A tie? Ugh. Fuck a tie. Just 'cause I can clean up doesn't mean I want to."

Okey fills up my glass, then takes my hand. "Mr. Monster...."

"That's Laird Monster to you," Matt snickers, in between bites of cake. "Derek's daddy was a Scottish laird."

"Matt, 'laird' isn't really a title. It just means someone who owns—"

Matt nudges me. "Don't spoil my fun, honey. Everyone loves a title. Your daddy owned a castle and estate in Scotland, right? He was the chief of his clan, right?"

"Really? How impressive," Okey says, sipping his drink. "Then you might wear a kilt and tuxedo jacket?"

"I might. In fact, I intend to."

"Derek looks mighty sexy in a kilt. You should see him."

"I'm sure he does. Laird Monster, would you escort a grand lady to Grand Hotel?"

"You want to go to a *vampire* convention?" says Matt. "We had to beg you to let Derek in the damn door."

"You did call me a crab louse in human form," I remind Okey.

"We just got off on the wrong foot is all." Okey bats his eyes and purses his lips, then breaks off laughing. "I'm serious. Sweet-talking aside, I'd love to go with you. If you're really going to try to charge an amulet with vampire blood, I should be there to oversee the process. Unless y'all have your own vampire witch?"

"I seriously doubt it."

"So does that mean I can go?"

I smile. "Yes, it does. You are formally invited to accompany us to Grand Hotel. I like you, Mr. Okey. A lot. You're funny and ferocious, and you obviously love Matt. I know you're juberous about my kind, but I still think we're going to be fast friends."

"See? I told you y'all'd get along," Matt says, topping off his own glass.

"I must warn you, though. You're not likely to be a very popular addition to the convocation. Witches make vampires very nervous. I'll need to get permission from Marcus for you to come, and I'll need to protect you, in case there are any young hotheads who object to your presence."

"Oh, horrors! I might die? Is it worth the risk?"

"You'll be a guest of Marcus Colonna, and you'll be escorted by Derek Maclaine. The risk is minimal to nothing, I assure you."

"Well, shit," Matt groans. "Really? Okay, if that's the way it's gonna be, then I gotta go too. To help watch over you and keep you company."

"And join me for sumptuous meals in the fancy dining room while the fanged fiends sleep? Drink stiff cocktails on the grand porch, get gently stewed, and watch the summer light fade? Stroll through the lawns and the cedar woods like Mr. Christopher Reeve and Miss Jane Seymour?"

Matt's face lights up. "Yeah. All that might even be worth having to put on goddamn dress clothes."

"You'll both be fine, guys," I assure them. "You'll be under my protection. I'm going to ask Cynthia to attend too, and no one's fool enough to fuck with the two of us. She can be as ruthless as I am. But one thing. Okey, you'll be expected to wear a suit and tie. You're not a woman."

Okey's face falls. "Well, fuck. Fuck, fuck, fuck! I already had a series of exquisite ensembles planned. So close and yet so far!"

"Unless…."

"Unless what, Mr. Monster? Er, Laird Monster? Er, my sweet, handsome friend Derek?" Okey clasps his hands in suspense. "Tell me!"

"Unless I can convince the humans there to overlook your outrageous and unseemly cross-dressing."

Matt lifts his glass to me. "Derek's mighty good with the hypnotic stuff. Glamouring, enthralling, mesmerizing, compelling…whatever you call it, it works."

"Also, I seriously doubt that hotel personnel would dare accost one of Marcus's guests. He goes there annually, and the vampire convocation occurs there every three or four years, contributing significantly to the hotel's coffers."

"Oh, mesmerism would be wonderful. Then I can wear what I please?"

"Yep," I say. "I'm curious to see what you come up with."

"I'll be enchanting, I promise. Will you boys dance with me, if there's a band?"

"Hell, yes," Matt says.

"Hell, yes," I say. "I haven't danced with an elegant drag queen since Paris in the thirties."

"So we're set," says Matt, "except I gotta buy dress clothes. Uck."

"Guess so," I say, smirking. "Matt's idea of dressing up is wearing a shirt with denim overalls instead of going bare-chested. He's a hopeless hillbilly."

"Bullshit. You may be a laird, but you're just as much of a hillbilly as I am," Matt says, taking another bite of cake, then pointing his fork at me. "As I recall, *you* were the one strutting around the house all bare-chested in overalls, just a few days ago."

"True. I'm teasing you. You're hot no matter what you wear, and you know it."

Okey titters. "I gotta admit, for a mixed marriage, y'all are pretty cute together. So, where y'all living these days?"

"Way out in Pendleton County," Matt says. "Derek has this great farmhouse near Spruce Knob that looks out over German Valley."

"Sounds real pretty. How long a drive?"

"From here?" Matt rubs his chin. "About four and a half hours."

"And can you travel during the day?"

"I have a travel crate in the back of our van," I say. "In the day, I sleep and Matt drives."

"Well, tonight I need to do some research on that demon, but…when are you going to Grand Hotel, Laird Killer-in-a-Kilt?"

"Nice nickname. As soon as possible. Within the next few nights. I think the convocation's about to begin. Matt can drive. We'll pick up Cynthia on the way to Michigan."

Okey sips his drink. "I never, ever thought I'd ever say this to a vampire, but…why don't y'all stay over? Tomorrow, Derek can snooze in my basement in his box, and Matt and I can indulge in a perilously fattening bruncheon at the nearest Tudor's Biscuit World, then hit Macy's in the Barboursville Mall and get him all spiffed up."

"That's real kind of you, Mr. Okey," says Matt. "Derek?"

"It is kind. Let's do that. In fact, Matt, use that credit card of ours to buy not only your clothes but a new gown for Okey. As fancy and costly as you can find."

"Really?" Okey gasps.

"Yes, indeed."

"Oh, most generous night horror! I'll pick out something appropriately Gothic. Then, after our frenzied shopping spree, Matt can drive us all up to your mountaintop eyrie and y'all can regale me with a romantic evening in the Hirsute Hideaway…and after that we can get on the road to Mackinac Island, listening to the *Somewhere in Time* soundtrack all the way. Mercy, how rude. I just invited myself. Can you butch boys tolerate a delicate drag queen in your man-cave bear-den?"

"Delicate? Shit," says Matt. "You could beat my ass, and you know it."

"My ass too, if I were still human."

"It does pay to be a big girl when ungentlemanly types are around. Do I need to bring that brick in my purse?"

"Wouldn't hurt," I say, chuckling. "You may be a drag queen, but you're as much of a warrior as we are, aren't you?"

"Hell, honey, my first role model was Wonder Woman. Some of the fiercest warriors I've ever known have been drag queens. We gotta be. Let's us have another round of drinks, and y'all tell me everything about this demon. Then I'll get to my books and call my coven over to help me charge two amulets, one for you to protect your mountain getaway and another to use against Satan's Slime-mold…though, come to think of it, you might want to make yourself scarce, Laird Hungry-Horror-in-the-Night, at least while my fellow witches are here. I don't feel like expending hours of energy trying to explain why I've agreed to help a vampire."

"Probably a good idea. I haven't fed tonight anyway. Any hot cubs in the neighborhood?"

"Oh, my. Are you asking me to be an accomplice to devilish bloodletting?"

"He won't hurt anyone. Just a few sips, right, honey?"

"Yep. I promise."

"You'd better promise," Matt says, thumping my arm. "I have a welcome-home present planned for you, so don't spoil your appetite tonight."

"Excellent." I can't resist flashing a fang. "Then I will definitely be abstemious this evening."

Okey produces a theatric shudder. "Lord. Teeth like a grizzly bear. What that present is, I don't want to know. Check out Rotary Park, Laird Tear-You-A-New-One. There're always boys cruising there. At any rate, back to the infinitely more attractive topic of fashion. Tomorrow, the magic of Macy's will transform this surly, backward, scruffy, unsophisticated, rough-edged ridge-runner of a ruffian into—"

"Please," drawls Matt. "I prefer 'hick,' or 'hayseed.'"

"Or rump-ranger? As I was saying, Macy's and the fine taste of this here chic queen, Ilene Over—"

"That's still your drag name? I love it."

"Stop interrupting, brash bear-boy. Tomorrow, come hell or high water—"

"Or lots of sulking and complaining," I add.

"No doubt." Okey grins at me, then returns his gaze to Matt. "Tomorrow, you will become a stylish Southern gentleman worthy of escorting a grand queen to the dance floor."

Groaning, Matt drains his glass. "Oh, Jesus, I'm screwed. Hand here another piece of that cake."

CHAPTER THIRTY-SIX

I wake to a man's husky grunting and delicious scents: armpit sweat, crotch tang, ass-crack musk. My fangs emerge. I lick my lips and open my eyes.

I'm in my travel crate, which, I can sense, rests in the crypt room at Mount Storm. Good to be home. Even better, when I push open the crate's lid, to discover the source of those arousing stimuli.

It's my newest thrall, Zac, lying on the floor. He's naked, struggling feebly, his green eyes full of a confused mixture of discomfort and desire. His hairy torso and well-muscled upper arms are trussed up in complicated webs of black rope knotted in the style of Japanese bondage. He's lying on his side, hands tied behind his back, wrists bound to ankles, body bent into the painful geometry of a hogtie. His erect cock and balls are bound up as well. Around a bit-gag, he mumbles my name. Drool drips from the side of his mouth, puddling on the floor.

"Great Eros," I sigh, standing. "Aren't you pretty? My own hairy Hercules, my own roped and gagged demigod." Bending, I stroke his saliva-sodden beard and then his pulsing hard-on. Zac gives me a pained grin and thrusts against my palm.

"Hey, honey," says Matt. He's naked as well, leaning against the crypt's open door and stroking his hard-on. "Zac there's been giving me quite the show for the last half-hour, straining and groaning and rolling around. Like the fancy rope work?"

"Woof! I sure do." I tug at the ropes digging into Zac's plump pecs. "Tight. Beautifully done. How'd you learn this?"

"While you were away, I was reading those hot, hot comics by that Japanese manga artist, Gengoroh Tagame, and decided I'd study some *shibari*, some *kinbaku-bi* sites online. I convinced ole Zac here to be my guinea pig while I learned the ropes…literally. I picked it up pretty fast."

"You surely did. *Kinbaku-bi*…'the beauty of tight binding.'" I finger Zac's nipples, both of which bulge inside diamond-shaped frames of taut cord. "Just the kind of aesthetic I most appreciate."

"So, welcome home! You ready to take this ass-virgin for a ride?"

"Hell, yes," I say, stripping off the clothes I've been wearing since that night at Club Diversity. "Zac, you up for that?"

Zac grunts, flexes his big arms, arches his ass, and nods.

"He should be ready. Last few days, I've been breaking him in with lots of butt-eating, finger-fucking, and dildos. I think he's pretty eager to take something bigger up that chunky rump of his."

"Then let's get to it." I free my thrall's ankles, haul him to his feet, and propel him down the hallway to the dungeon room. There I push him belly-down over the paddle bench and secure him to it with more rope.

"There you go," I say, ever so lightly stroking his furry buttocks with my palm. "Feel good? You sure look good."

Zac gazes back at me, bites down on the rubber bit buckled between his teeth, releases another long string of viscous drool, and nods.

"Fuck, I love it when a gagged guy slobbers. Matt, honey, open him up now."

"Gladly." Matt kneels behind Zac, spreads his rear cheeks apart, and buries his face in the bound man's fuzzy butt-crack.

"Ummmm mmm!" Matt enthuses. "Tasty, tasty. I could do this all night."

I lean against the wall, relishing the sight of two burly bears conjoined in such a delicious manner. Zac grunts, nods, and sighs, pushing his ass back against Matt's face.

Matt takes his sweet time. Finally, he smacks his lips and stands. "Okay, Zac, K-Y time."

Humming, Matt applies a good dollop. Pushing a lubed forefinger up Zac's asshole, he begins a slow probing. Zac humps the bench, lifts his head, and moans. Matt adds another finger. Zac rocks back, bound hands clenching. Matt thrusts steadily in and out, then adds a third finger and works Zac's hole a few minutes more.

"You ready, bud?" Matt says, pulling Zac's roped genitals back between his thighs, rubbing his cockhead and licking it.

"His dick's hard and his butt seems nice and open," I say, lubing myself. "Looks like he's more than ready to me. What do you say, Zac? Want my dick to be the first inside you? Want your new Daddy to plow you now?"

"Hehhhhhhh, yehh."

"'Hell, yes?' Right answer."

Matt moves aside, stroking his own prick as I take my place behind Zac, position the tip of my cock against his moistened butthole, and push. Zac flinches, nods, and shifts the angle of his ass. Gradually, I slide inside.

"Uhhhh. Ohhh, yes. Outstanding," I groan, gripping Zac's thick hips. He whimpers, trembling against me.

You all right, boy? You hurting?

Zac nods. *A little, boss. That's all right. I've wanted this real bad. Please go slow at first, but please don't stop. Pound my ass as hard and as long as you want.*

The perfect surrender of a slave, one of the Old Gods' greatest gifts. If only the entire cosmos were as accommodating.

Good boy. Good boy. I bend over, embracing his trussed torso and picking up my prick-pace. I nuzzle his neck and pierce it, taking shallow sips.

"Can I plow him too? Once you're done?" Matt stands in front of us, jacking himself, rubbing his cock against Zac's beard and bit-gagged lips.

"Most definitely," I mumble, mouth full of Zac's brimming blood. "After we both come inside him, we're going to string him up and clamp his tits. Then you're going to flog his butt and back black and blue, then jack him till he's good and hard, and I'm going to suck him off. Sound good, Zac?"

"Uhhh huh," Zac mutters. *Do whatever you want, boss. Now I live for you.*

Zac's very wobbly. He's difficult to dress and even more difficult to guide up the cellar stairs and into the den. He rubs his recently pummeled butt, plops heavily onto the couch and, smiling with contentment, closes his eyes.

"Oh, Lord. Dare I ask?" Okey enters from the kitchen, bearing an umbrella-topped cocktail. "The latest in a long series of sex crimes?" He's dressed in a pink and tangerine caftan, with a white turban and fuzzy pink slippers. Timmy follows him, carrying a blender full of frozen drinks.

"Chips. Onion dip. Crab dip," Timmy says, pointing to three bowls on the coffee table. "Dive in. Dinner'll be ready shortly."

"'That one's a natural-born cook," Okey says, nibbling on a chip. "We've been picking delicately on his sumptuous snacks while you sex-crazed hooligans noisily entertained yourselves in the basement."

"Oh, hell, you could hear us?" Matt groans.

"Honey, all that hollering? Why, the walls shook! The china tinkled! The rafters rattled! I feared y'all were going to bring the house down around us. It was a seismic event of the first order of magnitude."

"It was indeed. Mr. Okey, you *are* a drag queen," I say, studying his outfit. "I thought it was just a shocking rumor."

"Honey, please. It's 'Ilene Over,' and you don't know shocking. Later, I'm gonna give you ursines a fashion show in preparation for my glorious debut at Grand Hotel. What happened to this poor boy?"

"We leather guys get a little rough sometimes," Matt says, patting Zac's shoulder. "He's fine, I swear."

"You *undead* get a little rough," says Okey, peering at the raw wound on Zac's throat. "Ain't y'all going to bandage that? It's enough to put a lady off her dinner."

"I'll handle it," says Matt, heading for the bathroom.

"There'll be no folks being put off dinner," Timmy says. "I've worked too damn hard to make a good meal to celebrate our daddy's homecoming." He squeezes my shoulder and kisses me on the cheek. "I heard you made it to Hiiii-wahhhh-yah, sir. Lucky bastard. I made piña coladas just for you. I know you don't care about vittles, but—"

"*I* do," blurts Matt, returning with hydrogen peroxide and a box of Band-Aids. "I just worked up a major appetite. What's for dinner?"

"I made macaroni salad, Hawai'ian style," says Donnie, ambling into the den. "*Lots* of mayonnaise. And coconut pudding. Welcome back, Derek!"

"I made *kālua* pork," Timmy adds.

"Sounding better and better. I'm damn glad I bought y'all that new cookbook for Christmas," says Matt, doctoring Zac's neck.

"Thanks, man," Zac mumbles drowsily.

"You have quite the household," Okey says. "A bear ranch of sorts. Do they all…?"

I take a seat beside Zac. "Butt's sore," he mutters, resting his head on my shoulder.

I squeeze Zac's knee. "Do they all provide for my appetites, both gastronomic and erotic? Yes."

Okey adjusts his turban. "Greedy monster. Not a triad or a quartet, but a…quintet? All of you burly bears too. A scandalous case of demoniac debauchery, I'd say."

"A sextet, actually," Matt says. "Where's Nate? He's our security otter, er, officer."

"He should be back from Harrisonburg any minute," Timmy says. "He went down to get more ammunition, just in case those Alpha fuckers get any ideas about messing with us up here."

"Gay gun-toters?" Okey drawls. "I can just see y'all using homophobes' testicles for target practice. Could you ferocious boys arrange a show like that for a lady's amusement?"

"We might have to do that," I say, snickering. "So how's Nate's arm?"

"A *lot* better," Matt says. "Out of the sling. He's really taking his new job here seriously. He's been borrying Zac's Jeep and driving down to Brandywine for target practice, trying to get his trigger finger back in shape. After what Alpha did to him, he's pretty damn pissed. He's also studying on explosive devices and such like. If they do decide to come up here, he'll make 'em regret it."

"Good to hear," I say. "Okey, Nate used to—"

"*Ilene*, honey. Please. You're welcome to call me 'Ilene' in or out of drag."

"Sorry. Ilene. Ilene, Nate used to work as a security guard for Alpha Coal, but then—"

Matt interrupts. "But then Derek enthralled him, and—"

Ilene frowns. "Enthralled? Are all these boys hypnotized?"

"No. Not presently. I've used my mental abilities on all of them, even Matt, to varying degrees, and my bite gives me control over them, if I so choose, and makes them devoted to me. But all of them, except Zac here…." I pause to stroke his hair. "He's new. He's adjusting. I'm still manipulating his will somewhat. But the others, I gave them their willpower back long ago. They're free to come and go as they please."

"We're all glad to be here, Mizz Ilene," Donnie says, scooping up crab dip. "Derek's our Daddybear. He takes care of us. He helps us with money. He protects us."

"All of us have been real lonely in the past," adds Timmy, heading for the kitchen. "This here's a true community. That clan Derek's always talking about. He's given us all a home and a family."

"Well, Laird Orgy-on-the-Mountain, I guess you're a sexual predator and a sexual Samaritan too. You boys do look like a happy lot. Would one of you fuzzy gentlemen fix a lady a plate? And pour her another drink? Oh, here comes your sixth, I do believe."

The back door opens and in comes Nate, toting a box of ammunition. He stops abruptly, staring at Ilene. "Uh, howdy. Ma'am?"

"Well, hello, you must be Officer Otter. Aren't you a long, tall drink of water?"

"Nate," I say, standing, "this is Mizz Ilene. She's the witch who made the amulet for Matt, and now she's made one to protect Mount Storm. She's going to help us against Alpha."

"Well, great. Anybody who'll help us blow Alpha into bits is pure gold in my book." Nate puts the box in the corner before bounding over to me to exchange vigorous hugs. "No Hawai'ian tan?" he says.

"No. A couple of brawny island meals, though."

"Dinner's ready," Timmy yells from the kitchen.

"Oh, good." Ilene finishes her cocktail. "This queen is peckish to the point of peevishness. Shall we, Matt's Muscular Monster?"

"Certainly." I rise and take Ilene's hand.

Matt shakes Zac awake. "C'mon, buddy. Time to chow down. I could eat a horse."

I sit back at the head of the table, sipping Pinot Noir and watching everyone eat, laugh, chat, and dive into second helpings. I'm feeling fortunate to have such companions, but I'm feeling melancholy too, remembering their mortality, wondering how each of them is fated to leave me.

"I cherish every one of you," I say, as soon as Donnie's doled out the coconut pudding. "I'm glad we're all here together."

"Uh, oh, Derek's about to get serious," Matt says, lowering his fork.

"Only because the next few weeks will be dangerous. After we return from Michigan, hopefully with some of Marcus's associates, I intend to go after Alpha. I'm going to raid the Sodeski compound again and use Ilene's charm to try to destroy the demon."

"We wolves got your back, Derek," Donnie says. "Me and Rebekah, we'll tear 'em up."

"You sweet little thing," Okey sighs. "I can't believe you're a werewolf. I need to get to my books. Maybe I can help you lift that curse."

"Not till Alpha's dead," Donnie says. "I wanna be useful, and I'm loads more useful as a wolf. So, you *are* gonna attack during the full moon, right?"

"Yes. There's a full moon on the first of next month. That's when we'll strike. Ilene, do you think your coven can conduct a ritual that night and send us what protective energies you can?"

"Highlander from Hell, do you even need to ask? Of course we will."

"What about us?" asks Matt. "Timmy and Nate and Zac and me? Cain't we help?"

I shake my head. "You all are human. Alpha nearly killed two of you already. I don't want y'all getting near that battle."

"Derek, you know me better'n that," Matt grumbles. "I'm the reason you're in the war with Alpha. I ain't staying at home doing nothing."

"Me neither," Nate blurts. "I'm a good shot. You know that. Those Alpha guys tried to murder me, and I want to get even. Surely I can help take out some of Sodeski's guards. Hell, some of them might be the very guys who buried me alive."

"I'm a good shot too, and I've been known to kick some ass," says Timmy. "I'm a good boxer and I know some karate. Let us come along."

"Me too," says Zac, flexing a big arm. "C'mon, boss. Think about it. God knows I know my way around the Sodeski compound."

"You stubborn, plucky little shits. All right. I'll think about it."

"You damn well better," says Matt, glowering. "I'm tired of you taking all the risks. Donnie, bud, cut me more of that jiggly pudding."

"Honey, they done ganged up on you!" Okey exclaims. "I guess you'll feel obliged to paddle 'em all now. So when are we leaving for Michigan?"

"It's a very long drive. Twelve hours. Tomorrow night, I think. We'll need to pick Cynthia up, then get to Mackinac City. You two can take the ferry over. She and I will fly over after dusk. With as many vampires as are likely to be arriving for the convocation, the skies above Lake Huron might be thick with bats."

"Oh, Law! Bats?" Ilene clutches her turban, as if a hook-taloned night-creature were already tugging at it. "Why can't you turn into a pretty luna moth or a hummingbird?"

"Hell, Okey, urm, Ilene. Nothing manly about those kinds a' critters," Matt says around a spoonful of pudding.

"Well, sometimes manly is nasty. Laird Needle-Teeth, you tell your leather-winged friends to stay out of my wigs. Or I'll fill my atomizer with holy water and spray it in their eyes."

"'Laird Needle-Teeth?' I love it. Keep it up with the titles. Goddess knows we need the comic relief. As for my *draugr* compatriots, I'll do my best to warn them, but you should know that holy water won't work. Now, I guess if you steeped rowan blossoms in alcohol...." I make a face. "Ouch."

"Recipe duly noted. Back to our perilous and romantic adventure in the Grand Hotel and the swarm of undead horrors soon to congregate there. Mr. Matt and I can take turns driving...and stopping for toothsome treats at roadside diners and truck stops. Right now, I'm standing in need of another sip...perhaps a tasteful liqueur served up in a lovely old glass. Or some sophisticated sherry or port. Y'all got any of that, Hell-Laird's Hairy Hillbilly Harem?"

"We do," says Matt, rising. "Let me clean the table first."

"I'll do that later," I say. "Fetch the Empress of All Things Elegant her cordial."

Ilene slaps my arm. "Now you're doing it, Sultan of Satanic Satyriasis."

"I am indeed, Princess of Pornographic Pulchritude."

"Flattery will get you everywhere. If you think I'm pulchritudinous now, wait'll you see me in my new gown."

"So the shopping jaunt was a success?"

"Shit," grunts Matt, taking a liqueur glass from the corner cupboard. "It sure was. A lengthy success. We were in Macy's for two hours. I about went out of my mind."

"Oh, we got Matt some dress shirts and camp shirts and ties and slacks and shorts and suit jackets. Even some precious boat shoes to go with the shorts."

"Some prissy boat shoes. With ridiculous little socks. I look like an idiot in them. If you'll let me wear my cowboy boots with the dress pants, why the fuck cain't I wear my hiking boots with the shorts?"

"Hiking boots at Grand Hotel? Heaven forfend. Fashion is esoterica the hopeless rustic ne'er can comprehend. You just take my word for it. You'll look more stylish on Mackinac Island than you've ever looked in your life."

"For the last time in my life, I hope."

"Maybe not. If I ever find a goddamn husband, you can wear one of those outfits to my wedding. Why don't we all retire to the parlor—"

"The den," corrects Matt. "Here's your drink, madame. I hope black sambuca will do."

"It will. Why don't we all retire to the *parlor* and Matt can model his new clothes for us?"

"The hell I will. Man, you drag queens wear me out."

"How about you model your new gown, Mizz Ilene?" I ask, piling up emptied plates. "You found a nice one?"

"Jesus fucking Christ, did I ever! I mean…why, yes, kind sir, I did. A black and red number. It was obscenely expensive, but Matt said you wouldn't mind."

"I don't, I assure you. I've been amassing wealth for nearly three centuries. So, do we get to see it?"

"Yeah!" says Timmy.

"C'mon," Nate urges.

"No! You must wait. It will be part of my much-applauded debut on Mackinac Island. You, Laird Fatal Fangs, must live in bitter suspense until then. The rest of you bearded, beautiful brutes may see it upon my return from that land of lapping lakes and lavish living. Perhaps a coming-out banquet is in order?"

"Coming-out party? I could do with that," mutters Zac. "Before I met Derek, I didn't have the guts to admit I wanted men. Then he kissed me on the neck and it was all clear as a bell."

"A therapist, a social worker, a darksome wonder, all rolled into one thick-pec'ed package! You're the bikers' messiah, whose touch can raise the dead! Derek, honey, you need to go talk to those poor brain-damaged Christians who think they can cure us and work your charms on them."

"That might be fun," I say, licking a canine tooth. "Though I think I'd do a little more than talk to them. Matt, did you see the gown?"

Matt pours two glasses of Scotch, hands one to me, and sips the other. "I did. He…she looks like an evil queen, a Maleficent, who used to wrestle for a living: glamorous and intimidating at the same time. You should've seen the salesgirl's face when Ilene came outta that changing room."

"True. Poor provincial thing nearabout had an apoplectic fit. So no glimpsing of the Supreme Gothic Gown for you boys tonight. However, I do have a sky-blue dress I brought along…and a red, sequined number…and innumerable accessories."

"Hell, let's see 'em," says Zac, shifting uncomfortably in his chair. "Long as I can sit on the couch."

"I'd love to see a fashion show." Nate stands. "Let's do it."

"Then so we shall." Ilene stands as well. "Y'all get settled in the parlor and put on some sexy music I can shimmy to. Officer Otter, would you help me get dressed?"

"You bet," Nate says, taking her hand.

"Go on, guys. I'll be there in a minute," I say. "Let me snuffle a little night air first."

Noisy with excitement, everyone heads into the den after Ilene. Good to enjoy some fun and boisterous camaraderie. A pause before the storm, I fear.

I open the French doors and step out onto the back patio, where pots of night-blooming jasmine and nicotiana fill the night with fragrance. I sip my Scotch, then step off the patio and stride into the center of the standing stones. There, I pray.

Dark Mother in all your forms—Corn Maiden, Madame Pele, Moon Goddess, Cerridwen, Hecate, Hertha, Habondia, Freya, and the Morrigan—and Dark Father in all your forms—Horned One, Lord of the Forests and the Mountains and the Beasts, King of the Rising Sun and the Savage Storm, Eros, Cernunnos, Thor, Frey, Battle-Father Odin—help me protect my people. Give me the strength, the luck, and the cunning to smash my enemies and end them forever. Give me the allies I need to triumph, to save your sacred land from further desecration. Guard my family from harm. Let me survive the coming battle. Let me survive to defend my clan as long as Norn-necessity demands.

I gaze out into the woods and up at the sky. Then I kneel, take another sip of Scotch, and pour the rest onto the ground.

"Get in here, honey," Matt shouts from the patio. "Ilene's gonna start in just a little bit."

"Coming." I tap my breastbone three times, then head toward the house.

Chapter Thirty-seven

The hotel's a wonder, a bulk of white columns looming over the island. Cynthia and I approach slowly, absorbing the view.

Mackinac Island, set in Lake Huron between the upper and lower peninsulas of Michigan, is thickly wooded, with a little town lining the southern edge. Along the docks, the lights of stores gleam, and tourists swarm the streets. Here and there, equestrians clop along, or a horse-drawn carriage. No cars are allowed on the island, which gives the place a charmingly old-fashioned atmosphere. Cynthia and I loop over the town's roofs, then flap inland, toward the white hotel at the crest of the hill.

At a little over six hundred feet, Grand Hotel's porch is the longest in the world. At one end of it, a group of vampires congregates among the three-story-tall columns. At the other end, a smaller group of humans drinks and laughs. In the center, my husbear sits in a rocking chair, sips a beer, and watches the sky.

Cynthia and I glide down onto the dark lawn below the porch. We shift, taking on human forms already dressed for the elegant setting. I'm in my kilt, dress socks and shoes, jabot, and coatee. Cynthia's wearing a man's black tux with a black shirt open at the collar.

"Quite the place," says Cynthia, sniffing one of the huge lilac bushes that bloom around us. "Don't you look dashing?"

"The same to you, perverse transvestite. Let's up to the porch. I saw Matthew waiting for us there."

I lead the way up several sets of lilac-shaded steps to the carriageway, then up onto the porch. Matt rises when he sees us, knocks back the last of his beer, steps forward and hugs me heartily.

"Figured y'all would get here right after sunset," says Matt, tugging uncomfortably on his collar. He's wearing his Macy's garb: tan dress pants, white shirt, red tie, and tan jacket. The only visual reminders of the rough-edged mountain man I love are his shaggy hair, thick beard, and black cowboy boots. "You both look mighty fine. How you been, Mizz Cynthia?"

Cynthia smiles, giving Matt a quick hug. "Devouring lovely ladies right and left. Don't you look handsome in a suit and tie?"

"Oh, ugh. This monkey suit? I feel like I'm in drag."

"I'm the one in drag," Cynthia replies, stroking the lapel of her tuxedo jacket.

"Yeah. But it looks good on you. I look like a retard."

"Hardly. I hear you've become quite the environmental crusader. I'm impressed. Derek says you've been very courageous."

"Someone had to do it." Matt shrugs. "Luckily, I've had some help from my ferocious honey here."

"You'll be getting a lot more of that kind of help, if I can convince Marcus," I say. "Where's Okey?"

"Ah, he's in his room, which is real, real nice, by the way. Between the crew of vampires"—Matt nods to the left—"and that crew of bankers who're having a convention here"—Matt nods to the right—"he's been afraid to come out in his, uh, finery. He's been waiting for you two to arrive."

"Okay," I say. "Lead the way."

Matt directs us past a line of prettily potted red geraniums, across the well-appointed parlor, and up carpeted stairs to the long corridor on the third floor. He raps on a door.

"Okey? Ilene? It's Matt, with Derek and Cynthia. You here?"

"Thank God! Come on in," is the muffled reply.

Matt opens the door, revealing a pink room with floral wallpaper and a wide view over the water. Ilene's in her turban and housecoat, face already made up, sitting by the window in an armchair. She rises as we enter.

"Laird Night Horror! Don't you look fabulous in your kilt? What a pretty tartan. And that jabot is exquisite." She steps closer to fondle the kilt fabric. "The texture of that wool...."

"I'm glad a fashionista like you approves. Ilene Over, this is Cynthia Skala. She's an old friend who's given Matt and me much help and support over the years."

"Oh, yes," Ilene says breathlessly, taking Cynthia's hand. "Matt's told me all about you! You're the nightmarish butch dyke who helped Laird Nibble-in-the-Night cut down those abominable crosses that beastly millionaire had erected all over the Mountain State. Talk about civic improvement."

"Yes, that was grand fun," Cynthia says. "And you're the witch whose talents have helped my favorite coterie of bears withstand Alpha's demon. Well done."

"This romantic weekend's my reward," says Ilene, gesturing to the lake view. "It's everything I dreamed of. The broad blue waters. The groomed horses and fancy carriages. The white columns. The lovely flowers…have you ever seen lilacs so humongous? Only one crucial thing's lacking. An escort! A protector! Will you be my escort, Laird Kilted Glory, while I promenade in my sequined beauty? Else I might be harassed by your fangéd undead or, far more horrible…by heterosexuals. And, even worse than that, bankers. Good God, who can endure their banal conversations? Or their attendant brats?"

"Yeah, it's Straight Central around here," says Matt. "At least as far as the human guests go. Ilene and I are the only queers in town, from what I can tell."

"I do believe the ferry boats have queer detectors on them," Ilene says, "which give the alarm when Our Kind appear. Most of us have probably been escorted off and sent packing. Thank God that didn't happen to us. They'd have had to remove me kicking and screaming. I was determined to walk the fabled paths where Miss Jane Seymour strolled."

"Hell, you'd have knocked the shit outta them with your brick purse," Matt drawls. "Guy as big as you, you'd have tossed anybody who gave you trouble overboard."

"Matthew Taylor! Do you think I'd descend to unladylike behavior?" Ilene stabs the air with a painted fingernail.

"In a second," Matt says. "That's one of the things I love about you."

"Damn right I would," Ilene says, clenching a fist. "It's a short-lived fool who gets between a grand drag queen and her dream. Speaking of which, do I have an escort or not? Honestly, I've been afraid to appear in public—"

"Until we got here. Yes. I understand," Cynthia says. "I doubt that many cross-dressers have graced the halls of this historic edifice, but there is, as they say, a first time for everything. Lady Ilene, I believe you have several escorts at Grand Hotel."

"You bet you do," says Matt. "Derek paid a lotta money for these damn dress clothes I have on, so I intend to strut around this hoity-toity place and show 'em how a West Virginia redneck can look when he decides to clean up. You get dressed, Ilene, and we'll all head down to the porch to take the breeze and have us some more drinks."

"And then a sumptuous feast in the grand dining room?" says Ilene, pulling a wig from the several travel cases scattered about the room. "I'm starving."

"Yep," says Matt. "Drinking. Then feasting. Then dancing. The schedule says they got a band lined up for the Terrace Room later tonight. Might as well go all out while we're here."

"Superb! All right, y'all git on out of here and give a lady time to dress," says Ilene, waving us away. "I'll call y'all when I'm ready."

Matt leads the way out. "I got a room just down the hall," he says, pausing to admire a portrait of Jane Seymour on the wall. "But I'm not sure what sort of, uh, accommodations you day-sleepers might have. D'you know how to get hold of that Marcus guy?"

"I'm sure he knows we're here," Cynthia says. "Some of his minions should appear soon."

She's right. We've no more than entered Matt's room, a spacious one decorated in forest green with another fine view over the lake, when a soft knock sounds at the door. When I open it, I suppress a snarl of lust.

"Laird Maclaine?" says the boy. He's dressed in a gray suit with white shirt and black tie, and he's one of the best-looking cubs I've ever seen.

"Wow," says Matt from over my shoulder. "Damn. Who the hell are *you*? Is there a porn convention going on here?"

The boy blushes and grins. He's around five foot eight, in his late twenties, with short dark hair, dark eyes, and a neat brown beard. Just the sort of beautiful, bashful boy I most like to hurt.

"No, sir. I do model some, but tonight, I'm here on behalf of Mr. Colonna. May I come in?"

"Hell, *yes*, you can come in." Matt moves around me to take the boy's hand and lead him into the room. "This is Derek, er, Laird Maclaine. This is Cynthia Skala. I'm Matt Taylor, Derek's partner. Who're you?"

"I'm Aidan LaFlamme, one of Mr. Colonna's employees here at Grand Hotel. He wanted me to welcome you. He, uh, chose me very specifically to, uh, serve you while you're here. I'm to make sure that you gentlemen are, uhm, provided everything you require. My colleague Tiffany has been assigned to do the same for you, Ms. Skala."

"Marcus chose you specifically?" I say, grinning.

"Serve us, huh?" Matt says, grinning.

"Ahh, uh, yes. Mr. Colonna said that I might, uh, appeal to your tastes, sirs." Aidan shuffles sheepishly. He couldn't be more adorable. Or more desirable.

"He chose accurately," I say. "Where is Marcus?"

"He's busy with preparations for tomorrow night's grand convocation, but he might be by later. Are your accommodations pleasing, Mr. Taylor?"

"Huh?" Matt shakes his head. He's been so busy ogling the boy he probably hasn't heard half of what's been said since Aidan entered the room. "Oh, yeah. Real nice. Great view. You wanna have a drink with us? Or dinner? Or a shower? There's a shower stall in the bathroom big enough for three."

Aidan flushes. "I'm up for whatever you prefer, Mr. Taylor. I do what Mr. Colonna tells me to, and he's told me to make your stay at Grand Hotel as memorable as possible. Drinks and dinner would be a pleasure. But first, Laird Maclaine and Ms. Skala, if you'll come with me, I'll show you to your sleeping quarters."

"Hurry back," says Matt, patting my butt, "and bring that boy with you. I think I'm gonna like this highfalutin hotel a lot better'n I expected…especially after all the dress clothes come off."

Aidan leads us down the hotel's central staircase, then along a short passage branching off the first-floor corridor. He unlocks a door, leads us into a tiny room, then carefully locks that door behind us. When he touches a spot on the wooden wall, the paneling slides aside, revealing an elevator. We enter it and descend a long way. When we exit, another short passage gives us access to low vaults beneath the hotel.

The long space is illuminated by many candles. Vampires of various shapes, sizes, and ethnicities, all of them stylishly dressed, stand by carved wooden coffins, conferring in groups of two or three. There must be a hundred sleeping coffins here. All the other *draugar* must be prowling the night or enjoying the hotel's many entertainments.

"Here, sir," Aidan says, pointing to an ornately carved box of dark walnut. "This is your, umm, bed of sorts. Mr. Colonna said that you might not prefer the, umm, group dormitory arrangement, so he has a private crypt arranged for you, if you would prefer."

"I would prefer. I'm sure Cynthia would as well."

"Indeed." Cynthia's nose wrinkles. "I'm not accustomed to sleeping in a sea of strangers."

"Then I'll have your two coffins moved before dawn," Aidan says. "As Mr. Colonna says, whatever pleases you is my command."

"Mr. Colonna's a true aristocrat and a superb host. This is the largest convocation I've ever attended," I say, turning to Cynthia.

"I as well. I tend to avoid such gatherings."

"Me too. Crowds make me nervous. Give me my high mountain refuge any day."

"We're both loners. Just another thing we have in common. And who is this?"

A buxom young woman in her thirties approaches us, smiling broadly. Her voluptuous figure reminds me of Cynthia's werewolf thrall, Rebekah, though this woman is Asian, with long black hair framing her angular face. She's wearing a red satin gown and a string of jade beads.

"Ms. Skala, this is Tiffany, your maidservant for your sojourn here," Aidan explains. "Mr. Colonna says to enjoy her in good health."

"Ms. Skala," Tiffany says, giving a slight bow. "This is your sleeping box. I've taken the liberty of filling it with soft fabrics perfumed with sandalwood."

Cynthia chuckles. "Normally, that would be a little too femme for me, but I'm sure to enjoy it nevertheless."

Tiffany blanches. "Oh, I'm sorry, miss. Should I—?"

"Leave it as it is, please. A little scented pampering isn't likely to dull my edges. Tiffany, would you care to join us for a drink on the porch?"

"Would you prefer to drink here, miss?" Tiffany, trembling, steps forward and exposes her neck.

"Aren't you a solicitous darling? No, no. I meant a cocktail."

"Oh." The girl's relief is apparent. She's apparently a novice when it comes to waiting on the undead. "Oh, yes, miss. That would be lovely."

"Let's all go," I say, taking young Aidan by the hand. "It should be fun, shaking up a bunch of financiers."

The moon's nearly full. It rides high above the cedar trees covering the slope below the hotel. Soon enough, when the moon's pearly circle is complete, it will be time to take my wolves and make another assault on Alpha, hopefully with a battalion of Marcus's minions at my side. For now, however, it's time to enjoy the cool evening, the scents of lilacs, the view over the lake, and a good single malt.

The far end of the porch is still busy with partying bankers, but most of the vampires at this end have dispersed. The few who remain regard us dubiously and keep their distance. I enter the Geranium Bar long enough to order drinks, which soon enough a smiling waitress carries out to us: Glenmorangie for me, a beer for Cynthia, a gin and tonic for Aidan, a white wine for Tiffany. We've settled into wicker chairs when my cell phone buzzes.

It's Matt. "Hey, honey, you still with that preeminently fuckable cub?"

I regard a smiling Aidan and lick my lower lip. "Yep. No way we're letting him get away."

"Great. Look, Ilene's ready. Will you meet us at the bottom of the stairs? In case any mesmerism's required?"

"Absolutely. What would the two of you like to drink?"

"Ummmm...." There's a quick conversation at the other end. "I'll have a beer, and Ilene'll have a daiquiri."

"Got it. See you two in a minute."

I hang up and stand. "Mizz Cynthia, I need your help for a little mass hypnotism." I squeeze Aidan's shoulder. "You keep the fetching Tiffany entertained. We'll be right back."

"Yes, sir," says Aidan. What a smile. No wonder the boy's done some modeling. If I have my way—and I certainly shall—he, Matt, and I will be starring in our very own fuck flick later tonight.

"I like that 'sir.' Keep that up," I say, stroking the boy's dark-bearded chin.

"Yes, sir," Aidan says, giving me a shy wink.

Cynthia and I enter the white-columned parlor, which sports antique furniture, ceramics, chandeliers, and thick carpets decorated with red geraniums. It's beautiful, albeit a far cry from the rustic remoteness I'm accustomed to. More to the point, it's scattered with heterosexual humans, and a very large drag queen's about to descend the stairs.

"Shall we?"

Cynthia nods.

We move slowly through the room, focusing on face after face, manipulating mind after mind. One by one, the hotel guests give us blank smiles, blink, and pause in their conversations. None of them has the willpower sufficient to resist us. Overcoming their personalities is like swatting a swarm of gnats.

We've just completed our circuit of the room when Matt appears at the bottom of the stairs. "Ready?" he says.

Cynthia nods.

Matt steps back with a flourish. "Behold!"

Ilene peeks around the corner of the staircase, then picks her way down the steps very slowly. Her pace is due to trepidation, I'm sure, not the inability to walk in high heels.

"Lord Protector of All Things Polymorphously Perverse," she says, pausing, "and you, Ferocious and Fangéd Dyke of Doom, is it safe for a lady to descend? Have you tamed those surly peasants?"

"They are tamed," says Cynthia, stepping forward and offering a hand.

"You look glorious," I say, grinning. "Come on down, madam. Your daiquiri awaits."

"Kind sir, I do believe I will," says Ilene, descending. She's dressed in a skin-tight crimson gown sparkling with sequins, a dark beehive of a wig, a rhinestone tiara with matching necklace, a black clutch purse, and slingback pumps.

Cynthia takes Ilene's hand and leads her out onto the porch. Matt and I follow. "I cannot fucking believe this," he whispers, as we head over to Aidan and Tiffany. "This is fucking priceless."

"I agree," I say, taking his hand. "Mesmerism is truly among the greatest vampiric gifts. One of the largest drag queens I've ever known just entered the lobby of one of the most conservative and refined hotels on the planet, yet the other guests continue with their vapid socializing as if nothing were amiss."

We all take seats. The waitress arrives with Matt's beer and Ilene's daiquiri. At first, the girl's wide-eyed and stammering. After a little mental rearranging, she leaves with a serene smile on her face.

"Mercy, Mr. and Ms. Monster, you certainly know to make people behave," Ilene says, satisfaction softening her voice. "This is indeed a dream come true. I can't believe I'm sitting out here in all my finery, taking in such a fabled view. Y'all ought to go into politics."

"Derek's been into several politicians," Matt says, grinning. "Once we've socked it to Alpha Coal, he's liable to be into a few more."

"A follow-up visit to Congressional leaders might be in order," I say. "Especially if they're handsome, like Aidan-cub here."

"You *are* a toothsome child," Ilene says, patting Aidan's thigh. "I shudder to think of what your fate might be tonight, considering the presence of these barbarous bears. They tend to get frightfully rough. Why, they might just split you in half."

"I'm tougher than I look," Aidan says, blushing.

"We'll take good care of him," Matt assures her with a salacious smirk. "So, Mizz Ilene, why don't you tell us all about the history of this hotel and that movie you like so much?"

"Oh, yes!" blurts Tiffany. "I'd heard a very romantic movie was filmed here, but I know nothing about it. Please do tell us, miss."

"Honey, I will. Then let's head in to dinner. The menu looks top-notch. I plan on enjoying an intimate rendezvous with a tasty hunk…of prime rib."

Ilene, Matt, Tiffany, and Aidan are full of rich food and Cynthia and I are warm on good wine by the time the meal's done. Whoever's in charge of dinner service tonight must have been instructed to segregate, for those few of us *draugar* in the dining room have been seated together in our own area, thankfully remote from the bustle of the bankers, their wives, and their noisy offspring.

"Oh, Lord, look. Precious, precious, *precious* little demitasse cups," Ilene says as we re-enter the parlor. "And a pianist. Mightn't we indulge in a little coffee before retiring for the night?"

"Coffee sounds good," says Matt, winking at Aidan. "I ain't quite ready for sleep just yet anyway. Might have to take a shower here soon."

"Take a seat, m'lady," says Cynthia. "I'll get everyone a cup."

"Out on the porch, I think," Ilene says, eyeing the room full of guests and sidling toward the door. "I know you razor-toothed night horrors are keeping these wealthy Republicans in line, but my nerves are still shot."

"I got a flask up in the room you can borry," offers Matt. "For your nerves, y'know. Medicinal."

"Oh, honey, that'd be much appreciated. A little sip or two might help me sleep."

We've settled back into wicker chairs and sofas on the porch, now blessedly free of humans, when Cynthia appears, carrying a small tray of fragrant cups. She doles them out before taking a seat.

"To the end of Alpha Coal," I toast. "To the end of its demon-slug, its sea cucumber from Hell."

"Hear, hear," says Matt, clinking his cup against mine. "Time those bastards went down."

"A sea cucumber? How loathsome!" Ilene shakes her head and adjusts her tiara. "Once I saw some dried in an Asian market. Can you imagine eating the things? They resemble engorged leeches. If your demon looks like that, Laird Ravenous Cub-Ravisher—"

Ilene's interrupted by a shrill squeal. A boy of about ten has rushed up the porch stairs, followed by his shapeless father and shabbily dressed mother, both in their forties. Now he's running around in a circle and howling while his parents, oblivious to his obnoxious behavior, chat with another couple of the same ilk.

"Little horror," Ilene mutters, sipping her demitasse. "So ill-bred these days. And look at that woman's outfit. Finery? Hardly. I can't abide a tacky paisley. I have a mind to dial up the Fashion Police. Miss Joan Rivers would be rolling over in her grave if she—"

Ilene's interrupted yet again. The child yells, "Hey, lady!" and runs toward us. "Hey, are you a lady?"

I'm about to grip the brat's mind when Cynthia nudges me in the side. "The evening's been too peaceful. Let's have a little fun."

I nod, snickering. "Yes, let's."

Up rushes the holy terror, staring and pointing at Ilene. "You're not a lady!" he shouts. "You're not a real lady! And you," he adds, pointing at Cynthia. "I think you're a lady, but you look like a man!"

He shifts his attention to my kilt. "And you. A big guy with a beard, but in a skirt." He circles us, chewing on his lips and smirking. "Guys dressed like ladies, and lady dressed like a man. Freaks, Daddy! Look! I found some freaks!"

Ilene rises, face twisted, one hand cupping her capacious bosom as if warding off a projectile. This is, I know, the kind of response she's been dreading all evening. "Hateful child!" she gasps. "How ugly."

"I'm not ugly. You are!" The rapscallion sticks out his tongue.

"That's very bad behavior, darling," Cynthia says, eyes narrowing.

The child sticks his tongue out again. "I'm not bad. You are!"

Cynthia bends down to the little monster's level and looks him in the eyes. "If you stick that tongue out again, I'm going to take it home with me," she purrs. "I've always been partial to chopped tongue for breakfast."

The child stiffens, the contempt in his face shifting into a gape of fear. He takes a deep breath and begins to bawl.

"And the noise has simply increased," Cynthia observes with a sigh.

"There's your comeuppance, you ill-mannered urchin," Ilene says, taking her seat and patting her wig. "That'll teach you to mess with a real lady, especially when she has darksome protectors around."

"Howie? What's going on?" The parents, finally aware of their spawn's shenanigans, stumble toward us.

"The portly parents approach," Cynthia says. "Would you like to field this?"

"With pleasure," I reply, putting my cup down.

"Oh, Jesus, here we go," Matt says, trying to suppress a grin. "Just don't hurt anyone, honey."

"Don't worry. Just a little advice on parenting."

I cross my arms and regard the straight couple as they shamble closer. The child rushes toward them, wrapping his arms around his mother's waist. "Those freaks said they were going to eat my tongue!" he squeals.

"Good Lord, what sort of people *are* you?" the man says, staring at the massive drag queen in the sequined gown, the lesbian in the tux, and the muscle-bear in the kilt.

"What sort of folks are *you?*" sniffs Ilene, crossing one leg over the other and sipping her cup. "Your child has the manners of a rabid hyena and the looks of one as well. Were you all brought up in a barn? You clearly were born without the benefit of my genteel upbringing."

"My son was right," the man says, brow furrowing. "You're cross-dressers and freaks. I'm going to speak to the people at the front desk and—"

"No, you're not," I say, reaching into his mind and almost immediately finding the spot where I might tamp down his will. Who knew that bankers were such an easily compelled lot? This information might come in handy later. "You're not going to do that. Do you know what you're going to do?"

"Ahhhhhh, no."

"Would you like me to tell you?"

The man gives me a slack smile. "Yes, I would. Please tell me."

"Rodney?" the wife says. "What's wrong with you?"

I'm tempted to order the man to tear his brat's tongue out himself, but anything that extreme might alienate Marcus, which would defeat the entire purpose of this visit. I must, disappointingly, settle for a less entertaining option.

"You're going to spank your child right here and now. He's a public nuisance. Do it."

"Gladly," says the man. The eagerness he evinces is far deeper than any mesmerism of mine might evoke. It seems as if I've just given him an excuse to do something he's been dying to do for ages.

"Daddy? Daddy, no!" wails the child as his father grips his arm.

"Rodney, no!"

"Ma'am, may I borrow your seat?" Rodney asks Ilene.

"Most certainly, sir," Ilene replies, rising. "Anything for a good cause."

The man sits on the sofa, hauls the brat over his knee, and begins whaling on his butt. The child screeches and the wife begs, tugging on her husband's arm.

"It's fearfully noisy all of a sudden," Ilene says, finishing her cup. "I do believe I'll avail myself of your flask, Mr. Taylor, and then call it a night."

"Good idea," says Cynthia. "Tiffany, your hair smells like jasmine. That's a lovely scent. Why don't we have a nightcap in the Cupola Bar? And then another in your quarters?"

"Yes, miss," Tiffany says, brushing satiny black hair from her face. "I would like that."

The child's howls increase in intensity. The wife screams. The husband curses. Security officers appear at the door and head in the sadly troubled family's direction.

"Derek, how about we take Mr. Aidan on up? I'm ready to git outta these hot clothes and take a nice long shower. Maybe get a little exercise in before bed?"

I'm about to answer Matt when I hear the voice in my head, a voice I haven't heard in a long time.

"You two go on up," I say, kissing Matt on the cheek. "Get started without me. I'll be up soon."

"Well, okay. Sure. I'll warm him up for you," Matt says, wrapping an arm around Aidan's shoulders. "C'mon, cub. Daddy Matt has big plans for you."

I'm stepping off the porch when three security guards seize Rodney and grapple with him. Giving the mother and child a blithe wave, I disappear into lilac-scented dark.

chapter thirty-eight

B
eyond the wide lawn of Grand Hotel, the cedar trees are thick, casting a deep gloom beneath their branches. I wander among them, listening to lake water lapping on the shore just down the hill. I stop in a clearing and look up at the stars. I close my eyes and concentrate.

You called me, sir, and I am here. Thank you for inviting my companions and me to this beautiful place. I need your help badly, as you know. Appear to me, Splendidus, Aquila Aurea. Help me vanquish my foes.

There's a long soughing of wind in the boughs, and then a rustling to my right. Before I can turn, I find myself slammed face first against a cedar trunk. A hand's clamped over my mouth and my right arm's twisted behind me.

"There you are, my hairy Enkidu, my Caledonian brute. Once again you are my captive."

Marcus. I should have known he'd ambush me. Grunting and growling beneath his hand, I strain against his grip, knowing how much he'll savor my struggles and the utter futility of them. He was turned in the time of the Caesars: he's much, much stronger than I.

"Ah, yes, you know me well," Marcus says, tightening his hold. "You know how much I love your hapless squirming. Coatee and jabot? You look like quite the gentleman, boy. Not quite the tattooed-biker look you had in Rome." He nuzzles my neck. "You came here for my help, eh?"

Yes, sir, I say telepathically, nodding against his hard hand. *These are foes I can't best without you.*

Marcus nicks my throat with a fang and presses his erection against my rump. "The convocation meets tomorrow night. They will not want to help, I think, but I can sway them. For a price. I will convince them…on two conditions."

And what are they, sir?

"You may be a mountain barbarian, but you're an intelligent one. I'll bet you can guess the first."

Marcus buries his face in my hair and breathes deep. "Ah, what a scent. Here's a hint. In return for permission to taste the delights—and the shaggy little messiahs—of Rome, you swore me your fealty. You willingly surrendered to me, to my fangs, to my appetite, to my body, to my might. You swore to submit to me…when you were in Rome. Am I correct?"

Yes, sir. You are.

"You swore me your fealty…but only when you were in Rome. I want more. Your fealty must be made complete."

Again I try to twist free. Again Marcus slams me against the tree. His fingers dig into my bearded cheek. He nips my neck again, chuckling.

"We are no longer in Rome. We are together in this resinous forest on this remote northern isle, and I want your submission again. I want your bodily surrender always. The price for my help is just that. You will submit to my hunger anywhere and anytime I want…though some musky struggling and moaning would be most welcome, some small show of resistance."

I growl, thrash against him, and try to bite his hand.

"Yes, yes, very good," Marcus says, twisting my arm until I yelp. "Exactly like that. Do we have a deal?"

He kisses my cheek and neck. The fingers pressed over my mouth stroke my beard.

"If I provide you the army you need for your crusade against the demon, you will give me your hard, undead body to use and abuse whenever I please. You will be my—how is it said?—my butt-boy, my…bitch, whenever and wherever we meet. And I will be your master."

I hesitate, leaving off my fight. *I've never made such an oath, sir. I've lived independently since Sigurd turned me.*

"I know that. Which is why this will be most delicious. Why do you hesitate, prideful one? You and I both know that you relished surrendering to me before. How you groaned and shook beneath me on the Palatine Hill, as I ravished you and drank from your neck. How honeyed was your handcuffed helplessness. You felt ecstasy, did you not?" Marcus rubs his hard cock against my rear. "Surely you remember the rapture we both felt? Have you not come to love me?"

I…I did feel ecstasy, sir. I do remember. And I…I have indeed come to love you. I treasure those nights in Rome. I've missed you since we parted.

"Then this complete fealty I mention will simply guarantee you more of the same delights, my musky Highlander. Do you agree to my terms?"

You mentioned a second condition. What is that?

"If I send my men to aid you, you must be willing to fight for me in future conflicts. You will be one of my knights. You will slay my foes, just as the little army I'll provide will drive the demon you detest back into whatever grimy oblivion from which some misguided magus summoned it."

That seems fair, sir. You fight for me; I fight for you. That's what kinship's about.

"So you agree then? To my mastery?"

I lean back against Marcus and sigh against his hand.

I must, sir. I can't defeat my enemies without you. And this enemy must be defeated. Otherwise, the forested highlands I love will be destroyed. Yes, sir, I agree.

"Swear. Give me a prettily formal statement, one befitting Scottish lairds and Roman patricians."

I, Derek Maclaine, of the Isle of Mull and of Mount Storm, pledge my fealty, loyalty, and faith to you, Marcus Colonna, warrior and senator of Rome. My body is yours to use, and my sword-arm is yours to command.

"Very good." Marcus nibbles my ear and releases me. "Your obedience begins now. Be silent and lean against that tree."

I turn toward him and for a long moment study his aristocratic good looks: the ash-blond hair, blue eyes, high cheekbones, cleft chin, high brow and arrogant smile I remember so well from our past assignation. Dressed in a light blue suit, white shirt, and scarlet tie, he has his intimidatingly large penis out and he's stroking it. I turn back toward the tree, bend over, lean my right forearm against the trunk and rest my forehead against my forearm. I steady myself, placing my left palm against my left knee, preparing for the pounding to come.

Behind me, Marcus heaves a satisfied sigh and moves closer. "You have no idea what pleasure this triumph brings me," he says, stroking my face and lifting the back of my kilt, exposing my ass. "I have half a mind to thank the demon-conjurer instead of dispatching him."

A moistened finger parts my buttocks and probes. I groan and tremble, aching for his invasion. Soon, he's gripped my hard cock and pushed a finger up inside me, roughly working me open.

"Your *mentula*, so stiff, already dripping. Ah, how badly you want this. How badly you need this, forest trash," Marcus murmurs as he nudges his cock between my ass-cheeks and against my hole. He bends me over further and again he presses a hand over my mouth.

"I can take you slow and easy, or fast and hard. Which do you prefer? I believe I know."

You do know, sir.

"Excellent."

Without further ado, Marcus shoves his immense cock into me. I gasp, stiffen, and whimper. For a few seconds, the pain I'm feeling's as massive as the sword of undead flesh that pierces me, but now Marcus is stroking my cock, and my pleasure begins building in tight, shuddering waves. As it was on the Palatine, his hard thrusts have found that spot inside me that maddens me with surrender and the ache to be taken. Growling, I cock my rump and buck back against him.

God, yes, sir. By horned Herne, ride me hard!

"Ah, you are glorious. Just as it was in Rome: first ferocious resistance, and then sweet, complete compliance, the snarling hunger to be ravished. What a smelly treasure you are. No need for handcuffs now, eh? Clamp me from inside, barbarian, as you did before. Ahhhhh, yes. So skilled, you Scots savage. Such a superb *culus*. Ahhh, yes. I own you, do I not?"

You do, sir. Take me. Fill me full of you.

"I shall. And as I fill you, so you shall fill me."

His teeth sink into my neck. In a few moments, the great vortex of his ancient appetite tugging at my heart, my knees buckle. In another moment, his soft laugh tickling my throat, I've passed out.

I come to in the great cedars' fallen debris. I'm lying on my side, kilt still pulled up, butt exposed to the chilly northern air. My asshole's raw and burning, but inside me I can feel the glow and rush of renewed power as my *draugr* body absorbs Marcus's semen and with it some of his immortal might.

For the moment, though, I'm weak after being fed upon so ruthlessly. It takes me a few minutes and the aid of a cedar trunk before I manage to get to my feet. I brush off needles and twigs, adjust my clothing, then stagger through the darkness of the cedar grove, across the lawn, up the long white stairs, through the rich odor of blooming lilac, and into the parlor of Grand Hotel.

It must be late, for few humans are around, though several vampires are confabulating here and there. I contemplate the stairs, think better of it, and take the elevator to the third floor. My head's swimming, but the blood-loss has sharpened my appetite considerably. Luckily, not one but two men wait for me tonight.

When I enter Matt's room, neither he nor Aidan are in evidence, though the scents of soap and steam drift from the adjoining bathroom. My husbear must indeed have enjoyed a late-night shower, and if I know him, he wasn't alone in his ablutions. I peel off my coatee before peering into the bathroom.

What a superb sight. Hairy, naked, bearded men: one of the Horned God's most glorious gifts.

Matt's been practicing his Japanese knotwork again. Poor little Aidan's bound as prettily as Zac was when he served as my welcome-home gift. Aidan's hands are tied behind him, his torso and arms bound in artistically arranged webs of black rope. A black bandana's tied between his teeth, distorting his pretty mouth. He leans up against the bathroom wall, eyes closed, moaning. Matt kneels before him, sucking his cock.

I move closer, taking in the bound boy's beauty. His are the sort of innocent looks that most powerfully bring out my sadism. By the time I'm done, he's going to be chafed and sore in all the right places.

Aidan's skin is very pale, his body shapely and hard, not so much from visits to the gym but from good genetics and healthy youth, his lean hips etched with Apollo's lyre. Dark brown hair dusts his lower belly and the shallow cleft between his pecs, thickening around his big, soft nipples. He opens his eyes, bites down on his gag, and stares at me. The look of shy hunger, desperation, and vulnerability in his dark-bearded face is almost enough to make me come. Almost.

"Eros is perpetually generous. Looks like you're warming him up just like you promised."

"Hey, Derek," Matt says, releasing the cub's prick. His face's flushed, his eyes wild. "Where'd you go?"

"I met with our host, Marcus. Are you happy with our servant?"

"Hell, yes! This boy's the perfect bottom. Loves to be tied up. Loves to be fucked. Whatta prize. You gotta thank Marcus for me."

"I already have, in a manner of speaking," I say, rubbing my butt. "He just shoved me up against a cedar tree and ass-raped me. In return for his help, I promised to be his bottom whenever he wants, and to fight for him if necessary."

"Wow. Really?" Matt blurts, standing. "So my Top has a Top? My Daddy has a Daddy? How do you feel about that?"

"Seems like a small price to pay to save our mountains. Besides, I trust him."

"Hell, you love him. You admitted that to me when you got back from Rome. I told you that was fine by me. It's still fine."

"Good to hear. I've got to admit it's very hot to submit to a *draugr* so much stronger. Plus it can't hurt to have a permanent ally with his power and influence."

"That's great news, then. And yum, I'd love to have seen him ride you."

"At some point, that probably will be arranged. He drank from me too, so I'm very thirsty. Do you mind if I join you?"

"Mind? Hell, no. Git over here. I've already ass-fucked this kid once—whatta ride!—and I'm just about to do it again. How about we take turns? How's that sound, Aidan?"

Aidan continues to stare at me, brown eyes full of fear and pleading. He slumps against the wall and nods. Then he turns, bends over, and presents his ass. It's plump, smooth, and white, with a flare of hair in the crack.

"See?" says Matt. "The boy can't get enough dick up his butt. Get naked, honey."

"Marcus chose him well." In a trice, I've tossed my clothes off and joined them in the steamy space.

"He's all nice and open," Matt says. Gripping Aidan by the shoulder, he works two fingers up the boy's hole. Aidan nods and groans.

"Fuck yourself," says Matt, and Aidan obeys, rocking back and forth on Matt's fingers.

"*Good* boy. Damn, you're hot," Matt says. Removing his fingers, he plunges his cock up the trussed kid's ass. Aidan grunts, sighs, nods, and bounces back against Matt. Matt grips Aidan's shoulders and pounds him violently. I stand by, jacking myself, relishing the godsent sight. Is there anything more arousing or beautiful than one strong, hairy man rump-ravishing another?

"Ohhh, fuck, you're a real man-milker, ain't you? Already...I'm.... Here... we...go."

Matt stiffens, his face twists, and he's done, spouting come up Aidan's butt. For a long minute, he rests, panting atop the boy's back, before standing up and pulling out.

"More," Aidan begs against his bandana-gag, the word muffled but intelligible. "Please, Laird Maclaine. More. Fuck me."

"Gladly," I say, my previous weakness subsumed by raw lust. I tighten a hand around his throat, another about his bound hands, and shove into him. His ass-muscles clench around me, silky and sticky, full of welcome, pulsing tightly: the very technique I used earlier this evening to pleasure Marcus. It's almost as if his butthole were a keen mouth, sucking my member.

"Oh, sweet Pan, you're so fine," I hiss. I thrust in and out, snarling, savagely plowing him. Aidan squirms and nods, urging me on, mumbling muffled pleas against his gag.

"Harder, sir. Hurt me. Love me. Split me in half."

"Just what I wanted to hear. And so I shall."

I kiss his smooth back, wrap my arms around his torso, and torment his plump nipples till he's flinching, whimpering, and gnashing his gag. I ride his ass and torment his tits for a long, long time, rumbling with rapture, varying my rhythm from hard and shallow to slow and deep, delaying my inevitable release.

"I need to feed, Aidan-cub. May I do so now?" I whisper, lapping the artery-throb in his neck.

"Yes, sir," Aidan mumbles. "Drink from me, please. Pump my ass full of come."

What a savory parallel to my recent ravishment in the cedar grove. Bending over, I sink my fangs into Aidan's neck. His blood's thick and sweet, tinged with alcohol. Immediately after the first mouthful, I spurt seed, finishing inside him. When I slurp down a second mouthful of blood, and then a third, Aidan goes limp in my arms. He's swooned.

"Follow me," I say to Matt.

Tossing Aidan over my shoulder, I carry him into the bedroom. There, I stretch him out on the bed, lick his neck, and will him awake. He comes to, smiling groggily, eyes glazed.

Matt joins us on the bed. He sucks the boy's nipples—swollen even larger after my loving abuse—then moves to his cock. I wrap Aidan in my arms, sipping carefully from the bound boy's neck, while Matt sucks his prick and Aidan trembles and thrusts. Soon, Aidan's sobbing against his gag and pounding come into Matt's eager mouth. Immediately after his climax, the boy loses consciousness.

"Jesus," Matt moans, rolling onto his side and snuggling against our insensible captive. "I think I'm in love."

"Curl up with him, Matthew. Keep him roped and gagged till dawn. I want to sip some Scotch and watch you two sleep," I say, slipping off the bed. "Just before daybreak, screw him again. Hoist his legs in the air, bend him double, and fuck him mercilessly, till he's hurting and his eyes are brimming with tears. Will you do that for me?"

"You bet, honey," Matt says, giving me the wicked smile I cherish. "I think this ole man has one more load left in him."

"One more thing. When I rise tomorrow night, I want him hogtied on this bed, with a plug up his ass. I want him gagged with a pair of your piss-soaked underwear, tied in place with about two yards of rope, rope pulled so tight it makes the corners of his mouth bleed. I want to fuck him and feed on his neck and pretty nipples before we all go down to dinner."

"Christ, you're in major sadist mode. You're getting me hard again." Wrapping an arm around Aidan, Matt yawns, kisses the boy's pale shoulder, and closes his eyes. "You got it, Daddy. G'night."

CHAPTER THIRTY-NINE

Tonight's the vampire convocation. But first, Cynthia and I keep our human friends company in the hotel's dining room as they feast on another big dinner, baked whitefish with roasted potatoes and beef medallions with polenta. Matt's looking smug and satisfied after another day spent with Aidan. Tiffany's looking awed by the refined surroundings, expensive silverware, and solicitous service. Ilene's looking vastly content, clearly delighted to wear another glamorous outfit, this one a satiny sky-blue gown with a white shawl. Aidan, who's been walking somewhat crooked this evening, is drowsy after my recent assault on his nipples and neck. His brown eyes, full of devotion, move back and forth between Matt and me. There's been no need to enthrall him. The boy must have a true fetish for Daddybears.

Now the mortal members of our party disperse, Tiffany to her quarters, Okey to change gowns for the meeting, Matt and Aidan no doubt to get naked and grow frisky again. Poor little Aidan might need a walker by the time Matt's done with him. My husbear seems to be seriously infatuated with the cub, which is fine with me. The more sex-slaves, the better. Variety truly is the spice of life, for human and vampire alike, especially when it comes to the erotic. Semi-annual trips with Matt to Grand Hotel to luxuriate in the surroundings and spend time in bed with Aidan might be a pleasant change from our Mount Storm routines.

Cynthia and I are taking the air on the porch and I'm catching her up on last night's pact with Marcus while sparing her the salacious sodomitic de-

226

tails when we encounter another unwelcome human disruption to the night's peace. A very pregnant woman clad in a slinky dress and shawl and holding a puling infant in her arms steps out onto the porch and begins chattering banalities into her cell phone. The baby gurgles, then begins to cry.

"Oh, for Thor's sake," I spit. "Here we go again. As Matt said earlier, this is Breeder Central."

"That's quite the morsel she has there," Cynthia observes, lapping a fang. "Plump little butterball. Wailing meatloaf. Just a few sips…and the rest is silence."

"Don't fool me, madam. You're addicted to buxom femmes and steely-jawed bull dykes. You're nothing like those baby-swilling hussies in Stoker's misogynistic tale."

"True. Still, some peace and quiet to steady ourselves would be most welcome before we try to bend a convocation of the surly undead to our will. Shall you? Or shall I?"

"I'd be glad to. What shall it be? Mesmerism? A nasty squall? Or…I know."

Gazing down toward the shore of Lake Huron, I focus, sending out a silent call of command. The woman alternates between her phone conversation and casual attempts to silence the baby, which only squeals louder. Cynthia regards me, one eyebrow cocked, waiting.

An erratic cloud veers over the front lawn. Human ears couldn't make out the high whine from this distance, but vampire ears can.

"Lovely," says Cynthia. "A flock of tiny wampyresses, hungry for blood. These northern woods are rife with them in summer."

The mosquitos descend, voracious. The mother blinks, shakes her head, slaps the air, and utters a foul word. The baby claws at the air and screams even louder, an obnoxious crescendo. The mother slaps her forearm and then her calf. Finally, she pockets her phone, clutches the little darling to her breast, and rushes inside, still cussing and cuffing the air around her.

"Well done. But now it's time," Cynthia says, consulting her pocket watch. "Let's gather our redoubtable sorceress and make our way to the convocation."

When we enter the Brighton Pavilion, a large meeting room, it's already packed with bustling *draugar*. Most of them seem to know one another, making Ilene, Cynthia, and me a trio of outsiders whom they regard pointedly, some with curiosity, some with hostility, a meager few with indifference.

The presence of a human witch certainly nonplusses many of them. And who could overlook Ilene, considering the way she's dressed tonight? At last she'd donned the legendary outfit she and Matt found at Macy's and bought just for this occasion.

Her gown's tight, black and blood-red, sequined and bugle-beaded. Her wig rises in an impressive updo. Her lips and nails are deep scarlet, as are her high heels. A long slit in her dress shows off her shapely legs and black fishnet stockings. Jewels glitter about her neck and wrists. She carries a beaded clutch purse. She's elegance incarnate, with both the sensuousness of Aphrodite and the stern strength of Athena.

"I'm not wearing any silver, just as you suggested," Ilene says in a stage whisper as we make our way through the crowd. "I didn't want to seem hostile."

"Good. You got that customary brick in your purse?" I say, whispering back.

"Hell, no. What good would that do me here? I do have a protective charm, though. And an atomizer full of that *eau de sorbier*, uh, rowan-blossom water, as you suggested."

"You won't need it, m'lady," Cynthia assures her. "Derek and I will rip the limbs and head off anyone who dares show you impertinence."

Cynthia's promise couldn't be better timed. Here comes a young hothead, his face scarlet with high dudgeon. The boy's big-built, but he looks sixteen. He exudes the crass overconfidence of a fledgling, of a *draugr* turned only in the last few decades.

"Why have you brought this witch here?" he snarls. "We all hate witches. This is a convention of vampires, not cross-dressing sorcer*esses*!"

His accent and syllabic emphasis proclaim him British. His effrontery proclaims him unwise.

"I beg your pardon?" Ilene says, reaching into her purse. Emboldened by the presence of her escorts, she's gotten her dander up. No doubt she's contemplating the pleasant possibility of giving this git the vampiric equivalent of a face full of mace, but that would disrupt everything and cause hostilities to mount. Not what I need on a night when this undead congregation might agree to help me against Alpha.

"No, Mizz Ilene," I say. "Why should a maiden, even one so powerful, have to defend her honor when she has protectors at hand?"

I face the scarlet-cheeked cipher. "What's your name, child?"

He scowls. "I'm Unferth, and I'm not a child."

"Yes, you are," I say, putting as much threat into my smile as possible. "You're also a rude whelp. Best watch yourself, little Unferth. Marcus Colonna himself extended an invitation to this witch to attend tonight. She's his guest. The three of us have important business to discuss with your convocation."

"I don't believe you. Witches have no business—"

"Are you a *cretin?*" Cynthia breaks in. "Have you any sense of the strength Laird Maclaine and I possess between us? Get back to your hole, you larva."

The boy falls into a sputtering fit that's conveniently cut off by the entrance of Marcus Colonna. In response, everyone takes a seat around the tables, which are set in a great rectangle in the center of the room.

"Y'all showed him," Ilene says, tucking her voluminous skirts beneath her as she sits. "As my Irish grandmother used to say, 'What do you expect out of a pig but a grunt?' Or 'Better good manners than good looks,' and, bless his heart, that little turd doesn't have either."

When Marcus raises his hand, the room falls silent. The man looks magnificent, as usual. Every time he overpowers me and pummels my ass, the love I feel for him grows stronger. I am a lucky, lucky *draugr*, to have so many fine men in my undead life: a husbear, a bevy of boys, and a master like Marcus, gleaming like gold and ivory at the head of the room. Yet again I close my eyes and send up a grateful prayer to the Dark Lady and the Horned One.

"Good evening, my friends. What a pleasure to see you all here." Marcus smiles, brushing a lock of blond hair from his eyes. "I trust you've been enjoying your time at Grand Hotel…and the human companions I've assigned you. Tonight we have much to discuss. But first, let me introduce three guests of mine who have business with us. Two are solitary vampires. One is a human witch. All three, I might emphasize, are under my protection."

"See?" Ilene hisses at Unferth, who's sitting near us. She sticks her tongue out at him before recomposing her dignified expression.

"Laird Derek Maclaine, Ms. Cynthia Skala, and…the Lady Ilene Over." Marcus runs a hand over his faint goatee, as if trying to conceal his smile. "Guests, will you please rise?"

"Goddess protect me," Ilene mutters.

The three of us stand. The room of *draugar* studies us. Several are grim-faced, most likely objecting to a witch's presence, but none has the gall to complain now that she's been proclaimed Marcus's guest.

"Welcome them, please," Marcus says, giving the audience a stern look.

Half-hearted applause breaks out. Unferth claps once, scowling, crestfallen. Ilene smirks.

"Derek, would you care to explain to this august assembly why you've come?"

"Gladly, master." It is, I realize, the first time I've called Marcus "master" in public. It feels somehow humiliating and somehow right. "I'll be brief, since you have other matters to decide tonight. I'm trying to stop a demon named Aldinach. It and its human allies, a company called Alpha Coal, are devastating the landscape in my region, the mountains I love. They're determined to murder my human partner. I've tried to stop them, and I've failed. When I assaulted their compound, the humans were armed with rowan-wood bullets, indicating that they are aware of my vampiric nature and its weaknesses. The demon's very powerful, capable of spitting a virulent, fiery poison."

"What then do you want from us?" says a blond vampiress to my right.

"I want two things. First, I need as many of you as are willing to contribute your blood to a charm. Lady Ilene here has brought an amulet her coven's charged. The more blood that anoints it, the more efficacious it becomes. If it were to be bathed in the blood of every vampire here, it should possess the power to diffuse the demon, send it back to the astral realms, perhaps even destroy it for good."

"You want us to contribute our *blood?*" Unferth rises, fuming. "How do we know this isn't a trick? Some spell this witch has connived to sap our strength and—"

"You know it's not a trick because Lady Ilene's a member of my clan, and because I'm a man of my word," I say evenly, fighting back the urge to rip his throat out.

"Derek is a man of honor, yes," says Marcus, frowning. "Last night, he swore his loyalty to me in return for our help in this matter. He's agreed to be one of my knights when necessity demands. There's no reason not to trust him and his friends. I vouch for him. Is that not sufficient?"

Unferth, the truculent pup, grumbling, subsides into his seat. In future, I might have to arrange some set of circumstances conducive to his beheading.

"It's sufficient," says the blond vampiress. "Continue, Laird Maclaine."

"Thank you, madam. In addition to your help empowering the blood-charm, I'm asking for volunteers. I need a small army of warriors to help me raid Alpha's compound on the next full moon. My maker, Sigurd Magnusson, a very powerful Viking *draugr*, has agreed to be part of this army, as have two werewolves of my acquaintance and my good friend here, Cynthia Skala, whose ferocity's unmatched. We'll need to bring down the compound's many security guards, seize the CEO of Alpha Coal and the magus working for him, and destroy the demon. Once all that's done, I'll be free to destroy the technology Alpha uses to level my native mountains."

"Such a raid sounds parlous. Why should we risk our lives for this crusade of yours, Laird Maclaine?" says a vampire in archaic garb to my left. He looks askance at Marcus. "I mean no disrespect, may I add."

"Because, in return, I will—" I begin, before Marcus, glowering, interrupts.

"Because I am your leader, and I wish it. Derek has been a solitary for all of his undead existence, but now he has pledged himself to me. If you agree to fight for him, he will in future fight for us. He is very strong. He possesses some of my strength, for we have shared blood, as he possesses some of Sigurd Magnusson's strength. Derek's a fine warrior, one of the best. He will be a most powerful ally. Are you afraid of little men with rowan-wood bullets, my people? Are you afraid of that unnatural grotesquerie, Aldinach? Surely not. Surely not."

"Thank you, master. May I add something more?"

"Yes, you may." Marcus sits back, boring into me with his blue-blaze eyes.

"You all have homes, do you not?" I say, moving my gaze over the room. "We have that in common with the humans we once were: our love of home. Some of you might hail from the wintry wastes of Iceland, some from the seaside, some from the moors of England, or, like I, the Highlands and the Western Isles of Scotland. Some of you might dwell in the mountains of China, or the jungles of the Amazon, or the great Hungarian plain, or the Black Forest. Others might nest in cities: Paris, Prague, Berlin, New Orleans, San Francisco, Moscow, Cairo, or Rome."

My eyes meet Marcus's. He smiles. *Go on, my boy, my sweet-rumped Enkidu,* he intones in my head.

I smile back, then return my attention to the crowd. "I left Scotland when I was turned in 1730. A man I loved deeply had been murdered there, and the memories of his loss were too bitter for me to stay. I found a new home, in the Appalachian Mountains of America. It's one of the loveliest regions on the planet. My mountains are green-gold in spring, brimming with wildflowers. In summer, they're jade, and the fertile soil's fruits and vegetables nourish the humans we need to survive. In autumn, the hills burn with leaf-fire: purple, burnt orange, blood-red, and gold. In winter, snow shrouds the rocks, blankets the meadows, lines the gray limbs of the maple and the green boughs of the pine. It's those forested steeps that this demon and its human allies are destroying. They're felling the trees, driving off the wildlife, poisoning the water, and befouling the air. I'm asking you to help save my home. I'm asking you to help me save what I love. In return, if called upon, I will do the same for you."

"You have heard him. I would advise you to support him." Marcus stands. "Lady Ilene, have you the amulet?"

Ilene starts, surprised at being directly addressed by such a formidable personage. "Oh! Oh, yes, Lord Colonna. Senator Colonna. Oh, mercy, how should I address you?"

"'Marcus' is fine," he says, chuckling. "And you will save me a dance later this evening? Everyone's invited to the Terrace Room for music after this convocation disperses."

Ilene flushes. "Oh, yes. I'd be delighted." She fumbles in her purse, then pulls out an earthenware cup, a curved knife with a white handle, and, attached to a neck-chain, a jagged bit of crystal, very dark in hue.

"Black tourmaline," she announces. "As Laird Maclaine's explained, it's already charged. All it needs is blood to magnify the spell." She holds the stone up for everyone to see, then places it in the cup, puts the cup and knife on the table before her, and steps back.

"Let this be done then," says Marcus, approaching. He rests a hand on my shoulder and kisses my brow.

I take up the blade, slice my wrist, and bathe the dark crystal. As the lapis charm had before, it hisses and steams, drinking in the blood.

Cynthia goes next. Marcus follows.

"Next?" he says, lapping at his rapidly healing wrist and raking the room with his gaze. Beside him, the cup fumes and sparks. "Who among you are willing to help my new liegeman? Come forward now, those of you who are."

Silence falls. Then the blond vampiress I'd addressed before rises. So does the *draugr* in archaic clothes. One by one, my undead compatriots come forward. Only a handful pointedly decline, including petulant Unferth, who shakes his head and retreats into a corner. By the time the last *draugr* has contributed his blood, the cup's glowing red and smoking. Ilene pulls a black-handled knife from her clutch, touches the stone with the blade's tip, and whispers an incantation. Violet light cascades from the cup, the astral twin of liquid nitrogen, swirls clockwise, coalesces into a spouting flume, splashes back into the cup, and vanishes.

Ilene shakes her head in wonder and lifts the crystal. It flickers violently in her hand, then returns to its normal appearance.

"Quite the spectacle," Cynthia whispers.

"It's done," Ilene announces, handing me the tourmaline pendant and returning her tools to her purse. "The amulet's super-charged now, thanks to you preternaturals. This should blow that slimy critter of Alpha's all to hell."

Marcus chuckles. "Well put. Good to hear. Thank you, my people. Now, how many of you are fearless enough to join Derek's army? I'll consider it a personal favor to me if you do so."

Another long pause before members of the group respond. Of the hundred or so here, a third stand.

"So few?" Marcus rumbles.

"Enough." Smiling at the crowd, I don the pendant. "My thanks are boundless. We'll take no more of your time." Turning to Ilene and Cynthia, I beckon toward the exit. "Shall we leave them to other agenda items?"

"Why, certainly," says Ilene. "I'll see all y'all later in the Terrace Room," she adds, with a gay wave, as if this room of immortal killers were a crew of gentlemen callers vying for her attentions. "And Marcus, honey, I'll save you the first dance."

"Excellent, my lady," Marcus says, briefly taking her hand before turning back to the convocation. "On to the next order of business."

I hold the door open for Cynthia and Ilene. Passing me, Cynthia mutters, "If I ever encounter that little toad Unferth again, I'm going to disembowel him with my bare hands." Passing me, Ilene mutters, "Sooooo many fangers. Jesus fucking Christ. I almost pissed myself. Goddamn, do I need a drink."

"Private Party" says the placard outside the Terrace Room. Two humans dressed in black, no doubt chosen for their intimidating bulk, guard the door, but they move aside respectfully when little Aidan escorts our group inside. The room's full of sophisticated-looking *draugar*, laughing, chatting, and dancing. Their reaction to our arrival is much different from the chilly one they gave us earlier. This time, I sense either admiration or begrudging respect. Unferth and the few others who refused to donate their blood to the amulet are nowhere to be seen, meaning that Cynthia won't have to besmirch her handsome outfit with his sticky entrails.

Aidan leads us to a table in the corner, away from the band and at a distance from the dance floor. Immediately servers slip up to us and hand out flutes of champagne. Cynthia's glass and mine are noticeably pink.

"To success," I toast.

"To new friends," Cynthia says.

"To the end of Alpha," adds Matt.

"To opulent and romantic settings in which to wear gorgeous gowns!" blurts Ilene. "And to my savage protectors."

We all drink. Cynthia and I grin, recognizing the individual essences enriching our refreshments.

"You precious dear," Cynthia says to Tiffany. "What a nice touch."

"You too, cub," I say, squeezing Aidan's knee. "It's the taste of celebration."

"Thank you, sir. I'm going to miss you and Daddy Matt a lot. Do you have to leave tomorrow?"

"We do," Matt says. "We have an important battle to fight. But we'll be back one day. Right, Derek?"

"Absolutely," I say, taking another sip. "And here's our host."

Marcus strides up, a golden knockout as usual in a blue-gray suit with a dove-gray tie. "May I join your table?" he says, a faint smile curling his lips.

"Please, sir," I say. "I know you have many other allies to speak to, but we'd love the pleasure of your company for as long as you can spare it."

"Let me second Derek," Cynthia says. "You were wonderfully persuasive this evening. We're forever grateful."

"We're grateful, and you're fabulous! Oh, honey, what a stylish suit," Ilene says. "So debonair."

Matt, wide-eyed, clears his throat and stands. "Howdy, Mr. Colonna," he says, extending a hand. "I'm Matt, Derek's husbear. I too wanna thank you for all your help. It means so much to all of us, and soon it'll mean a lot to a whole slew a' folks back home."

The two men shake. "So you're the wild mountain man who's stolen this Scottish monster's heart. You look just as I imagined: the perfect combination of rough-edged, big-built, shaggy, and sweet."

"Ah, th-thanks," Matt stutters, retaking his seat. "You're pretty fine yourself. Real regal. You were a duke or something, right?"

"A Roman senator. Several thousand years ago. Now I'm a vampire wrangler and playboy philanthropist who enjoys helping his friends. Have you enjoyed your time at Grand Hotel?"

"Hell, yes," Matt enthuses. "Other than having to wear dress clothes, which we country boys ain't much into. Pretty place. Great food. Plus, uh, Aidan's, um, service has been top-notch. He's been great at making us feel right at home."

"I suspected as much. Thanks to my time with Derek, I have some sense of your aesthetic. I felt sure you would find Aidan beautiful and his acquiescence appealing. And speaking of beauties…Lady Ilene, would you care to dance?" he says, offering his hand.

"Oh, honey, would I?" Ilene stands, patting her wig. "I've been waiting twenty goddamn years for a man with your looks to ask that. Y'all watch my purse now. This big girl's about to waltz with a blond god just like she's always dreamed." Grabbing Marcus's hand, she pulls him along behind her toward the dance floor.

The dancing goes on until the wee hours. The band's apparently been instructed to play music that ranges from the Middle Ages to the present, as would appeal to beings who have survived for centuries. Marcus and Ilene waltz, then move into a medieval round with other couples. Cynthia and I foxtrot. Matt and Aidan gyrate to seventies disco. Cynthia and Tiffany slowdance. Cynthia and Ilene tango. Copious amounts of champagne are quaffed. Around four in the morning, the tipsy roomful of *draugar* begins to disperse.

"Lady Ilene, thanks for the dance." Cynthia rises, with Tiffany on her arm. "Marcus, my thanks again. Derek, I'll meet you on the porch an hour before dawn."

"Mercy, I hate to leave!" says Ilene. "It's been truly magical. Y'all have made me feel like Miss Jane Seymour. It's been a dream come true."

"Perhaps we should make this an annual reunion," Marcus says, kissing Ilene's hand. "Would you like that?"

"Oh, fuck, yes! I mean, mercy, yes, please. Is that possible?"

"It is," says Marcus. "But now, Derek, perhaps you and I should discuss the disposition of your little army, especially since the full moon occurs in only a matter of days. How about a nightcap in your room? You and Matt and Aidan and I?"

"Oh, Lord," Ilene says, kissing Marcus on the cheek. "I think I know what that means. Marcus, thank you for a night I'll cherish till the day I die. It was perfect in every way. And Aidan, honey…I'll pray for you, child, since I think preying of a far different kind is about to occur. I shudder to think of it. Goodnight, butches and gentlemen." With a happy wave, Ilene sashays off.

"Honeyed dreams," Cynthia says. "Come, my jasmine goddess." Nuzzling Tiffany's hair, Cynthia guides the voluptuous Asian off.

"Lead the way, Aidan-cub," I say. "It's time for a wee dram to end the evening."

Aidan nods obediently. Our little group heads up the hotel's central staircase. Matt, following Aidan, reaches up to squeeze his ass. Behind me, Marcus, chuckling, does the same to me.

In Matt's room, my husbear pours us all glasses of Scotch. We stand in a small circle, eying one another.

"This time together has been very productive," Marcus says.

"It sure has. I'm so glad your people are going to help us fight," says Matt. "Thanks to Alpha, the coalfields are all tore up, and folks there are suffering bad."

"So Derek has told me. But it's not just my people who'll be helping you. I plan to be there too." Marcus smiles. "I intend to enjoy my share of destruction. Now that Derek's my liegeman, I owe him that."

"That would be wonderful," I say. "Your strength will be much appreciated in the battle to come."

"Your 'liegeman,' yeah. I heard about your all's deal," Matt says, lapping liquor from his mustache. "I, uh…top Derek once in a rare while, but…I gotta admit, the thought of him submitting to you gets me hard as a rock."

"Is that so?" Marcus raises an eyebrow.

"Yeah, it is. He told me you ass-fucked him against a tree. Wish I'd been there to see that."

"I as well, now that you mention it." Marcus chuckles, stroking his goatee. "You're as much of a satyr as your partner, I see."

"Yep. That's one of the reasons we get along so good. Inveterate horndogs." Matt slugs back his drink, then wraps an arm around Aidan's waist. "This sweet lil' cub has sure kept us both super-satisfied. I'm going to miss him."

"He'll be here, waiting for your return. Won't you, boy?"

"Oh, yes, sir," Aidan sighs. "Daddy Matt and Laird Maclaine have made me very happy. Please come back whenever you can."

"I think we need a memorable goodbye," Marcus says, taking a chair. "It's time for the three of you to remove your clothes."

What can we do but smile and obey? A few minutes of hurried stripping, and we stand before Marcus, our master for the evening.

"Kiss now," the blond Roman commands, relaxing into his seat. "Make love. Your lord wills it."

We need no further prompting. Matt, Aidan, and I embrace. Matt and Aidan kiss passionately, groping each other's nakedness, then Aidan and I do the same. Aidan falls to his knees and sucks our pricks while Matt and I kiss.

I stretch out on the bed. Aidan drops onto his elbows and knees between my legs and sucks my cock while Matt eats Aidan's ass and jacks himself.

"Lovely, my men," Marcus says. Rising, he loosens his tie and pulls it off, then unbuttons his shirt. "Matthew, would it please you if I topped your husband now? While you take our little friend Aidan from behind? Shall we ride them together?"

Matt lifts his face from between Aidan's butt-cheeks long enough to gasp, "Ohhh, Jesus. Fuck, yes! Let's do it."

Beards nuzzling, fingers intertwined, Aidan and I rock and moan, kissing passionately. We're on our elbows and knees in the center of the bed. Behind me, Marcus kneels, driving his cock inside me. Behind Aidan, Matthew thrusts, his balls noisily slapping the boy's butt.

"Fuck me, Daddy Matt," Aidan pleads before sucking my tongue into his mouth.

"Goddamn, this is hot," Matt grunts, gripping Aidan's hips and increasing his rhythm. "This boy's asshole is pure paradise."

"As is Laird Maclaine's," Marcus says, digging a fingernail into my left nipple, making me grit my teeth and whine. "He really starts rearing like a stallion and squeezing my sex from inside when I torture his nipples."

"Yeah, Derek likes to hurt there." Matt pauses, leaning over to kiss Aidan's back before returning to his sweaty exertions.

"I like to hurt him there," Marcus says, raking my chest with his nails, leaving bloody grooves just as he did on the Palatine. "Matthew, you two should come to Rome together. We could string Derek up and push pins through his flesh."

"Whoa. Intense. Really?"

"Uhh! Sounds great to me," I rasp. "One of the many advantages—uhh!— of a rapid healing process—huuhhh!—there's no such thing as too rough. Master, would you please stop chatting with my husbear—ummm!—and plow me harder?"

Marcus laughs, slapping my ass and giving my hole a vicious prodding. "Shut up, you impertinent savage, or I'll gag you."

"Hell, that ain't no threat," Matt says. "Derek'd love that."

"Daddy Matt," grunts Aidan. "I'm pretty close."

"Don't you dare come before I do," Matt says. "If you touch your prick again, I'll tie your hands."

"Well done," says Marcus. "I admire a man who's as stern a master as he is an eager slave. Like Derek here. He has this technique—"

"Oh, yeah, I know. This boy too. Milk me, cub. Yep! Ain't gonna…be too long, if you…keep…that up. How you doin'…Derek?"

"I'm…in heaven, of course, filled up with a prick so huge," I say, wiggling my butt against Marcus's lean loins. "Th-thank you for this private convocation, Marcus, sir. Uhhhh…I'm getting close too."

"Pound him, Marcus," Matt says. "Make him hurt bad."

"With pleasure," Marcus says, bringing an open palm down hard on my right ass-cheek. He pulls his fat penis out, only to slam into me again. The tourmaline pendant around my neck sways crazily back and forth, bumping my breastbone.

"Uhhhh! Praise Herne," I groan. "The hunter become the hunted." I fist my prick and buck back onto Marcus's cock, impaling myself even deeper.

"Ohhhhh, fuck!" Matt gasps. "Here we go, lil' guy."

With a roar, Matt climaxes up Aidan's ass. Aidan works his dick hard and fast, then, trembling and whimpering, spurts semen onto the sheets and slumps back against Matt.

"Such a sweet spectacle," Marcus says, shoving in and out. "Caledonian, here comes Roma's seed. But first…." Marcus wraps his arms around my torso and sinks his teeth into my neck.

"Ah, yes, by Mithras! Ah, yes! What vast pleasure you give me. I love you, my boy," Marcus mumbles against my throat, gulping my blood and inside me simultaneously jetting his semen.

"I love you too, sir," I moan, before the suction of his appetite robs me of consciousness.

"Drink," Marcus says, pressing his smooth chest against my mouth. Rumbling gratefully, I bite his nipple, suckling for a long interval from his hard pectoral.

"Thank you, sir." I withdraw my fangs, feeling the intoxicating glimmer of his power—both blood and semen—pulsing inside me. Beside us, Matt and Aidan sleep, the bigger man curled around the smaller. Marcus and I roll onto our sides and take the same position, the tall Roman embracing me from behind.

"Your man's nearly as splendid as you," Marcus says, stroking my hair. "As I said, you should bring him to Rome. He'd love the culinary delights of my city. Besides, your thrall Francesco misses you greatly. He's kept your tower in perfect shape, and his old mother is thriving, thanks to your generosity."

"All that's good to hear. A trip to Rome would be wonderful. Have you feasted yet on that waitress you favored? Nigella?"

"Oh, yes, though she's become a bit possessive. Very strong-willed. Almost impossible to control. She became quite petulant when she learned that she was not going to accompany me to Michigan but that you would be here."

"She's jealous of me?"

"Most definitely. I think she'd lace your Chianti with rowan-flower water if she thought she could get away with it. I believe she senses how much pleasure I take in mastering you, in treating you cruelly."

Marcus pats my rump, runs a finger down my ass-crack, locates my lubed hole, and commences to tease it. "Speaking of which, the three of us came, but you did not. Am I correct?"

I arch and tremble as he works a finger up inside me. "You…are, sir. But it's nearly dawn. Should we not strategize before…?"

"There's no need for that now. Now is still the time for hungers fulfilled." He kisses my shoulder and pushes a second finger up inside me. "You need choose only the appointed night and the appointed place." Marcus begins finger-fucking me steadily. "We will be there. It will be time for death, for utter destruction, for the righteous annihilation that gives men like us such rich exhilaration. Your wolves will be there, and Cynthia Skala in all her ruthlessness, and your mighty Norse maker, and my savage people, and you and I. We will make your enemies pay. We will make them regret ever crossing you, or harming your handsome mate. Have you any doubt?"

"I…do…not, sir," I say, masturbating slowly, riding his fingers.

"Finish yourself, sweaty Highlander," Marcus says, nibbling my torn nipple. "Soon enough, I swear to you, your foes will be howling in agony. Soon enough, we will end them."

CHAPTER FORTY

We soar together beneath the full moon, a flock of forty *draugar*. Below, set in the Boone County hills, the Sodeski compound sprawls. Here and there, an Alpha thug walks a guard dog. The security seems sparse. It's been weeks since my last attempted invasion. Perhaps Sodeski and his magus assume that the ass-whipping I received has dissuaded me from future attacks. They would, of course, be perilously wrong. Like Atlas, I have broad shoulders. I can carry a grudge to the crack of doom.

It's doom we bring tonight. Thanks to Nate's knowledge of explosives, we're armed with more than the immense strength and sharp fangs customary to our kind. And thanks to Okey's magical talents, one particular piece of ammunition I carry should wreak havoc on our astral foe.

Time to begin this battle. I dip down toward the roof of the house. There, on the widow's walk, a solitary guard's dozing. I unburden myself of a deadly parcel. It drops straight and true, hitting the floor behind him and bouncing. He jolts awake and looks around. A second later, there's a thunderous explosion. The widow's walk disappears in a spasm of flames. The roof surrounding it shudders and collapses. No perch for snipers there.

On the lawn below, men shout and dogs bark. A warning siren starts up. Another explosion reverberates in the garage. Seconds after that, other explosions dwarf the earlier ones. Sodeski's fleet of cars combusts one by one, devastating that end of the house.

Flames swirl up the walls. I glide down onto the lawn, transforming into human form—bare-chested, girt with kilt, claymore, and dirk—and stride toward a flock of guards. In me, undead adrenaline's rushing: the bloodlust, the thrill, the ache to kill. An Alpha thug spots me and takes aim. I have no desire to tolerate the foul pangs of rowan-wood bullets. I focus for only a second, and then his dog's turned on him, savaging his thigh. The man shrieks and goes down.

Across the lawn, one by one, the dogs turn on their masters. Sodeski was a fool to keep animals in his compound. About me, Marcus and his horde of minions descend, taking human form. All are, by design, very, very hungry, ready to feast on our foes.

"Well done, Derek," Marcus says. Streaking off to my left, he seizes the nearest guard and snaps his neck before returning to my side. "Have you any instructions for us? If so, now is the time to deliver them."

"Yes, I have. Listen, my people," I shout. "The portly man and his corpulent wife, spare them for the present. And the magus, if you find him. Slaughter all the rest. Leave none alive. No talebearers may escape. Leave the demon to me."

"You heard him!" Sigurd roars. "So often in this world, to keep the peace, we must restrain ourselves and our appetite for blood and death. Not tonight! Do what you will!"

A few vampires cheer. Somewhere a human screams. We're dispersing across the lawn and I'm heading for the front door when guns sound and a poisonous bullet grazes my shoulder, leaving a gory groove.

"There! Beware!" I bellow. A small battalion of guards flanks the burning garage. They pause, aim, and fire.

Four vampires snarl with pain and rage. Beside me, Marcus doubles over, then drops to his knees. "By Mithras!" he hisses, digging at his belly and pulling out the bloody projectile. Growling, he lobs the toxic thing into the grass.

Another round of bullets. Around us, five vampires go down. Smoke roils around our attackers. "Again," their leader shouts.

"Stay here, sir." I pull my dirk and move as fast as I can. In another second, I've run my blade through the leader's guts, then pulled it out and drawn it across the throat of his nearest comrade. Before I can reach for a third, something even faster has flashed through their ranks and downed every one.

"Sigurd!" I say to the grinning Viking who grips my shoulder. "Many thanks! It's been decades since you and I dispatched—"

Another explosion, this time at the compound's gate. Beyond the wall, there's the flare of headlights, and the high howl that excited redneck boys make as they release long-trammeled energy for good or ill. Zac's Jeep speeds up the road and smashes through the remains of the gate.

"Your human friends are here," Sigurd says. "Help Marcus. I'll take care of the stragglers." Baring his teeth, he streaks off.

I lope back to Marcus, sheathe my dirk, and haul him to his feet. The Jeep careens up to us and screeches to a stop.

"Howdy, boss!" Zac clambers out of the vehicle, pistol at the ready. Behind him, Matt, Nate, and Timmy do the same. All are armed. Every damn one of them's dressed in some shade of camo. Every damn one of them's beautiful.

"Couldn't resist a little Rebel yell," says Zac, caressing his crumpled bumper. "Always wanted to be one a' those ole boys from *Dukes of Hazzard*."

"Mr. Colonna," Matt says, rushing forward, "you're hurt."

Marcus grips Matt's hand. "I'm very old, my friend. I'm already healing."

"You hillbillies sure like your dramatic entrances," I say.

"Effective entrances, I'd call 'em," Zac counters, clapping my back and scanning the scatter of corpses. "Looks like y'all have cleaned up the first batch."

"These assholes have fucked with the wrong folks," Timmy says, brandishing his rifle. "We been practicing at the shooting range. We're all aching to hand out some old-fashioned mountaineer butt-whipping."

"Seems like the place to do it," Nate says, smiling with satisfaction at the flaming ruins. Somewhere in the direction I last saw Sigurd advancing, more men are screaming. "Looks like my explosives came in handy. Just the Hell-on-Earth smoking chaos I was hoping for."

"Honey, you're hurt too," Matt says, gripping my arm and examining my wound.

"I'm fine, Matt. You all stay out of the thick of fighting unless absolutely necessary. Promise me?"

"Yep." Matt grimaces. "Though the least we can do is pick off a few of these thugs for you. Me and Nate in particular have some grudges to settle."

I nod. "You're mortal, though. Remember that, for Odin's sake."

"We promise," Timmy says. "Meanwhile, your friend Cynthia, she's—"

Another explosion, toward the rear of the house. A vampire's death scream, most likely a rowan-wood bullet to the heart. The front door of the burning mansion flies open, and another group of armed men emerges. One spies us and fires. Another does the same. One bullet zings past my ear. Another breaks the Jeep's driver's-side headlight.

"Shit!" Timmy says. "Get behind the Jeep, guys!"

We take cover. Bullets pepper the vehicle. The other headlight shatters. Tires deflate. Zac wails. "Oh, hell. My baby."

"I'll buy you a new one," I drawl. "Y'all stay here now. Bullets can't do much against a green mist. Let me—"

Suddenly Sigurd's at my elbow. "We destroyed the back of the house, at the cost of several *draugr* lives. No one will escape from that angle; it's burning hotly. I think Sodeski's retreated to the cellar."

"He has a safe room there, where he escaped me before. But he's unlikely to stay there with the house burning down around him."

Another round of bullets tears into the shelter of the Jeep. "Then he'll come out the front or the side," says Marcus. "Those men on the porch are trying to make a path for him."

On the far side of the hill, the distinctive flapping of a helicopter nears.

Marcus nudges Sigurd. "The cars are demolished, so our quarry hopes to take to the sky? In the midst of night-winging *vampiri*? *Imbecille*! *Cretino*!"

"Does that mean retarded?" Timmy says.

"In a manner of speaking," says Marcus, chuckling.

"Ragingly stupid." Sigurd nods. "Delightfully desperate."

"Shall we?" Marcus gestures skyward. "I'm in the mood to harry."

"You've recovered sufficiently?"

"Close enough," Marcus replies, rubbing his abdomen. "Let's go, Orcadian."

"Yeeow!" Zac gasps, as Sigurd and Marcus take to wing and zip into the sky. "Y'all can all do that?"

Another round of bullets rakes our makeshift barricade. "Shit," says Zac. We better retreat. If one a' those bullets hits the fuel tank, we're all fucked."

"Good point," I say. "Why don't I get their attention while you all get out of harm's way? Move beyond the compound wall until I can—"

A series of popping sounds fills the air. A canister rolls around the vehicle. I seize it and lob it back.

"They're trying to gas us, the fuckers. I can do better than that," Nate says. Pulling a grenade from his haversack, he offers it to me. "Derek, you want to go airborne with this?"

More popping. Several canisters drop around us. Racing about, I manage to retrieve three and toss them over the Jeep. The others explode, spewing corrosive smoke.

"Goddamn it!" Timmy cries. "Tear gas!"

"Mixed with rowan essence," I gasp, as burning tears my eyes. "Let's go, boys, before—"

Hold your ground, Derek. It's Cynthia, sounding inside my head. A sharp wind picks up, dispersing the noisome fumes, driving them in the direction of the house. Above us, thick clouds congeal, veiling the summer sky. In the woods behind us echoes a low howling.

"Excellent," I say. "Cynthia and our lupine friends approach."

"Oh, shit. Donnie's never really let loose around me," Timmy says. "This I gotta see."

"Look, Derek! Look!" Matt says, wiping his face and pointing. "They're here."

Cynthia takes slow form just outside the smashed shards of the gate. She's dressed as she was at Grand Hotel, and she's smiling broadly. On her right lopes the half-man, half-wolf that Donnie becomes. On her left strides a bristling black beast, all wolf: Rebekah. The lycanthropes regard us, snarling.

"Not them. Those are friends." Cynthia fondles the black wolf's ears and points toward the smoking mansion. "Those men over there, those are the ones you want. Rend them. Tear out their throats."

The beasts race forward. Cacophony mounts: snarling, screaming, the popping of guns. With one hand, I rub wet from my eyes. With the other, I grip Cynthia's hand. "Perfect timing, those storm-gusts of yours."

"Thank you. After the wolves clear the way, we should enter the house. Where are Sigurd and Marcus?"

"In the air. Sabotaging Sodeski's escape vehicle."

"The helicopter? Oh, good. Have you encountered the demon? Surely the magus will rouse it."

"No sign of Aldinach yet. But I have the black tourmaline." I pat the stone, hanging on its chain about my neck. "I'm ready to use the blood-charm whenever the thing appears."

"This particular saga shall be called, 'Derek, Cynthia, and the Sea Cucumber from Hell.' Listen. The gunfire's ceased. Shall we?"

Cautiously, I move around the ruined Jeep, every sense on alert. The mansion's porch is cluttered with bodies. I move up the steps, nudging aside corpses left in the wolves' wake—staring eyes, torn necks, black blood. The door stands wide open. Somewhere in the house, another bout of snarling erupts, then another bout of shrieking.

"Jesus," Timmy murmurs. "Donnie-boy, you and your friend are tearing 'em to pieces." His tone's part horror, part admiration.

"I want Sodeski alive," I say, leading my little pack into the spacious entrance hall. More bodies scatter its tiled floor.

"How about the magus?" Matt says. "The guy who summoned that slug thing? He's gotta be here. Derek, how about us boys take care of him?"

"No, Matt. He might be dangerous, especially if Aldinach's near."

"I'll keep the wolves off Sodeski and his wife till you return," Cynthia offers. "I can smell her vulgar perfume. They can't be far. Let me—"

Screams erupt in the yard behind the house. Not human screaming. Vampires. Vampires in great pain.

"Something's very wrong," Cynthia says.

"It's here," I say.

"Sir!" someone shouts behind us. Raffaello, one of Marcus's men, a lean Tuscan with styled black hair and a square jaw, rushes into the entrance hall. "Laird Maclaine, the demon! It's out back. It's enraged! It's brought down nearly all of us. Please come. Please help us!"

"Stay here," I say, gripping Matt's elbow. "Do not follow me. Cynthia…."

"Yes. You stop that thing, and I'll fetch your prey."

"Derek!" Matt pulls me into a quick hug and kisses me hard on the mouth. "Please be careful."

"The same to you. Don't take any chances," I say, kissing him back. "Lead the way, Raffaello."

The Tuscan and I speed out the door and around the house. "There," Raffaello says, pointing, but there's no need. My hell-spawn of a foe is all too apparent, shimmering and ballooning in flares of firelight.

"Go back inside," I say, staring at the thing. "Help my friends." Another second, and Raffaello's fled.

Aldinach's pulsing fog-shape is larger than it was before, a palpitating malignance looming at the opposite end of the patio. In the space between, fallen *draugar* are slumped, unconscious, or rolling about, howling, their bodies splotched with the foul acid I remember all too well.

"Scum," I snarl, drawing my dirk. "You've interfered with my homeland long enough."

It recognizes me now, and the rush of auric hate is so strong it ripples the air and shoves me backward a step. The side of the Lovecraftian blob purses like a mouth and launches its foul essence toward me.

I dodge the satanic spit. Beside me, patio flags are spattered. They hiss, steam, and crack. I launch my dirk through the air toward the demon. Might as well see how solid its form is. The denser it is, the easier it will be to hack its remains into gobbets.

My dirk disappears into its slimy flank only to make an audible clatter as it hits the patio's flagstones. Aldinach does no more than shudder. Fumes roil from the thing, concentric waves of noxious gas no doubt as corrosive as its projectile slobber. I slide into bat form and rise above the threat.

Tentacles take shape, snapping out at me, seeking to snag my legs. More saliva's spat my way, narrowing missing the high veer of my wingspan. I flap over the center of the thing, claw off the pendant, and drop it. Let the charm anointed by the blood of many vampires do its work.

To my horror, the stone stops with a clinking sound a good yard above the hell-slug. Sparking violently, it makes a slow arc to the patio, as if sliding down something curved, invisible. Gods damn it, Aldinach must be surrounded with some sort of chitinous shield.

Snarling, I skirt the nebulous horror, snatching the tourmaline up in my claws and rising again, only to be caught in the right wing and in the belly with acid.

Agony floods me. Reverting into human form, I fall, smashing into the grass of the lawn. Another spume of venom coats me, burning off my garments, dissolving my sword belt. When I rise, roaring, my claymore drops from my waist, its scabbard melted away, its metal smoking.

Damn it, where's the charm? There, to my left, sparking again, as if leading me to it. I dart over, grasp it in my hand, and hurl it at the horror. Again, the stone ricochets off an unseen shell, clattering across the patio. How do I gut this thing with the amulet if I can't pierce its protection?

I leap back onto the patio, searching for the tourmaline. Another gout of slimy toxin splashes my back, eating into my skin. Here's the sparkling charm, beckoning me. It wants to be used. I can feel it.

Only one possibility left. Otherwise, this thing will reduce my homeland to a heap of broken rocks and my people to a mound of burnt bones. I clutch the charm, stumble forward, and take up my scorched claymore. I will enter this thing's body, whatever the consequences, and I will take the charm with me.

"By Odin, I am the end of you," I snarl, swinging the blade. The first blow's deflected by its shell, then the second. Acid hits me in the face, agonizing. Half-blinded, I swing again. The sword blade flashes with violet light—the color of Okey's magic. Beneath my blow, something gives. Something brittle turns soft. I slice again and again, staggering forward into a stinking viscosity. The demon contracts, writhing about me, emitting psychic screeches that burn my brain. Its every movement flays my skin.

A great force hits me in the face like a battering ram, and I go flying backward off the patio. Still clutching claymore and charm, I hit the ground, shoulders furrowing the dirt.

I shake dizziness from my head, trying to gather my wits. Before me, the thing tumbles down the steps of the patio in pursuit. I rise on one elbow, sprawled in cool grass. There's no sight in my left eye.

Aldinach streams forward, pulsating. It is, I sense, preparing to spew more acid in my face. One more well-placed gout of venom, and this spitting cobra from the pits will have me blind and at its mercy. But then it pauses. It shifts, as if uncomfortable. It contracts and retreats, as if it's recoiling. But from what? Certainly not my considerably diminished strength. Back up the patio steps it surges, hissing, thwarted. Why?

Derek! It's Matt's voice in my head. Great Herne, I can tell he's badly hurt.

I'm scrabbling to my feet when Aldinach twists, quivers, and expands. One tentacle arcs through the air and snaps around my neck.

"Goddamn you! Get off me, you fuck," I spit, clawing at the taut slime that grips my throat.

Derek, Matt groans. *The magus....*

The demon's tentacle tightens, cutting off my breath. I go wild, kicking and clawing. "Goddamn you. Goddamn you," I gasp. "Lemme loose."

Do it, Derek! Matt bellows in my head. *I love you. Do—*

Matt's passed out. I can sense it. I've got to get to him.

Again Aldinach emits a voiceless shrieking. Its grasp tightens, twitches, and then, to my surprise and relief, goes entirely slack. The foul appendage about my throat liquefies, splashing me like a chemical-fouled brook. The demon, flickering shades of red, purple and gray, backs up, turns away, and begins to thrash.

Something's happened. Something's different, and I don't know what. My foe suddenly seems addled and directionless. It's ignoring me while it throws the demonic equivalent of an hysterical fit. Whatever the cause, I need to take the advantage while I can.

Staggering to my feet, ignoring the burning pain of my wounds, I swing my sword once more. There's no chitinous skin now. The foggy astral mess cleaves open like a freshly slaughtered loin of meat. Gripping the tourmaline in my left hand, I shove the charm inside.

There's a blinding flash of crimson light and a percussive thunderclap that knocks me backward, off my feet. Aldinach screeches, then that screech rises, stretching out into high keening. The thing rears up and spasms. It tumbles off the patio and plops into the grass with a sickening squelch.

Clambering to my feet, I leap onto it, slashing it with my claymore. To my pleasure, the blade encounters solid substance, its sharp edge cleaving off chunks of the thing. That's how the coven's magic has worked! The tourmaline's made the demon's etheric, protean matter a solid substance, something that can be wounded, dismembered, gutted, and destroyed.

Exhilarated, I heave a shout and swing again, amputating a pseudopod. Shrieking, flinching, it slithers away. I pursue it, driving it over the lawn. When it backs up into a boxwood hedge, it cringes. Its gray surface shudders, as if it were brushing up against barbed wire or a wall of thorns. By the Gods, is the thing allergic to leaves?

Chlorophyll. Of course. No wonder it's dedicated to wiping out the woodlands wherever it goes.

"Hah! I know your secret now, you loathsome germ. This forest will be your grave," I snarl, giving it a vicious stab. Squealing, it reels away. I hack at it. It backs up. I hack at it again. I drive it into the woods. It writhes, agonized by the thick undergrowth. By the time we reach the cliff over which I flew the first night I came here, it's limping and oozing, and I've managed to slash off nearly a quarter of its mass.

On the edge, it comes to an abrupt halt. It lunges at me once more time and then slumps into itself, hissing and sighing.

"Enough. My lover needs me. I have no more time for you. Let the greenwood finish you." Gripping my sword in both hands, I grit my teeth. I bring the blade down as hard as I can, cleaving the squirming thing in half. Screeching, its remains roll off the edge and drop a hundred feet into the thick leaves of trees below. There's a series of crashing sounds, a low wailing that tapers off, and then there's nothing to hear but wind in summer boughs.

"The revenge of the Green Man," I say, hawking scorn-spit over the drop.

"Matt!" Half blind, naked, a good three-fourths of my skin burnt black, I stagger back toward the burning house.

CHAPTER FORTY-ONE

Sodeski's house is a holocaust. Any human being still inside will be burnt to ashes.

On the patio, still scattered with wounded vampires, I snatch up my acid-corroded dirk, then skirt the flaming house, searching for my clansmen. Human corpses sprawl in the lawn, nearly thirty of them, their throats ravaged by the teeth of werewolves or vampires.

Where's Matt? Where's Matt? Nearby. I can sense him. I can smell him. I can smell his blood.

There they are, my boys. They're huddled together on the front lawn. Lanky Nate's pacing, eyes narrowed, watching the perimeters, gun at the ready, though no enemies appear to be left. Timmy's wounded, sitting cross-legged, holding a bloodstained rag to his shoulder. Matt's slumped on his back in the grass. Zac's on his knees at Matt's feet, sobbing.

"Jesus, Derek," Nate gasps, studying the extent of my damage. "You're burned so bad."

I reel closer, dropping my weapons. "Matt. What's happened to Matt?"

"Derek, oh, God." Nate steps aside.

A ragged stab wound in Matt's chest is welling gouts of bright blood. He's unconscious. He's still breathing, but he's fading fast. His inhalations are faint and shallow.

"Oh, Odin. Oh, no." I drop to my knees and take his hand. "What happened? What happened?"

Timmy scowls. "We found the magus. Damn fool was hiding in the base-ment, in some kinda ritual room, mumbling who knows what sorta evil shit? When we broke in, the bastard shot me. He nearly shot Nate in the face. Matt grappled with him. He was clutching something, some kinda charm we fig-ured was important 'cause he was protecting it so fierce. It was a scroll of some sort, wrapped around a...a human finger bone, and it was set in silver, I guess 'cause he knew you vamps wouldn't be able to wrassle it away from him."

"But Matt did," Nate says. "The guy put up a helluva fight, but Matt tore it away from him. That's when he stabbed Matt in the chest with a knife."

"I hit the motherfucker in the head with a candlestick," Zac says. "I remem-ber him. Mr. Mathers. Up here all the time. Nasty as hell to everyone 'cept the Sodeskis. He hurt Matt so bad. I couldn't stop hitting him. I bashed his skull open. He's still inside. Burnt up by now, the bastard."

"Matt smashed the charm before he passed out," Nate says. "The thing fizzed with some kind of red foam and exploded."

"That's my brave warrior," I say, stroking Matt's slack face and fighting back tears. "What he did weakened the demon enough for me to use the coven's blood-charm. Where's Cynthia?"

"She's good," Timmy says. "Her and the rest of Mr. Colonna's men have the Sodeskis locked up in the potting shed."

"Donnie and Rebekah?"

"Both of them took bullets," Nate says. "But that only seemed to irritate them. There are dismembered limbs all over the compound. They must have taken down three-fourths of Sodeski's men."

"Just the bloodbath I dreamed of," I say, examining Matt's injury. The wound's very deep. The dagger pierced a lung, and, from the brilliant crimson oozing out of him, an artery too.

"Derek? Is he going to...?" Nate whispers.

"Yes." I run a finger over Matt's face. "The only chance he has is if I turn him. But...."

"But?" Timmy says.

"But...I don't know what he'd want. We've been together for a long time, and he's never wanted me to change him. Only lately has he even mentioned the possibility."

"You can't think he'd rather die? Leave you? Leave us?" Nate says.

"No. I think he'd rather stay. Even…changed. But I don't have the strength, boys. I'm damaged badly. And I've never transformed anyone before. Ever. I—"

Another explosion jars the air. Distant, but prodigious. The sky to the west lights up, as if the sun were setting twice this evening.

"Christ," Zac grunts. "What the fuck was *that?*"

"Marcus and Sigurd. The helicopter. Marcus and Sigurd. Marcus and Sigurd!" I say, choking on frantic laughter and sudden hope. I close my eyes, clutch my head, and call out to them. *Master. Maker. Come to me as fast as you can. Matt's dying. I need your strength.*

Matt moans and gasps. Bloody foam edges his wound. A scarlet bubble swells and pops. Then another. Then another.

"Oh, God, boss!" Zac whimpers. "He's about gone!"

The wind picks up again, and a thin drizzle prickles my burnt face. A flapping fills the air. Boughs sough around us. A strong hand grips my right shoulder. Another hand grips my left arm and pulls me to my feet.

Two men loom over me, the blond Roman and the blond Viking. "We're here, Derek," Sigurd says, stroking my face. "Drink from us, boy, and be whole."

Sigurd offers his neck. I lunge. I drink. I drink. I drink. The old blood shimmers through me, effervescent with might. Vision seeps back into my blinded eye.

"Enough now. Come to me, Caledonian." Gently, Marcus pulls me away, wraps me in his arms, kisses my cheek, and presses his throat to my mouth. Again, I gulp and gulp, till Marcus is shaking and slumping against me.

"Enough," Sigurd says, pulling me off. "Your love has little time. Turn him. The Norns have given you this chance. I suggest you take it fast. Do you remember how I turned you? The extra potency of the seed?"

"I remember well," I say. My smile makes my healing skin smart.

"Hurry. Over there. That outbuilding's empty. You'll need privacy. Go."

Matthew groans as I lower him onto the floor of the tool shed. I sink my teeth into his neck, taking only the tiniest mouthful of blood, since he has so little to spare. Then I slice my left breast and nipple with the dirk and press his mouth to my wound.

For an agonizingly long moment, Matt doesn't respond. *Herne. Cerridwen. Hertha. Cernunnos. Eros. Freya. Frey. Please. Please. Allfather Odin. Osiris, raiser of the dead. Please. Please.*

Matt moans. He shivers violently. His eyes flicker open. He licks my bloody nipple. "Derek?" he pants, nuzzling my chest hair. "That, that you?"

"Yes, sweet lover."

"Um, thought I was done for. Hard to breathe, but…. Umm, you taste good," he says, lapping at me. "That…that your blood?"

"Yes, Matt. Drink it now. Drink from me, or you'll die."

"Will I become…?"

"Yes. Sorry, honey. Not much choice now. Vampire or corpse. Up to you."

Matt fingers his chest wound, flinches, and moans. "Ohhhh, shit. Okay. Here goes." Wrapping a weak arm around my back, he pulls me closer and begins to suck.

"Good. Good," I sigh, running my fingers through his mussed hair. "Take as much as you please."

It's many minutes before Matt lifts his head. His eyes are glazed, his mouth curled in a blood-smeared smile. "Oh, wow. Wuuuuhhhfff."

"Now this," I say, pushing my cock against his cheek. "Suck me."

"Ummmmm. You bet, baby," Matt says, taking me onto his tongue as if I were some hairy Host, then wrapping his lips firmly around my shaft and sucking softly.

Gripping his head, I grow stiff fast. I ride his face until I've climaxed in his mouth. He swallows my load, humming with satisfaction. Giggling, he licks his lips.

He drowses. He sweats. He tosses and shakes. He passes out. He comes to with a start.

"Whoa, man," he groans, shaking his head. "Drunk as shit. Weak. Hit by a freight train. This the way it works?"

"Yep. One last thing," I say. Tugging his pants down around his ankles, I roll him onto his belly and lube us up with sweat, blood, and spit.

"Relax now, Matt. Open up for me, okay?" I say, patting an ass-cheek and prick-nudging his hole.

"Hell, yes," Matt grunts, nodding weakly. "Put it in me."

I lie atop his sweaty back and spread his thighs with mine. Slowly, I ease my cock into his ass.

Matt tenses and sighs. "Ohhhh, yeah. All the way. All the way in now. Sweet. Damn, so sweet. Fuck me, Derek. Fuck me, Daddy."

"In blood and semen are the mystery and the magic," I whisper, nuzzling his neck. "My strength will make you strong."

"Oh, Derek. Oh, honey man. Oh, hell, yes," Matt groans, arching back against me, slipping into the delirium of the change. "Yeah, fuck me, Daddy. God, gimme your rod. Sheath that big Scottish sword of yours." Humping the floor, he reaches back with both hands and spreads his fuzzy buttocks wider. "Ohhhh, yeah, use my ass. Gimme your seed. Gimme your life."

"Matt's passed out again," I say, as Zac hands me a pair of army-green cargo shorts retrieved from the back of his Jeep. "He'll sleep for a good while now."

My anxious boys surround me in such a tight pack it's hard to pull the shorts on. "But he made it, right?" Nate says, handing me my claymore.

"Yes." I shake out my hair and study the house, which has fallen into black-ening embers. "Matt made it, thank the Gods."

"He'll be different, though? Like you?" Zac asks.

"Yes. Tomorrow night, he'll awaken, strong, healthy, and whole, with no sign of a wound, and he'll be a *draugr*."

"Hmm. Two vampires at Mount Storm?" Timmy rubs his neck. "We better find a few new housemates to, uh, spread the, uh, hemoglobin? Hemoglobin donations out?"

"Successful, I hear," Cynthia says, striding up. Her usually calm face is grooved with concern. She gives me a hearty hug. "I feared I'd lost you both."

"Not tonight, praise the Gods…and praise all of you. We should finish this business and get out of here. I'd imagine Sodeski had cops on his payroll who—"

Cynthia smiles. "Who rushed up here when the alarm went off. Yes. Who then rushed back to Madison to carouse all night, having entirely forgotten who Stanley Sodeski ever was. Marcus, Sigurd, and I have already taken care of that potential inconvenience for you. So there's little left to do. And what little is left I've saved for your delectation."

"Yes," I say, lifting the claymore. "Let's end this and get home."

Sodeski rises when we enter. Potted geraniums and marigolds bloom brightly around the man personally responsible for the destruction of so much Appalachian flora and fauna. In the corner, his wife's wedged, blubbering and squealing.

"You son of a bitch! I'll see you dead," he blusters, but the smell of terror rolls off him like swamp-stink.

"Stan, give these people whatever they want," his wife begs. Cynthia was right about her perfume. It's cheap, abominable. I can taste it on the back of my tongue.

"One last lark before this saga is done?" Cynthia says, raising an eyebrow.

"Indeed." I raise my sword. Sodeski backs up and whines.

"Go," I say, lowering my blade and moving aside.

Sodeski gapes. "Praise the Lord," his wife sighs. Sodeski grips her hand and they make for the door. Cynthia and I step outside to watch their mad flight.

"Dogs, I assume?" I say, grinning.

"Yes. Long night. Sheer convenience. You?"

"I have a surprise."

The Sodeskis are halfway across the body-strewn lawn when barking begins. Guard dogs swiftly converge. Only yards from the gate, they bring Mrs. Sodeski down and begin a savage ripping of flesh.

Mr. Sodeski pauses not a whit. Ignoring his wife's screams, he barrels past Zac's bullet-riddled Jeep and out of the compound.

"So?" Cynthia says, frowning.

"Follow me," I say. Side by side, we stride toward the gate. We're nearly there when shrill sounds of terror delight our ears.

Just beyond the gate, the coal mogul's huddled against the wall, eyes bugging out of his head. A very large black bear confronts him, baring its teeth.

"Well done," Cynthia says. "Perfection achieved." Chuckling, she crosses her arms.

"I thought you'd approve."

Sodeski snatches up a fallen tree limb and waves it at the bear. In normal circumstances, this might be successful, but not tonight, when a very angry vampire's will goads the beast to especially violent action. Soon, the bear's charging toward Sodeski, and Sodeski's staggering along the wall. The animal's on him in a trice.

The mauling goes on till I'm weary of it. "Stop, brother. Enough," I say.

The bear gives the quivering, blood-soaked form one last swat, then pads up to me.

"You have given me a great boon, brother," I say, stroking its moist nose, wiping blood from its mouth. "Go now, and live a long life."

The bear grunts. He nuzzles my hand, then lumbers off into the woods.

"The revenge of the God of the Beasts," I murmur.

"Indeed," says Cynthia.

I stand over my foe. He's still conscious, dull glance flickering up at me. I would stay to watch him suffer and bleed, but dawn's approaching, and I want to take Matt home.

I lift my claymore and strike off Sodeski's head. Then I call the many small, hungry mouths of the forest to finish what's left.

CHAPTER FORTY-TWO

When Matt wakes at sundown, we're snuggled together in my cellar nest.

"Home. We're home?" Matt says, taking my hand. His face is drawn, very pale.

"Yes," I say, brushing hair off his brow. "Sodeski's dead, and Aldinach's gone."

"And I'm...like you, right?"

"Yes. I'm sorry. We've lived together long enough for you to know what that means."

"Yep. I'll miss the sun for sure. But don't be sorry. It had to be done. But, man, I'm thirsty. For...for blood, I guess?"

"Yes." I slip a forefinger into his mouth, probing his gums. He chortles and bites down.

"There you go," I say. "Full-fledged fanglets."

"Wow. Really?" he mutters around my finger. He pushes his own finger in beside mine, probes, and gasps.

"Ohhh, man," he says. "You're right. Sharp as hell."

"You're ready to feed. Here," I say, pulling him to me. "Let me be your first."

Still stunned from the change, like a butterfly recently emerged from its chrysalis, Matt nods. Shyly, tentatively, he nuzzles my neck.

"Go on. You won't hurt me. To quote you from last night, 'Put it in me.'"

Matt chuckles, his beard tickling my skin. "You got it," he says, sinking his teeth into me.

I flinch and sigh. He drinks from me, mumbling with wonder. The vampiric intimacy has us both hard. We fondle each other's dicks, swaying together. He takes shallow sips at first, then deeper draughts, till I'm light-headed.

"Enough for now," I say, pulling away.

"Amazing. Tastes better than I ever woulda dreamed." Matt rubs his hand over his mouth and slumps back onto the bed. "Uhhhfff. Now I'm sleepy again."

"You're still changing. The process takes a while. Why don't you take a nap? I have something to do, but I'll be back soon. Just rest here, all right?"

"Yeah, sure." Smiling, sated, Matt passes out.

Rising, I pull on T-shirt and cargo pants and collect what paraphernalia I'll need. Slipping out the back door of the cellar, I climb into the van, start it up, and head down the mountain toward Petersburg, West Virginia.

A guitar and Civil War musket are propped in opposite corners of the bedroom. A sheathed Bowie knife's resting on the dresser, a Confederate uniform's hanging in the closet. The boy's sprawled in bed, sound asleep. Wearing nothing but white briefs, he's lying on his side atop the sheet, sweating in the efficiency apartment's stuffy air. A rotating fan hums on the dresser.

I stand over him, snuffling his aroma, studying the fetching details of his face and physique. No wonder Matthew's been raving about how cute he is. Hunter Hedrick's pale and lean, with freckled shoulders, lightly muscled arms, a full chestnut-brown beard, and the curvaceous pecs and buttocks Matthew and I both savor on a man. He's about twenty-five, I'd guess, around a hundred sixty pounds. I hope he gives me just a little fight.

I bend down and touch his cheek. The boy grunts, rubs his face, and rolls over onto his belly. Just the position I want him in.

I leap upon him. His arm's twisted behind his back and my hand's clamped over his mouth before he can do or say anything. Gasping, he starts to struggle.

"If you scream, I'll snap your neck," I snarl. "I'm about fifty times stronger than you."

The boy shouts and kicks. I wrap my legs around him and wrench his arm hard. He yelps with pain against my palm.

"Shut up, damn you. If you don't, I'll break your arm, and then I'll smother you. I'll gut you with your own Bowie knife. I'll slaughter anyone who might be foolish enough to come to your aid."

I clamp my hand harder, squeezing his nose shut, stifling his breath. He whimpers, tossing his head and fighting for air.

"Do you want to die?" I say, brushing his bearded cheek with mine. "If you do, keep fighting me. If you don't, stop fighting me. If you stop fighting me, I swear I won't hurt you."

The boy trembles beneath me. He emits a hoarse moan and falls still.

"Good. You're not going to cry out if I take my hand off your mouth?"

The boy slowly shakes his head.

"Good," I say, lifting my hand off his face. While he gasps and coughs, sucking in air, I pull cord from my cargo pants and rapidly bind his hands behind him, then tie his feet together.

"W-who…w-who are you?" he stutters, rolling onto his side. He gazes up at me with terror so abject it thrills my heart and hardens my crotch.

"I'm Derek Maclaine. And you're Hunter Hedrick," I say, running a hand over his close-cropped hair. "My partner Matt's told me a lot about you. He's admired you at several Civil War reenactments. I can see why."

"M-Matt? M-Matt Taylor? You're his—?"

"Yes. He has need of you. I'm going to take you to him now."

"Hell, if M-Matt needs me…I w-would have come with you if you'd asked. Why'd you j-jump me and tie me up?"

I run a hand over his narrow shoulders, then trail a finger over his flat belly and compact pecs. He's fuzzy in all the right places.

"Because I felt like it. Because I enjoy your fear and your futility, your body struggling against me. Because I like to see you tied. Because you wouldn't have come willingly if you knew what Matt needed." I pull a rag and a roll of duct tape from my pants pockets.

Hunter stares at what I hold. He licks his lips. "Wha…what does M-Matt need?"

"He needs your blood."

"My blood? What do you mean?"

"You'll see."

Clutching the back of his head, I cram the rag into his mouth, cutting off a wail of protest. When he resists me, shaking his head and twisting in his bonds, I backhand him twice. Then I muzzle him: several feet of tape wrapped around his head and over his mouth, several more feet layered under his chin and over his scalp, immobilizing his jaw.

"Time to go," I say, hauling the dazed boy to his feet. "Keep quiet, or no one in this building will live to see the morning. All right?"

Hunter stares at me with wide green eyes. He nods, and then, to my delight, begins to cry.

"Matt has excellent taste." Bending, I throw his slight weight over my shoulder. "He's going to relish you."

I carry Hunter through his apartment. Pausing at the front door, I listen. No one near is awake, I sense, so I slip out into the hall and lope down the stairs.

Outside, the night air's surprisingly cool for July, sharp with the first indication of approaching autumn. I open the van's back doors and lay Hunter gently on a blanket. He curls into a ball, squints his eyes shut, and begins to sob in earnest. I take in the rapturous sight—a slender, bearded, bound and gagged youth whom terror has broken down entirely—then close the door, climb into the driver's seat, start the engine, and steer the van out of the parking lot.

By the time we reach Mount Storm and I've dragged Hunter from the back of the van, the captive boy's weeping has ceased. His face is still wet with tears, though, warm and welcome brine I lap up before carrying him through the side door of the cellar.

Matt wakes as we enter the crypt. He rubs his eyes and grins.

"Holy shit, I cain't believe it," he groans, sitting up and staring at my winsome armload. "You just went in and kidnapped the kid?"

"Hell, yes." I lower Hunter onto his roped feet, then shove him forward onto the bed. "Why not? Why waste time? One of the great glories of being a *draugr* is the ease with which you wreak your will upon the world. You need to feed. He's all yours. Haven't you been wanting him naked and in your arms for months?"

"Ohhhhhh, fuck." Matt slides over to Hunter, wraps an arm around him, and pulls him onto his lap. When a fang snags on grinning Matt's lower lip, Hunter begins to whine.

"Poor kid. All taped and trussed up. You're scared shitless, ain't you?"

Hunter whimpers and nods. He's shaking violently.

"You want me to let you loose?"

Hunter bows his head and nods. He seems unable to look Matt in the eyes.

"Not just yet," I say, pulling off my clothes.

"Naw. Not just yet," Matt says, eyes gleaming. He growls low in his throat. He licks Hunter's neck. Hunter closes his eyes and sniffles.

"Ohhh, man, Derek. I want him so bad." Matt pinches Hunter's right nipple and squeezes his buttocks. Hunter flinches and squirms.

"The boy's beautiful, is he not?" I say, joining them on the bed.

"God, yes," Matt murmurs, voice full of hunger and awe. Smiling, he strokes Hunter's hair and nibbles at the skin over his carotid. "So, so beautiful. His beard. His pretty eyes. His sweet little body. His tight little ass. His skin's so soft. I've never felt anything so soft. And the smell of him? It's driving me crazy."

"So beautiful that you'd like to keep him around? Make him your slave? Or shall we both feast on him till he's drained dry?"

At these words, Hunter huddles against Matt's chest, shakes his head, and again begins to sob.

"Ah, naw. Ah, naw. Don't cry, Hunter baby. I don't want to kill nobody." Matt rocks the boy in his lap, fondling his tape-swathed face, kissing his brow. "Don't be afraid. I'll take care of you. Don't cry. Don't cry."

"Look into his eyes, Matt. Now you can do what I do. Convince him he's in no danger."

"Umm, okay, I'll try. Hunter? Hunter, sweet boy?" Matt cups our prisoner's chin in his hand, kisses him on the nose, and gazes into his eyes. "Stop crying. You hear me, Hunter? Stop that crying now. Ain't no reason to cry."

Hunter stops weeping. He visibly relaxes. He stares at Matt, tears dribbling down his tape-plastered cheeks.

"I need something from you, Hunter. Okay? I need it bad. I ain't gonna take it by force. That'd be rude, right? I'm asking you for it, man. 'Cause we're buddies now, right?"

Hunter blinks long-lashed eyes and nods.

Matt nudges Hunter's chin with his own. "I need to drink from you, buddy. That all right? And then I wanna make love to you, okay?" Matt kneads Hunter's crotch though his briefs. "I wanna make you feel good. After I feed from you, I wanna fuck you so slow and sweet and tender. You want that? That okay with you? You want me inside you where you're all slick and warm and tight? You want me to ride you hard, till we both come?"

Hunter hesitates for a long moment. Then he rests his brow against Matt's furry chest, rubs his groin against Matt's hand, takes a deep breath, exhales, and nods.

"There's my guy. Yeah, there's my little guy," Matt sighs, exposing a fang and raking the white skin in the pit of Hunter's neck. "It's time, ain't it? It's time. I gotta taste you now."

"Go ahead, Matt," I say, clasping his shoulder. "I'll stop you when I think you've taken enough."

"Good. Don't let me hurt the kid." With a bass snarl, Matt exposes his new fangs and sinks them into Hunter Hedrick's snowy throat.

"About an hour till dawn," I say, running my fingers through Matt's belly hair, snuggling against him from behind. Hunter—thoroughly assfucked, unconscious from blood loss, still tape-muzzled and bound—is wrapped in Matt's arms.

"It was so hard to stop," Matt says, squeezing my hand. "Thanks for pulling me offa him. I would never have forgiven myself if I'd killed the lil' guy. Will it always be so hard to stop?"

"No. You'll learn. We'll feed together for the first year or so, till you can control yourself."

"So what we gonna do with him?" Matt says, lapping at the raw wound on the boy's throat.

"We're going to carry him upstairs here in a little bit and let Timmy and the others take care of him. He's your thrall now. Your first thrall. You can send him home, or you can keep him here. Whatever you want."

"I figure we got enough of a harem here, and, besides, the boy's trying to finish a degree. How about we just have him up every month or so? To snack on and plow cross-eyed?"

"Sounds good to me. You and I have shared Nate, Timmy, Donnie and Zac sexually, so now we can share them in another way. I gather from all the slurping and groaning and yum-yum-yumming you were doing that you enjoyed Hunter's blood?"

"Enjoyed? Better'n a sausage, mayo, and 'mater biscuit. You were right about how much richer and tastier than any food a hot guy's blood and semen are. Never thought I'd say that. No more gray hairs in my beard, huh?"

"Nope. You're perpetually forty-seven, unless you don't feed."

"Guess you're stuck with me for longer than you thought, Laird Maclaine." Matt chuckles, rubbing his bare ass against my groin. "You saved my life, that's for sure."

"And you saved mine. When you destroyed that magus's scroll, it weakened the demon so much that I was able to use the coven's charm. If you hadn't done that, its acid might've blinded me, and then we would all've been done for."

"So Sigurd and them didn't find any trace of that fucking thing at the bottom of the cliff, huh?"

"Nothing. Just scorch marks on the side of a boulder and some very lush vegetation. I think the power of that blood-charm and the strokes of my claymore reduced Aldinach to particularly rich plant fertilizer."

"Poetic justice, I'd say, after all the forest that fucking thing helped Alpha tear up. So what're we gonna do about what's left of Alpha?"

"Now that their demon mascot's gone, now that you're a *draugr*, we can do what we please."

"I have a few things in mind, followed by a big celebratory party. We'll invite Okey, and lil' Hunter here, and Cynthia. All the clan."

"Clan Shadow. Our friends and kin. I would never have been able to defeat Aldinach without their help, or without you. I would never have been able to turn you without Sigurd's and Marcus's healing blood." I kiss Matt's shoulder and grip his hand. "Now you'll never age and never die."

"Well, fuck me. Talk about a happy ending."

"I believe I will fuck you, Mr. Taylor," I say, patting Matt's chunky butt, sliding a finger through his crack-fuzz. "Hurriedly, since it's so close to dawn. Then we'll free your new boy, take him upstairs, and introduce him to the household. Then you and I will sleep the day away here in this cozy crypt, wrapped in one another's arms. For the next few nights, I'll coach you in your new abilities, and then...."

"And then," says Matt, grinning sunnily, cocking a leg and wiggling his ass against my hand, "you and I are gonna take on what's left of Alpha."

CHAPTER FORTY-THREE

The night before Yule, the mountains of Mingo County are covered with snow. Frigid flurry-gusts buffet us as Matt and I wing over the last ridge, angling our way closer to Alpha's mountaintop removal site at Rawl.

There below is the usual mess, the usual disemboweling: acres and acres of ripped-up earth, security lights and fences, a huge dragline poised to create more damage in the morning. Thanks to the bitter cold, there are no guards patrolling the perimeters. They're all inside a long trailer at the far end of the compound, no doubt huddled around heaters. They're probably praying that what's happened to their compatriots over the last several months won't happen to them. If so, their prayers are in vain.

Matt and I glide down onto a huge heap of snowy shale just outside the fence and shift. I'm in my usual battle garb: kilt, dirk, claymore. He's in his pissed-off-redneck-about-to-whup-some-ass outfit: work boots, camo pants, tight black T-shirt, and WVU baseball cap. The haversack over his shoulder is heavy with explosives Nate's manufactured.

For a long, grim moment, we stand in the snowfall and survey the man-made disaster. "Last one," Matt says, beaming at me. "Alpha's last goddamn dragline."

"Yes," I say, wrapping an arm around his shoulder. "We've had a very productive autumn. Dynamite lobbing. Persuasive trips to the state legislature and Congress. Not to mention that…intense visit to the White House."

Matt snickers, fanging his lower lip. "Yep, that was a shitload of fun. Who knew how easy it would be for two undead mountain men to change history? Well, back to the job at hand. All the nasty diseases that folks around here been suffering from, all those coal-sludge chemicals in their water.... No more a' that shit, here or anywhere else in Appalachia. Let's tear this place up."

"Which would you prefer? Driving off the guards or...."

"Let's do that together." Grinning, Matt pats his haversack. "But this time the damn dragline's mine."

"After the massacre at Sodeski's and all we've managed to do this autumn," I say, "the guards in there are probably armed to the teeth: rowan-wood bullets, silver bullets, rowan-gas grenades. You know that, don't you?"

"Yep, I know. Let's just take 'em fast and then scoot outta here. Try not to hurt 'em too bad, honey. They're just good ole boys like me, trying to make a living."

"You're far more than a good ole boy now, fledgling," I say, clapping him on the rump. "Just be careful."

"You too. Let's do it."

Together, we shift. Together, we soar over the security fence. Together, we resume human form. Matt pauses long enough to place his haversack on the ground outside the trailer, then together we smash in the trailer door. Together, we zip through the space, punching noses, slamming men's bodies into walls, and seizing weapons. Only one of the six manages to get off a shot, a rowan-wood bullet that narrowly misses my head and shatters a window behind me. One guard escapes, rushing out into the snow, shrieking in a less than manly manner. I'm poised to go after him when Matt grabs me by the arm.

"Let him go, the poor bastard. Let him call for help. By the time anyone else gets here, it'll be too late."

My husbear and I leave the unconscious guards to their guilty dreams and stride out into the snow. Before us the monstrous dragline looms. Snow powders its bulk. Flurries snake and scurry about its pontoon feet.

Matt takes up the haversack. "Plant them just where I taught you," I say.

"Yep, got it." Matt speeds over the snow and races up the side of the huge machine. In less than half a minute, he's darting back in my direction, bushy-bearded face flushed and gleaming. His laughter's that of a little boy's.

"Go, go, go!" he shouts, leaping into the air and taking wing.

We soar together—up, up, up into the frigid air—then level out into a wide circle, Matt in the lead. Thickening snow frosts our fur. *God, Derek, I love you. I love our life together*, Matt's voice rumbles in my head.

The first explosion rocks the air. The dragline's bucket shatters in a flare of golden light. The second explosion tears the crane into fragments. The third blast rips apart the cab, sending up a fountain of fire and a shower of metal shards.

Triumphant, Matt and I spiral, watching smoke rise, fires blaze and pop, and a couple of stunned guards stagger from the trailer, waving and shouting. Above us, a new moon and a wide swath of stars slip out from behind diminishing clouds.

Matt flits up to me and nuzzles my snout. *C'mon, honey, we're done here. It's a long flight back to Mount Storm, and I got a Yule party to plan.*

I grin and nod, baring a fang. Matt and I wheel higher and higher over snow-clad hills, then, veering northeast, bathed in winter starlight, my lover and I head home.

ABOUT THE AUTHOR

Jeff Mann grew up in Covington, Virginia, and Hinton, West Virginia, receiving degrees in English and forestry from West Virginia University. His poetry, fiction, and essays have appeared in many publications, including *Arts and Letters, Prairie Schooner, Shenandoah, Willow Springs, The Gay and Lesbian Review Worldwide, Crab Orchard Review*, and *Appalachian Heritage*. He has published three award-winning poetry chapbooks, *Bliss, Mountain Fireflies*, and *Flint Shards from Sussex*; five full-length books of poetry, *Bones Washed with Wine, On the Tongue, Ash: Poems from Norse Mythology, A Romantic Mann*, and *Rebels*; two collections of personal essays, *Edge: Travels of an Appalachian Leather Bear* and *Binding the God: Ursine Essays from the Mountain South*; three novellas, *Devoured*, included in *Masters of Midnight: Erotic Tales of the Vampire, Camp Allegheny*, included in *History's Passion: Stories of Sex Before Stonewall*, and *The Saga of Einar and Gisli*, included in On the Run: *Tales of Gay Pursuit and Passion*; six novels, *Cub, Country, Insatiable, Fog: A Novel of Desire and Reprisal* (which won the Pauline Réage Novel Award), *Purgatory: A Novel of the Civil War* (which won a Rainbow Award), and *Salvation: A Novel of the Civil War* (which won both the Pauline Réage Novel Award and a Lambda Literary Award); a book of poetry and memoir, *Loving Mountains, Loving Men*; and three volumes of short fiction, *Desire and Devour: Stories of Blood and Sweat, Consent: Bondage Tales*, and *A History of Barbed Wire* (which won a Lambda Literary Award). In 2013, he was inducted into the Saints and Sinners Literary Festival Hall of Fame. He teaches creative writing at Virginia Tech in Blacksburg, Virginia.

CPSIA information can be obtained
at www.ICGtesting.com
Printed in the USA
LVOW10s0305170518
577523LV00004B/283/P